Other Novels by Steven Hamilton

Dragon Slayers

McSally and Company

From Where I Stood

Coming in 2020

Quite by Accident

Journey Home

A Novel
by
Steven Hamilton

ISBN: 978-1-7338778-3-1

Cover Art: BespokeBookCovers.com

<u>Dedication</u>

As I write this, our society seems trapped in the grip of violence in a way that I have never experienced in my long years. Behind the headlines and the debates, there are real people—fellow human beings—struggling with grief. Parents, sons, daughters, spouses, brothers, sisters, and all manner of relations and friends trying desperately to find solace and peace, a way through the darkness. I humbly dedicate this work to those out there that, even at this moment, are coming to grips with the reality that they will never see that loved one again. Nothing in my effort, indeed, nothing that I could ever say, can make things right. There is no way to bring back one that we cherish when their life has been so brutally ripped from them. My heart goes out to all of you.

<u>With Gratitude</u>

I want to thank my lovely wife, Mary, for her continued support and for her unfailing insistence that we give it "one more read-through" (I think that brings the total to… well, I've lost count). And, as always, I am grateful to Peter and Caroline O'Connor with BespokeBookCovers.com for their inspired work on the cover.

Prologue
<u>Monday, August 15, 2005</u>

Silence deafened the room. Carol Tullis sat on the couch next to her husband, Chris. She waited. They waited. It had been two days. The first few hours she had been furious that their mischievous twelve-year old, Jenny, had wandered off at the mall. By nightfall, she directed her fury at Chris for not being there with her to help watch the kids. It was his fault.

During that first twenty-four hours, she had cycled through every possible explanation and emotion. With each tick of the clock, she became more and more certain that any moment Jenny would walk through the door with a uniformed police officer who would then scold the parents severely for allowing their daughter to be unsupervised.

As the second day dawned, Carol ran out of explanations. So here she sat, staring at the front door, waiting. As a homicide detective of five years she had made the journey up several walkways to steps leading to porches where she rang a doorbell. She had wondered at the time whether the people inside were expecting her. The detective in her had practiced the words before ringing the bell. The mother's heart that beat inside her had ached for the pain she knew was coming to whoever answered the door. As it turned out, Carol didn't have a clue.

With their seven-year-old son, Jason, at a neighbor's house, the couple sat and waited. Her eyes surveyed the room. A framed photograph hanging on the wall adjacent to the stairs caught her attention—the four of them on vacation

1

along the Columbia River in Oregon. Jenny had been eleven and Jason six. *If she comes back—No! When she comes back, we're going there again. We can leave tomorrow.*

***

The nude, lifeless body lay peacefully before him. Twelve was such a precious age. A mere twenty-four hours earlier, her brilliant blue eyes had danced with laughter as she teased her younger brother. Even two hours ago, her gaze darted frantically around the room trying in vain to understand what was happening. Now those eyes stared lifelessly at nothing.

He sighed. It seemed a waste that such a beautiful young girl should die so early. But he had given her the most precious gift she could ever hope for—himself. Surely, she had appreciated that. All of his planning, anticipation, and hard work had brought the two of them together for a few precious and exciting hours. And after all, this experience could never be matched again. Everything after this would have been a disappointment anyway. Better that she leave this life now.

The room in which he stood diverted his attention. He hated this place. The dust, the fungus, and the smell violated the sanctity of the love he had shared with so many beautiful young girls. He vowed, as he always did, to find another place, a sanctuary worthy of what they shared.

Turning his attention back to his prize, he felt pangs of regret. They never really understood what was happening. He longed with all of his heart to see the realization in their eyes that they knew what was coming, that they understood the inevitable. He wondered whether working with women

2

might be more satisfying. But that was a decision for another day.

Reluctantly, he began preparing the body for its return to the world. In the past, he had lacked self-confidence. He had hidden the bodies of his young protégés in places where they would never be found. With experience, though, he gained the skill and knowledge that allowed him to give some closure to the parents. After all, they had created and raised these beautiful creatures all for his pleasure. It seemed only right that they get the bodies back when he was done. He pulled a new, sealed blue plastic tarpaulin from the closet.

***

The rhythmic ticking of the miniature pendulum clock on the mantle defended against complete silence. The summer sun had passed its zenith and crept relentlessly toward the horizon, which was obscured by houses and trees in the suburbs south of Seattle. Carol could see shadows on the curtain—flies, bees, and other assorted winged insects buzzing around outside. They went about their lives as if nothing was amiss.

The sound of the doorbell intruded. They stood, husband and wife—father and mother. Chris stepped out in front, striding across the room to open the door. About a minute later, Carol began to disintegrate. Her bedrock fractured. Her remaining strength crumbled. The periphery of her vision darkened. The details of the room blurred.

She slipped over the edge into the abyss.

Chapter 1

Things would be all right again. *It's been over ten years. I can do this.* And it wasn't like this day was the anniversary or anything. September 27, 2015—an unremarkable date. The equinox had come and gone, but the summer had decided to hang around a while longer.

Carol Tullis had paced around her house all afternoon. She had obsessed about returning to work the next morning. She started to get her things ready at about eight that evening. The beige linen coat looked good over the butter cream yellow blouse layered on the hanger. The linen would wrinkle easily but she could take her coat off once she got settled in at the station. She laid them down on the bed next to her forest green cotton slacks and nodded her approval.

Apprehension bordering on fear gnawed at her stomach, though. Eight and a half years off the job—likely a lot had changed at the Seattle Police Department Homicide Division. The one thing that had not changed was that the demons continued to haunt her day and night. She had clung to the job for a year and a half after Jenny died before self-destructing. And it had been a long road back.

What else? She pulled her dark brown flats from the bedroom closet and put them on the floor next to her nightstand. That was everything.

Nope. She moved the scarves and folded blouses around on the shelves in her closet. *Not here. Where would I have put it?* She checked the coat closet in the living room. Not there either.

Of course. She headed down the hallway from the living room, stopping about halfway. Reaching up, she pulled down on a small chain. The ladder access to the attic dropped and she climbed up. At the top, she reached instinctively to her right and located the light switch. As she flipped it up, dim light intruded on the darkness. Although the sun had been down for hours, the heat generated by its pounding on the roof had not yet dissipated.

Layers of dust coated boxes that were strewn haphazardly. Some had large handwritten letters on the side noting the contents. Some had lids; others didn't. She made her way over to the far side, careful to walk on the rafters. Planks laid across would have made for easier walking but that was one of the "to do" items that had not gotten done.

Carol spotted the suspect box hiding in a corner. But a smaller box sat on top of it—*the box* she dared not open. She knew that far too much grief hid inside. With every ounce of effort and will she could muster, she gently moved the smaller one and retrieved the container she wanted.

She lifted the lid. "There you are." *So many years.* She could see the worn areas of the leather on the shoulder holster, testament to the service it had seen before she had banished it to the attic. She would get her sidearm along with her badge when she reported for work. Things would be okay again.

After a quick shower, she stood in front of the bathroom mirror assessing what she saw. Touches of gray highlighted her short brown hair at the temples. She tried to recall when that had happened. She knew that turning gray was inevitable but forty-two seemed too young. The image staring back at her looked older than that, though. Hazel eyes sank into her gaunt face. She noticed the lines starting to make their way from the corners of her eyes and mouth.

As she stepped back, the top part of her body came into view. The mirror confirmed what her clothing had been telling her for the past few years. She had shed weight, giving her already trim frame a wasted look. It had been a hard decade.

But things would change. She was going back to work as a homicide detective. Carol entertained a passing thought that a celebration would be nice, except that she had no one with whom to celebrate.

Chapter 2

Carol left her home, located south of SeaTac Airport, around six in the morning. Anticipating heavy work traffic on I-5, she needed to leave in plenty of time to make the eight o'clock meeting with her new boss. Captain Dale Peterman had taken over as the head of Homicide Division during her forced hiatus. She had no idea what to expect, so she figured better early than late.

As it turned out, traffic moved along at a good clip. She strode through the door to the Homicide bullpen, which was mostly deserted, just after seven. One detective sat with his ear glued to the phone and his eyes focused on whatever sat on his desk. Another sat near the center of the room, glancing up as she entered. She nodded to him. He stared for a moment and then went back to his reading.

Friendly bunch around here. She studied the large open area. A few things had changed over the years. The desks were arranged in pairs facing each other with about four feet of empty space between the groups. The phones looked new. But then there was the same old dry erase board at one end. A corkboard with photos, drawings, and notes occupied the other end of the bullpen. The taupe carpet appeared old and worn, but clean. The familiar institutional odor of disinfectant and mustiness permeated the still air.

Carol had no idea which desk would be hers. Standing in the awkward silence, she considered wandering into the break room for coffee. Instead, she found herself in the stairwell headed for the basement—case archives. With each step, a voice reminded her that it was a horrible idea. Still she descended.

When they approved her return to work, the review board had reminded her not to get involved in Jenny's yet unsolved case. But looking at the file wasn't really the same as getting involved. Besides, the case probably wasn't active. As far as she knew, there hadn't been another child serial killing in nine years. She'd seen nothing in the paper about it. It was probably buried down in the belly of the building in a box covered with dust.

The archive room had not changed. An overpowering musty smell hit her when she opened the door. The sickly green walls looked as though they had seen no paint or cleanser in her absence. The dark green linoleum floor appeared clean and polished in the center, but she could see a build-up of dirt in the corners.

Carol approached the guardian of the kingdom, an overweight uniformed man who looked to be in his early sixties. She eased up to the counter, pulling him from whatever held his interest. "Hi. I'm Tullis from Homicide. I was wondering if I could take a look at one of your files?"

The man considered her for a moment. "Carol Tullis?"

She didn't recall ever meeting this particular guy before. "Yes. That's me."

"Forget your badge this morning, did you?"

Carol rolled her eyes and shifted her weight. "Today's my first day back. Been gone for a while."

The man glared at her. After a moment he shrugged but maintained the scowl. "You got a case number?"

"Case number? No. Sorry. It's the child serial murders from about ten years ago." She knew that most of the detectives at the time referred to it as the *Kiddy Killer* case. She could not bring herself to say those words.

He folded his arms for a moment, appearing undecided about how to respond. Finally, he shook his head. "Yeah. I know the one. Not down here anymore. It's up in Cold Storage."

"What? Cold Storage?"

"They keep older unsolved cases there. It's on the third floor. Your file is up there." After another short moment of glaring at her, he turned his attention back to the papers on the counter in front of him.

She exhaled loudly. "Okay. Well, thanks."

He continued to study whatever was in front of him in silence.

Carol left, shaking her head as she departed. She felt as though she had stepped into some alternate universe where everyone was programmed to ignore her. *Third floor. Cold Storage.* Cold cases kept in Cold Storage. She got it, although it irritated her. They kept Jenny in Cold Storage.

She checked her watch—not yet seven-thirty. She could go back to Homicide and be uncomfortable. Or she could check and see what this third-floor place looked like. The review board's cautionary words flashed across her mind again. And again she ignored them.

Stepping out of the stairwell, she wandered down the hall, which opened up into a large bay, subdivided into cubicles. The lights were on, but the space seemed oddly quiet. Carol reminded herself that it was still early. She noticed shadows moving in a cubicle on the right-hand side.

As she approached, a man turned to face her. "Can I help you?" His gaze started at her eyes and worked their way down her legs. He looked to be in his early thirties, wearing dark brown slacks, a white shirt and a chocolate brown tie. His sandy hair was long and shaggy on the sides but thinned to nearly bald on top.

She shook off the momentary discomfort. "Yes. I'm Detective Tullis from Homicide. I was wondering if I might be able to have a look at the file on the serial child abduction and killings from about ten years ago?" She tried to make the words come out as routine.

He narrowed his eyes. "Detective Tullis, huh?" He surveyed her body again. "Yeah. I know the case." He looked around the space and then up at the clock. "I'm in the middle of something right now. If you come back later, I'd be happy to sit down and go through the file with you." His face brightened.

"I'd really appreciate it. But I don't want to trouble you."

"No problem at all. Why don't you drop by around five? I'll have plenty of time to take a look then."

"Thanks. Maybe I will." She turned and headed toward the hallway.

As she rounded the last cubicle, she nearly ran into another man. He looked to be sixtyish and stood about five ten. His charcoal wool slacks, French blue shirt, and maroon tie signaled that he was not just another detective. She stepped aside to avoid him, but he moved at the same time blocking her exit.

"Can I help you?" His face presented a cold veneer, his mouth drawn into a tight line.

Carol's alarms went crazy. "No thanks. I was just checking on something."

"What would that be?" He showed no signs of moving out of her way.

"Uh, just an old homicide case. Nothing urgent." She moved to the side to pass and he moved with her, again blocking her exit.

"So, you're Homicide?"

Her stomach revolted and her legs trembled. "Yes."

He stared and said nothing.

"Detective Tullis." She shifted her weight from one foot to the other.

"This is Aged Cases. Homicide's on the second floor."

"Yes, sir, I know. Thank you." She just wanted out of there.

He stepped aside and Carol took full advantage, fighting the urge to break into a run—prey running from a predator.

Chapter 3

In a rare instance of good timing, Carol walked through the double doors into the bullpen at precisely eight o'clock. Although activity had picked up, nearly half of the seats still remained empty. Easing across the space toward the captain's office, she tried to ignore the stares and awkward silence. She kept her eyes focused on the destination.

Peterman's office was a glassed-in section of the bay. Vertical louvered blinds were affixed for those *special occasions* where privacy was needed. Carol recalled the washed-out memory of her own such occasion. Her old boss, Captain Walsh, had called her in one Friday afternoon to go over the few options remaining after she had so effectively painted herself into a corner. With a sympathetic look in his eyes, he explained that she could either resign, agree to enter treatment for her alcoholism, or be placed on unpaid leave until such time as she could demonstrate her capacity to return to duty.

Maybe in another time or place the showdown would have been traumatic. But coming on the heels of her liquid lunch, she had simply shrugged. Tossing her shield on the desk, she had taken out her Glock-19 nine-millimeter side arm, removed the ammo clip, and locked the slide back. She set the weapon and ammunition on his desk.

Carol had abandoned her dream job as a homicide detective with the same casual, matter-of-fact attitude with which she had ended her fifteen-year marriage to Chris. "Later," she shot over her shoulder as she sauntered out the door. Luck was with her that day. She arrived early for happy hour at O'Malley's.

12

She snapped back to reality as she approached the open door. Inside, a man appearing to be in his late fifties or early sixties sat with the telephone receiver to his ear. Without missing a beat, he spoke into the handset and beckoned her in, motioning toward a chair beside his desk. "Certainly. And thanks for calling." He put the handset down.

"Tullis, I assume?" He leaned back in his chair, fingers steepled in front of him.

Carol squirmed a little to get comfortable in the chair and took a deep breath. "Yes sir."

His face betrayed no emotion or judgment. "Forgot to get off the elevator on the second floor, huh? Ended up on the third?"

Christ, word travels fast around this place. "Yes sir. I ended up in Cold Storage." She tried to spin it as happenstance, an accident.

"Aged Cases." The words came out measured but stern.

"Sir?"

Captain Peterman narrowed his eyes as he spoke. "Aged Cases. It's the Aged Cases Division. Their offices are on the third floor. Captain Tarrant runs that office. I think you met him. Homicide is on the second floor. You need to remember that."

"Yes sir."

"Good." He paused and turned his attention to the file folder in front of him. "Says here that the board approved your return to full duty. The doc says you're okay." He glanced up, as if doing his own assessment.

She wasn't feeling any great welcome coming on. "Yes sir."

"And you have a copy of the union agreement and department policies?" The inflection at the end signaled the question.

"Uh, yes, sir." She immediately regretted that she'd left them in a manila envelope on the kitchen table.

"We have copies out in the bullpen if you need them, along with Homicide-specific policies." He paused but continued before Carol could acknowledge.

"You'll be partnered with Detective Ramirez. You'll find him out in the bullpen. He'll help you get settled in a desk and point you in the right direction to get your phone, computer access, and such." He paused and opened a drawer on his desk. Reaching in, he pulled out a shield and set it on the desk between them. "This is yours, I believe. The armory will issue your sidearm. You need to re-qualify, both proficiency and judgmental. Allow a couple of days for that. Don't go out in the field until you do."

Carol reached across and picked up the shield. She looked at it for a moment before closing her fingers around it. "Yes sir." This was turning into a very one-sided conversation.

He turned his attention to the folder. "You also need to swing by Payroll. Get that done today." He paused for a moment. "Any questions?"

Given the reception she'd gotten thus far that morning, Carol opted to remain as silent as she could. "No sir. None right now."

"Good. You were a homicide detective before, and you know the drill. I'll spare you the 'our work is important' speech. But I'll leave you with this. You were here under Captain Walsh. Good man. But I run things a little differently.

It's pretty simple though. I'm the captain and you're the detective. I assign the cases. You work on those cases. You don't work on other cases. Don't offer your services to other divisions and don't go snooping around in their business." He stared without breaking his emotionless expression.

"Yes sir." She got up to leave.

"Tullis."

She turned at the door to face him.

His eyes took on a different, more intense but not totally unsympathetic look. "I know someone on the board probably told you this but, in the interest of clarity and just to make sure that there is no misunderstanding, I'm going to tell you again. Stay away from your daughter's case."

Her heart fell. Yes, they had told her, and she understood it. But having the captain say it felt different, more personal. "Yes sir." She turned toward the door and then stopped. "Captain, respectfully, would it be possible for me to at least get an update?" She felt a little like it was going out on a limb. On the other hand, members of the public could ask for an update under similar circumstances.

His eyes briefly took on a far-away look. "I'll call and ask for one."

"Thank you, sir." Carol took a deep breath and turned to go.

"Tullis." The voice, softer now, floater over her shoulder. She turned again to face the captain.

"Yes sir?"

"It may take a day or so. In the meantime, you can probably assume that the case is pretty much where it was when you left."

Carol lowered her head. She had expected as much. "Yes sir. Thank you." As she left, she felt more confused than anything. The captain certainly wasn't the warm and fuzzy type but something in that last statement struck a chord with her, although she wasn't quite sure what it was.

Chapter 4

Carol approached the man from behind as he typed notes into a computer. "You Ramirez?"

He swiveled around and faced her. Apparently in his early forties, he had a full head of black hair, neatly trimmed, was smooth shaven with a dark complexion. His piercing brown eyes locked on hers. "Yeah. Tullis?"

"Carol Tullis." She extended her right hand.

Detective Ramirez took her hand briefly with a strong grip and then motioned her to a chair on the other side of the adjacent desk. "That'll be your new home. Most of the stuff you need should be there—stapler, hole punch, like that." He closed the folder in front of him and leaned back in his antiquated office chair. "You finish with the captain already?" While not unwelcoming, he didn't come across as particularly glad to see her.

"I guess you could say that."

"Something wrong?"

"Oh no, unless you count me wandering up to the third floor as something wrong. By the time I got back into his office, I was already on his shit list." She ran her hand over the corner of the desk nearest her. All of a sudden, sitting here at this desk with this detective seemed wrong, not what she had expected.

He considered her for a moment before responding in a matter-of-fact tone, "Yeah, well, that'll do it."

Back in the old days—*before*— her partner would have commiserated with her over the injustice of the ass-chewing. Things had apparently changed. "I guess." She sat up in her chair and scooted up closer to the desk. "The captain said you'd clue me in on the schedule and getting things set up."

Ramirez gestured around the room. "Pretty simple, really. We work eight-hour days with an unpaid hour for lunch. This division has flex hours so you can come in at seven and leave at four. Or you can come in at eight and stay until five. Some come in at ten and leave at seven. They try to keep someone here seven to seven with the bulk of us here between nine and five. So far, the captain lets us work it out ourselves. He just wants the coverage. We also have on-call duty once every ten days to cover after hours."

"Sounds reasonable. Do partners work the same schedule?" Carol mentally ticked through her own preferences. Early was better than later.

"Goes both ways. Sometimes partners like to spend all their time working together. Sometimes they work different shifts to minimize the time they have to put up with each other. Just depends on the individuals, I guess. I work eight to five."

She drummed her fingers on the desktop as she considered the options. "Okay. Thanks." She preferred an earlier shift, maybe seven to four. That would give her a better shot at avoiding work hour traffic. But that decision could wait.

Ramirez tapped something into his computer. "I'll put in a work order with IT to get you set up with network access. They'll get you a cell phone too. You going to be around the rest of the day?"

"Probably not. Captain says I have to go by payroll, to the armory to get my weapon, and then re-qualify. It'll probably take a couple of days." Carol's discomfort grew by the minute. She felt as if she was talking to a machine rather than a human being. This whole day was starting to feel like one big mistake.

"Before you head out, I'll fill you in on our caseload. We have three active cases right now." He tossed a file folder across the desk in Carol's direction. "First one's a double homicide…."

This entire place is like some automated production line. No humans here, just machines.

"…suspect in custody but…."

Jenny's file is sitting up there gathering dust. Nobody here gives a shit.

"…we have an APB out…."

She stared out across the bullpen, which now looked close to capacity. Nobody interacted. They all seemed huddled into their own little worlds.

"Detective? Detective Tullis?" The stark words and loud volume intruded.

"What? Yes." She pulled herself back into the moment and snapped her head around to face Ramirez.

He glared at her. "I'm sorry. Was I boring you? Are these dead people not important enough for you?"

It all came down to this. It had started the moment she entered the bullpen that morning. Since then, it had gone steadily downhill. She snapped. "Fuck you!"

If Ramirez was shocked, he gave no evidence. "Snappy comeback. I give you ten for delivery. You've apparently used that one before. But you get a one for creativity. You're going to want to put a bit more thought into your retorts." He arched his eyebrows but otherwise sat perfectly still.

Carol became aware that the room had fallen silent. She glanced around and then back at Ramirez, who wore the most patient, unassuming look. This was like some alternate universe. "What is it with you people? Has everybody here been forced to attend some kind of asshole indoctrination?" She shook her head and turned away from her partner.

Instead of answering, Ramirez went back to his file folders. "Why don't you go get your stuff done. We'll try this again later."

Chapter 5

Carol processed through payroll in less than fifteen minutes. A scant half hour later she left the Seattle Police Department Armory with a Glock 19, two clips, and two boxes of ammunition.

Once inside the indoor shooting range, she grabbed a set of hearing protectors and made her way over to a bench where she loaded the clips with bullets. Initially intending to move straight into the qualification process, she opted instead to spend the rest of the morning practicing. She found a spot at one end of the line. Donning her "ears," she began firing round after round at the target.

She started with ten yards and worked her way out to twenty-five over the course of the morning. After the first few cycles, she settled into a comfortable, almost mindless routine. The recoil on the Glock was enough to reassure her of the weapon's power but was much gentler than the 45 that she'd initially trained on. The odor of burnt powder reminded her of earlier, mostly happier days.

She relentlessly cycled through, firing seventeen rounds, inserting the second clip, seventeen more rounds, stop, check the target, reload the clips, rinse and repeat. Her mind wandered, though. Things were not going as expected. What *had* she expected—smiles, pats on the back, at worst no notice at all? Was she so naïve as to expect that somehow her past would go unnoticed?

It's none of their business. But people had a way of making things their business when they wanted. *Why should I have to justify myself to them?* Because she wanted to be a part of them. *Bullshit. It's not fair.*

21

Fair? That was the best card she could play? Fair? There was no *fair*. Where was *fair* when Jenny was killed? Where was *fair* when her case got shipped off to Cold Storage?

Carol roused herself from the internal argument just before noon. It seemed a good place to stop for lunch. Grabbing her things, she headed out into the fresh air and high overcast of the late September morning.

Entering the small deli that cops frequented, she toyed with the notion of a sandwich, chips, and a drink. She left carrying only a bottle of water. Food held little appeal and she failed to see the point in spending money for something she didn't want. She parked on a bench near a small pond, set her purse beside her, and untwisted the plastic cap on the bottle.

She allowed herself to return to the problem of her partner. If circumstances had been different—if she wasn't just returning from a nightmarish lapse in service, if she had the option of dealing with her old captain—she would have been inclined to barge into her boss' office and demand a different partner. *I guess that's not going to happen.* Somehow, she'd. have to learn to live with Ramirez.

***

Carol set her purse on the desk and dropped into her chair. "Anything going on?" She looked across at her partner, who had his head buried in a file when she approached.

"Oh, hi. How'd things go at the range?" He leaned back, hands interlaced behind his head. His demeanor—the faint smile and gentle eyes—suggested that whatever words had passed between them earlier had been forgotten, or at the very least, forgiven.

She opened the file drawer on her desk and pulled out a blank folder. "Not bad. Got the proficiency stuff done. Just need to do judgmental tomorrow." She labeled the file *Qualifications* and slid a copy of her pistol proficiency record in. "Anything new on the cases?" She wasn't sure what would constitute "new" since she hadn't paid attention when he went over them that morning.

"Nada. Oh, the IT guy said to stop down there and pick up your phone. And they got your computer all set." He pointed toward the monitor on her desk. Glancing at his watch, he stood. "It's a half-hour till quitting time. Let's go get a coffee."

But rather than heading for the coffee pot, he grabbed his coat and started for the door.

Carol caught up with her partner as he entered the elevator. "You want to tell me where we're going" She laced the question with as much venom and hostility as she could muster.

He turned and considered her for a moment. "You know, fifty years ago we'd be headed out looking for free doughnuts and such." The elevator door closed, and he punched the button for the ground floor. They rode the few seconds in silence.

The door opened and they strode toward the front door of the building. Once outside, he turned right and made his way down the crowded sidewalk. "As it is, we're headed to Starbucks to pay twelve bucks for a latte and a stale scone. The times they are a changing, as the poet said."

"Yeah. Dylan. I know. But why?" Carol hurried to keep up with him.

Ramirez laughed. "Why are the times changing or why are we going to Starbucks?"

She didn't answer. It didn't matter anyway.

Chapter 6

This particular Starbucks was like every other that she'd been in—soft new age music, a line to place the orders, and young baristas with a variety of body markings and piercings. Carol opted for a small black coffee at three bucks. True to his word, Ramirez sat down with a latte grande and what looked like a black currant scone.

She blew across the surface of her coffee, looking at her partner through the steam. "So, you going to tell me why we're here?"

Ramirez' face softened and his eyes seemed to convey sincerity, something she hadn't seen much of in anyone this particular day. "The bullpen is a great place to solve crimes. We discuss cases and work on ideas. But you have to assume that anything you say there is for general consumption. Someone's always listening, and people talk. Most of the time, it's okay. Some subjects, though, require more discretion." He gestured in the direction of the mass of people in the coffee shop. "Here, nobody cares about our silly problems. They have their own."

Carol's guard went up. What could they need to talk about that he didn't want others to hear? "So, what? You just get up and walk out on an extended coffee break anytime you want?"

"Pretty much, within reason. We're allowed two fifteen-minute personal breaks a day—one in the morning, one in the afternoon. I just figured we'd combine them into one break, since it's so close to the end of the day."

She shook her head. "Okay. What's so sensitive that you need to spend money on crap like that?"

"Hey, this is good stuff. Well, it's a little on the stale side." He studied the scone as if it was about to impart some crucial piece of information before turning his attention back to Carol. "Now, where were we? Oh yeah, *fuck you*. Now I remember. You want to know what's going on with everyone, why they're all treating you like you have some communicable disease. Well, here it is. Some of the guys were here when you were. When we got word you were coming back, they spared no effort to ensure that all of us knew the story—the full, unedited version." He took a sip of his latte. Breaking off a piece of his scone, he popped it in his mouth and chewed slowly.

"Some of it likely was accurate. Some probably embellished or exaggerated. Almost certainly some was outright lie. Problem is, though, that once the word is out there, it is *the word*." He looked down at his scone as if considering whether to take another bite.

"We pretty much got it all—your daughter was murdered, your marriage tanked, and then you crawled into a bottle." His mouth opened as though he had something else to say, but evidently decided against it. He leaned back and cupped both hands around his ceramic up.

"Shit." She shook her head and looked down at the table.

"You know, within an hour of the word getting out, most of the guys went to the captain to make sure they had nothing to do with you. I hear tell that some even lobbied hard to have you reassigned to another division or precinct."

"And what about you? How did you manage to draw the short straw?"

"I don't know. I'd been without a partner for a few weeks, so I guess the captain felt I was the logical choice."

So, this was what it was all about. No one trusted her or wanted to work with her. "How'd you feel about that?"

He blew across his latte and took another sip before answering. "I shared my reservations with the captain."

She moved her coffee cup to the side and placed her hands flat on the table between them. "And those were?"

"Two reservations, really, although I only shared one. Fact is, Tullis, I need a partner with her head in the game. We have three cases that are biting at our ankles and there are more on the way. I don't need a partner whose mind is on something else, some other case."

"I was a homicide detective before you were even on the force. I know how to keep my mind on the job." She shot her response across the table without blinking.

"All evidence to the contrary. You ended up on the third floor looking for your daughter's case file before you even got your desk assignment. All things being equal, I'd say your mind is probably there."

She started to tear into him again but thought better of it. She exhaled and bit her tongue.

"Nothing personal, Tullis. None of us can know what it's like to be in your shoes and I'm certainly not criticizing you for it. I'm just saying that I need my partner to have her mind on our cases. Those victims all have families and friends. They deserve answers, justice. I just worried that you wouldn't be able to do that for them."

Carol stared at the top of the table feeling defeated. "And what did the captain say to that?"

Ramirez chortled. "The same thing he probably told you this morning, something about him being the captain and me being the detective." His laughter softened and his words took on a more serious tone. "But he did say that you were a good cop and that I should give you a chance."

She considered his answer. "And are you?"

"Am I what?"

"Going to give me a chance."

"I'm not giving you anything. You have a shield, which means you're a homicide detective. You happen to be my partner and I don't have any say in the matter. Where it goes from here isn't up to me. But I'll promise you this. I'll be up front with you. I won't lie to you and I won't keep things from you. I won't stab you in the back and I won't gossip about you. I'll stand up for you as long as you deserve standing up for. I'll respect you. I'll pull my share of the load. When the time comes, I'll have your back. I expect the same from you. If we can do that, then, who knows?"

She watched him for a moment before responding. "Fair enough. So, what was your other reservation?"

Ramirez's demeanor became more serious. He considered her for a moment before averting his gaze. He rubbed his index finger around the rim of his half-empty cup. "I have three kids—one daughter. She's five. I have trouble imagining her even being in danger. The idea of losing her is unthinkable to me. But the idea of losing her like you lost your daughter and then having the case go unsolved is beyond anything I can imagine. I'm sitting here looking at you and you look cool, collected, and composed. But your eyes, I can't see into them. It's like they've got a coating of rime ice on them. Under that frosty veneer, I wonder if maybe there's a seething cauldron of rage. I worry about the day that something sets you off and everything comes spewing out leaving us with a bloodbath." His voice trailed off.

"Sounds a bit melodramatic, don't you think?"

"Maybe. But thing is, it won't happen until it happens and then it'll be too late to worry about it. Tullis, I believe that there's some rage in there and I can't blame you. I just need to know that, between us, you're going to have some kind of pressure relief valve. I guess I'm hoping that you can talk to me as we go along. Don't keep it bottled up with no place to go until the cork pops."

Carol exhaled and allowed her shoulders to slump. "I can do that." She checked her watch. "We can continue this tomorrow." She stood to leave. "Oh, and sorry about the 'fuck you' thing."

"Not a problem. I'm actually glad that you know how to push back. You're going to need it." He paused before adding, "Oh, and in the interest of full disclosure, pretty much everyone knows about the Royston thing."

Chapter 7

*R*oyston. She brooded all night, tossing and turning, rarely falling asleep for more than an hour at a time. Of all the things she never wanted to think about again, this ranked somewhere near the top. But why bother to explain? It was none of his business. Come to think of it, why did she need to tell him anything? He was a detective. She was a detective. In terms of total service, she probably had him beat.

By dawn though, she decided to come clean—not just about Royston, but everything. After all, if everyone already knew, there was little point in letting things fester between her and her partner.

After the morning at judgmental weapon training, she met Ramirez for lunch. They sat on a bench in the small park. He munched on a homemade sandwich he'd brought with him. She sipped on water from a plastic bottle. "What I'm telling you is between you and me. Right?" The futility of that statement struck her the instant it took form. Once she told him, she had no control at all over what happened to the information.

"Of course."

Carol closed her eyes briefly and began. "Yes, my daughter, Jenny, was murdered. The case has made its way up to Aged Cases, where it is apparently at about the same place it was when I left. I assume that there's not a lot of dispute over those facts." She forced her words out as calmly as she could.

Her partner's eyes betrayed a softness, but his face remained neutral.

"The marriage. My marriage didn't tank. *I* destroyed it. Chris and I divorced about a year after Jenny's death. The details are private and have nothing to do with the job." She arched her eyebrows and waited for an acknowledgement.

Ramirez nodded.

As calmly as if she were describing a cookie recipe, Carol moved on to the alcohol. "My drinking. Yes. Well, everything you heard about it is probably true, and then some. I started drinking a few months after Jenny's death—something to dull the pain. Way back when, I used to enjoy a glass of scotch from time to time, although I typically never finished a drink. By the time I parted ways with the department, I had graduated to vodka—drink of choice for any self-respecting alcoholic. It's cheap and lends itself to drinking on the job without getting caught. I was up to a couple of pints a day. Well, a couple of pints during the day and then another at night, just for good measure."

She shifted in her seat, scratched the back of her head as she finished the rest of the story. "I quit the booze about six months after I left the department. I haven't touched it since." She took a deep breath.

"And that brings us to Royston—Detective Joe Royston. I guess I'm a little baffled, though. I realize that having an affair with a married co-worker was stupid and wrong. But I have to say I'm a little surprised that it made the cut, in terms of things people hold against me. It's not like we were blatant about it and we weren't partners." Even though she tried to downplay it, the memory left a bitter taste in her mouth as she uttered the words.

Ramirez scrunched up his face and narrowed his eyes for a moment as he appeared to process the information he'd just heard.

Exasperated, Carol stared at him. "What?"

Her partner exhaled, opened his mouth, and then closed it. He looked confused. Finally, he spoke. "That's not exactly the version that floated around the bullpen. What we heard was that you didn't have an affair with him."

She offered a sarcasm-laced retort. "Now that's a real crime. I didn't have an affair with a co-worker."

"What I mean is that he claimed you were obsessed with him, that you wanted to sleep with him. He said you wanted him to leave his wife and marry you. When he refused your advances, you called his wife and lied to her, telling her that the two of you were in love and having an affair. They got divorced not long after that. He blamed you."

For the first time in years, Carol laughed, and it felt honest. "Talk about your alternate universe. That's fantastic." She shook her head. "No. I wasn't obsessed with Royston. I didn't love him. Hell, we didn't really even like each other. We each got what we wanted out of it. He got free, no-strings-attached sex. I got an hour or two a week of not having to think, feel, talk, or even care. We'd hook up in a hotel room after work, spend an hour together, get dressed, and then go our separate ways."

She paused, thinking back on the whole affair, to the extent that she could peer back into the alcohol-induced haze that defined that part of her life. "Apparently his wife found out, how I don't know. But she called me one afternoon, hysterical. She ranted about me sleeping with her husband and calling me pretty much every name in the book. Not that

I didn't deserve it. Actually, everything she said was true. And, had it been another day, another time, I might have done things differently. I might have deflected her remarks. I could have hung up, tried to reason with her or, hell, I might have even lied to her. But, fueled with a pint of vodka for lunch, I unloaded on her. Told her what she could do with her marriage and her husband, in very graphic terms."

A wave of sadness swept over her, not for Royston or his wife. She shuddered at the depth of her attempts to avoid pain. She didn't give a shit about him or his marriage. She knew, though, that if these detectives all knew about the affair, then likely her ex-husband, Chris, had heard the stories too. Although they were long divorced by then, she could only imagine the humiliation and pain it must have caused him. If she had eaten any lunch, it would certainly have come back up at that moment. She closed her eyes and took a deep breath as she recaptured her composure. "And that was it. I left the department about the same time. As far as I know, the affair had nothing to do with my disciplinary action. When I re-applied here, I did check to make sure he was gone."

"Fair enough. It's a start, I guess. So, you got sober and turned things around. I assume things got a little better after that."

Carol looked at him for a moment considering the question. "No. Actually, that's when things really got hard. But that's a different story for a different day. And it has nothing to do with the job." She stood to leave.

Ramirez leaned forward and turned toward her. "Oh, I forgot to tell you this morning. You know that serial rape murder case?"

"Yes. I read about it. Are we on that one?"

"No. That's over in Sex Crimes and they keep a pretty tight rein on it. But you may end up getting called out on your duty day. I've never had to go on one but several of the guys have. You just help canvass for witnesses, secure the scene, and hold things together until one of their detectives shows up. You should be aware of it, just in case."

"I'm not sure when I'm going to pull an on-call day."

"Oh, that's easy. You're going to be with me for a couple of mine before they turn you loose on your own. I'm on a week from this Saturday. Not much to it. You just keep your phone handy and be ready to go."

"Okay. Well, actually, that sounds good, except that a week from this Saturday is my weekend to have my son." She exhaled loudly. "I'll work something out."

Chapter 8

Carol trudged through the front door to her aging single-story wood frame house ten minutes before seven that evening. Heavy work-hour traffic and construction plagued the drive. She tossed her keys into the small basket sitting on the hallway teacart.

Removing her shoulder holster, she sat it on the kitchen table along with what remained of her last box of ammunition. A sense of apathy regarding dinner suggested cold cereal—quick, easy, and inoffensive. *Maybe later. Get this thing cleaned up first.*

The answering machine light blinked incessantly. Taking a deep breath, she went over and pressed the "play" button.

"Hi. It's Chris. Give me a call please."

They didn't speak often; mostly coordinating weekend visits for Jason, their son. She was working hard at rebuilding that mother-child relationship but the seventeen-year-old seemed ambivalent most of the time. He was never overtly nasty, but their time together left little doubt that the visits were not the highlight of his life.

The message ended and the next one started. "Hi, this is Ben Sturgis. I'm going to be renting the apartment you have out back. I just finished up with your agent and he said I'd need to meet with you before we finalized it. I'd be happy to drop over. Just let me know what time's convenient for you. Thanks." She shook her head. He'd neglected to give his phone number. Fortunately, the machine recorded it. She called him back. He said he'd be over within the hour.

Carol sighed as she picked up the phone again and dialed her ex-husband's number.

"Hello."

She sat down at the kitchen table and tilted her head back. "Hi, it's me. You called?"

His voice sounded tired but amicable. "Yes, thanks. I wonder if it'd be possible for you to take Jason this coming weekend rather than the following one. We're going down to the Oregon coast."

Her initial reaction was annoyance. She'd reached the point in her life where schedule changes irritated her. Then it occurred to her, this was perfect. She could do the visit this weekend, leaving her free for on-call the following Saturday. "Sure. No problem. When are you leaving?"

"We're going to try and get out of here on Friday morning. If you could pick him up on Thursday night, that'd be great."

"I work on Friday. But if you're okay with him being here alone for the day, I can pick him up after work on Thursday." She had no idea how Jason would react to being stranded in her somewhat austere home for the entire day. She had only basic cable and just a few movies. Maybe he had games on his phone.

"That'd be okay. See you then."

She disconnected and sat the phone down. She thought about his words. "*We're* going to try and get out of here…" *We. Chris and Shelley.* She fought back the resentment and pain. She had done it to herself. And he had waited nearly six years before dating again.

***

Carol considered the prospective tenant. He appeared to be in his early to mid-thirties with a boyish appearance. His full head of brown hair covered about half of his ears. The slightly disheveled look made him sort of attractive. His green eyes seemed to laugh as he spoke. At about six feet tall, he had an average build but filled out the faded, worn jeans and the Hard Rock Café tee shirt nicely.

She motioned toward an overstuffed chair in her living room. "What do you do for a living, Mister Sturgis?" Her property management agent took the application, did the background checks, and handled all of the details. She insisted on meeting her tenants but didn't get involved in the details. She took a seat on the couch.

"I'm writing a book."

Carol studied his face for a moment. "Yes, so what do you do for a living?"

He laughed. "Ah, I see what you're getting at. I have about two years of resources saved up. I'm hoping to get my book published and on the shelves by then. If that doesn't work out, I'm a licensed clinical psychologist. I can always open up a private practice in the area."

"Where are you living now?" She knew that this, along with just about everything else she would ask was in the completed application. Still, it was good to talk to him just to get a sense of who she'd have living out back.

"I'm in the process of moving down from Bellingham. Right now, I'm paying a weekly rate for a small efficiency unit about twenty minutes from here. I'd like to get out of there within the next day or so—save me a week's rent."

"Why the move?" She chided herself as she asked the question. After all, he wasn't a suspect to be interrogated. People move. It happens. She quickly added, "if you don't mind my asking."

"Not at all. I taught at Western Washington for the past few years. I resigned at the end of last semester. All in all, I'd just rather be in Seattle. More going on." He opened his mouth as if he was going to continue but stopped.

Carol started to ask why he'd quit but figured that was one question too far.

Before she could respond, Sturgis continued speaking. "Teaching was okay but kind of restrictive. Everything revolves around class schedules, students, and regular research and publication. It's just one big never-ending machine. Time to step out and do things my way for a change." He grinned.

She got up from the couch, signaling the end of the interview. "Okay then. I appreciate your coming by. I'll call Tony tonight and clear it. He has the keys so you can start moving in whenever you want."

He stood but remained still for a moment. "You're a cop."

She did a double-take. "Why would you say that?"

He laughed. "You ask a lot of questions. You pay attention to details. I could see you sizing me up. You're suspicious. In fact, you're a detective."

She arched her eyebrows.

"Yeah. You listen more than you talk. You seem to carefully consider my answers, almost as if you were analyzing me, although not in the psychological sense, of course."

"I'm sure Tony told you, no pets, no smoking and no loud parties. It's a quiet neighborhood."

He got an animated look on his face. He took a deep breath and widened his eyes. "The book I'm writing is about mental health issues in serial killers. I wonder if I might interview you sometime?"

"You can get the keys from Tony. Thanks for dropping by Mister Sturgis or, I guess it's Doctor Sturgis." She started over toward the door.

"Oh, just Ben will do." He extended his hand, a broad smile on his face. If he was disappointed by her non-response to his inquiries, he gave no clue.

"Have a good evening, Doctor Sturgis."

Chapter 9

Chris' neighborhood never failed to impress Carol. The well-manicured lawns complemented what she was sure were million-dollar homes. Mercedes and Volvos occupied the driveways, She pulled into the double driveway of his two-story garrison just outside Bridle Trails State Park at four-fifteen. Parking her older Honda Civic, she sat behind the wheel taking it all in. She closed her eyes, took a deep breath, and got out of the car.

"Hi, come in." Chris opened the door and stepped aside.

"Thanks. Jason ready?" Since the divorce, she'd never mastered the art of small talk with her ex. Whenever she came over to get Jason or return him, she felt as if the weight of the world was crushing her heart.

"He just ran out to get a new game for his PlayStation. He should be back shortly." He shook his head. "Gets his driver's license and looks for any excuse to drive the car."

God. He has his driver's license already. Why the surprise? She knew his age. She just couldn't quite grasp where the lost years had gone. "Oh, okay."

The room décor diverted her attention—upscale. Steel gray carpeting and pale blue walls complemented a navy couch and matching armchair. Pen and ink sketches of children at play adorned the walls. One featured a young girl that Carol knew just had to be Jenny, although of course it wasn't. She fought back the pain.

Chris took a seat on the couch and motioned her to the chair. "You started back to work this week?"

"Yes, I did." She wasn't sure what else to say.

"How's it going so far?" He had seemed genuinely happy when she told him that she'd been rehired.

She gazed at the window as she spoke, more to avoid meeting his eyes than to see what was outside. "Well, let's see. Monday and Tuesday, I re-qualified with my weapon. Yesterday and today I've just been coming up to speed on my cases. So, I guess not too bad, all things considered."

"That's good. Uh, anything going on?" He seemed to search for the words.

Carol knew exactly what he was asking. She'd come prepared. Opening her purse, she took out a piece of paper and handed it to him. "I asked for an update on Jenny's case. I got this today. They are working it up in the Aged Cases Division, you know, cold cases. Nothing has changed since I left."

He took the paper and studied it for a moment, his eyes growing moist. "Thanks. I guess it's good they're still working on it—still on their radar." He handed the paper back.

"Yeah, I guess—"

The sound of the front door opening and then closing interrupted her. She watched her son walk in from the front entryway with a plastic bag in one hand.

She stood and went over to hug her son. "Hey you. I've been looking forward to this."

He dropped his bag on the coffee table and limply put his arms on her shoulders only to immediately drop them to his side. "Hey Mom." The words sounded pained, forced.

"So, grab your things and let's try to beat the traffic."

***

41

Carol focused on driving but occasionally shot Jason a glance. He sat with his head against the passenger window looking silently out the side. "I guess you're off the whole weekend." A stupid statement, she knew, since he would obviously be at her house in South Seattle until Sunday night. She just couldn't think of much else to say.

"Yeah." His stock answer, although he alternated frequently with "I don't know" and "I don't care," depending on the question.

"What do you say we grab a pizza for tonight?"

"I ate while I was out." With his face pointing away, his voice was muted.

"Maybe later then. It's still early."

She drove in silence for a few more minutes. The clouds that had dominated the day finally delivered on their threat. A gentle rain started to fall. As she switched on the wipers, Carol felt comforted by the rhythmic swiping. If nothing else, it broke the uncomfortable silence.

Out of the corner of her eye, Carol saw Jason twist his head toward her. "Why did you and Dad get divorced?"

The question stunned her. She felt his glare bearing down on her. Searching for the right way to truthfully answer it, she opted for a stalling tactic. "What did your father say about it?"

"I'm asking you." The words came out laced with a combination of insistence and distaste.

She cleared her throat. "I'm guessing that 'it's complicated' isn't the answer you're looking for."

Silence.

Carol took a deep breath. "Yeah, I thought not. Tell you what. Let's talk about it when we get to the house. I don't think I can navigate the traffic and that subject at the same time."

Silence.

She made the turn off 520 West onto I-5 south and joined the hordes of commuters bound for the suburbs. Their progress went from good to okay to slow dealing with the rain and construction on top of work traffic. They pulled into her driveway at six-thirty.

Once inside, she shed her work clothes and opted for a pair of jeans and a sweatshirt. The September rain and wind injected a chill into the air. "You want a cup of cocoa or something?" She spoke loudly as she put the kettle on for tea, hoping to reach his ears in the living room.

No answer.

She sighed. *Three nights of this.* She should be used to it by now. Most of the weekends they spent together passed that way. It seemed like just some obligation he had to suffer through every few weeks.

She put the teabag in her cup and doused it with boiling water. Dipping it a few times, she removed it and put it in the trash. Carrying the ceramic mug into the living room, she sat on one end of the couch. She hoped that one day he would come sit beside her. It was not to be this evening, apparently.

He sat in the armchair staring out the window. "So, are you going to answer my question now?" His words seemed not so hostile as they had in the car. They came out more as a resignation.

Carol closed her eyes and took a deep breath. "Yes, Jason, I will." Over the last year, she had decided that she needed to talk to him about what had happened and to apologize. She never seemed to be able to find the right words or even the right opportunity. Fate, apparently, had intervened.

She opened her eyes and turned to face him. "When we lost Jenny, your father and I, we both suffered. Our lives were shattered. After about six months, though, he was able to start functioning more or less normally. He started doing things around the house, fixing meals for us, and even suggesting that we all go out to movies and things." Memories flooded back. Tears filled her eyes.

"I couldn't do it. I crumbled. Your father tried, God he tried. He took care of you. He took care of the house and everything. He even tried to take care of me. But I couldn't come back." She reached over and took a tissue from the box on the coffee table, wiping her eyes and nose.

"I started drinking. The more your father tried to help, the more I drank. I got angry with him for getting better. And I got worse. Finally, I told him to leave." She stopped. Silence settled in for a moment. Carol peered into the late afternoon light, barely able to make out the falling rain.

"I guess if there's one thing I want you to know, it's that your father did everything he should have done. He tried to hold it together. I destroyed it. Everything that's good in your life right now is because of him. All of the pain you have is because of me." She stared down at the coffee table and shook her head. The tears continued to flow down her cheeks.

Carol glanced up to see Jason looking out the window, a flat expression on his face. "Were you cheating on Dad?"

She felt as though the wind had been knocked out of her. "What? Why would you even ask such a question?" The words came out almost as a shout.

"So, is that a yes?" He turned and looked at her, venom in his eyes.

She stared wide-eyed at him. "No, that most certainly was not a yes. I want to know why you're asking that question. Did your father say I was?" She was frantically trying to understand where this had come from and what it meant.

He leaned forward, suddenly looking years older than he was. "It's a simple yes or no question. Why won't you answer it?"

She continued to stare, slowly shaking her head. "No. It's not a simple question. And it's not a question I expect to hear from my son. Why are you asking that?" She repeated the question for the third time.

He kept the confrontation going. "This is what people do when they have something to hide. They answer questions with questions. So, I assume that you were." He glared.

Carol grabbed hold of her mind and bore down. "You can assume anything you want but unless you answer my question, this is going nowhere. Now you can sit there and spin these things in your head all you want, or you can tell me what's up and we can discuss it. Your choice." Her voice hardened.

He blinked and turned away. "I got friends whose parents are divorced. They say that their moms and dads cheated. They say it's no big deal. They joke and laugh about it. I just want to know if that's the way it was between you and Dad." His voice shrunk to a near whisper.

"Is that what you think—that it's not a big deal?" She lowered her voice to match his.

He shook his head.

She relaxed. "No, Jason. I did not cheat on your father and your father did not cheat on me. I have never been unfaithful to him. And just so you're clear on this, when we divorced, there wasn't even a hint of anyone else in my life. And I don't believe there was anyone in your father's either." She watched him for a moment, as he appeared to process the information.

"Hon, our problem wasn't that we didn't love each other. God, I loved your father more than you can imagine. I would never have betrayed him, and he wouldn't have betrayed me either. Things just fell apart and it was all my fault." She wiped the tears from her face and blew her nose.

"And now he's going to marry Shelley." His words came out soft and sad.

"Jason, listen to me. Your father deserves all the happiness he can find. If Shelley makes him happy, then I think it's wonderful. More than anything else in the world, I want the two of you to have a good life."

He smirked. "Do you have a boyfriend?"

She took another deep breath and tilted her head back, looking at the ceiling. "No. I don't. I dated someone briefly a couple of years after your father and I divorced. But it just was not going to work for me." The statement wasn't really a lie, although it wasn't the truth. She had sort of dated Joe Royston, but it was hardly an attempt at a relationship. She left it at that.

When Jason spoke again, the harsh, accusatory tone and words took Carol by surprise and cut deep. "Did you screw that up too?"

She couldn't breathe. She bent over to catch her breath, her eyes filling once again with tears. She got up from the couch. "I need to get a shower and get ready for work tomorrow." She left, terrified to say anything else for fear of completely breaking down.

***

Carol stood in the shower, hot water pounding her face. Her tears mixed with the water as it rolled down her body. With every passing minute, she more fully realized just how badly she had messed things up. She had ruined not only her life but also the life of her son and husband. She wondered if there would ever come a day when Jason wouldn't hate her. She closed her eyes and prayed to the great beyond that she could make it through the night and then the next three days.

After her shower, she put on a robe and sat on the bed trying to focus on filing her nails. She noticed them being a little long when she was firing her weapon at the range. She just hadn't gotten around to trimming them. This seemed a good opportunity.

She could hear the sounds of a video game coming from the television in the living room. He was in there killing monsters while the demons attacked her in the bedroom. The tears came first, then the sobs. She dropped the nail file to the floor and covered her face with her hands. With her elbows resting on her knees, she broke down. It had been a while, but this meltdown reminded her that things were never going to be okay.

Gradually, the crying subsided. She could feel her eyes swollen and imagined what they must look like. Having her son hate her was like having the last vestiges of anything worthwhile in life ripped from her. The lump in her chest returned and her eyes began to fill again.

The door opened after a quiet knock. She didn't look up. She couldn't bear to see the hatred in his eyes.

Carol felt a hand on her shoulder. Jason sat on the bed beside her and put his arm around her. "I'm sorry, Mom." He squeezed her tight.

The sobbing returned with a vengeance as she burst into tears. She turned and hugged her son fiercely. She had screwed everything in this life up and he was in here apologizing to her. How wrong was that?

Chapter 10

Monday morning in the homicide bullpen offered respite for Carol after the weekend with Jason. Tossing her purse in the desk drawer, she dropped into her chair and leaned back with a sense of relief. "Morning, Ramirez."

Tom looked up from the file folder. "Did the weekend get any better?"

She had commiserated with him on Friday after the Thursday night experience. "Yes and no. It's kind of crazy. He'd be sullen, mean, and nasty and then an hour later he was hugging me and telling me he was sorry." She shook her head.

He laughed. "I think it's called being a teenager. The cure, or so I hear, is turning eighteen."

Carol sighed. "We can only hope."

A booming voice coursed out over the room from the direction of Captain Peterman's office. "Ramirez, Tullis. Come."

She looked over at Tom, eyebrows arched in question.

"We've been summoned." He stood and trudged across the room. Carol followed.

They both knocked and entered Peterman's office. "Yes sir." Ramirez stood erect before the boss as he spoke.

Peterman motioned them toward two chairs that sat across the desk from him. "We have a division meeting with the folks from Sex Crimes this afternoon, but I wanted to talk to the two of you first."

He narrowed his eyes and continued. "This serial rape murder case, we're going to be more involved from here on. The division, as a whole, will just be doing more of the same—support, helping onsite, and maybe some

49

interviewing. But I'm specifically adding this to your caseload. Just so there's no confusion, though, Sex Crimes keeps the lead on this. They call the shots. The brass are looking for a fresh set of eyes and new ideas. The lead detective will let you know what they need. My take on it is that you should be second-guessing their assumptions. The case has hit the brick wall, so to speak. It may be that they just need to keep butting their heads against it until it shatters. Or, it could be that they're looking in all the wrong places. Whichever it is, I can pretty much guarantee that they need your help and are none too pleased with that reality. Tread carefully."

Carol stared back across the desk at the captain trying to read the underlying message. His eyes locked on hers. His face looked relaxed, his mouth a straight line betraying no emotion—nothing.

Peterman signaled the meeting to an end. "Okay then. That's it. Let's get to it."

Carol and Tom stood to leave but the captain spoke again. "Ramirez, you can go. Tullis, hold up." He kept his eyes on Carol as Ramirez left, closing the door behind him.

"You going to be okay with this?" The captain's voice came out steady and without an air of accusation.

Carol sat down. "Yes sir. Why wouldn't I be okay?"

Peterman leaned forward into the desk, his hands folded in front of him. His voice edged closer to a confrontational tone. "Don't play dumb with me, Detective. You know damned well what I'm talking about."

Carol lowered her head and closed her eyes. She did indeed know what he was talking about. This case, while different from Jenny's, was still focused on a serial killer and it stirred her emotions. "Yes sir. I'll be okay."

Peterman ratcheted up the tension. "That's the answer I expected. But I'm telling you straight up, Tullis, don't get yourself drawn into this. Do your job. Leave the personal stuff at home."

Carol bristled at the apparent implication that she couldn't remain professional. "I got it, Captain. I understand. You don't need to lecture me."

"This isn't a lecture. When you get one of those, you'll know it. This is me giving you direction. Remember, I'm the captain and you're the detective. I call the tune. You dance the dance. Don't forget that." His face retained that neutral, matter-of-fact appearance despite the hard edge to his voice.

Right. Like I could forget. "Yes, sir. Got it." She left it at that.

"Good. Now go."

Chapter 11

The first-floor conference room was arranged with roughly forty folding chairs facing a lectern. A blank dry erase board hung on the wall behind a speaker's podium. Although Carol knew what was to come, the room itself gave no clue to the subject of the meeting.

She and Ramirez parked in seats about midway between the front and back. She surveyed the room, which had begun filling up. Some of the faces she knew from Homicide. Others were unfamiliar.

Several people in the front row caught her attention. Although she could only see the backs of their heads and a tiny bit of their facial profile, a couple of them looked familiar. One in particular, a woman in her late forties or early fifties, sat almost dead center in the front row. Her blonde hair fell on broad shoulders. From what Carol could see, the woman looked stocky but not fat. Something about her face and demeanor, at least what was visible, struck a chord but the detective couldn't place her.

At five after two, Captain Peterman entered and took station at the podium. "Looks like we're all here. I'm going to turn this over to Captain Fredericks with Sex Crimes in a minute but before I do that, I want to go over a few preliminaries. Starting today, Homicide is going to be more involved in the serial rape murder case. You'll get the details on that involvement shortly. I have assured Captain Fredericks that we will provide whatever support is needed. I want to be clear that Sex Crimes retains the lead. They call the shots. Any questions?"

He paused for a couple of seconds. "Hearing none, I'll pass this off to Captain Fredericks." He nodded to a tall, slender man looking to be about fifty.

"Thank you." Fredericks reached up and adjusted the knot of his navy tie. His intense blue eyes surveyed the audience. "The case at hand has been active now for just over two years. We've done a thorough job of documenting the MO and developing a profile. Unfortunately, we're still coming up short. I'm going to leave it to Detective Sullivan to fill you in on the details. But what I'm hoping is that bringing fresh perspectives will give us something new." He rubbed his hand across the short-cropped gray-brown hair on the side of his head. The intense light from the overhead fixtures reflected off the bald top. "With that, I'll turn this over to Sullivan. Again, thanks." He grimaced as he left the podium.

A tall, slender black woman stood and walked to the podium carrying a notebook computer. She picked up a small device and half-turned toward the board behind her and clicked. A projection screen descended from its hidden compartment in the ceiling. The woman opened her computer on the small table beside the lectern, punched several keys, and an image appeared on the screen.

"Thank you, Captain Fredericks. I'm Detective Brenda Sullivan and I'm the lead on this case. I've been on it from the beginning. I'll be going over what we know." She gestured toward the stocky blond woman in the front row. "We also have Doctor Hoskins from Western Washington University Psychology Department with us. She's been working on the profiling and she'll fill you in on that."

The name hit Carol hard. She remembered the woman now. Hoskins had done the profiling in Jenny's case, a case that had never been solved.

Sullivan began plodding through the case point by point. All twenty-three victims were adult females. Ages ranged from twenty-three to fifty-five. Most of the women were white. Two were African American and one was Asian. Four were married, the rest single—some never married, some divorced. Professions varied from attorney to barista.

Carol shook her head at the lack of a clear pattern. Nothing seemed to connect these women.

Sullivan projected a map of the greater Seattle-Tacoma area with a series of red stars scattered across it. "These are the locations where the bodies were found. As you can see, there doesn't seem to be any discernable pattern. We don't have any way of knowing at this point how far away from each site the actual murder scene is. We have, in most cases, identified the abduction sites." She reached over and hit a key on the computer, overlaying a set of blue stars on the map.

"The only thing we see in common here is that all of the women were abducted in public places. What is interesting, though, is that the specific locations where we know the abductions occurred have no video cameras. Now, this is important. The outside areas in general do have some limited coverage but not enough to help us. We assume the unsub is very aware of surveillance. Doctor Hoskins will speak to this in greater detail."

Sullivan presented another slide, this on a standard presentation style format with bulleted points. "Here are the key points that are always consistent. First, the unsub always covers the victim with a brand new, fresh out-of-the-bag nine by twelve blue tarpaulin. This never varies. The exact brand and product number are the same. You can find those in the case notes." She reached over and pressed a key on the notebook, bringing up the next bullet.

"The victims were all raped. Afterwards, they were killed with a precision slice through the carotid artery. The bodies were cleaned and prepared as if for display." Sullivan's eyes hardened and she clenched her jaw. She advanced the display to the next bullet.

"The ME has found the same two drugs in all victims. The first is rohypnol, a common date rape drug. We suspect that this is used to get the women out of the public area to a more private, secluded spot."

She swallowed hard and looked down at the podium briefly. Looking up, she continued, "The second is an obscure synthetic paralytic substance known as naelosaxitoxin. This one paralyzes the individual. They can see, hear, and feel. They cannot move or speak." She closed her eyes briefly before continuing. "We believe that the unsub uses this so that they can be aware during the rape. There are signs of preliminary sexual assault, including biting of nipples and trauma in the genital area."

She paused again, shaking her head almost imperceptibly. "This is followed by penetration. The unsub uses a condom. Again, from the analysis of the residual spermicide, he uses the same brand and type every time. No variation." She took a deep breath before finishing. "This all occurs while the victim is alive and aware. Only after all of this is over are they killed."

Silence dominated the room. Carol stared at the bullet points on the screen. Technology allowed the display that they all hoped would help solve the case. And yet it provided a coldness, a loss of connection that removed all trace of humanity from the victims. She wondered if Jenny's case had been discussed this way. Sullivan's voice interrupted her thoughts.

"Finally, the victims are cleaned up. They are laid out in unpopulated areas." She paused for a few seconds, looking around the room. "One other thing, and this is a fact that we've withheld from the press. It will allow us to separate out any copycats. In each case, the unsub lays a length of royal blue silk cloth across the breasts and the pubic area of the victim."

She reached over and punched a computer key, bringing up a photograph of one of the victims laid out. "The size of the cloth is one foot by three feet. We've identified the manufacturer and checked for distribution. What we found is that a large hobby and crafts shop in Des Moines, Iowa, was burglarized about four years ago. A large amount of merchandise was taken including nearly two hundred linear yards of this cloth. The break-in was never solved. We assume that this is where the material came from, although we have no idea whether our unsub was the actual burglar or not."

"Before I turn this over to Doctor Hoskins, I have one other thing for you. Tomorrow marks day thirty since the last killing. If the pattern holds, and we have no reason to believe it won't, the unsub has already selected his next victim."

Chapter 12

His eyes followed her every movement. She glided through the crowded mall as though in a trance. Her gaze alternated between the area in front of her and the floor at her feet. She cut out of the crowd into the small, crowded bistro where she took a spot in line to place an order.

Jessica was forty-seven and never married. He felt her pain. She clearly wanted love in her life, but nothing had worked for her. She was not a completely unattractive woman. She had taken good care of her body. It remained trim and well-proportioned despite the years. Her mousy brown hair just covered her ears. In the front, she kept it brushed to the right side, giving a clear view of her cream-colored forehead. Maybe plain, but certainly not ugly.

He watched her fidgeting with the bill in her hand, probably a twenty. She never looked up at the menu, though. No need to. She was here at the same time every evening after work. She typically hovered over a latte for about forty-five minutes. She had no need to hurry, though. There was no one waiting at home.

He started toward the bistro for his practice run. Standing in line, he studied the menu, glanced at Jessica, then the crowd, and back to the menu. He confirmed the lack of surveillance in this area of the mall. Over the years he'd learned how to spot even the most obscure video cameras. He congratulated himself, as he always did, on his attention to detail. And he reminded himself of how much he'd grown—how he'd perfected his craft.

He took a seat and sipped his cappuccino, watching Jessica and dreaming about what they would enjoy together the next evening.

Chapter 13

Carol rolled into the squad bay at exactly eight o'clock the next morning. Ramirez was apparently running late. As she hung up her coat, a familiar voice came booming across the room. "Tullis, come." She shuddered.

Grabbing her pad, she made her way across to the captain's office. Stepping just inside the door, she paused. "Yes sir?"

"Close the door. Have a seat." He motioned toward a chair beside his desk.

Odd. Normally he keeps the desk between him and me. Carol sat down tentatively.

Peterman sat for a second, his hands perfectly still on the desktop in front of him. "How's the serial case going?"

"Well, I just got the briefing yesterday and you were in the room with me. I guess I'd say that you know as much as I do right now." She wondered if maybe he'd expected her to go over the case notes that she'd been given at the close of the previous day's meeting.

He fell silent for a moment. When he continued, the characteristically hard look on his face relaxed. "I want you to keep me in the loop on this."

Something seemed off. He got regular briefings so there should be no need for her to keep him advised. Still, he was the captain and she was the detective, as he was so fond of reminding her. "Yes sir." Her curiosity got the better of her. "If I might ask, Captain, what kinds of information are you looking for? I assumed that Captain Fredericks would keep you up to date." She cringed, waiting for the onslaught.

Instead of a rant about him being the boss, he responded quietly. "Yes, well, he probably will keep me posted. But I want to know what's really going on. I'm not talking about the case as it's doctored up for general dissemination."

Alarms sounded in her head. She felt like she was getting sucked into some kind of conspiracy. "Well, very good, sir. You want me to also pass this along to Ramirez?" Some company would be nice.

"No!" He paused, his next words coming softer. "I only need one of you and you're the one. This is between you and me." He narrowed his eyes and clenched his jaw.

Carol trembled. Just over a week back and she was being drawn into something that felt wrong. "Yes, sir."

Peterman leaned back in his chair, hands laced behind his head. "Tullis, I can see the wheels turning in there. Don't make more of this than is there. I'm giving Sex Crimes a good chunk of resources. I'm doing it partly out of professional courtesy to Captain Fredericks. But mostly I'm doing it because the Commissioner thought it would be a good idea. Every minute we spend on this case is a minute not spent on our own cases. All murder victims deserve justice, not just victims of serial killers."

Carol felt sick at her stomach. This felt wrong in every possible way. Still, maybe he was right. Homicide was going to invest time and energy into the case. Surely the captain deserved to know how it was going. She told herself that she was just being paranoid.

Chapter 14

Carol felt more than a little self-conscious coming out of Peterman's office. Closing the door behind her, she immediately spotted Ramirez watching her, a somber almost suspicious look on his face.

"You and the captain are getting to be best buddies."

She forced a laugh. "Not in this lifetime." She plopped into her seat and sighed. "If you don't have anything lined up, I'd like to go over the video of Doctor Hoskins' profile presentation from yesterday."

"Why, we watched her presentation and you have the case file?" The words came out more as a casual observation than a challenge.

She turned and looked at him, wondering to herself why she wanted to see it. "I don't know. I just think that there's more to learn in the presentation and I always tend to see new things a second or third time around."

Carol queued up the video for viewing on her desktop monitor as she waited for Ramirez to get back from the coffee pot.

What he brought back was closer to sludge than coffee. "Here you go. Enjoy." He chortled.

"Thanks." She started to take a sip but the stench of swill convinced her otherwise. "Okay. You ready?"

"Where's the popcorn?"

Carol clicked the "Play" icon and the screen jumped to life. She watched as Doctor Hoskins bumped into a chair on the way to the podium. The profiler wore a pair a dark-colored slacks, either navy or black, and a cream blazer over a pale lavender blouse. A silk scarf in muted tones of pink and purple obscured her neck.

Ramirez leaned back with his arms folded in on his chest. "You'd think those professor types would be used to getting up in front of people. I mean, they teach every day."

Tullis studied the image of the woman on the screen. The doctor's overall appearance suggested an age in the mid-fifties. Standing about five foot nine, her figure was full, maybe stocky, but not fat. Her blond hair fell on broad shoulders. She fumbled through some notes in her hand, apparently searching for the right place to begin. At one point, her papers, scattering on the floor around the lectern. She could hear the soft laugh from the audience, who had gotten a chuckle at the good doctor's expense.

As Hoskins regrouped, papers in hand, Carol could see her eyes surveying the group, much like a teacher would consider a classroom full of students before beginning.

"This is what's wrong with education in this country." Ramirez's voice added commentary to the scene. "She's a disorganized klutz who's supposed to be the head of the Psychology Department at Western Washington."

Carol's laugh came out abbreviated. The profiler came across as uncoordinated and almost clueless. Yet there seemed a sharp, almost predatory look in her eyes. It was as if the disorganization and dropping the papers were a part of the presentation itself. The detective thought back to her own days in college. Each professor seemed to have their own little act that they used to engage students. *I guess that's how they do it.*

Chapter 15

Carol watched as the psychologist made one last visual sweep of her audience before beginning. The scene reminded her of those last few moments back in college before a professor began a lecture.

"Good afternoon." The smile seemed a token offering of cheer amidst a horrific situation. "I know some of you already but for the rest of you, I'm Doctor Marge Hoskins. I've worked in profiling on a number of cases over the years. I've been on this case since the third victim."

Carol stared at the woman's steely gray blue eyes, wondering how she coped with the gruesome nature of profiling work. She surely must have some defense mechanisms in place to buffer herself. Did she de-personalize or de-humanize the victims in order to protect herself? Did she de-personalize Jenny all those years ago?

"I'm going to be going through the profile this afternoon. Now, I'll tell you up front that much of what we've come up with is based on certain assumptions, which I will identify. So, as I go through, I'll cite the evidence where we have it." She paused and cleared her throat.

"As you heard from the Detective Sullivan and Captain Fredericks, we're hoping for some fresh ideas."

Carol smirked. She'd yet to meet a consultant or contractor in this field that welcomed any challenge to their ideas. She tried to envision how that conversation would go. A sarcastic laugh almost escaped.

Hoskins shuffled through the papers that she'd set on the podium before beginning.

Carol caught herself shaking her head but stifled it. *This woman's a caricature of a nerdy professor. No wonder she couldn't solve Jenny's murder.* But of course, it wasn't the profiler's job to solve the case. The detective mentally whisked away the disdain and went back to watching the video.

Ramirez, meanwhile, sat with his right elbow on the desk and his head propped on his fist—the picture of boredom. He did make the occasional note on his pad but that seemed the extent of his interest.

Shifting her weight from one leg to the other, Doctor Hoskins waded into the substance of the presentation. "Let's start with the basics. We're dealing with a Caucasian male. I say Caucasian simply because statistically most of these kinds of crimes are committed by whites. So, this is one of those assumptions I spoke of. We have no evidence other than trend data on other similar crimes."

Carol paused the video and made a note to check crime statistics and affirm that. If they were coming up empty, unwarranted assumptions were a good place to start. She clicked on the play button to continue.

"I estimate the age of the unsub to be early to mid-thirties."

Carol mused at how the academic had picked up the lingo of profilers that littered the serial killer television environment. She could swear that Hoskins was enjoying this.

"If you think back to Detective Sullivan's description of the crime scenes and the elements, you can see that this individual is highly disciplined, patient, and possesses a great deal of self-control. The incidents are spaced exactly thirty days apart—never early, never later. He meticulously cleans

64

and prepares the bodies for display never varying his routine. The length of time between abduction and killing, at least for those victims where we can closely approximate the time of abduction, is consistently about six hours. During this time, there is no physical torture or abuse that we can detect. A younger man doing this would be more likely to rush things or even escalate the frequency."

A tight knot formed in Carol's stomach. *No physical torture or abuse? What the fuck was rape and killing?* She felt bile rising in her throat. Maybe eating lunch rather than sucking down a cup of coffee would have served her better.

The doctor continued, her voice intense and animated. "There is, of course, the possibility that the unsub could be older but that would beg the question, what have they been doing up until now? It's rare for a person in, say, their late forties or fifties to suddenly turn to serial killing. We've checked regionally and nationally to identify any older cases, perhaps in other areas, where similar strings of killings have occurred. We've found nothing to indicate that this person has been active before." She paused for a moment and then asked, "Any questions so far?" Silence.

"And so, I'll move on." She shuffled the papers again and briefly donned a confused look before continuing. "Yes, the next thing I want to cover is the apparent sense of awareness of video coverage. But it's really more than that. This individual doesn't make mistakes. Avoiding cameras is certainly a part of that. But also, he doesn't leave any trace of himself on the victim. He picks his abduction sites in a way that allows him to make contact and get the woman out not only without being recorded but also apparently without being noticed. And given that his schedule is so precise, we have to conclude that it's not a trial and error methodology. He's done it successfully now twenty-three times. So, he knows what he's doing. Very possibly he has a background in or currently works in law enforcement. Maybe not as a police officer but perhaps in a support capacity such as forensics or technology services." She paused and looked around the room.

A hand shot up from a male Homicide detective, Williamson, as Carol recalled. "Doctor, is it possible that we might be looking for someone who wanted to be a cop but washed out of the academy or got drummed out of the force? Maybe wanting to throw this in our face?"

Hoskins lightly rubbed her chin as she appeared to consider the question. "Possibly. But I don't think so. The unsub doesn't seem to taunt the police. And I think that Detective Sullivan will tell you, we've tried to bait and taunt him, hoping to force him into a mistake. But it's like he doesn't notice. He keeps to the schedule and method. Almost as though he considers the police irrelevant." She arched her back, as if she were stretching. "Anything else?" Silence.

A thought jolted Carol out of her concentration. *Is it possible that the killer could be someone connected to the investigation team?* She shuddered. That would mean that everything said in meetings was being shared with him.

"I want to finish up by discussing what I see as his social skills and status. Let's look first at the actual crime. He abducts the women not by grabbing them and tying them up or hauling them out physically, but by using a drug. Then they leave willingly with him. During the ordeal, he seems to go out of his way not to cause any physical pain. He uses a chemical rather than a physical restraint. As I said earlier, there is no sign of torture. Instead, he engages in what we might call foreplay, albeit in a rather bizarre approach. After foreplay, he penetrates them vaginally but there is no sign of trauma, tearing, or bleeding. He uses a lubricant in addition to that found on the condom. Again, it is as if he wants to avoid causing physical pain. Finally, when he kills them, the death is quick and painless. It appears that he walks around and stands at their head as they are lying there. He reaches down and slices the carotid artery in a way that the victim likely does not see it happening. So, we probably say that he is not without some empathy."

Carol had broken out in a sweat and her nausea intensified. She was sitting there listening to this doctor describe a horrific assault and murder process as if it was some ordinary sexual encounter. Images of Jenny's body flashed across her mind. She sprang from her chair and bolted for the restroom. She barely made it to a stall before vomiting her coffee. She coughed, spitting out phlegm. A splash of cold water gave some relief. A breath mint also helped.

Ramirez watched her as she trudged back over to the desk. "You okay?" He got up as she approached.

"Yeah, I'm okay. Just, you know, nature calls." She lied.

He grunted and shook his head, returning to his seat.

Carol clicked the play icon again. Tom had apparently paused the video when she'd deserted the scene. The image of Doctor Hoskins, frozen in mid-gesture, came to life again.

"The last thing that we need to look at is the selection of victims. Now, as Detective Sullivan explained, there is no pattern in terms of race, age, marital status, or occupation. But look closely at the photographs of the women." She looked over at a young man sitting with a notebook computer in the front row. "Could you put up the photos please, Carl?"

A set of three DMV photos appeared on the screen. The doctor remained silent for a few seconds. "Next set please." And so, they sequenced through all twenty-three victims.

"What do these women all have in common, other than being female?" She paused and looked around the room. "None of them are what we would call ugly, but neither are any of them beauties. They are all unremarkable. Some married, some single, some divorced. What we know, though, is that none of the single women had love interests and from what we've been told, the married women were in basically loveless marriages. Assuming that our unsub can learn this, we may be looking for someone who sees themselves as providing love to these women. This is consistent in his activities with them."

Another hand shot up from the front row, this time a female that Carol hadn't met before. "Are you suggesting that the killer made contact and possibly established some kind of initial relationship before abducting them?

Hoskins reverted to the same mannerism she'd used with the previous question. She rubbed her chin and appeared to focus on some distant point in space. "I'm going to say no. If this were the case, it would be very likely that at least one or more of the victims would have spoken about it to someone they know. So far, no one interviewed has indicated that this was the case. I conclude that the individual made contact and abducted them at the same time."

The questioner wrote something on the pad in front of her.

"In all likelihood, the individual has strong social skills. He's probably a good conversationalist. He's able to get into their space, sit down with them, and converse without drawing any attention. When he leaves with them, again, it seems very natural or we would have people noticing. In conclusion, then, we're looking for a white male in his early to mid-thirties. He works in or around law enforcement. He's intelligent, very self-disciplined, and affable but not so much as to attract unnecessary attention. And, I guess I'd also say he's probably not married, although that's also an assumption."

Carol clicked on the pause icon, freezing the doctor's face on the screen. The night separating the presentation from the video viewing had not helped to dampen the disgust. "I don't get it. She talks about this monster like he's just an ordinary guy picking up women."

Ramirez swiveled his chair around to face her. "Easy, Tullis. She's a psychologist doing her job. We all know the killer's a monster. We don't need the doc to tell us that. We need to know what we're looking for and at least she's giving it to us straight."

Carol remained unconvinced. *I don't know if I can do this.*

Chapter 16

Carol skipped lunch and managed to sneak out of work an hour early. Watching the interview with Doctor Hoskins had destroyed any sense of well-being that she had.

She rolled into the driveway of her south Seattle home about five-fifteen. The rain had softened to a constant drizzle and the low clouds obscured the setting sun.

As she entered the house, she tossed her keys into a basket sitting on the tea cart. After putting her weapon away, she trudged toward the kitchen in hopes that something in the refrigerator or pantry would strike her fancy. She'd not planned anything for dinner.

While taking stock of the dinner options, she heard a sharp knock on the back door. Looking out a side window, she saw her tenant standing on the back porch with the screen door open.

She opened the inside door to face him. "Good evening, Doctor Sturgis. Everything okay back there?"

He was dressed in a pair of faded jeans, a burnt orange long-sleeve pullover, and gray and white sneakers. "It's Ben, please. And yes, everything's fine. Well, except the bedroom overhead light's not working. I was wondering if you had a step ladder."

Carol moaned inwardly. She had a property manager specifically to deal with things like this. "You can call Tony and he'll take care of it. I'm sorry for the inconvenience." She stood square in the doorway.

Sturgis laughed. "Oh, come on. That'd cost a fortune for a licensed electrician. If you've got a ladder, I can at least check it. I did construction during the summers while I was in grad school. Likely nothing more than a disconnected wire." He shrugged, letting his arms hang loose at his side. "Oh, and since I'll shut off the breaker, maybe you could hold a flashlight for me."

She closed her eyes and exhaled. "Okay. Give me a minute. I'll open the garage door. The ladder's in there. You'll have to go around the side to get to it." She knew that having a tenant willing to take care of small things would save her a lot of money in the end. Still, today was not the day. She sighed and inwardly sucked it up, deciding to just get it done and over with.

Carol retreated into the hallway, opened the door into the garage, and hit the opener switch. Flashlight in hand, she made the ten-yard journey in the light rain across the back lawn to the small apartment. Sturgis came around the side of the house carrying the ladder.

He opened the door and moved straight through the combination living and dining room into the small bedroom. He had already moved the bed out of the way. After setting the ladder in place, the young man went over and turned the light out before going to turn off the breaker. "Be right back."

The remainder of the lights, all of which drew power from a single switch, went out. "Okay, let's get this done." He climbed up the ladder, putting his hand on her shoulder. "If you could shine the light right up here, that'd be great." He began taking the housing down using a screwdriver that she'd not noticed.

He twisted on the ladder just slightly and leaned over. "Damn I hate being left-handed sometimes. Right in here, if you can."

Carol adjusted the flashlight to illuminate the dark opening where he was pointing. "That do it?"

"Yeah, perfect." He twisted his body again and cocked his head as he looked into the hole. "There's the culprit. Yep, the neutral's disconnected." He put the screwdriver in his back pocket.

Carol cringed, imagining what would happen if he fell and the blade, pointing up, went into his back. "Be careful up there. I can do without an ambulance call."

"No problemo. It's just the twisting. Just a little more... and, voila. All done." Sturgis straightened up on the ladder. Carol, could you go hit the breaker for me, make sure that did it, please?"

Something about the way he said her name irritated her, a little, but maybe not so much. Not many people called her "Carol" these days. After resetting the switch, she called in from the far corner of the kitchen. "Okay. Done. Try it."

Illumination poured forth from the bedroom. "That did it. Thanks."

She came back to find him resetting the housing. He again put his hand on her shoulder as he came down the ladder. Carol was sure she felt a slight rub on her shoulder as he descended. An involuntary shiver coursed through her body. She stepped away from him immediately.

As he folded up the ladder, she noticed a set of very light indentations on the carpet. From the look of it, he had placed a dining room chair in that spot within the past hour and stood on it for a few minutes. She closed her eyes and smiled. He'd disconnected the wire himself, just to get her into the bedroom. "Thanks for fixing that, Doctor Sturgis. I appreciate it. I'll put the ladder back."

He laughed. "Ben, please. And you're very welcome. Say, I've got a fantastic bottle of Glenlivet Scotch here if you'd care to join me."

Ladder in hand, she looked at him. The pick-up line was cheesy, but he did fill out his jeans nicely. Still, much too young. *Not so much.* "I appreciate the offer, Doctor Sturgis, but no." She turned for the front door.

That laugh again—youthful and genuine. "Okay, but my feelings are hurt. And it's Ben."

She shook her head and laughed as she turned the handle on the front door. "Good night, Doctor Sturgis."

Chapter 17

He sat in his parked Forest Green Toyota Camry with the engine running and the windshield wipers on intermittent. The steady rain of the previous evening had lightened to a sparse drizzle. Three-thirty in the morning was a special, almost magical time. Most of the world slept, hopeful that the new day would bring joy, love, riches, or whatever else they desired. He was alone at this special time in this special place with Jessica, if only for another hour.

From the unobtrusive parking spot, he studied the gate that interrupted the chain link fence. A rather hefty looking lock secured the chain, which connected the gate to the post. The chain, lock, and fence were of no importance. But the rain and mud exacerbated an already troublesome issue.

He could not, in good conscience, leave this lovely woman in a soiled condition. She deserved better. And yet he needed to return her to the world. A thought drifted across his mind. Seattle and the surrounding environs were not the best suited for his affairs. Perhaps it was time to consider moving. Arizona, with its large population centers and drier climate would be perfect.

He roused himself out of the thought train. Relocating was another problem for another time.

Surveying his surroundings again, he could appreciate the genius in his choice of locations. This particular worksite was still in the planning stages. The architects, engineers, and other professionals would wander in around nine, after their morning lattes. Workers would not be here for another few weeks at best. No danger of anyone showing up early to interfere. Still, he could be assured that Jessica would be found before the day was done.

After cutting the lock, he made two trips between the car and Jessica's resting place. In addition to transporting the body, he had the tarp, silk cloth, and some towels and washcloths to make sure that he left her clean. The mere idea of leaving her in an embarrassing condition was revolting.

Selecting a piece of higher ground so that water from the continuing drizzle would not collect, he laid out a four by six sheet of clear visqueen. This was a first for him. In the past two years he had never had to deal with rain. That realization struck him as odd. With the climate of the area, the weather had miraculously cooperated every time. It was as if Nature herself smiled on his love. And, maybe tonight was Nature's way of gently nudging him—it was time to move on.

He laid Jessica out, wiping off a few traces of mud that had splashed up as he had carried her. He quickly covered her breasts and pubic area as delicately and with as much dignity as he could. After removing the protective shower cap and brushing her hair, he gave his love one last look to make sure everything was perfect. He slit open the package protecting the blue tarpaulin. He spread the cover over her, folding down the part that would cover her face. Her lifeless eyes called to him, but he resisted the urge to kiss her one last time. He pulled the covering over her face.

Chapter 18

Carol awoke with a start. Her heart pounded as she checked the clock—three forty-five. Whatever bad dream had haunted her proved elusive. She laid her head back on the pillow, eyes closed and willing her heart to slow down.

A thread of disquiet hovered at the edge of her conscious thought, something just beyond her grasp. After a few minutes of futile effort to sort it out, she gave up and opened her eyes.

She knew from long, bitter experience that sleep would not return this night. Throwing the covers back, she got up and went to the kitchen to put on a pot of coffee. The night-light plugged into the outlet next to the sink was enough that she could see what she was doing. The gurgling sound of production signaled about a ten-minute wait for the first cup—time for a quick shower.

She paused briefly at the backdoor window. Looking out at the small apartment, now dark, she thought about the events of the previous evening and the young psychologist cum electrician and his touch. A fleeting sensation that she'd last known nearly a decade ago coursed through her body and then disappeared.

Too young, too pushy. She swept the thoughts of him from her mind.

As she made her way down the hall, it hit her. The previous evening was the thirty-day mark for the killer/rapist. A jolt of nausea hit her stomach and she stopped mid-way to the bedroom. If the schedule held true, a woman had died several hours ago and was now laid out waiting to be found. She closed her eyes and hung her head. Despair set in.

***

Carol pushed through the double doors into the bullpen at five minutes to eight. Peterman sat at his desk but appeared to take no notice of her arrival. Tom's desk sat empty. Her partner prided himself on not arriving early.

The prevailing sense of quiet and order in the bullpen struck her. About half the desks were occupied, their owners all engaged in reading, typing on the computer, or making notes the old-fashioned way. If a body had been dumped the previous evening, it had not yet been found.

Maybe the schedule won't hold. Maybe he decided to skip a month. She felt as though a massive shoe hung precariously over her head, about to drop at any moment.

Two cups of coffee later, she found herself in the women's bathroom, hunched over the sink and splashing cold water onto her face. Turning the water off, she kept her head bowed over the sink and closed her eyes tightly.

A female voice intruded on her party. "Rough morning?"

Carol turned to see a short, stocky woman in her early thirties. Her dark brown hair just barely covered her ears. She was a homicide detective although the name proved elusive.

"Just thinking about the serial killer case. Yesterday was day thirty. I guess I'm dreading the phone call." After an awkward few seconds of silence, she slid by the woman to depress the button on the paper towel dispenser.

"You're Tullis?" The woman's voice was quiet, even, and dispassionate.

Carol turned to face the woman and extended her right hand. "Yes, Carol Tullis. Sorry, you're not catching me at my best."

The young detective eyed Carol up and down for a few seconds and then shook her hand briefly with a noticeable lack of enthusiasm "Jessie Collins." As she turned to go, Carol could see the disdain in her eyes. *I guess my reputation does precede me.*

By mid-morning, she allowed herself a meager dose of hope. She was just about to share the thought with Ramirez when her cell phone rang. Looking at the caller-ID, her heart fell.

Chapter 19

Ramirez drove and Carol stared out the passenger side window at the guardrail posts zipping by as they sped down I-5. She mused that her luck at the ritual coin toss had been nothing short of extraordinary. Other than the first time, when her partner had obviously cheated, she'd won every toss. He was getting a lot of practice driving. This constituted the one small corner of her life where things always seem to go right.

The rain had stopped altogether and a small break in the clouds ahead suggested that some early October sunshine might make an appearance. Still, the roads were wet from the night before and Tom had to turn on the wipers periodically to swipe away the dirty film accumulating on the window. The hum of the road, the occasional swipe of the window, and the visual effect of the moving landscape induced something of a trance in Carol.

About ten minutes into the trip, Ramirez intruded on her reverie. "You're pretty quiet today."

Carol closed her eyes and let her head rest against the passenger side window. "We're on the way to the body of a woman who was alive yesterday but is dead today." She knew it made no sense. It's just that small talk seemed so screwed up at this moment.

Silence for another few seconds. "You're a homicide detective. What did you expect? Without murdered people, you have no job." The argumentative words contrasted with the soft, almost gentle tone of her partner's voice.

She exhaled and let her gaze out onto the countryside slip out of focus. "Yeah, well, I'd gladly give up the job if the murders would stop." She thought about her statement even as she spoke. Would she really be happy to give up her job? She'd heard other professionals spout similar statements— addiction therapists, rape counselors, child service workers— all of them glad to leave their careers behind if the misery of their chosen fields ceased to exist.

In fact, there were entire industries built up around human misery, crime, and sickness. Billions spent on the prison industry, fortunes made in the pharmaceutical industry, and hospitals that only thrived when people were so sick or injured that they couldn't be helped in physicians' offices. What would the world be like if there was no need for these institutions?

I guess I could have been a chef or an accountant or maybe even a teacher.

The car jolted to a stop in front of a chain link fence without Carol even noticing that they'd exited I-5 onto an obscure side road. A strip of yellow crime scene tape blocked access to what looked like a combination construction site and junkyard.

"We have arrived." Ramirez announced the obvious.

They approached a uniformed officer standing on the outside of the yard. Tom lifted his badge as he spoke. "Ramirez and Tullis. Is Sullivan here yet?"

The officer, who appeared to be no older than his mid-twenties, gestured in the direction of the yard. "She got here about ten minutes ago."

Carol lifted the tape to walk under. "Do they have things taped off inside? She looked into the yard and saw only tape around the broad perimeter. Mud, multiple footprints, and standing pools of water dominated the scene.

"Naw. The guys who opened up here this morning noticed the cut lock, but figured it was just vandalism, or so they said. They destroyed the scene walking around before they noticed the tarp covering the victim."

Tullis made her way around the outer edge of the yard toward a blue tarp that sat alone on a slightly elevated piece of ground. She noticed that, in contrast to mud and standing water around the area, the lone small spot stood above it all. The killer had chosen well.

As she approached, she saw Sullivan berating a forensic technician, a hard, angry look on her face. Carol only picked up the last few words of the discussion. "...all of it. I don't want to have to tell you again. Now get it done." The Sex Crimes detective turned abruptly and stormed off in the direction of the work site entrance.

Tom touched Carol's shoulder. "Come on, I'll introduce you."

The forensic tech knelt on one knee as he coaxed some bit of something into a small plastic evidence bag. With his back to the two approaching detectives, he apparently didn't hear their approach.

"So, how's the resident redneck this morning?" Tom chortled as he blurted out the greeting.

The technician turned and a grin found its way onto his sullen face. "Jose, the man! How does this good morning find you?" He stood and stretched.

"Bubba, this is my new partner, Detective Tullis." He nodded toward Carol and continued. "And this is Sam Johnson, Forensics. You're going to get to know him really well."

"Carol Tullis. Nice to meet you, Sam."

Ramirez intervened. "I think he only responds to Bubba. It must be one of those inbreeding things."

"That coming from a certified wetback." Johnson smirked. He offered a warm, genuine smile. "A pleasure to meet you, Ma'am."

Tom pointed toward the front gate, where Detective Sullivan had apparently accosted someone else. "What did you do to get her so riled?"

"Who knows? Maybe it's my accent." His smile faded and he sighed. "But I guess I might be a bit touchy too in her shoes. This makes, what, number twenty-three or twenty-four? And, if you ask me, we're not getting any closer. Gotta be hard on her."

"Yeah, well that's her job." Tom didn't appear long on sympathy for the detective.

Sam kept an eye toward the front gate. "I'd better get back to it."

Sullivan, apparently finished with her intimidation at the entrance, sloshed through the mud over to where Tom and Carol stood near the body.

Careful to make sure that her badge was visible, she approached the still-angry detective. "Hi. What do we have?"

Sullivan turned and stared for a moment. "A dead woman. What did you expect?" She turned and slugged her way toward a man taking crime scene photographs.

Carol knelt beside the tarp and pulled it back. As she looked at the dead woman's face, a loud voice interrupted her thoughts. "Hey, get away from there." She turned to see Sullivan glaring at her. "I don't want anyone touching that until the forensic guys are done." She stood, eyes blazing with her hands on her hips.

"Sorry." Carol got up and stepped back. She decided to overlook what she thought was a gross overreaction. After a few seconds of a staring contest, she turned away and walked toward the gate. She really wanted to lay into Sullivan, but Captain Peterman's admonishment came to mind. *It's their case. They call the shots.*

As she walked, she turned her head to look back at Sullivan, who by this time had returned her attention to the photographer.

Ramirez alternately took notes and surveyed the scene as Carol approached. He pointed in the general direction of the gate. "I have to say, this guy has it down cold. He comes down I-5 and, zip, he's off onto a side road with no houses, businesses, or any other buildings. There's no way any kind of surveillance would have picked this up. And look, this place is surrounded by trees so, once inside, he'd be out of sight."

"Yeah. You're right. This is how he manages to have the time to attend to details. I wasn't able to look at the body long, but it looked immaculate, given the conditions out here."

Tom turned and trudged toward the site entrance. "Let's have a look at the lock." He tucked his pad into his jacket pocket as he made his way across the muddy field.

Carol inspected the chain drooped around the metal post that framed the gate. "Look. The chain's intact. The guy cut the lock. Smart. To anyone passing by, everything would look normal. No one was going to notice anything until the workers got here." She turned to the uniformed officer. "Who called this in?"

The young cop standing beside the gate pointed toward a small group of civilians. "That guy over there, in the denim jacket. He's in charge." He took a pad from his pocket. "Jamison's his name."

She considered going over and talking to him but, recalling her recent encounter with Detective Sullivan, she opted to check first. Pacing across the yard, she approached the woman from behind. "Detective."

Sullivan turned and stared but said nothing.

"If it's okay, I'd like to start interviewing some of these guys." Carol gestured toward the group of men gathered near the entrance.

"I'd rather you didn't." The words came out quiet and even but laced with contempt.

Carol glanced away briefly as she gathered her thoughts. "Okay, could you at least tell me what's going on here? We were assigned to help you. What would you like us to be doing?" She stepped up closer to Sullivan so that she stood face-to-face with only a few inches separating them.

The Sex Crimes detective remained perfectly still, not flinching at all. "Nothing. That's what you can do for me."

This caught Carol off-guard. As she tried to organize a coherent response, the woman interrupted.

"I don't need your help. And my captain doesn't particularly want your help. But his boss seems to think we do, so here you are. I can't prevent that, but I can keep you from mucking up the works. So just sit back and watch." The volume and the hostility in her voice notched up.

"And frankly, if I did need help, you'd be the last one I'd call." Sullivan inched in even closer.

Carol felt her face turning red. Her breath came short. She opened her mouth to reply. Ramirez stepped in, touched her on the shoulder, and then took Sullivan by the arm and pulled her aside. Carol could see him dominating the conversation although she could not hear the words. He punctuated with his finger not quite hitting her chest. She had never seen him with such fire in his eyes.

She could see the lull in their conversation. Sullivan's back was to her but the stiff posture, arms folded in front of her left no doubt that the woman was not happy.

When the confrontation ended, Tom strode across yard past Carol, calling out over his shoulder, "Come on, we've got better things to do."

Chapter 20

Carol seethed as she stared out the passenger side window at the landscape zipping by. A smudge on the glass caught her eye. She'd rested her head there as she stared out the window on the way to the scene. The thought crossed her mind that she was spending all of the drive time staring blankly at whatever happened to be outside the window. Still, she was pissed.

"You know, I don't need you to fight my battles for me." She tried to keep her tone neutral but could feel the hostility leaking out.

Ramirez glanced briefly at her and then back at the road ahead. "It wasn't *your* battle. It was *our* battle." He tapped his fingers on the steering wheel as he continued. "The captain sent us out here as a team. They don't get to pick and choose which of us gets to play in their little sandbox."

She realized that her entire body was tense. Allowing her shoulders to relax and droop, she responded, "But I'm the one she called out."

"Yeah, she did at that. Look, her problems run deeper than just having you there. Something else is going on. Most likely, it's got nothing to do with us. You were just a convenient target."

Carol hadn't considered that. She tried to visualize the pressure on Sullivan—two years on this case and they had ceased to make any progress. The news outlets weren't cutting the department any slack on it and, as they say, shit rolls downhill. Sullivan was at the bottom of the hill. "I guess."

She fell silent for a few seconds. The image of the dismissive look from Detective Collins in the restroom earlier in the morning flooded into her mind. She glanced over at Ramirez, reminded that he'd warned her about her reputation. "I was hoping that getting out into the field would ease things. I mean, around the bullpen there's constant tension." She felt a little adolescent complaining about it.

Her partner shook his head. "It's likely to get worse before it gets better." He shot her a quick glance. "Look, Tullis, thing is, most of the guys are watching you. Some are curious. Some are hoping you screw up. And some are just waiting for you to blow up. Keep at it. Don't give 'em the satisfaction. You'll be fine."

Her mouth tightened into a thin straight line. She clenched her jaw and gritted her teeth for a few seconds. "I shouldn't have to prove myself to those assholes."

Ramirez laughed. "Yeah, and there shouldn't be any wars or hunger or crime. Human nature, Tullis. Human nature."

Chapter 21

Carol pulled into the driveway just before six. The promising break in the clouds earlier in the day produced a beautiful sunset with a few stars making their appearance. She opened the garage door and pulled in. Just as she got ready to close it, though, she remembered that the next day was garbage day.

She rolled the container down the driveway to the edge of the street. Turning toward the house she encountered Ben Sturgis bringing his container down. She nodded as she passed him.

"Evening." The voice floated from behind.

Carol turned to see that he had also started toward the house. "Hi." She started to resume her trek to the house when she sensed him hurrying to catch up.

"Hey, Carol, I meant to ask you." He caught up and walked along beside her. "Are you working on that serial killer case?" The words came out matter-of-factly.

She laughed and kept walking. "Doctor Sturgis, surely you know enough about police work to know that there's no way I would ever discuss an active case with you, whether I was working on it or not."

He shot back quickly. "Could you just call me Ben, please. That's my name." He offered a mischievous grin. "So, if I wanted to know more about the case, who would I ask? I mean, as research for my book?"

Carol gestured with her index finger. "Oh, that's easy. Seattle PD Public Affairs Office. Anything that's released for the public is available there. If it's not available there, then it's not released for the public." She turned toward the house again.

He hurriedly caught up. "Well, crap. Say, I still have that bottle of Scotch and it's early."

She stopped and turned to him again, this time offering the best scowl she could produce. "I'm sorry, I don't drink."

Sturgis grinned sheepishly. "Don't drink? Or don't drink with me?"

Carol laughed. "Yes."

"Aha, a recovering alcoholic." Standing with his hands in the front pockets of his jeans, he arched his eyebrows.

"That's why people don't like to talk to shrinks. Always with the analysis."

He hung his head. "Sorry. Old habits. Maybe we could just talk over coffee or something."

Carol exhaled and shook her head. "I'm not trying to be mean or anything, Doctor Sturgis. It's just that I'm a landlord and you're my tenant. Let's keep it at that level."

Ben shot her a serious, sincere look that she'd not seen from him before. "I get it. I know. It's just that I live alone and don't get to converse much these days. And I know you live alone. I guess it'd just be nice to have some adult company once in a while."

She explored his eyes as she considered his words. "Maybe another time. It's been a rather brutal day for me." She turned and continued toward the house. "Good night, Doctor Sturgis."

"Ben. My name is Ben. Goodnight, Carol."

Chapter 22

As she booted up her computer the next morning, a notice appeared on her calendar—a nine o'clock meeting at the Sex Crimes office. She shuddered at the prospect of having to deal with Detective Sullivan again. *Might as well get used to it. I'm saddled with her until this is done.*

Ramirez came in wearing the look of a man without a care in the world. His pace was brisk but not hurried, with a bounce in his step. "Morning, Tullis."

Carol sighed as she slumped in her chair. "Yes, it's morning."

He laughed. "Oh, come on now. It's a great day to be alive." He looked over toward the window into which rare October sunshine was beaming in. "Feel the sunlight. Breathe the air."

She smirked as she gestured at her computer monitor "Whatever. Looks like we got a party invitation."

***

Carol decided to go early and try to smooth things over with Sullivan. The confrontation at the crime scene the previous day left her with a distinct feeling of unease. She found her way to the detective's office. The door was open, so she knocked and entered.

Sullivan looked up from whatever she was reading and her face immediately tightened into a hostile mask. "What do you want? The meeting's not for another fifteen minutes." The words came out laced with venom.

Ignoring the tone and look, Carol pulled a chair over to a spot just across the table from Sullivan. "Maybe I'm missing something here, but I've been assigned to help you. It's your case and you call the shots. But I'm not here to take abuse from you. So, I need to know that, at least as far as the case goes, you and I are okay."

Sullivan leaned in to the desk and returned the hostile stare. "And what gives you the idea that you and I are okay?"

Nothing made sense to Carol. She had no history with this woman. In fact, she'd never even heard of her before this case. "I have no idea where this is coming from. But if you've got that much of a burr up your ass about me, just call over and get me removed. Won't hurt my feelings in the least. I've got plenty of work in my own shop."

Sullivan smirked. "Yeah, right. I've already tried that. I'm stuck with you." She leaned back and folded her arms on her chest. "So, if there's nothing else, I have a few more things to do before the meeting." With that, she gestured toward the door and went back to whatever she was reading.

***

Carol studied the collection of people in the room. Sitting to one side of Sullivan were two detectives, one male and the other female. The faces were familiar, but the names escaped her. Doctor Hoskins, sitting adjacent to Sullivan on the other side, seemed immersed in a document. Noticeably absent was Captain Fredericks, the head of Sex Crimes. Ramirez occupied a seat next to Carol and sat idly tapping his fingers on a blank pad of paper.

Sullivan paused her note taking. "I guess it's time. Let's get started." She slid an eight by ten photograph to the center of the table. "Jessica Brunnell. Age forty-seven. Single, never married. Worked as an accountant at Peabody and Swartz in Bellevue. We found her car at the Bellevue Square Mall. We're still going through video surveillance footage from the general area. It appears, though, that there was no coverage in the coffee shop, where we believe she was abducted. We might catch a break and see something from external cameras, but we're not counting on it." Her voice sounded unenthusiastic. "I'll update you if we find anything there. The MO's the same—nothing new." She paused, as if considering whether to rehash the details. Instead, she glanced to her left. "Doctor Hoskins can update us on how this fits with the profile."

The doctor straightened the papers in front of her. "Thank you. As Detective Sullivan noted, there's no change in the way the unsub goes about this. What is interesting is that this is the first time we've had a victim placed during a period of significant precipitation. In all of the previous instances, the weather has been either clear or, at worst, overcast." She paused and looked around the room, narrowing her eyes.

"We get an even deeper insight into the individual here. Despite the rain and the muddy environment at the site, he kept the woman's body immaculate. If any mud splashed during the placement, it was carefully wiped off. Her hair was dry, which means that, in all likelihood, he had it protected as he carried her. This highlights the fact that the unsub is trying to show respect for the women, at least in his own mind. If you look at the crime scene site, you'll notice that he chose to place her on a spot that sits higher than surrounding areas. He likely did this to keep water from pooling around the body."

Carol felt a rising annoyance. The doctor was making this guy sound like a considerate lover. She closed her eyes and took a deep breath.

If Hoskins noticed Carol's discomfort, she didn't let on. "In terms of sexual contact, the patterns we discussed previously are the same in this case. There seems to be evidence of genital stimulation, both manual and oral. As in past cases forensics found evidence that the individual used a bleach and water solution to clean up the genital area, removing any trace evidence." She cleared her throat, lowered her head, and took a deep breath. "So, our prior impressions hold. I believe that the intent of the person is to provide pleasure, maybe even love to these women. We've said it before, but it bears repeating, it would appear that killing is not the intent. Most likely that is merely a means of removing the victim as a possible witness."

Carol's rage boiled over. "What the hell? Why can't we just call this what it is—a brutal rape and murder? Why do we call this guy 'a person' or 'an individual?' He's a monster." With her hands clenched in front of her and her knuckles turning white, she felt the heat of anger rising in her face.

The room fell silent, all eyes on the enraged detective. Sullivan glared across the table and appeared ready to unleash her anger.

Hoskins, voice quiet and slow, intervened. "Detective Tullis. Tullis—the name rings a bell but I'm not placing it." The look on her face reflected a combination of sadness and compassion.

Carol, aware that she'd just lost her self-control, felt the rage subside. She looked down at the table for a moment and then up at the doctor. "Yes. Well, my daughter Jenny Tullis was one of the victims of the child serial killer ten years ago." She left unsaid that Hoskins had been the profiler on that case.

The doctor closed her eyes and exhaled, slumping in her chair. The silence in the room was deafening. When she spoke, it was with the same soft, understated voice. "Could you all excuse us for a few minutes please?" She remained seated while the others stood up and filed out. Ramirez put his hand briefly on Carol's shoulder and squeezed as he left.

The two women sat across from each other without speaking for a few seconds before Carol broke the silence. "I apologize, Doctor Hoskins. I was out of line." But she felt more conflicted than out of line. She regretted the outburst but she still seethed with anger.

Hoskins gently waved her hand in front of her as if brushing away the apology. "There is no apology necessary, Detective Tullis, Carol." She looked across at the detective's ID.

The doctor took a deep breath and leaned in folding her hands on the table. "Between the two of us, I'm going to be more forthright than I might be in a group. The evidence in this case is not taking us anywhere. Twenty-four victims and we don't know any more than we knew after the second or third. You can tell from Sullivan's briefing today that she learned nothing new this time." Hoskins jabbed her index finger on the tabletop as she made her next point. "The only way we solve this case is by getting inside the guy's mind. And inside his mind, this is not rape and murder. It's an act of love. Inside this guy's mind, he's not a monster but someone who is kind, considerate, and loving." She suddenly leaned back gesturing with her open hands in front of her. "The police—you, Sullivan, the forensic guys and even the ME—you can all think of him anyway you want but I don't have that luxury. I have to be able to see the world through his eyes. I have to be able to envision how he sees himself. That's what I do."

Her next words came out as almost painful. "I'm going to share something with you, Carol—something I've never shared with anyone. Your daughter's case was my first as a profiler. I thought I was ready for the job. I wasn't. I allowed myself to feel the rage, the pain, the utter disgust of what I was dealing with. I thought of the unsub as you painted our present perpetrator—a monster. As a result, I never got into his head. We never caught him. There are lots of possible explanations but, I fear that the failure rests at least partly on my shoulders."

She approached the table, her eyes flashing with anger and her voice escalating. "I will never let myself do that again, ever." She sat down, exhaled, and lowered her head. Her voice reverted back to its quiet, even tone. "Before I came to Western Washington, I did grief counseling in my private practice. Despite years of experience, I still find myself at a loss for words when I come face-to-face with tragedy like this. I can only force myself to do what will ultimately catch this guy."

Carol sat, silent and numb. She somehow knew all of this was right. But still the pain was unbearable. "Yes, I know. I'm sorry." She started to add that she wouldn't let it happen again but wasn't sure she could guarantee that.

As the group re-convened, Sullivan cleared her throat. "One more thing. I got word this morning that we have asked the FBI to formally join the task force. The captain and I have a teleconference with the main behavioral unit in Quantico tomorrow. I expect they'll show up early next week. I'll give you more information when I get it." There was no mistaking the pain and dejection in her voice.

As the meeting wrapped up, a thought occurred to Carol. Sitting in her chair as the others filed out, she jumped up and hurried down the hall. "Doctor Hoskins, could you hold up a minute, please?" She made her way around the forensic tech to catch up to the doctor.

Hoskins turned around. "Yes."

"I wonder if you might be able to give me some information? Do you know a Doctor Ben Sturgis?"

The doctor took a step back, her eyes wide. "You think Ben Sturgis is somehow involved in this?"

Carol laughed. "No, no. Nothing like that. I have a small detached apartment that I rent out. Doctor Sturgis is the tenant. My property manager does all of the screening, but I like to get to know the people as best I can. He said that he was at Western Washington until just recently so I figured you might know him." *But what do I really want to know about him?*

Hoskins nodded but said nothing.

"I was wondering if you know why he left his position there."

"That's a question you should ask Doctor Sturgis. But, honestly, I don't recall the details of his resignation. And, in any event, even if I did, I couldn't discuss them. You know, privacy and such."

"Of course. Just thought I'd check. Thanks anyway." She started to turn but the doctor continued to speak.

"But I can tell you that, from a landlord-tenant perspective, I don't know of any reason for concern, if that's what you're worried about."

"Thanks. Yes, that's helpful. I appreciate it." Carol started to leave but paused. "And I'm sorry for my outburst."

Chapter 23

The knock on the back door came about thirty minutes after Carol got home from work. She could see Ben through the back window. Opening the door, she struggled not to show her weariness. "What can I do for you, Doctor Sturgis?"

"I was headed up to Snoqualmie Pass this Saturday, kind of a day trip. Wondered if you'd like to join me. We could have lunch up at the lodge."

She wondered whether this was about getting her to talk about her work or perhaps... something else. Either way, it didn't seem like something she should be doing.

"Thank you for the offer but I'm on call this weekend. Maybe another time." She could have been more specific and said she was on call Saturday. But she was afraid that he would suggest Sunday.

His smile faded. "Oh well. Maybe another time."

Carol spoke before she could stop herself. "Ben, really, I mean that. Look, I'm not much of a social person. Lots of reasons, none that I want to talk about. But if it's just coffee or lunch and conversation, then maybe. But nothing more. I just need you to know that up front."

"Certainly. We can do that. Another time then."

"Good night, Ben." As they parted, it occurred to her that she'd slipped over a boundary. He was now *Ben*. And it was maybe not a bad thing. There was no need to be so formal. *Ben* was, after all, his name.

"Night, Carol."

***

98

Rush hour traffic took its toll the next morning and Carol walked in fifteen minutes late. Tom looked up from his desk as she came through the doors. As he caught her eye, he nodded over in the direction of the captain's office. "He was asking about you."

She shook her head as she put her purse in her file drawer and hit the power switch on her computer. "Freaking traffic. I swear, I-Five is perpetually under construction." She plopped down in her seat. "Any idea what he wanted?"

"Not a clue."

Their conversation was interrupted by a familiar booming voice. "Tullis, come."

Carol sighed and forced herself out of the chair. "Wish me luck."

She knocked and entered. "Yes sir?"

He motioned her to the chair beside the desk. "Working banker's hours today, are we?" It was as close to humor as she'd ever heard from him.

She started to recount the traffic story but decided against it. *No point.* "Sorry, sir."

He gestured with his hand as if waving away the apology. "What's up on the serial case?"

Carol mentally processed through what they'd discussed the previous day. "Nothing new, really. The victim fits in with the rest. MO's the same. Just nothing. Well, other than the fact that they're calling in the FBI's behavioral unit. Sullivan didn't seem too keen on the idea." She tried to recall if Hoskins had added anything new. Nothing came to mind.

Peterman slouched in his chair and leaned back. "Yeah. I knew about the FBI thing. Tell me about Sullivan."

The question took Carol by surprise. "What do you want to know about her? I mean, I don't really know her that well and I've only interacted with her a couple of times. She seems to be doing okay, I guess."

The captain stared as if looking through her. "There's more than that. You know what I'm talking about."

Ah, yes. Sullivan said she'd requested my removal. "I guess you're talking about her dissatisfaction with having me on the team?"

"So?"

Carol sighed. "I don't know what to tell you. She doesn't like me. Makes no bones about it. But she didn't say why. Part of it, I gather, is that she feels help is being forced on her and she doesn't think she needs it. But as for her personal dislike for me, I honestly have no idea what it's about."

Peterman rubbed his chin. "Yeah. Oh well. She'll have to get over it, I guess."

Carol decided to take a chance. "Captain, if you don't mind my asking, if they're that unhappy, why not just replace me?"

He smirked. "Because I'm the captain and she's not. I make the decisions about who gets assigned from this division. If their captain wants to forego Homicide involvement, so be it. But he doesn't get to pick and choose like at a pizza buffet."

Nice to know that he uses that logic on everyone. "Yes sir. Well, in that case, I guess we'll see movement of some type when the feds show up. She said it's probably going to be early next week."

Peterman laughed. "Oh yes. I suspect there'll be movement all right."

Chapter 24

Saturday morning brought a brilliant azure sky and a brisk wind out of the north. The high-pressure system that had set in over the Pacific Northwest promised a beautiful autumn weekend.

Carol sat down at the kitchen table in her robe with that first cup of coffee. Looking out the window, she mused at how nice a trip to Snoqualmie would have been. It had been ages since she'd taken a "road trip" with another human being other than her trips to crime scenes with Ramirez. The image of her sitting in the front seat next to Ben watching the scenery whiz by felt warm, comforting.

The warm feeling disappeared when her cell phone rang—Central Dispatch. Her on-call day was starting early. She connected and put the phone on speaker mode, setting it down on the table. "Tullis." She grabbed a pen and pad from the counter.

Carol took notes as the voice on the other end recited the details—an adult female body, construction site near SeaTac, uniforms on-site, and the rest. She scanned notes to make sure she had everything she needed.

Thirty minutes later, she pulled up to a secluded lot surrounded by a slatted fence. Parking outside, she flashed her badge to the patrol officer standing by the gate. "Tullis, Homicide. Is Detective Ramirez here yet?"

The officer shook his head. "You're the first. Looks like the serial killer—blue tarp and all." He pointed in the direction of the yard. "Dispatch notified Sex Crimes, so they'll probably show up soon too."

Carol shuddered. *Sullivan on a Saturday*. "Thanks." She took a pair of latex gloves from her jacket and donned them as she walked into the yard. The ground was hard packed, so footprints weren't likely. She stopped after several steps and surveyed the scene. A different uniformed officer was blocking off the area with yellow crime scene tape.

Satisfied with the process, she knelt over the covered body. *Might as well take advantage of the fact that Sullivan's not here yet.* But something struck her as wrong. She stood and stepped back away from the tarp. The blue covering appeared to be new, just like the ones at the other scenes. But something was different. The fact that it was less than a week since the last murder also fueled her alarm. *Something's not right.*

She bent down and lifted the plastic, revealing a nude female body with two pieces of blue silk cloth covering the breasts and the pubic area. The woman appeared to be in her mid-twenties. Her blonde hair appeared to be colored rather than natural. With her fingers about an inch from the skin, she traced the cut on the woman's neck without actually touching it. *Something.*

"I told you to keep your hands off until forensics finishes." The unmistakable voice intruded.

Carol glanced around but didn't bother standing.

Sullivan's confrontation tone diminished. "So, our unsub jumped the rails, finally. Less than a week since the last one. Hopefully he's made some mistakes and we can catch a break."

Carol turned her head back toward the body. "Nope. This isn't our guy."

An awkward silence followed her remark. Sullivan slipped around to the other side of the body. "How do you know?"

Carol stood, leaving the tarp pulled back to reveal the body. "First, look at the tarp. Yes, it's blue and it looks new. But check closer. See those grommets? Aluminum. Our unsub uses tarps with gold grommets. The white powder looks like deterioration residue. This tarp's been out of the package for some time. Maybe even used and cleaned to look new."

She knelt and touched the cloth covering the breasts and pubic areas. "And these, first, the blue color seems a little deeper. We can have forensics check that. But look at the cuts—ragged with stray threads. And look at the placement. Our unsub always positions the cloth over the body but tucked beneath the arms at the victims' sides. Here you can see that the cloth is draped over the arms. Look at the hair. It's matted and dirty. Our guy would have cleaned it up and brushed it. Finally, the cut on the neck has some jagged spots, almost like either some tearing or like it was done with a serrated edge. Cuts on the others are smooth, likely from a very sharp smooth blade." She pulled the tarp back up over the body and stood.

Sullivan stared down at the covered body for a moment. "Okay. So, it's not ours. I guess Homicide's got themselves another case." She turned to leave.

Carol called out after the departing detective. "Hang on a second. How do you know this isn't a sexual assault? It's not the serial killer but it may still be yours."

"Not my problem. If the ME says sexual assault, my captain can assign it to whoever he wants. But, right now, I'm going home."

As Carol watched her go, she noticed Ramirez coming through the gate. As he passed Sullivan, he turned his head, watching her recede. He approached, looking alternately at the tarp and back toward Sullivan's retreat. "This what I think it is?"

Carol smirked. "No. This may be an even bigger problem."

Chapter 25

By four o'clock that afternoon, Carol and Tom had followed the meager trail of evidence to an apartment in a large complex near SeaTac Airport. After the manager let them in, the two detectives stood in the living room surveying the scene, which left little doubt about the events that had played out there.

Carol pulled on her latex gloves as she scoped the place out. "I'd say we found our murder scene." A large patch of bloody carpet dominated the center of the room. Splatters covered a part of one wall. The killer had apparently tried to wipe them off but only managed to smear some of them before abandoning the task.

A new voice with a heavy southern drawl drew Carol's attention to the front door.

"Christ, Jose! Why do you have to do this stuff on a Saturday?" Sam Johnson lifted the yellow crime scene tape and slipped inside.

Tom smirked. "Hiya Bubba. Any chance to screw up your weekend makes for a good day."

The tech surveyed the room and let out a soft whistle. "Must have been one hell of a party."

Tom squatted down and depressed the stained carpet with his gloved hand. "The body was found at a worksite to the north. Looks like it started here. The carpet's beginning to dry but it's pretty saturated. What do you think, maybe last night?"

Johnson, who had been kneeling while he gathered samples, stood and arched his back, stretching his arms out to the side. "I'm getting too old for this stuff." The strong southern drawl added a leisurely feel to the statement.

"Christ, Bubba, you're all of, what, twenty-five?"

"I'll have you know that I turn twenty-seven next month."

"Just right around the corner from retirement, eh? But back to the matter at hand. Any idea on the time?"

Johnson studied the room, his arms folded on his chest. "Well, I reckon you may be right, Jose. Blood starting to dry around the edges and turning hard. Still soaked in the middle, though. Once we get samples back to the lab I'll know more. And the doc can tell you the time of death. But, yeah, I bet my brother-in-law's pick-up that we're looking at last night."

The chaotic state of the room struck Carol. The coffee table was shattered, apparently during the struggle. Several broken vases littered the floor along with a framed photograph with broken glass. "Whoever did this didn't spend a lot of time cleaning up."

Carol walked into the kitchen. "Hey, I found her business card on the fridge—Cassandra Devon. Looks like she worked as a hair stylist over at J and M Salon." She took the card off the refrigerator and tucked it into a plastic evidence bag. "We can show the photo to the owner over there and get confirmation." She glanced at her watch and sighed. "Probably too late today. We can get the owner's home contact info since the place is probably closed tomorrow. I'll take care of that if you can finish up here."

Ramirez looked over the few dishes in the sink, opening the cabinets, and looking in the trash. "Yeah, I guess. It's going to take me the rest of the evening here." He turned to Johnson, who appeared to be dusting for prints on the kitchen counter. "You finding anything, Bubba?"

"Some smudges here, maybe partials. I got some samples of what's likely semen from the bedroom and some hair from the pillows. That should tell us something."

Ramirez said, "Hopefully we can get some results back early Monday. Something tells me that this one's going to go fast anyway."

Carol sighed. "Yes, and I'm afraid that I'm not going to like the direction it goes."

Tom stopped and turned to her, eyebrows arched. "What?"

"Think about it. We have a perp who knew about the MO of the serial killer. Pretty sloppy, lots of mistakes, but, specifically, he knew about the blue cloth. That means that he's seen at least one of the bodies. That cloth was a hold-back—never put out in the press. So only those people connected with the investigation or who have been onsite knew about it. Possibly someone who found a body, but I'd call that unlikely. Civilians who find bodies generally are pretty rattled. I wouldn't expect them to remember the details."

Ramirez's eyes widened. "You thinking somebody on the investigation?"

Carol shook her head. "I don't think so. Someone involved would get it right. It looks like this was spontaneous and the killer made a feeble attempt to make it look like the serial killer. I may be wrong but I'm thinking there's a strong possibility that our guy is a uniformed officer, maybe a first responder or one who helped out on scene once or twice. He would have seen the layout but would not be privy to the fine details."

Tom leaned back against the kitchen counter and stroked his chin. "Could be. But it could also be one of the ME staff who transported the bodies or a forensic guy."

Carol glanced toward the living room where Sam Johnson continued to collect samples. "Maybe, but I think if it had been someone like that, they'd have been more detail-oriented too. But either way, I don't like where it's headed."

Chapter 26

After working all day Saturday and brooding about the new case on Sunday, Monday morning felt like a continuation of the previous week for Carol. Coming through the double doors, she could see Peterman in his office already poring over papers on his desk. *Funny, I never see him focused on the computer monitor—old school.* Although he didn't really look to be more than ten years older than she.

Ramirez already had the phone glued to his ear. He shot her a glance as she plopped into her chair. She caught the tail end of his conversation. "Okay. We'll be right down." He turned to her as he stood. "Bubba's got something."

Carol hustled through the double doors behind him. "Oh, by the way, I confirmed the hair salon connection. Our vic is Cassandra Devon."

"You talk to the owner?"

"Yeah, but she couldn't tell me much. There's a co-worker that was good friends with her. She's out of town until Wednesday."

"This friend have a name?"

"Tiffany Clarke."

"Okay, I guess we talk to Miz Clarke on Wednesday." He shrugged as he ambled down the corridor. He seemed relaxed, like he was at peace with the world. She wondered how he did it. After all, he worked Saturday and likely had a much more hectic Sunday than she did, what with three kids. "How was the weekend?"

He laughed without breaking stride. "You mean after we spent all day Saturday on the job?" He shook his head. "I

110

guess it was okay. Sunday was church and then brunch out. I did manage to catch the last half of the Seahawks game."

No wonder he's relaxed. She visualized his day. In contrast, she'd spent the day drinking coffee and brooding about the new case, about the probability of having to interrogate fellow police officers, and her relationship with Detective Sullivan, which sat squarely in the toilet.

They pushed through the doors into the forensic lab to see Sam Johnson typing case notes into the computer. He turned to greet the two. "Howdy, folks. Come on in and drag up a chair. Be right with you." The twang of his southern accent conveyed lazy cheerfulness. He turned toward the keyboard to continue his work.

Carol pulled a chair over closer to Johnson's desk. Ramirez parked his butt on a nearby table, legs dangling.

About a minute later, the tech swiveled around to face the two detectives. "We got ourselves a break here. The blood type matches Miz Devon. I got pubic hair from the bed—some hers, some his. I also found some hair on the pillows. Finally, I got a few partials from the smudges around the house. So, all in all, we're in pretty good shape. I'll get DNA started on this. But unless he's in the system, it won't help us find him. So far, nothing useful on the partial prints."

Carol stared at a point on the wall, her eyes out of focus, as she processed what she'd heard. "We have other things working here. So maybe we can get the preliminary indication and use these results to confirm. This is great work, Sam. Thanks."

"My pleasure, ma'am."

***

Carol listened as Doctor Blount, the medical examiner, gave his preliminary thoughts. So far nothing she'd heard surprised her.

He took his wire-rimmed glasses off and polished them as he spoke. "I'll finish the autopsy today and have something more definitive. But for now, I think it's probably safe to say that the cut to the neck was the likely cause of death. In my initial exam, I found semen in the vagina and no signs of trauma in that area. So, I'd say, at least at this point, it was probably consensual. Things turned sour after that."

Just as the doctor finished speaking, Ramirez's phone rang. "I need to take this. Looks like the hair salon returning my call." He pressed the screen and put the phone to his ear. "Detective Ramirez."

He nodded as he listened. "Okay. Thank you. We'll do that." He turned back to Carol and the doctor. "The owner's in and available to talk to us." He tucked the phone back into his shirt pocket. "We can head over and get the basic info as well as the contact information for the co-worker, who's due back on Wednesday." He eased off the table. "Thanks Doc. If you could, give us a shout when that autopsy report is ready."

Carol's phone pinged and she pulled up a text message. "Looks like I have an invitation to the briefing with the FBI team. The meeting's scheduled for one o'clock tomorrow afternoon over in Sex Crimes."

Ramirez checked his phone. "Yeah, same here. Come on, let's head over to the Hair Salon."

Chapter 27

As she pulled into the driveway that evening, Carol noticed that she wasn't feeling quite as tired as she had been on previous evenings. *The routine is starting to click.* It felt good.

As she made her way through the house, first tossing her keys in the basket and then hanging up her coat, she heard a knock on the kitchen door. She didn't need to see through the window to know that it would only be one person.

Opening the door, she offered a smile without moving to let him in. "Good evening, Ben. What can I do for you?" She felt oddly okay that he was there.

"Was wondering if you might be up for that rain check on the ride up to Snoqualmie. Not many weekends left until the snow hits and I don't ski."

"Thank you for the offer but I have my son this weekend."

"You seem to have a whole bunch of excuses."

She considered him for a moment and then shook her head. "No, what I have is a life. I have a job and a son. Those things come first." She paused for a moment and then continued, "Look, I appreciate the offer, really, I do. And maybe sometime that will work out. But for now, I have to take care of what's important."

***

The next afternoon, Carol and Ramirez found seats at the opposite end of the table from where the head honchos would be. She could see stacks of papers and file folders occupying that area. "This should be priceless." She recalled Sullivan's demeanor last time the FBI had entered the conversation. The Sex Crimes detective had seemed less than thrilled.

Tom slouched in his chair. He'd made no secret of his opinion that he and Carol should be working on their own cases. Their most promising lead would not return to town until the next day. Carol could barely make out his mumbling. "Come on, come on. Let's get on with this."

"Patience, my good man. Patience."

The conference room door opened, and Detective Sullivan slipped in and stood beside a chair at the far end of the table as others filed in.

Two men and a woman that Carol had never seen before came in first, followed by Doctor Hoskins and Captain Fredericks. Once everyone was settled, Sullivan began, "Thank you for coming. As I mentioned last week, we have the FBI Behavioral Unit joining the investigation. I have nothing new on the case specifically, so I'd like to turn it over to Special Agent Slattery."

The agent was tall and slender. His white shirt and solid maroon tie seemed in keeping with his short-cropped brown hair and quiet, piercing look. He appeared to be in his late forties. He introduced his two associates before plowing ahead into the case.

Several of the Sex Crimes detectives sat with their forearms resting on the tabletop, apparently paying close attention. Sullivan stared coldly at file folders in front of her. This was apparently no fun for her. Doctor Hoskins sat beside the detective, toying with the end of a beautiful sage and rose silk scarf wrapped around her neck.

Captain Fredericks, though, appeared the epitome of boredom. He tapped his fingers quietly on the tabletop. If he even heard anything that was being said, he didn't let on.

Slattery consulted some papers in front of him before continuing. "Another member of our team is still in DC finishing up on a case. He'll be joining us around the middle of next week."

Carol listened to the agent but kept her attention on Fredericks. Something didn't fit. This was his division's most pressing case. He had just brought in the cavalry. And he seemed as if he didn't really give a damn.

She heard Slattery continue to speak. "Our profiler, Doctor Charles Irwin…" and then she saw something. A darkness, some deep-seated panic, seemed to sweep over Fredericks. His body tensed visibly. He clenched his jaw. His gaze locked briefly on the senior agent and then dropped to the tabletop, where his knuckles had turned white gripping the edge. *What the…?* The shift in appearance had coincided with the announcement of the profiler. *Some connection?*

"…but we've looked over Doctor Hoskins' profile work. It's very impressive and we feel comfortable working from that." He turned and nodded to the doctor, who smiled in return.

Fredericks remained for about five more minutes before excusing himself. "I'm sorry. I have to leave. I have another meeting in a few minutes. Sullivan, you can brief me later." And with that, he stood and left.

Chapter 28

The behavior of Fredericks bothered Carol for the rest of the day. By the time she arrived home from work, a number of different scenarios had floated across her mind. She kept coming back again and again to the stark visual change in the Sex Crimes captain at the mention of the FBI profiler.

As she tossed her keys in the basket, she sorted through the day's mail. *Junk, bill, junk, junk....* She sorted it all into two stacks with one piece left over. The postal carrier had mistakenly left one for Ben Sturgis in her box. She tossed it on the kitchen counter and went over to the pantry to get a box of cereal—her dinner of choice most days. Opening the refrigerator, she reached for the milk but decided against it.

She picked up Ben's mail and strode across the back lawn to the small apartment. Carol could see lights and rang the bell. The young man's backlit profile came into view through the translucent curtains. When he opened the door, she was taken aback.

He wore a pair of jeans and nothing else. His hair was wet and disheveled, like he'd just stepped out of the shower. His bare chest glistened with moisture. He had a cell phone at his ear and spoke animatedly as he motioned her in. He turned his back to her and walked toward the kitchen, continuing to talk.

"Yes. I know. I realize. Middle of next week at the latest. Absolutely." He paused and looked around at her, holding an index finger up. "Okay. Yes. And thank you." He disconnected and sat the phone on the counter.

116

"Sorry about that. I got an agent for my book and she's pushing me to get the first half to her." He ran his hand through his wet, tangled hair. He glanced down at his bare chest and his face turned red. "Oh. Crap. I just got out of the shower. Let me get some clothes on." He turned toward the bedroom.

Carol felt flustered. Her heart beat faster and she felt herself blushing. "No need. I just came to drop this off. The mail guy left it in my box by mistake." She handed him the envelope.

He took it and looked at it briefly before tossing it on to the counter. "Thanks." He came closer.

She turned to leave. "I need to get back. Oh, and congratulations on your book."

He touched her shoulder. "Wait." He pulled his hand back suddenly. "I mean, you don't need to go just yet." He moved even closer, his face only a couple of inches from hers. He softly touched her cheek with his hand.

Carol trembled. A shiver coursed through her body. "No, Ben." But she didn't move.

With his hand on her cheek, he kissed her gently on the lips, a kiss lasting only an instant. His other hand went up to caress her other cheek.

She closed her eyes. *No, please.* But she didn't speak. She put her hands on his shoulders to push him away. His skin felt soft and warm. Rather than pushing, her hands slid over his shoulders and around his neck.

His lips touched hers again, this time lingering. She felt his tongue and parted her lips. His arms enveloped her.

Carol pulled her hands back to his shoulders and, with every ounce of effort she could muster, applied gentle pressure to move him away. She pulled her face back, breaking the kiss. "No."

Ben opened his eyes and pulled his face back, keeping his arms around her. "Carol. Why? What?" She could see the confusion in his eyes.

She closed her eyes and shook her head. "Just no." The words came out gentle, soft. "No." She pulled back away from him and turned toward the front door.

"Wait, Carol." His voice sounded distressed. "Please. Don't go."

"No." She moved quickly outside, closing the door behind her. "No."

***

No. But why not? *Just no.*

She was an adult. They were both adults and both single, as far as she knew. *No.*

Her body revolted against the decision, the trembling, the shivers. *No.*

But it had been so long—years. *No.*

Carol struggled with herself. Why shouldn't she? He was attractive, young, and affable. She closed her eyes and imagined what it would be like. Her body shuddered at the pleasurable image.

And so her evening went. By ten, she felt emotionally spent and more than a little depressed. The worst part was that she could not come up with a single reason not to. But the answer was always *no*. Finally, she gave up. Getting undressed, she put on a nightgown and crawled into bed.

Carol rolled over. She flipped the pillow and rolled again. A glance at the clock told her it was ten forty-five. She pounded the sides of the pillow to fluff it up and then buried her head in it. Up to use the bathroom and then return to the tossing and turning.

Finally, she threw the covers back and looked over at the clock—eleven fifteen. She brushed her teeth and shed her nightgown. Slipping on a pair of jeans and a tee shirt on her nude body, she made her way barefoot down the hall into the kitchen.

Looking out across the back lawn, she could see lights on in the small apartment. Shadows moved reassuring her that Ben was still up. She closed her eyes and once again imagined the scene, what it would be like, after all this time. The shivers and trembling returned. Opening her eyes, she continued to stare at the apartment for a few moments before turning and dragging herself back to the bedroom.

It would be a long night.

Chapter 29

By dawn, Carol had made peace with herself. Ben was not going to happen. The realization came slowly, but it finally arrived, accompanied by the dull, grey overcast beginning of the day. He was not what she wanted.

Dragging herself into the squad room just before eight, she leafed through the papers in her inbox—DNA and lab reports on the Devon case along with the autopsy report. Nothing new jumped out at her.

She powered up her computer just as Ramirez walked through the door. "Morning. Did you confirm the friend at the hair salon?"

"I did indeed. Tiffany Clarke's her name. She's due into work at nine."

Carol jumped up from her seat and strode toward the door. "Then let's get going. We can grab a coffee on the way. With the traffic, we should be just about right."

From behind she heard the familiar command. "Call it."

"Heads."

"Dammit."

Another good day.

***

Carol leaned back on the desk looking expectantly at the young woman. Tiffany was Caucasian, maybe twenty-five. Her short frame made the few extra pounds she carried noticeable. Tattoos circled both wrists, flowers and leaves. The ring in her nose did little for her appearance.

"You knew Cassandra Devon?"

The woman wrung her hands in her lap and shook her head. "God, yes. Cassie was like my best friend. I can't believe this."

Carol continued to question the witness while Ramirez looked on. "When was the last time you saw or heard from her?"

Tiffany spoke slowly at first. "We both worked on Thursday. Friday was my day off." Then she picked up speed. "I tried to call her late Friday afternoon, but she didn't answer. I left Friday night for Vegas and didn't get back until last night." When she finished, she looked up at Carol, eyes red and questioning. "Was she really murdered?"

"Did she say anything, or did you notice anything that seemed to be troubling her?" Carol kept her tone even and volume low.

Tiffany shook her head. "No. I mean nothing really, not like that. She was always a little stressed about money but, hey, aren't we all?"

"Did she have a boyfriend?"

A light of recognition came on in the young woman's eyes, as if she'd just remembered something. "Yeah. She was going with this guy for like six months. They were going to get married as soon as his divorce was final."

Carol pressed, "Does this boyfriend have a name?"

Tiffany scrunched her face and slouched down in the chair. "Naw. I mean, yeah, I'm sure he has a name. It's just that Cassie wouldn't tell anyone. She said that if people found out about them, it'd screw up the divorce case."

The story struck a familiar chord, not that unusual. "Did you ever see him?"

The woman turned her head slightly to the side and scratched a spot on her jeans for a moment. "Well, not close up. But I did see him once from a distance."

Carol sighed. "What did he look like?"

"I dunno. Average, I guess. It was far away. Looked pretty much like any other guy."

"Was he white, black, Latino?"

"White. I think."

"Tall? Short? Heavy? Thin?" Carol probed for some morsel.

"Just average. I don't know. Average white guy." Her eyes widened. "Wait, I do remember something. He was wearing a uniform. I could tell by the belt with all the things hanging on it and stuff."

Carol shot a glance at her partner. She hadn't wanted to hear this. "What kind of uniform, like army or navy?"

"No, no. Like a cop, police officer. It was dark, I think Black. But he didn't have a hat on."

"Could it have been a security uniform, you know, like you see at malls?" Carol hoped.

"Yeah, I guess. I mean, it was just a uniform and I wasn't close enough to see any details."

Carol pushed harder. "What about his face?"

"Naw. He was turned away from me mostly and I wasn't that close." Her face brightened and she sat up straight. "Hey, I do remember one time me and Cassie was talking, and she called him her Danny Boy."

Carol snapped up the crumb. "So maybe his name was Danny or Dan?"

By this time, Tiffany was animated. She gestured with her index finger making her points. "Yeah. Like we were talking, and I told her this guy was just using her and he'd probably never get a divorce anyway. Even if he did, he'd probably dump her. Guys are like that." She shrugged. "Anyway, she said that her Danny boy would never do that. It was like the only time she ever said his name."

"Thank you Miz Clarke." Carol handed the woman her business card. "Take this and give me a call if you think of anything else."

***

The windshield wipers swept away a combination of drizzle and road grime. "So, what do you think?"

Without taking his gaze from the road ahead, Ramirez shot back. "You know damn well what I think. We'll set it up this afternoon and get started tomorrow morning.

She slouched in her seat and sighed. Not such a great day after all.

Chapter 30

Carol hung her coat on the back of her chair and flipped the power switch on the computer. "You got everything lined up?"

Ramirez, slouched down in his chair, beamed at her. "It's almost party time." He pointed toward the captain's office. "Union rep. I should've figured. My guess is that the captain will call for us any second now." He tilted his head back, closed his eyes, and nodded as if counting.

A booming voice carried across the bullpen. "Ramirez, Tullis, Come."

Tom laughed aloud as he stood. "Told you."

Carol smirked. "Right. Just what we need."

When they entered the office, the captain gestured toward the union representative, who was seated across the desk. "Talmadge here's going to be sitting in on the interviews. Extend every courtesy." He turned his attention to the sitting visitor. "And just to reiterate, this is a homicide investigation. I'm allowing you in there but remember that you're there to observe. If one of the guys has a question for you, fine, but no interrupting. Got it?"

"Yes, sir, and thank you."

"Good, now go, all of you." Peterman waved his hand as if brushing away a mosquito.

Striding back across the bullpen, Carol extended a hand to Talmadge. "Hi. Carol Tullis. You want to grab a cup of coffee before we head in?"

The union representative shook her hand, never breaking stride. "Jeff Talmadge and, sure. Cup of coffee would be great."

124

Ramirez piped up from behind them. "The first one up is Officer Daniel Thomas. He should be here in about ten minutes."

Cups in hand, the three of them entered a spare office that had been set up for the occasion. Questioning four different police officers who carried the first name of "Daniel" as their only connection to the case suggested a less heavy-handed approach than the interrogation room.

Ramirez placed a file on the table and opened it. "Just to make sure we're all on the same page. We're interviewing four officers today. We have just a few questions for each. None of them are under suspicion of anything. We're just following up on a lead. Something may come of it, or not."

Talmadge studied the list. "As I understand, the only link here is the first name?"

Carol responded from her standing position. "The best way to look at this is that we're just ruling these guys out. Even if our perp is a cop, there's no guarantee that he's Seattle PD. He could be from another city or even a state cop. We'll try to make it as fast and painless as possible."

"Good. Some of the officers are coming in on their time off and have to go back on shift later."

She couldn't decide whether his tone was laced with irritation or with condescension. Either way, the union rep wasn't particularly pleased. She didn't care, well, other than the fact that she didn't need to add more complications to her already shaky relationship with other officers. "I understand and we'll try to move this along quickly." An idea occurred to her as she glanced at Ramirez. "I'm going back out into the bay to meet Officer Thomas."

She walked out into the larger area just as a tall, stocky black uniformed officer entered through the double doors. She sighed. *Our perp is white. What's this guy doing here?* But, as she thought about it, better to be an equal opportunity questioner.

She glided over to intercept him. "Officer Thomas. I'm Detective Tullis. Thanks for coming in. We're set up in a back office and your union rep is already there. How about a cup of coffee?" She started for the pot without waiting for an answer. She poured one for the officer and one for herself. Handing a cup of steaming liquid to the man, she turned and headed for the office, confident that he was following.

When they entered the office, Carol almost laughed at Ramirez's reaction. He obviously had not checked the race of each of these guys. "Have a seat." She gestured toward a chair, taking a seat across the table. "This is Detective Ramirez and you probably know Officer Talmadge, your shop steward."

Thomas, who had not spoken to this point, took a sip of his coffee and set the cup aside. "Yes, well. What's this about? Am I in some kind of trouble?"

Carol stared at the officer's cup. He had just placed his DNA on the rim and there it sat, just waiting.

Ramirez placed an eight by ten photo in front of Thomas. "Do you know this woman?"

The officer looked closely at the photo and then at Talmadge, who didn't react at all. Looking across at Ramirez and Carol, he narrowed his eyes as he spoke. "No, but I have to say that she looks vaguely familiar. Not sure where I would have seen her."

126

It occurred to her that the victim's photograph had been in the newspaper. She whispered the fact to Tom, who nodded his understanding.

Her partner continued the questioning. "Officer Thomas, where were you last Friday night between about eight and midnight?"

The uniformed officer went rigid. "What? You suspect me of something to do with this woman?" His gaze darted quickly between the two detectives and the union rep.

Carol stepped in. "No, not at all. We're simply ruling people out." She could have just demanded that he answer the question but that seemed a bit harsh considering the situation.

The answer didn't appear to mollify the officer. "Why are you ruling *me* out? Why am I special?"

Well, shit. We're probably going to have to explain this to all of them. "Officer Thomas, we're trying to locate an officer with the first name of 'Daniel' who knows this woman. You're just one of a few in the department with that name. Sorry. Luck of the draw."

To her surprise, the officer relaxed. Leaning back in his chair, he responded. "Well, honestly she looks familiar for some reason, but I don't know her. As for last Friday, I worked graveyard, so I was asleep until about ten-thirty, when my wife woke me up."

Carol was certain that the last little bit was a way of saying that someone could vouch for him. "Okay then. That's all we need for now." She handed Thomas her card. "If it comes to you how you recognize her, could you give me a shout?" She got up to escort him out. *One down.*

***

She looked across the table at the uniformed officer who appeared old enough to be her father. "Thanks for coming in, Officer O'Riley." Her gut told her that this would be another dead end.

The older man took a deep drink of the coffee she'd gotten for him and cradled the cup on the table with both hands. "Yeah, yeah." He seemed the epitome of bored.

Ramirez slid the enlarged DMV photo in front of him. "You know this woman?"

O'Riley shook his head. "I wish. But at my age, it all looks good." He quickly glanced up at Carol. "Sorry. No offense intended." Looking back down, his demeanor became more serious. "Say, isn't that the woman that was murdered last weekend? I think I saw this same photo in the newspaper."

"No offense taken." Deciding to shorten the process, she offered an explanation of their interest. "Just so you know, what we're doing here is ruling out officers. We're looking for a man named 'Daniel' who knew her. Where were you last Friday night between about eight and midnight?" She felt stupid even asking the question.

The officer laughed. "Well, if I'd been with her, I'd remember. Naw, I was at home. Had a few beers and watched TV until about ten then went to bed."

Carol started to ask whether anyone was there with him but decided against it. No wedding band and a look of loneliness in his eyes. She could imagine exactly what his night had been like. "That's all we need for now, Officer O'Riley. We really appreciate you coming in."

"No problem. I'm on shift anyway. I'd rather sit here and drink coffee talking to you guys than the alternative." He glanced at his watch and laughed. "At least for the next forty-five days."

***

Carol watched the young man's eyes carefully. He seemed confident but wary. "I don't know her but, unless I'm wrong, that's the same photo that was in the paper, that murder victim."

Tullis watched him take a drink of his coffee. "Officer Miller, where were you last Friday night between eight and midnight."

His face flushed. "Why do you want to know?" She detected a note of panic in his voice.

"We're just ruling people out." She went on to offer the first name explanation.

After a long, uncomfortable pause, the officer responded meekly, "Uh, I was out. Got something to eat and then a few drinks. I was home by ten."

Ramirez leaned into the table. "Anyone verify that?"

The uniformed officer's panic appeared to deepen. His eyes conveyed desperation. "I was just out with a friend."

Carol noticed he was not wearing a wedding band. *Why do I always notice that?* "Your friend's name?"

Miller remained silent for a moment. "Michael." As if that would satisfy them.

"Okay, Officer Miller. Thanks for coming in." She handed her card and gave him the same speech about calling if he remembered anything.

129

After the young man left, Ramirez turned to her with a look of incredulity. "What the hell was that? Michael? That's it? You took that for an answer?"

Carol laughed. "Officer Talmadge, could you excuse us for a second?" She nodded to Ramirez as she stood and left the room. As he came out after her, she laughed. "Weren't you paying attention?"

Tom's voice carried an urgent note of frustration. "Know what? What are you talking about?"

She shook her head. "This guy had almost no reaction to the photo. And what he did have seemed genuine. But when we asked who he was out with, he panicked. He was out with Michael. Now, you tell me, what's going on here?"

She saw the light go on in his eyes. "Ah, gotcha."

Carol headed out to the bullpen to meet their final officer while Tom returned to the interview room.

***

The last candidate, Officer Daniel Shillings, fidgeted nervously with his cup of coffee. Carol watched him. *Go ahead, take a drink.*

The photo evoked a stark reaction. He glared at it as if not seeing it for a moment before answering. "No. Never seen her." He shook his head. "Should I know her?"

Carol's gut spoke to her. *It's him.* "Take a good look. Are you sure?" She prodded.

Shillings glared across the table at her. "I'm sure. I don't know her. I've never seen her before. I'd remember her for sure." He looked quickly to the side at his union rep.

Talmadge, who until this point, had been docile bordering on disinterested, sat up, alert. His eyes signaled recognition. He glanced across at the two detectives and then at Shillings.

"Do I really have to put up with this crap, Jeff?" The officer turned sideways in his chair looking directly at the union rep. He held on to his coffee cup, from which he had yet to take a drink.

Talmadge scooted his chair up closer to the table, his hands cradling his cup. "You're not under arrest or anything. They're just asking questions trying to rule out people. You know how it works. If you feel uncomfortable with this, just say so and we can get you an attorney. Otherwise, you can go ahead and answer their questions and get on with your business."

Carol gazed at the cup in the man's hand. "Officer Shillings, I'm sorry if that came across wrong. I assure you, we're just trying to rule you out so you can get back to work." She reached over discretely and touched Tom's arm, hoping he got the message. *Let's put some air in the conversation.*

Shillings remained silent.

Carol watched the coffee cup. The officer wiped his brow with his free hand. More silence. He lifted the cup to his lips and took a drink. *Bingo!*

She continued with the questioning. "Officer Shillings, first I want to tell you that we've talked to other uniformed officers today and we're asking all the same questions. So, there's nothing special about what we're asking you."

He nodded without speaking, so she continued, "Where were you last Friday night between about eight and midnight?"

His eyes widened. Carol noted the look of despondence that followed. They had him. "Uh, I was at home with my wife and kids. They can vouch for me. I was there all night." A bead of sweat appeared on his brow.

She tried to inject a note of lightness into her words. "That will do it for today, Officer Shillings. Thanks for coming in."

***

Carol, Ramirez, and Talmadge sat around the table finishing their coffee. She tapped her cup idly on the side as she spoke. "Well, that's it. We're done here."

The union rep stood. "What next?"

"We finish up. We have lab work coming in and we'll verify their stories. We just see where the trail leads us, I guess. You know the drill."

Talmadge lowered his head. "Okay. Thanks."

He knows too.

Tom waited until they were alone again to weigh in. "Why didn't we go ahead and sweat him. I mean, not much doubt there."

Carol stood and wandered over to the window. She spoke without turning around. "I don't know. I mean, he probably knows he's been made. Right now, I figure he's hoping against hope that it's going to blow over. I guess I was trying to feed that. Let him think he's off the hook. We got his DNA. We'll be able to get his cell phone records. Once we tie him to her, it's a done deal. Hopefully, we can get a rush on these." She waved her hand at the four paper cups, each labeled with the names of the officers.

Chapter 31

Carol walked through the doors to the bullpen on Friday morning already dreading the day. If DNA was back on the coffee cups, having to arrest a fellow police officer seemed imminent. On top of that, she had Jason to look forward to. As much as she loved her son and wanted to see him, his wild mood swings and caustic remarks cut deep.

Ramirez was already at his desk, the phone glued to his ear. He put his free hand over the mouthpiece. "Still waiting on DNA from the cups."

She took off her blazer, draping it across the back of her seat. "I'm going to grab a cup. Want one?"

He nodded as he returned to the phone conversation. "Okay. Yeah, I understand. Give us a call as soon as it comes in."

As she approached her desk, two cups of coffee in hand, she noticed a young man in his late twenties walk through the double doors, a large file box in his hands. He was dressed in navy slacks, a light blue shirt, with a navy and silver diagonally striped tie. He stopped and looked around, like a lost boy.

Carol set the coffee on her desk and walked over to greet him. "Hi. Can I help you?"

He smiled nervously. "Oh, yeah. I'm Russell Cartwright, coming up from patrol. Starting here today." He set his box on the floor and offered his hand.

She shook his hand. "Welcome to Homicide. I'm Carol Tullis. These are the rest of the criminals." She waved her hand around the bullpen and then pointed to the glassed-in office. "That's Captain Peterman. You'll need to check in with him first. He'll get you pointed in the right direction."

Before the young man could respond, a voice carried over from a corner desk behind Carol. "Hey Tullis, still looking for action in the bullpen?"

She whipped around and glared at Detective Art Mulroney, an overweight, fiftyish veteran. They had never really exchanged words, so the barb shocked her. As the blood rose in her face, Carol prepared to unleash the full measure of her fury. Her vision darkened along the periphery. Everyone else in the room disappeared and it was just her and her newfound enemy.

She walked over and grabbed a straight-backed chair sitting against the wall. Carrying it by the back, she set it down in front of Mulroney with its back to the desk. Straddling the seat, she sat glaring at the detective for a moment before she sensed her face relaxing. A sense of peace came over her. "You trying to fill in the empty spot in your love life, are you, Mulroney?"

He smirked. "You offering?"

Carol narrowed her eyes, looked up, and tightened her lips for a moment before answering. "Hmmm, tempting, but no. That does raise an interesting question, though. How does your wife feel about going without? Or, maybe she's made other arrangements."

Silence. Mulroney glared, his face turning beet red.

She leaned in to his desk and lowered her voice. "Is there more or are we done here?" She placed all the mental force she could into shooting daggers from her eyes.

No response.

135

Carol relaxed. "I figured as much." She stood and pulled the chair back over to the wall.

As she turned toward her desk and away from her nemesis, she heard his voice again, this time lower and laced with venom. "Fuck you, bitch."

She whirled around, eyes wide. "Bitch? You called me a bitch?" She looked around the bullpen feigning amazement. "That's it? That's the best you can do?" She relaxed. "I'm going to give you a ten for delivery. It's a complicated line, I know, and you've clearly used it before. But you get a zero for content. You've got to find some better material if you're going to keep up."

The bullpen erupted in laughter. Carol caught sight of Detective Jessie Collins toward the back of the room laughing with both thumbs up.

A booming voice interrupted the jubilance. "Was there a party scheduled? I didn't get the invitation." Peterman stood at the entrance to his office, hands on his hips. The room fell silent. "You Cartwright?" He stared at the new arrival, who looked stunned.

"Yes sir."

"Come. The rest of you get back to work." The captain gestured the new detective in and shut the door behind him. Around the bullpen, heads went down as everyone tried to get back to work.

Carol returned to her desk, plopped down in the chair, and took a deep drink of her coffee, which had cooled to near room temperature. She felt herself relaxing.

Ramirez looked across at her, a serious expression on his face. "You get a ten for delivery. Nicely done. But I can only give you five for content since you stole it from me." A grin cracked his face.

"Didn't anyone ever tell you that plagiarism is the sincerest form of flattery?"

Tom's ringing phone broke the conversation. "Ramirez." He listened for a moment before responding. "Okay. Muchos gracias, Bubba." He hung up. "And we have a winner."

Chapter 32

Carol's heart dropped as she considered what she had heard. *Shit.* She hung up the phone. "Shillings didn't show up for shift today. Didn't call in, either." *We had him right here. We should have just sweated him like Tom said.*

Ramirez stood up and grabbed his coat. "Got a home address?"

She took her armored vest off the hook and donned it, slipping her blazer on over that. The loss of weight over the past few years made for a comfortable fit. "Yeah. Just a few miles north of SeaTac. What's the chance of getting a couple of uniforms from that precinct to meet us there?" She pocketed her cellphone.

Tom responded over his shoulder as he started for the door. "Yeah, I'll call it in."

Carol stopped in her tracks. "Whoa there, cowboy. Where you going? Get that vest on." She glared at her partner.

"It's a tad snug. I need to take off a pound or two."

She laughed. "Yeah, well maybe so. But you're still going to wear the vest."

Ramirez stood and stared.

"You put that vest on right now or I swear I'll call your wife and let her talk to you about it."

He exhaled sharply and shuffled over to the wall where his vest hung on a hook. Carol almost laughed aloud when he sucked his stomach in to get it fastened in front. "There, you satisfied, Mother?"

"Yes, Son. I'm so very proud of you. Now let's hit it." She strode across the bullpen toward the door.

From behind she heard the command. "Call it."

"Heads"

"Alright! Finally."

She turned just in time to catch the keys that Ramirez had tossed her way. A wave of uneasiness coursed through her body and disappeared as quickly as it had come. Her day was already starting to unravel.

***

Carol pulled the sedan into the convenience store parking lot a couple of blocks north of Shillings' home. A patrol car sat waiting. She and Ramirez got out and walked over to meet the two uniformed officers exiting the car.

"Hi. I'm Carol Tullis. This is my partner Tom Ramirez." She offered her hand. "Appreciate the support, guys."

The taller of the two, a trim African American man, took her hand. "I'm Officer Dinkins." He motioned toward his partner, a petite young Caucasian woman. "My partner, Officer Jordan." His demeanor became serious. "They didn't give us any details. What do you got?"

She took a deep breath and shook her head slightly. "Well, nothing that's gonna be fun, that's for sure. We need to pick up a homicide suspect. He lives a couple of blocks down. Thing is, he's a uniform from the downtown precinct. Didn't make shift or call in today. Pretty good bet he knows we're on to him."

Both uniformed officers grimaced in unison. Carol understood. Arresting a fellow police officer was not high on anyone's list of favorite things to do.

Carol hesitated before adding the rest. "According to HR, he's got a wife and two sons. Not sure whether they'll be there or not but I'd say we assume worst case. Getting him separated from them should be first priority."

Officer Jordan stepped in closer. "So, how do you want to play it?"

Carol started to respond but decided to let Tom take the lead. The knot in her stomach tightened. *Too many ways for this to go wrong.*

Tom gestured in the general direction of Shillings' house. "We'll park on the street several houses down. We drove by the place earlier—nothing special sticks out. We make the approach on the sidewalk, up to the door. You stay on the lawn out of view of the window and door but in sight of us. We'll have to see where it goes from there, I guess."

***

Carol and Tom stood on opposite sides of the door. As Ramirez nodded, she reached up and rang the doorbell.

Nothing. She rang it again, this time with a double-tap. Nothing.

Carol knocked loudly on the door. "Officer Shillings."

"Get the fuck away." Loud and angry-sounding.

Carol closed her eyes and took a deep breath. "Officer Shillings, we just need to talk to you. Could you let us in? Don't want the neighborhood listening in on this." She kept the tone of her voice even and her volume just loud enough to carry inside.

"Get off my fucking porch, right now." Louder than the last response.

She thought about her options, not that she had many. "Officer Shillings, Daniel, come on now. You're a cop. You know we can't do that. We're doing our job, just like you do."

"Get out. I'm just sitting here with my family. Leave me alone." The volume dropped and a note of despair had crept in.

Shit. Her worst nightmare was unfolding.

Chapter 33

Carol pulled up the data that the dispatcher had sent. "I've got his phone number here. Let me give him a call."

Ramirez pulled the phone from his ear and covered it with his hand. "No, Tullis. The negotiator and Tactical are on the way. Just hold fast. Let's not get ahead of ourselves." He glared at her.

She shook her head. "That gives us fifteen minutes. Let's try to get his wife and kids out of there." The two uniforms stepped back, watching intently. She punched the icon to call Shillings' home number and put the phone to her ear.

"Goddammit, Tullis, I said no." Ramirez kept the volume constant, but anger infused his words.

Carol held her hand up to him as she waited for an answer. Tom turned his back and stomped a few paces, shaking his head vigorously.

"What do you want?" Shillings' words came out slow and even, laced with a touch of weariness.

Carol turned and walked away from the small group as she spoke. "Look, Daniel, I just wanted to reassure you that we're all back here at the car. No one's doing anything risky. We pulled back, just like you said. We're waiting for you." She kept her tone and volume low, trying to sound casual.

Silence for a moment and then, "Just leave me alone."

Carol closed her eyes and tilted her head upward. *Please, God, don't let me screw this one up.* "Daniel, you're a cop. You know the deal. The negotiator and the Tactical squad are both on the way. We have just a few minutes before

142

this takes on a whole new look. It's a chance for you and me to ratchet things down so that everyone walks away."

A sarcastic sounding laugh preceded his answer. "Yeah right. You're just looking to make the collar."

She took a huge chance. "Okay, you want to cut to the chase. A bottom-line kind of guy. So here it is. You're wrong. I don't give a shit about any collar. What I do care about, though, is that woman and two children in the house with you. This is not their issue. This is between you and us. Let them come out."

The snarky laugh repeated. "Sure thing. Then you and your storm troopers can launch the assault. No thanks. We're all in here together and that means that you're not going to do anything stupid." His words came out as an attempt at rationality laced with desperation.

Carol thought about it for a moment. Ramirez, by this time, had walked over and was standing next to her. "Okay, so in straight up terms, you need hostages. Tell you what, I have a one-time offer for you. You take me as your hostage and let them go." She braced herself for the onslaught from her partner.

"What the fuck! Tullis, no. Absolutely not. No." Tom moved over to confront her, their faces only a couple of inches apart.

She turned away from him, waiting for a response. For a moment, she wondered if perhaps the connection had been broken—silence. When the response came, it was slow, almost uncertain. "What, you think I'm stupid? I know you can't do that."

Carol tried to walk away from her partner, but he followed her, blathering on. "No. Tullis. Hang up. You can't do this. You're going to get yourself and them killed too."

She kept turning away from Ramirez as she carried on her conversation with Shillings. "Yeah, I know. But the fact is that you're holding the cards here. Look, neither of us wants your wife and kids hurt. It's the one thing we can agree on, right? So, a simple swap—me for them? I'll leave my weapon out here. You can even cuff me when I'm inside. Then you can take all the time you want. With a cop as a hostage, you know that no one's going to do anything stupid." She knew that the Tactical team would actually be more cautious with the wife and children inside but decided the lie was worth it.

Silence for a moment. "Okay. You can come in. Alone. Just you. And go over in front of the window first. Hold up your arms and turn around so I can see you."

"Okay. Like I said, you're calling the shots here. I'll be over in front of the window in just a minute." She waited for his answer but heard only a click. Removing her shoulder holster and handing it to Ramirez, she put her cell phone in her trouser pocket.

Tom grew animated and shifted back and forth on his feet as he took her weapon. "Tullis, re-think this, please. You're going to lose your badge over this. The captain's going to eat you alive. Come on. I was just starting to break you in good."

She put a hand on his shoulder. "It'll be okay, Tom. I'm sorry. Those kids, I can't let them sit there in the middle of this. The job? Screw it." She walked toward the front window.

Chapter 34

Once inside, Carol scrutinized the room, trying to assess the tactical situation. A young woman sat cowed on the couch with her arms around two boys who sat on either side of her. With eyes wide, they sat perfectly still leaning in against their mother. The two sons looked to be about seven and twelve, the same ages as....

An unwelcome image of Jenny in the grasp of her killer intruded as she looked at the three. A monotone, empty voice brought her back to the moment. "Turn around, back to me."

Carol lifted her hands above her head signaling compliance and slowly turned. Looking at the floor, she tried to conjure up an image of her jailer. His weapon was an automatic, most likely his issued sidearm, maybe a nine-millimeter Glock like hers. *Probably using issued ammunition.* Wouldn't that be an ironic touch? Using taxpayer funded bullets to murder a cop and three others.

"Take your cuffs out, set them on the table, and put your hands behind your back."

She dropped her arms and turned around to face Officer Shillings. She exhaled and shook her head. "Come on now. Really? You want to cuff me with my hands behind my back? Sitting here for maybe hours? No way to scratch? Geez. Can't we just cuff 'em in front?" She held her hands out, pleading.

Shillings smirked. "Yeah, right. So, you can jump me."

Carol rolled her eyes and tilted her head. Gesturing down over her body with her hands. "See this? Christ, you got a hundred pounds on me and it's all muscle. You got the gun and I don't. And I'm going to be handcuffed and sitting wherever you tell me to. I think it's safe to say you have me at a disadvantage here." She stood, shifting her weight from one foot to the other as she waited.

He narrowed his eyes and clenched his jaw. After a moment of silence, he relented. "Okay."

Carol pulled out her cuffs and offered them. "You want to cuff me, or you want me to cuff myself?"

He looked over at his family for a moment and then back. "You go ahead but make them tight."

With her wrists bound together, she returned her attention to the man. "Okay. You have me cuffed. Time to let them go."

He offered a twisted smile. "You're awfully trusting for a detective. Now I have four people in here and one of them a cop."

Carol noticed that he avoided using the word "hostage." She glanced over at the family again. If anything, the darkness on their faces had deepened.

She nodded at him with her head, gesturing him closer. In a low voice that the family could not hear, she challenged him. "We had a deal here. I come in unarmed and be cuffed. They get to go free. I've held up my end. It's your turn."

"No. I didn't agree to anything. I just said you could come in. I never agreed to let them go."

She moved one step closer and intensified her glare. "Don't split hairs with me, Officer Shillings. Neither of us is stupid here. Don't treat me like a complete moron." She relaxed, shot a glance at the family and then back to his eyes.

"You think by holding on to them you strengthen your position. Think again. Think like a cop. Yes, you have four hostages but in terms of negotiation, quantity does nothing for you." That was a stretch, but she said it with confidence. "On the other hand, you now have to manage four hostages, three of which are your family. That means feeding them, letting them go to the bathroom, and trying to anticipate their unpredictability. Truth is, all they do for you is increase the chance that you're going to lose control. With only one hostage, it's pretty easy to manage. Even better if that one hostage is a cop." Carol paused and watched his eyes.

He appeared, for a brief moment, to consider the point. Then the smirky grin returned. "Nice speech but I like things the way they are now."

She turned slightly away from him so that she was facing directly toward the family. They watched, silently, fear frozen on their faces. "Okay, if that's the way it is." She turned back and moved even closer to him. "Your word is no good. Got it. That means that you and I share no trust, no understanding at all."

Carol paused and glared, tossing daggers with her eyes. *Here goes.* "Those two boys over there, they didn't ask for this. They should get to choose whether they live or die. I lost my twelve-year old daughter to a serial killer ten years ago. She should have been able to live. But she wasn't given a choice. She was tied up and brutally murdered. As God is my witness here, Shillings, if you don't let them go, you better kill me now. If you don't, I'm coming at you the first chance I get." She kept her voice low so that the family could not hear.

147

The sarcastic look left his face. "And what makes you think I won't just kill you?" It sounded more like an intellectual inquiry than a threat.

"Dunno. I guess in the end, it doesn't matter. My life hasn't been worth much since then anyway. Besides, even if you don't kill me, I'm going to be fired on Monday."

He looked at her without speaking, eyes searching for something in hers.

"Look, Daniel, I don't know what's going to happen. I don't know what's going on with you right now. But I'm pretty sure that you don't want your kids killed. I can tell you from experience, it sucks. And I also think that, whatever you need to do here today, you probably don't want your kids watching it. Let 'em go, for God's sake." She pled with her eyes.

His face hardened. All sign of humanity vanished from his eyes as they took on an icy, glazed look. He spoke back over his shoulder without turning to look at his family. "Estelle, take the kids and get out." His voice remained steady and cold.

His wife's face screwed into a look of terror. "Danny, please."

Shillings shouted. "Get out. Now. Go."

Estelle shot off the couch, pushing her two sons in front of her. Within seconds, she was out the front door.

As the seconds ticked by, Carol and Shillings stared at each other, neither moving. The silence was broken by the sound of his telephone.

She sighed. "That will be the negotiator."

Chapter 35

Four-thirty already. Where had the hours gone? Carol watched as Shillings held the phone to his ear and muttered short grunts. "Yeah." Pause. "Yeah." He looked at Carol. "What about my family? Are they okay?" He nodded. "Okay. Just keep them away from here." His eyes narrowed as he listened. "No." Pause. "Okay, you can talk to her. I'll put this on speaker. We got no secrets here." He pushed a button on the phone and put the handset down on the dining room table. "Okay, go ahead."

"Detective Tullis, this is Walt Simmons. You there?" The voice came over with a soft tone and a slow, even cadence.

She sat on the couch, cuffed hands in front of her between her legs. "Yes. I'm here."

"You okay?"

She focused on answering the question as directly and succinctly as she could. "Yes. I'm fine." The one thing she didn't want was to perturb Shillings.

"Are there any other hostages in the house?" No change in tone, volume, or speed.

"No. There are not." Avoiding one-word answers was her way of assuring that there was no misunderstanding.

"Okay. Good. Is there anything you want or need right now?"

"No. Not at the moment." She looked over for a reaction from Shillings but saw no change in his flat affect.

"Are you hungry? Can we get some food for the two of you? Maybe something to drink?" The cadence picked up slightly and the words came across as upbeat.

Carol shrugged at Shillings.

He stared at her for a moment before blinking, like he had just awakened. "Uh, yeah, I guess that'd be okay."

"Good. What would you like? We can get you some pizza, sandwiches, soup or salad. What's your pleasure?"

Shillings raised his eyebrows as if giving her the option. Food was the last thing on her mind. But eating would occupy his mind for a while and possibly slow any emotional escalation on his part. "I don't care. Anything will do."

"I guess pizza's okay."

"Pizza it is. What kind? You have a preference?" Simmons' voice had taken on the tone and pace of a casual conversation between friends.

Shillings held the gun with both hands, barrel pointed down. "It doesn't matter. Anything. Pepperoni's fine."

Carol could see that the hammer was cocked. She couldn't see whether the safety was on or not.

"Will do. And we'll send in some water and soda with that. It's gonna be about a half hour. Anything else we can do for you in the mean time?"

"No. That's it." Shillings disconnected the call and set the landline handset back on the table. He stood and paced around the room, avoiding the window as he moved.

Carol watched him without speaking.

He turned and faced her. "They going to try to put some listening device in with the food?"

She considered him for a moment, not sure what would or would not set him off. "I don't work in Tactical, so I don't know. I guess I'd say that I don't see the point. After all, it's not like we're having discussions where you're telling me what you're going to do. They probably have no interest in hearing our little conversations." She raised her cuffed hands to scratch an itch on her face.

He eased over to the side of the window, moved the curtain back slightly with the barrel of his gun, and peered out at the lengthening shadows. His words came out soft and slow. "When do they assault the place?"

She almost laughed. "Why would they storm in? You aren't going anywhere? There aren't any deadlines. They'll wait you out. You're smart enough to know that."

Shillings said nothing for a few moments. As he moved away from the window, he sat in a chair facing the couch. "You seem pretty cool about all of this."

Carol turned her attention to the window and the world outside. She wondered idly about the weather. It had been partly cloudy earlier with a brisk wind. It had felt good on her face. "I got what I wanted. Your family is safe. What happens from here on is up to you." She glanced at the clock—past five. She'd missed the pick-up time for Jason. *Was he disappointed? Or did he just wait a respectable amount of time and then head out for a fun night with his friends? Did he even care?*

Silence descended to be broken only by the ticking of a small clock sitting on the mantle. Encased on a box of dark wood, maybe cherry or mahogany, a gold pendulum swung relentlessly, and the second hand made its way repeatedly around the face of the clock. The minute hand moved in discrete clicks, one mark at a time. The hour hand seemed frozen in place, although she knew that it would inevitably advance as well. Time would march on, whether she lived or not.

Her captor sat staring at a spot on the floor between him and her, tapping his right heel rapidly on the floor. He held the pistol with both hands, barrel down between his knees.

Shillings spoke softly. "I never meant this to happen. Any of this. Things just got out of hand. I never meant to hurt her." His eyes had a look of pleading.

She nodded but remained silent.

He shook his head. "I just don't know how to make this right."

Carol was surprised at the statement. Up until this point, his thought capacity seemed to be diminishing. Now, all of a sudden, he was talking about finding a way out. She decided to take advantage of it. "Not easy sorting these things out. But I can tell you from bitter experience that it helps if you just lay out what options you have."

He smirked and rolled his eyes. "I don't have any."

"Yes, you do. You may not have many and you may not like any of them. But you do have options. And the thing is, you *will* have to make a decision sooner or later." She kept her voice low and the cadence even.

He stared at her for a moment. "You're so smart. What are my options?"

"Hey, I'm not looking to argue with you. If you want to talk about it, I will. But I'm not here to provoke you."

His laugh came out laced with bitterness. "No. Please, feel free."

She closed her eyes and inhaled deeply. *Please don't let me say the wrong thing.* She knew she was far out of her element. "Okay. Well, first, you can't change the past and you can't control the future. You only have the present. Any decision you make is in the moment. Right now, you have three options. You can either place yourself in custody, which leaves you room to make other decisions in the future that may or may not help you. You can decide to go out in a blaze of gun fire and take me with you. Or, you can simply choose not to decide anything right now and wait for those guys outside to make a move."

"You're right. I don't like any of those options."

"Understandable. But all three are options that are open to you. Two of them will essentially remove any future decisions from the table. The only one that provides some future room to move is to place yourself in custody." She was careful not to use the term "give up."

He laughed. "Yeah, right. So rather than shoot me, they stick a needle in me. Same outcome."

She looked away and shook her head. "Oh, come on. Surely, you're not that out of touch. We've had a moratorium on executions for three years and the governor has introduced legislation to eliminate them. Your challenge is how to get the best deal you can."

He looked at her, his eyes narrowed and his head twisted slightly to the side.

Surely this guy can't be that dense. "Think back. You bring guys in and charge them. What happens? They end up getting a lot less than you think they should. Why? Because the DAs all have one thing in common. They're all looking for the deal. If they go to trial, they put the case at risk. Juries and witnesses are unpredictable. But if they do a deal, they get a notch on their gun with no risk. You get a good lawyer and exploit that."

He stared at her in silence.

The phone rang and Shillings picked it up. "Yeah." He looked over at the door. "Okay, have him bring it up on the porch. I'll open the door. Tell him to just slide it in." He disconnected and set the phone down. "Food's here."

He walked over and cracked the door. He stood with his back to the wall beside the opening, gun held in both hands, which were trembling. Within a minute, a large square box slid through the opening followed by another box with several bottles of water and soda. Shillings shut the door and picked up the box, taking it over to the table. "Come help yourself." He went back over and grabbed the drinks.

The sickening smell of the melted mozzarella cheese and pepperoni fed a wave of nausea in her stomach. "Maybe later." The thought occurred to her that this could be her last meal. *Pizza.* She tried to remember if she'd eaten anything earlier in the day. She didn't think so. If not this pizza, then what would be her last meal? *Oh, yeah, the cereal last night.* Forty-two and a half years of life and her last meal would be cold cereal.

I wonder what Jason's eating tonight. He and his friends are probably out scarfing down fast food burgers and fries. I'll bet when he's out having fun with them, he's a bottomless pit. She couldn't know, of course, because she had not really been a part of his life.

Her ringing cell phone interrupted the thought. She looked at Shillings, who had tensed up. "Who is that?"

She pulled out the phone and looked at the caller ID. Closing her eyes, she sighed. "My ex-husband. I was supposed to pick up my son at four. He was coming over for the weekend."

"You want to take it?"

The question took her aback. "Uh, with your permission, sure."

"Go ahead."

Carol clicked on the connect icon. "Hi Chris."

The voice coming over sounded worried. "Carol. Everything okay?"

She closed her eyes and took a deep breath. "Yeah. Sorry I didn't make it. I got caught up in something and couldn't get away."

"You involved in that hostage situation down south? It's all over the news."

Shit. "Uh, yeah." She looked at Shillings, who was watching her intently. "I can't really talk right now."

A tentative-sounding response followed a moment of silence. "Are you sure you're okay?"

"Yeah. I'm sure." She paused a moment and then added, in a voice so soft she could barely hear it herself. "Chris. I need you to do something for me. Please tell Jason that I love him very much. And that everything will be okay. I have to go. Good-bye." She disconnected the call.

Shillings stared at her for a moment and then stood. "Okay. Time to go."

Her eyes widened. "What?"

"Let's get this over with. We're going out." He walked over to the window, looking out once again from the side.

Carol was able to see that darkness had fallen and the house was illuminated from the tactical equipment on the street. The front porch would be like a stage with a massive spotlight. She struggled to put her thoughts in order. She hadn't expected this. "Okay. Well, at the risk of sounding presumptuous or pushy, might you consider we switch positions? You take the cuffs and I'll take the gun. It'll make the walk from the house to the car easier and faster." Perhaps she wasn't going to die.

He smirked. "Not a chance."

She shook her head. "Look, there are some good cops out there. But there are also some rookies who are about ready to crap their pants. I'd hate for one of those newbies to squeeze that trigger too hard. What about we toss your gun out before we go out just so there's no misunderstanding?" She stood and waited for his answer.

He stood by the front door waiting. "I'll give it to them once we're outside." His affect was completely flat, his voice monotone.

This doesn't feel right. "Okay. You're the boss. Can I at least call them and tell them we're coming out?"

He nodded.

She dialed Ramirez's number, not knowing the one for Tactical.

The voice sounded incredulous. "Carol? You okay?"

"Yeah. Fine. Let me talk to Simmons."

Silence for a moment followed by the familiar voice that had taken their pizza order. "Tullis?"

"Yes. We're coming out. I think I'm coming out first. I'll have my hands up." Holding the cellphone with her cuffed hands was a bit uncomfortable.

"That's good news. Good news. Can you get him to toss his gun out first?'

She glanced over at Shillings who stood, as if in a trance. "No. He's says not. Say's he'll give it to you when we get out there." She could feel the hope draining out of her words.

"Tullis, that doesn't sound good. You sure about it? Maybe you can talk him into it?" She could hear the concern in his voice.

"Sorry but no. This is it. We'll be opening the door. Probably in a minute or so."

When she had entered the house, she was prepared to die. She'd screwed up her life and the lives of her family. She'd humiliated herself. Dying to save the two kids seemed a fitting penance. But something had changed. She wanted to live. She wanted to hug her son again and tell him how much she loved him. She wanted to go to his high school graduation, and his wedding, and be there when his first child was born. But all of that could disappear within the next few minutes.

Carol walked over to the front door and stopped. Shillings took position behind her and with what felt like his left hand, he grabbed her vest at the top and held it tightly.

"What's up with that? The only place I can go is outside and we're going there anyway." She glanced over her shoulder.

He nudged her. "Open the door."

No. I won't let it go. She thought about the front porch and the steps. The porch itself was about two, maybe three paces if she remembered right. And then there were two, no, three steps down to the walk. She would take those two or three paces across the porch and then simply fall limp, rolling down the steps. He wouldn't be able to hold her with that grip and shooting a moving target wouldn't be easy. And she had her vest on so, to kill her, he'd have to hit a clean headshot—not likely.

"Move it, slow and easy." He nudged again, his grasp on the vest still tight.

She opened the door and stepped out onto the porch.

Chapter 36

The spotlights blinded Carol as she stepped across the threshold. She held her cuffed hands over her eyes, giving them time to adjust. Looking down at the porch, she confirmed her recollection about its size. *Yes. Two, maybe three paces.* She decided to take smaller steps and make it three for sure.

She felt a nudge in her back. Raising her hands over her head, she shouted, "Coming out." She took a second step. Her eyes had become adjusted and she made out the silhouettes of cars, vans, and people. She knew that scores of weapons were trained on the two of them. After all, with her in front, they wouldn't be able to differentiate.

"Keep moving." Another slight push with the hand firmly grasping her vest at the top back.

She took the third pace and glanced down at the steps below. *It's time.*

She took a deep breath and prepared to fall limp down the stairs. But at the last instant, she felt the grip on her vest tighten and another force, probably the gun or the hand holding the gun, in the small of her back. A massive push thrust her forward, downward toward the waiting sidewalk.

She sucked breath, eyes wide watching the concrete approach. She threw her arms up in front to protect her face. Her knees hit first, and pain shot through her body like a jolt of electricity. Her midsection and arms connected with the ground at the same time. The force knocked the air out of her lungs. Her forearms ground into the sidewalk, raking the skin away. The impact forced her arms to the side allowing her cheek to take the finishing blow. She felt pain explode in her head. The lights dimmed, to be replaced by vivid, whirling colors.

Roll! Roll! She tumbled quickly to her right. Coming to stop several feet from the sidewalk. She covered her head with her hands, waiting for what she was sure would come next. Other than the loud hum in her ears from the facial blow, she heard nothing for a second or two.

And then, "Drop your weapon, Officer Shillings."

Two deafening pops rang in her ears. A storm of gunfire followed. Carol scrunched and tightened the pressure of her arms over her head, as if that would protect her.

Silence. *Suicide by cop.* But he hadn't taken her with him?

She rolled over on to her side and started to sit up, pushing down on the wet, dirty lawn with her cuffed hands. As she sat, Ramirez ran up to her. "Here, let me get those." His voice sounded frantic as he unlocked the handcuffs.

She hung her head. "Thanks." She took a deep breath and stood.

"Detective Tullis. Are you okay?"

She vaguely recognized the voice as belonging to the negotiator that she had spoken to on the phone what seemed like a lifetime ago. She turned to face the short, wiry, balding man with black-framed glasses.

"Yeah. Good. Thanks." She tried to wipe the grass and dirt off her blouse and trousers, but it only smeared.

Walt Simmons eyed her for a moment before speaking. "Wouldn't want to be in your shoes on Monday morning. Good luck with that."

She exhaled and hung her head. "Yeah. I know."

His next words came out softly. "By the way, the wife and kids are safe."

As she looked up to make eye contact with him, she could see the compassion in his expression. "Good. Thank you."

He nodded. "You're welcome. Now, let's get you to the hospital. That facial wound looks pretty nasty."

Carol shook her head. "I'm fine. Just a little dizzy."

Simmons laughed. "Oh, I'm sorry. Did that sound like a suggestion or request? Get your butt in that wagon and do what they say." He turned and held up his hand, gesturing some uniformed medical techs over.

She lowered her head. "Can I make a quick phone call first?"

"Sure." Simmons walked away.

Turning and walking a few steps, she pulled her cellphone out, brought up her contact list. As she waited for the connection, Carol tried to think of the words she wanted to say. Nothing seemed right.

The call connected. "Carol? Are you all right?" The voice sounded frantic.

"Yeah. I'm fine. A little bruised here and there but okay." She had no idea how much he knew. She glanced around. The media wasn't allowed on the front line, but she knew beyond any doubt that they were just beyond her line of sight waiting for any tidbit.

"We heard an officer was killed. They just announced it. I was afraid…." He didn't finish the sentence.

"No. I'm fine." She decided not to elaborate. She was in enough trouble already without being responsible for dispensing information. "I guess Jason's out with his friends by now." She wondered whether he was with a girlfriend or just a bunch of guys. It occurred to her that she didn't even know whether he had a girlfriend or not.

The voice came across as soft and tentative. "No. He's up in his room. Pretty upset. Let me get him for you."

"No." Something needed to change, and Carol felt it was time for her to do something positive. "Chris, can I come over in the morning and talk to him and you? I promise, I won't take much of your time."

A tentative response followed an instant of silence. "Sure. He's usually out and about by about ten so, you know, maybe around nine?"

After disconnecting, she put the phone in her pocket and trudged over toward the waiting EMTs standing by the ambulance. "Let's go, boys."

Ramirez stood beside her, his hand on her shoulder. "I'll meet you there."

"Thanks Tom. But you need to get home to your wife and kids. I'll find my way back after they're done poking and prodding me."

He laughed. "I'm sorry. I don't need your permission. I'll meet you there."

She shook her head as the dizziness returned. Settling onto a gurney in the back, she closed her eyes and listened as the door slammed shut and the siren wailed.

Chapter 37

Carol winced as the physician cleaned the wound on her forearm, which looked like someone had smeared it with strawberry jam. "I'm fine. Just get this bandaged up and I'm good to go."

The young, swarthy doctor shook his head as he focused on his task. "Yes, we've done the x-rays and scans and, no, we haven't seen any damage. But I'd still like to keep you overnight for observation. Head injuries can be tricky."

She shifted nervously on the exam table. "Thanks, but no thanks."

"I can't force you. But you'll need to sign an AMA form since you're leaving against medical advice." His words came out matter-of-factly.

The clock on the wall caught her attention. *Nine already.* She wondered if Jason had gone out after she called. *Was he really upset?*

The doctor interrupted her reverie. "Okay. That's it. You can sign your form over at the admission desk." His voice came out with a tinge of resentment. Then he turned to her, the look on his face softer than his words. "If you have any dizziness, nausea, or any other symptoms, get back in here right away. Understand?"

She hopped down off the table and rolled her sleeve down over the bandage on her forearm. "Got it. Thanks, Doc."

As Carol took her first step, she almost collapsed on her left knee, the one that had broken her fall. She steadied herself with her hand on the exam table, and gingerly took another step, and then another. "I'm okay." She cringed, took a deep breath, and limped across the exam room, into the hallway, and down toward the admission desk.

Creeping along one strained pace at a time, she saw Ramirez standing at the far end of the corridor. His face seemed strained and his body slouched more than his usual poor posture.

She forced a smile. "Hey. You didn't have to wait here. You need to be home with the family."

He smirked. "Yeah, right. You look like shit, Tullis." Shaking his head, he continued, "Besides, Dani made some late-night snacks for us. I was instructed to bring you over to the house."

Carol stopped abruptly, searching his eyes. Why would he want to have her over to corrupt his family gathering? "You know, it's late. I should probably just get home."

"Of course, it's late. That's why she made late night snacks. Besides, if I don't bring you over, I'm in deep trouble and it never pays to be in deep trouble with my wife."

She shook her head. "I don't know. Anyway, let's head back to the precinct so I can get my car." She continued her journey toward the admission desk.

"Sorry, no can do. You're not driving." He kept pace beside her.

Carol rolled her eyes but continued the torturous transit. "What, are you my mother now?

He didn't miss a beat. "If need be. I'm going to pick up my car. *We* will then go to my house where we will partake of late-night snacks. After that, Dani, you, I, and the kids will pile into our van and go get your car. I shall drive you home with the wife and kids following. We will park your car. You can go in and go to bed. And I shall ride home in the van. That's the plan."

She sighed but kept walking, too bone weary to argue.

**

Carol limped through the front door into the living room. Three children stood staring. She remembered from her initial meeting with Tom that the girl was five. Her heart ached just to look at her. The two boys, both older, stood on either side. All three stared at the stranger in their home.

A tall, slim woman with shimmering black hair falling on her shoulders stepped from behind the children. "Hi Carol. I'm Dani and these three gawking children are Roberto, Isabella, and Alex." She turned to the kids. "Say hello to Miz Tullis."

The young girl crossed her arms on her chest and spoke as though conveying some profound message. "Bella. I'm Bella." The two boys mumbled greetings, their gazes at first fixed on her and then, almost in unison, dropping. Kids had a way of being genuine that adults could never seem to manage.

Carol summoned the best smile she could manage. "Hello and thank you."

Dani gently touched her arm and motioned toward the couch. "Have a seat. From the look of it, that has to be hurting."

Carol limped over to the couch and plopped down as gracefully as her damaged body would permit. "Thanks. Mostly it's just awkward."

The woman stood gazing at Carol for a few seconds. She looked as though she was sizing up the visitor. Finally, she nodded. "Tommy's right. You definitely need to eat more. I'll be right back." She started toward the kitchen but stopped, midstride and turned. "Oh, and what do you want to drink? We have some water and juice, apple and cranberry."

Carol relaxed into the sofa. "Water's fine. Thanks."

Tom, who until this point, had been standing silently to the side, walked over and touched her shoulder. "I'll be right back. Going to change clothes. Don't let the kids drive you crazy." He paused, gazing at her. "Seriously, Carol. You okay?"

She couldn't remember the last time that a friend had worried about her. In fact, she couldn't recall any friends since…. "Sure. I'm fine. Thanks."

***

"That's plenty." Carol looked at the small slice of homemade pizza on her plate. It was unlike the usual restaurant stuff. It had a thin, almost cracker-like crust. The red sauce was spread sparingly, and a few onions and peppers adorned the top with a small amount of feta cheese sprinkled around. Aromas of basil and oregano wafted from the steaming slice. A small green salad composed only of dark lettuce and olives sat on a small plate with small dispensers of olive oil and balsamic vinegar to the side. She splashed a little of each on the salad and stabbed a piece of lettuce with her fork.

The five members of the family watched her every move. The kids seemed fascinated. Dani seemed to be still in the assessment mode, which she made no apparent effort to hide.

Finally, Tom broke the silence. "I told you so." He shoveled a piece pizza in his mouth, gathering some salad on his fork as he chewed. "She doesn't eat enough to keep a bird alive."

His wife considered him for a minute and then turned back to Carol. "Pay no attention to him." She smiled broadly. "Anyway, we'll have a much better dinner tomorrow night and no doubt you'll be in better spirits by then."

Carol tried to decipher her words. *Was that a dinner invitation for the next evening?* She chewed the piece of lettuce until it was mush and then swallowed. "Excuse me?"

Dani laughed. "Tommy told me you'd say something like that. Dinner tomorrow night, of course. I'm doing chicken parmesan. We'll have that with a little pasta and fresh bread. You like tiramisu? I'm going to make some tomorrow. Haven't done it in years but I have my mom's recipe."

Carol wanted to decline. Better yet, she wanted the invitation to go away. But all of the words that came to mind seemed dismissive, even rude. "Thank you. That's very kind." Taking a deep breath, she picked up the small slice of pizza, wondering whether or not it would even stay down.

***

As the family packed into the van to go, Carol watched the kids banter and argue, eventually doing as they were told. Tom and Dani playfully interacted. He popped a kiss on her cheek, and she reached up and touched his. They smiled a lot.

I used to have that. Her heart was breaking. She remembered their times as a family. *Until he destroyed it. He killed Jenny and destroyed my life.* But she knew better. Yes, *he* had killed her daughter. But the destruction of the family she could blame only on herself.

As she moved to the van to get in, a smiling Dani took her aside. "Carol. Thank you for coming tonight. It means a lot to me. We'll talk more tomorrow night."

Chapter 38

Carol managed to drag herself out of bed, despite the aches and pains from the previous day's injuries and make it to Chris' house just before eight-thirty. Saturday morning traffic, or rather the lack of it, helped. Even as she rang the bell, what exactly she wanted to say to Jason eluded her. Mainly she wanted to hug him.

"Carol. Oh my God!" Chris stared, his mouth open. He shook his head as he appeared to be searching for some other words. In an instant, he threw his arms around her and squeezed.

She held him for a moment and then pulled back. "Looks worse than it is. No broken bones." She paused and looked up at him. "I was lucky."

He stepped aside and gestured her in. "Come in, please. I have coffee ready." He touched her shoulder. "Then it's true? You really were the hostage? How did that happen?"

"Long story and yes to the coffee." She started for the kitchen, speaking over her shoulder. "Jason up yet?"

The aroma of fresh brewed coffee, French roast, welcomed her. She took one of the cups out on the counter and filled it to the brim.

Chris followed her in and refilled a cup that was also sitting on the counter half-full. "Yes. I heard him stirring a few minutes ago." His brow furrowed and he chewed on his bottom lip. After eyeing her for a moment, he spoke again, his voice softer and slower. "He was worried about you. I've never seen him like that. From your appearance, his fears were justified."

She leaned back against the counter, taking the weight off her bad leg. "I'm fine, Chris. Things just went a little sideways." In truth, things were every bit as bad as he was making out. She conjured the memory of her desperation the afternoon before, when she was sure she would never see either of them again.

He shook his head but didn't speak.

A voice from the direction of the stairway intruded. "Is Mom here? I thought I heard the doorbell." Jason walked in dressed in jeans and a sweatshirt.

Look at him. He's grown up. Carol set her coffee cup down and pushed off the counter, limping toward her son. He hugged her tightly.

Ending the embrace, he stepped back. "Mom. What happened?"

Carol looked down for a moment and then up at her son. "Everything's fine. Like I told your father, it's not as bad as it looks."

Jason shook his head, his eyes widening. He gestured with his hands out to her. "How could that happen?"

She almost dismissed the question since it was not what she came to talk about. But his eyes begged an explanation. "Jason, there were two young boys in that house. There was a good chance that they and their mother might have died. Honey, I just couldn't stand out there and let that happen. No child deserves to die like that." *Especially Jenny.* "But that's not what I wanted to talk to you about. Let's go in the living room." She picked up her coffee and limped toward the sofa.

As they settled in, Carol made a last run-through of what she thought she wanted to say. "Jason, I wanted to talk to you, and your father, about your weekend visits." She shifted on the sofa to get a little more comfortable. "You know I love seeing you. And if I could, I would spend every spare moment of my life with you. But it's not fair. I can see that now. When you come over to my place, I'm taking you out of your world, literally out of your life. Everything you love to do, all your friends, and your job, all of that comes to a halt for the weekend. And I love having you there. But I realize that I'm forcing you to pay the price for my failure." She wiped at her cheeks again.

Jason looked over at Chris and then at her. "Mom, really, it's okay. I'm fine with it."

She waved his comments away with a sweep of her hand. "I know you are. And that really shows how much you've grown up. But that's not the point, Jason. I want to be a part of your life but not at the cost of you putting that life on hold. Look, what I have in mind is this. How about I come over every few weeks and we could go out for a burger or pizza, or maybe take in a movie."

"You'd be okay with that?" Jason's words came out as tentative and questioning. He left the chair where he had parked, sliding over onto the couch beside her. He put his arms around her and held her tightly.

Carol felt like her heart would explode. "Yes. I'm more than okay with that. Just to be a part of your life is the most remarkable thing in the world to me. I love you so much." She had turned sideways, her arms tight around his neck, wishing the moment would never end.

Chapter 39

Carol stood at her kitchen window looking through the light drizzle across the brown lawn at the small apartment. *What I wouldn't give to have someone to talk to right now.* The idea of sitting with Ben Sturgis over a cup of coffee and just carrying on a casual adult conversation almost drove her to the back door. But she knew that the price was too high. What he wanted from her was out of the question.

Her mind drifted back to the days before.... She and Chris had always found time to talk. Sometimes it was after the kids went to bed. Occasionally they would both be off work on a school day, and then they often found themselves in more passionate pursuits. Most often, though, they just managed to capture a spare moment where gentle, reassuring words could be exchanged, along with smiles and quick touches.

She pulled herself out of her reverie and looked at the clock on the stove. *Oh crap.* The hours had somehow crept by without her noticing. She had only forty-five minutes before she was supposed to be at the Ramirez home for dinner. And she wanted to stop on the way for flowers.

She limped into the bedroom to begin the painful process of changing clothes. Her cheek had swollen and her right eye was black and blue. But what hurt most was her knee. She had stiffened up and just the simple act of changing into another pair of slacks became a major operation.

I'll make it a short night.

***

Having rang the bell, Carol stood at the front door waiting. A bouquet from a discount grocery store occupied her hands. She did not look forward to the coming evening.

Dani greeted her, "Carol, come in. Oh, those are beautiful."

Carol knew better. The flowers were just a bundle of cheap. Looking around the room where she had spent some time the previous evening, the hominess and warmth struck her. The furnishings were by no means opulent. But the tabletops shone. The beige carpet looked clean. Throw pillows with a floral earth tone design were strategically placed on the chocolate couch. She felt embarrassed that she'd so thoughtlessly grabbed a random bunch of flowers just so that she wouldn't show up empty-handed.

"Thank you." She handed the flowers over and Dani put them to her face and inhaled.

"Perfect. Let me get them in a vase." She headed off toward the kitchen, calling over her shoulder, "The kids are in the den glued to the TV. I sent Tommy out to the store. He should be back shortly." Her voice faded as she turned the corner out of view. A few seconds later, she stuck her head into the doorway. "Can I get you something to drink? I just made a fresh pot of coffee. We also have tea, cola, and water."

Tom told her about my drinking. "Coffee would be great. Black. Thanks."

Dani returned by way of the adjoining dining area, where she sat the tall, antique looking yellow vase with flowers on the table. Rotating the vase first one way and then the other, she eyed the product of her work and then retreated to the kitchen.

A moment later Dani returned carrying two cups with saucers. Carol was used to mugs. They delivered the caffeine in much larger doses. "Thank you." She blew softly across the steaming liquid and took a sip—*interesting flavor. Tastes a little like Jamaican Blue.* She rested the cup and saucer in her lap, giving her something to do with her hands.

Dani paused for a moment and then became more serious. "Truthfully, Carol, I sent Tommy to the store with a rather long shopping list so that you and I could talk privately."

Carol felt her stomach roil. She already had misgivings about the dinner. Now there was this private conversation with relatively little doubt about its subject. She nodded without speaking.

The woman's words came out softly but carrying a sense of gravity and purpose. "I'll be up front with you. I know about your history. When Tommy told me you were going to be his partner, we talked about it."

You mean he filled you in on all the sordid details. Carol didn't trust herself to respond.

Dani continued, "It's easy, you know, for people to sit back and think that they'd have done things differently. I guess it's human nature. I have a five-year-old daughter in the other room. I tried to imagine how I would have done it. But my mind kept slamming shut. I couldn't get past the 'what if' part. So, I guess what I'm trying to say is that, while I may not like everything you did, I am at a loss as to how I would have done it. You're not going to get any judgment here. I just want you to know that."

That last sentence surprised her. She lowered her head. "Thank you. And, no, I'm not happy with how I handled things either. And, looking back, there are a thousand things that I should have done differently, or rather not done. Living with it is, well, not easy."

"I can't even imagine."

Carol had no idea where her next words came from or even why she said them. "And I suppose you know about Joe Royston too?" She felt herself blush at her failure to keep the words in.

Dani studied her for a moment and then shrugged. "Yeah, I know."

"I can't blame Tom for telling you, I guess." Carol now understood the reason for the conversation. *Can't have the partner in bed with the husband.*

The woman laughed. "Oh, Tommy didn't tell me. God. I've known Joe Royston for years, and his wife, well, ex-wife. I also know his brother-in-law. And I volunteer with his sister down at the Parish food pantry once a week. Yeah, I've heard several versions of the story." Her face took on a more serious look. "I can't say that I approve of what you did. But like I said, I can't know what it was like there in your shoes. And I also know that Joe could never keep his eyes in check or his hands to himself."

Carol sighed. She summoned every bit of courage she could muster and looked up. "Dani, I can assure you that those days are past. As for Tom and me…."

Dani burst out laughing. "I hope you don't think I was suspicious or jealous. Heavens no. Tommy and I are in a good place and that never even crossed my mind." She cleared her throat and looked away for a moment.

When she continued, the words came out stronger and more direct. "I come from a long line of cops. My father and grandfather were both Chicago police officers. I have two brothers who are detectives. I have another brother in prison so I guess you could say he was in law enforcement too, just on the other side of the fence, literally." She laughed as she spit out the last few words.

"I know how this works. I saw the look on my mother's face every time my father left for his shift. I could see the uncertainty about whether she would see him alive again. I've talked to my sisters-in-law about it. So, I knew what I was in for when I married Tommy."

As she continued to speak, a fire seemed to emanate from Dani's eyes. "Maybe I'm being melodramatic, but I believe in my heart that the day will come when you will be the only thing that keeps me from being a widow. I need to know that when that day comes, you won't fail Tommy or me."

Carol took a deep breath. "What I can promise you is that I will do anything—everything I can to protect him."

Dani's expression lightened. "After yesterday, I have absolutely no doubt about that."

Chapter 40

As the family of five and guest gathered around the dinner table, Carol looked over the fare. A deep casserole dish held chicken parmesan. Bubbly hot sauce with a thin layer of melted cheese on top gave off an array of mixed aromas—oregano, basil, and the pungent tang of parmesan cheese. A large ceramic bowl adorned with colorful flowers held the spaghetti. Another large bowl contained a green salad made of romaine lettuce, purple onion slices, and tomato wedges. The bread sat in a small basket wrapped in a white cloth.

She wondered whether her stomach would accept this. Her usual meals consisted of cold cereal with the occasional sandwich or cup of canned soup. *Just a little of each, enough to avoid insulting the hostess.*

As the family sat down, Dani nodded to her husband. "Tommy, would you please?" She bowed her head, as did the children.

"Bless us O Lord and these thy gifts, which we are about to receive from Thy Bounty, through Christ our Lord. Amen." He made the sign of the cross and looked around at his family, which had echoed the "Amen" and were crossing themselves.

Carol muttered, "Amen." Not being Catholic, she wasn't quite sure about crossing herself.

Tom passed the pasta bowl to her first and the other dishes queued up to come her way. She dished out small portions of each, although the chicken breasts were whole. She groaned inwardly as she looked at the large piece of meat. *No way can I eat all of that.*

177

Plates filled, the kids dug in. Silence followed a couple of perfunctory conversational exchanges. Tom cut up Bella's small piece of chicken. The two boys, both older, managed their own cutlery.

Carol speared a piece of lettuce and was chewing it when a small voice broke the silence.

"Don't you like pasketti?"

She looked up to see the young girl, her mouth surrounded in red pasta sauce and a fork of spaghetti stalled halfway to her mouth. The girl's bright brown eyes shone inquisitively.

Finishing the bit of salad, Carol wiped her mouth. "Yes. I love pasketti."

Bella tilted her head, her eyes still wide. The loaded fork remained half-way to her mouth, as though suspended in time. "Then why don't you eat it?"

Dani intruded. "Bella. That's not polite."

Carol laughed. "It's quite all right." She leaned toward Bella, consciously widening her eyes. "You know, your mom spent this afternoon pouring all of her love into this meal. It would be a shame to rush through it. I eat a little at a time and savor it so I can taste it."

"What does love taste like?

Carol put her fork down and folded her hands on the corner of the table as she spoke. "You know, it's hard to say. But if you take a small bite of food, close your eyes, and chew slowly while you think about your mom, you'll taste it."

Bella stared at Carol for a few seconds, looked over at her mom, and then down at the food on her plate. She looked at the fork full of pasta and then put it into her mouth. She closed her eyes and chewed slowly for a few seconds. Her eyes came wide open and she laughed. "I can taste it."

***

Carol sat on the couch feeling more relaxed than she had in years. She had managed to get most of the food down. Although her stomach had not fully committed to holding it, this night, the odds felt good. "That was wonderful, Tom. I don't know when I've had food this good." She cradled a cup of fresh coffee in her lap.

"Just good old everyday Italian fare." He laughed.

Dani walked through the living room on the way to the kitchen. "They're down for the night but I have to tell you, you made a friend tonight. Bella wanted to stay up with you."

A part of Carol felt warm and alive being here with this family. But seeing the young girl laugh, so alive, brought back painful memories, too.

As she struggled with the contrasting feelings, Tom intervened. "Maybe it would be a good idea if I talked to the captain first on Monday, you know, tell him how good things have been going with us." He leaned forward holding his coffee cup in both hands.

She felt a surge of gratitude but shook her head. "No. You can't fight my fights for me. I brought this on myself and I need to take it straight up."

"Oh, come on. I'm not going to fight your fight for you. It'll just be me and the captain having a nice, friendly conversation."

Carol laughed. "Right. You and the captain don't have nice, friendly conversations, remember? He's the captain and you're the detective. Besides, after Monday I won't ever have to put up with Sullivan again."

Dani, who had just come in and sat down, looked first at Carol and then at Tom. "Who's Sullivan?"

Tom shook his head. "She's that detective over in Sex Crimes. She really has it in for Carol, but we don't have any idea why. It's crazy."

Dani narrowed her eyes. "Brenda Sullivan?"

Carol tensed up, sitting forward on the couch. "Yes, that's her. You know her?"

"Let me get this straight. You two are detectives in Homicide, two of Seattle's finest, and you don't see what's going on?" She laughed and looked away. "Saints preserve us. Remind me never to call Seattle Homicide if I want any detecting done." Dani shook her head, as though in amazement. "Brenda Sullivan is Joe Royston's girlfriend."

Chapter 41

As Carol made her way from the parking lot up to the Homicide bullpen, a plethora of emotions coursed through her. She'd not made any friends there other than Tom. In fact, she knew of no one that even liked her. Well, maybe that other female detective, Jessie Collins. Even Captain Peterman seemed singularly unimpressed with her. Maybe this was for the best, especially after that run-in with Mulroney the previous Friday.

Still, something about the place felt almost like home, sort of. She came through the double doors into the squad bay at seven forty-five. She figured she'd get it over with. The captain would be settled in by seven fifty-five and she could go in, get fired, and be gone before the crowd hit. She could always call Tom later, maybe even go over and have some coffee with him and Dani sometimes.

As she eased into the room, she could feel the emptiness. Looking around, she saw Mulroney sitting at his desk scribbling something into a file folder. He looked up and then back down without even acknowledging her presence. *I really should.* No. He'd started it. She'd just given him a taste of his own crap. *Still, my last day here. Maybe I can at least leave on a good note.*

She walked over and grabbed the same chair she'd used when she insulted him. Pulling it up to his desk, she looked across at him. "Hey, Mulroney."

He looked up, his eyes narrowed, and his head turned slightly to the side. He kept silent.

"About last Friday. I was out of line. I wanted to apologize." She met his gaze.

He looked around the room as if he was afraid that he was about to be made the butt of another insult. "Captain put you up to this?"

She sighed. "No." The silence in the room held sway during the pause. "This job, it beats the shit out of us. We shouldn't be doing it to each other." She stood and picked up the chair. "Anyway, I'm sorry." Dragging the chair across the floor, a voice from behind interrupted her.

"Tullis."

She turned toward Mulroney.

He seemed to consider her for a moment and then lowered his head. "Yeah, me too."

"Thank you."

The captain had, by this time, settled into his desk, eyes glued to whatever paper sat on the desk in front of him.

Might as well do this. She started for his office and then paused. *I do hate to see it end this way, though.*

Mulroney's voice came from behind. "Hey, you okay?"

Carol turned toward last Friday's nemesis. "Get back to me in about ten minutes."

"This about the thing last Friday night?" His expression seemed sincere, his eyes locked on hers.

She nodded. "Yeah."

"I heard about it. Most of us have, I guess. We all...." He paused as if searching for the right words. "Good luck in there."

"Thanks." Carol took a deep breath and started toward her fate with a determined stride.

She knocked on the frame beside his open door and stepped inside. "Captain."

Peterman looked up at her, without expression or response.

She stood in discomfort, shuffling her feet.

He closed his eyes and exhaled loudly. "Tullis, are you modeling some new line of clothing or do you need something?" His tone oozed irritation.

The words took Carol aback. "Uh, you heard about last Friday?"

He gestured with both hands up. "Yes. And?"

More confusion. This had to be some kind of cruel joke.

His face lit up, his eyes wide. "Oh yeah. Let's see." He offered a sardonic grin. "You violated a number of department policies. You gave yourself up as a hostage. You put civilians at risk. You put the department in a very tough position. And, oh yes, we ended up with a body. I think that covers it. And now you're here expecting me to pronounce judgment from on high, right?" He arched his eyebrows as he waited for her response.

Carol shifted her weight off the bad leg. "Well, yes sir, the thought crossed my mind." She stared at the floor waiting for the boot to drop.

"Oh, well, okay. Here it is. You violated a number of department policies. You gave yourself up as a hostage. You put civilians at risk. You put the department in a very tough position. And, oh yes, we ended up with a body. Don't do it again." His attention returned to the paper on his desk.

Surely, she hadn't heard that correctly. "Excuse me, sir?"

Peterman pushed his chair back from the desk and gestured into the air with his arms. "For the love of God,

Tullis, what part of that was ambiguous? *Don't. Do it. Again.* Clear enough? Now, if there's nothing else, I have work to do and I'm sure you have murders to solve. Go." He gestured her out of the office while rolling his chair up to the desk.

"Yes sir. Thank you, sir." *I think.* As she reached the threshold of the door, she stopped and turned. "There is something else." She reached around, closed the door, and pulled a chair up to his desk.

His hard, caustic look eased into one of quiet interest as she recounted the meeting with the FBI agents. She saw a slight physical change in him, he seemed to tense up and clench his jaw when she described Captain Fredericks' reaction when the lead agent had told them the name of the psychologist.

"This psych got a name?"

"It's in my notes. Irving, or something like that." Carol had it on the tip of her tongue but couldn't quite get to it.

"Irwin? Charles Irwin?"

The captain was full of surprises. "Yes sir. That's it. You know him?"

Peterman turned to her with a determined, yet tired look. "Keep me posted."

Chapter 42

Carol limped out of Peterman's office in a state of bewilderment. Not getting fired was a pleasant surprise. Her chastisement seemed somewhat light-hearted even with the captain's sarcasm. Why would he just pass it off almost as if nothing had happened?

And what's with the FBI psychologist? His reaction befuddled her. *Keep me posted. Really?* She made her way over and plopped down in her chair.

Ramirez, who had arrived and settled in to work during her visit with Peterman, glanced up. "You finish with the captain?"

"For now, I guess." She powered on her computer.

Her partner grinned. "I see you still have your gun and badge. How bad was it?"

"Let's just say he has a way with words." She smirked. The truth was, she wasn't sure what any of the conversation with the captain had really meant. She wasn't ready to trust herself discussing it with anyone. "I figure I'll have to check in with IA and the shrink, though."

"Small price to pay."

"I guess." After checking her calendar and mail, Carol stood. "We should go check in with Sullivan. They may have something new since the Feds arrived." She grabbed her blazer off the back of her chair.

***

They found Detective Sullivan in her cubicle surrounded by stacks of paper. Carol knocked on the fabric-covered divider to announce their arrival. "Hi. Anything new yet?"

The detective swung around in her swivel chair and stared, first at Ramirez and then at Carol. "I thought surely you'd be well on your way to the unemployment office by now."

"Sorry to disappoint. So, you have anything?" Carol remained determined not to bicker with the woman.

Sullivan stared daggers. "If there's anything I need you to know, I'll send over a memo." She spat the words out.

"Okay. So, is there anything you need us to do right now?" She glanced at Ramirez, who seemed dumbfounded.

"In the unlikely event I want you to do something, I'll let you know. Until then, I'm busy." She turned around to the stack of papers.

"Fair enough. Let's go, Tom." She started down the hallway toward the exit. She stopped when she heard Sullivan's voice follow her.

"Wait." The detective came out of her cubicle to face them. "You know, I do have something for you to do. Doctor Irwin is coming in tonight and wants to go up to see Doctor Hoskins in Bellingham. Captain Fredericks was going to take him, but something came up. So, if you think you can handle it, maybe the two of you can chauffeur him around." She stood, hands on her hips.

Before Carol could offer a polite answer, Ramirez chimed in. "I don't know. That seems awfully complicated. You think two of us will be enough?"

Sullivan snickered. "Well, ordinarily I think one person could but, in your case, yeah, you might want to get a third. It is a rather complex task."

***

Carol walked in silence as they returned to Homicide. She focused on the opportunity at hand. They would spend the next day with Irwin. Maybe he could shed some light on the different reactions that she'd seen.

"I don't get you, Tullis. You know what's got her knickers in a bunch. Why didn't you just come at her? Why put up with her crap?" Tom walked beside but slightly behind her.

She stopped about halfway down the corridor. "Yeah. I know. But this whole thing—Friday, the weekend, and this morning—it got me thinking. I really like being a homicide detective. And yes, I'm taking some crap. But it's really my own fault. I did it to myself. All that stuff that I'd hoped was water under the bridge. Well, no, I still have to answer for it. If I'm going to get along here, I've got to repair the relationships. I can't expect others to just tumble on to me. And that includes the ice maiden over there. Sure, I know what's up with her. But there's no way to solve it. It doesn't matter a whit what I tell her. Besides, the time might come when she does need us, and she'll have to come crawling."

Chapter 43

He allowed himself the luxury of a few minutes staring out his office window. On bright summer mornings, the foliage stood out brilliant green against the deep azure Northwest Pacific sky. Now he gazed through the cold, gray October rain at the small stand of trees across the boulevard.

His thoughts wandered to his last outing, the first where he'd been forced to deal with rain and mud. Thinking back over the past two years, he realized he'd been exceptionally lucky. But the constant, gentle rain outside his window brought him back.

Yes, it's time for a change.

But these changes must be carefully managed. Clearly, he would stop the outings. But how long would it be before the police gave up chasing their tails and moved the case onto the back burner?

And even if they did suspend the case, he couldn't just up and move. Given his position, that would raise too many eyebrows. He knew it was going to take years. The last time it took eight. On the other hand, it had worked out well.

But the years were passing. Every year of abstinence would be a year lost that could never be reclaimed. Eight to ten years of his life at this point was unacceptable. He wondered in passing how many good years he had left.

What if they solved the case? He turned the idea over in his mind. If they caught the killer, or someone they thought was the killer, that would mean a closed case. And if that suspect was a dead one, even better.

This idea might have merit.

Chapter 44

Carol pulled into her driveway at about six-thirty, a full two hours after sunset. After hanging her coat up, she went out to check the mail. Returning, she grabbed a water outage notice from her door knob. It looked like the service would be out for at least two hours the next morning. It didn't matter much, since she'd be at work anyway.

She was about to toss it into the trash when she remembered Ben. She hadn't spoken to him since their near miss. Hopefully, he didn't harbor any ill feelings.

Carol flipped on the back-porch light and made the trek across the wet brown lawn. She could see lights on in the living room. When she came closer, she could see that the front door was ajar. She tried to peek inside but couldn't see anything. She knocked a couple of times with no response.

Looking around and seeing nothing, she eased the door open and stepped across the threshold. "Ben. You here?"

No answer.

She wandered over to the worktable he had set up in the living room. She figured on leaving the water outage notice there on his computer keyboard where he'd see it.

When she approached, her eyes gravitated to the screen, where the words "urgent changes" caught her attention. But they meant nothing to her. She started to drop the notice on the keyboard but was distracted by what looked like a journal. Some words leapt off the page but before she could process them, a loud angry voice boomed across the room.

"What are you doing in here? Get away from there."

She looked up to see Sturgis standing, glaring daggers at her.

Carol felt herself blush. "I'm sorry, Ben. I just came back to drop off this outage—"

He surged forward and interrupted her. "I don't care. You have no right to be in here. Just because you're the landlord, that doesn't mean you can break in any time you want. Now get out." His entire body appeared to be shaking with anger.

Carol quickly set the notice on the table and stepped away. "You're right. I'm sorry. I really didn't mean to invade your privacy." She eased toward the door taking care to keep her distance from him.

Her mind whirled. What was this about? Rage seemed to consume him. He literally turned his body to watch her move around him. He seemed tense, ready to pounce.

When she reached the door, she paused to face him. "Ben, really, I'm sorry. I just brought that notice. The water service is going to be off."

He glared in silence.

She left, closing the door behind her.

***

Carol sat in her living room staring blankly at the wall. She tried looking at the event in the apartment from different angles. Nothing made sense. Yes, she could understand that he might be irritated at her simply walking in. And of course, she had no right to be reading his private material. Still, his reaction bordered on psychosis, to the extent that she knew what psychosis was.

And the journal? Some words had jumped out at her. "I think she suspects." "…she'd see." "Will need to change things." But these phrases were disconnected and scattered among other writing that she hadn't captured in her mind. These could mean anything or nothing. Maybe they were part of his book. Or maybe he'd decided to write a novel. But why write in a journal? Why not just type them in the computer.

Who knows? And it's none of my business.

Chapter 45

Carol glared at Tom. "This is the last time I'm going to tell you, Ramirez. I catch you without your vest on again and I'm calling Dani straight away."

He rolled his eyes. "You're not my mother."

She smirked. "Yeah, your mother would probably kick your butt if she knew. Seriously, Tom, put the vest on. I promised Dani I'd keep you alive and I don't need you fighting me."

He exhaled and took his jacket off. He grabbed his vest, slipped it on and, with some apparent effort, affixed the cord around the waist. "There, satisfied, mother?"

She grinned. "Now, what do you say we get over to Sex Crimes and pick up our good doctor?"

When they arrived, their charge for the day sat at the table in the conference room drinking from a Starbucks cup. As they entered, he glanced their way and then continued speaking with Sullivan as though he hadn't even noticed them.

Sullivan nodded curtly. "Detectives Tullis and Ramirez, this is Doctor Charles Irwin." She glared at Carol. "Doctor Hoskins is expecting you at ten-thirty." She checked her watch although a large clock mounted on the wall in her field of view showed the time to be eight-thirty.

"Okay. That gives us plenty of time." Carol turned her attention to the doctor. He wore a brownish tweed coat over a yellow button-up shirt with a pair of jeans and casual walking shoes. Not the standard FBI wardrobe. "If you're ready, we can leave now, Doctor. Otherwise, give us call when you're set." She paused in the threshold of the door.

Irwin stood and picked up his cup. "Any time."

***

Carol's luck with the coin flip returned and Ramirez found himself behind the wheel on I-5 to Bellingham. The doctor had claimed the backseat.

The steady rain of the night before had subsided, but the wet roads provided a consistent film of dirty water on the windshield. The occasional swipe of the wipers broke the monotony of the steady hum of the tires. Irwin seemed preoccupied with his cellphone. He didn't seem to even notice his two traveling companions.

Carol stared out the window trying to develop a suitable line of conversation that might shed some light on Fredericks' reaction. She turned, her body facing Ramirez and craned her neck to look at the doctor. "I guess Captain Fredericks was originally supposed to drive you."

Irwin glanced up briefly and then down to the phone without answering. His fingers continued to work the screen. His lips, drawn into a tight line and a slight roll of his eyes signaled dismissal.

Nope. Need to regroup and try something else. "Do you know Captain Fredericks?" *Might as well try the direct approach.*

The doctor stopped his finger punching on the phone and glared at her for a moment. "Detective, Tullis is it? I'm trying to get some work done if you'll excuse me." The tone and words left no room for misunderstanding. He was not interested in conversation. And she and Ramirez were just chauffeurs.

***

The Psychology Department resided in a building nestled in the southeastern corner of the main campus just off of the College Way Loop. They found parking and made the five-minute walk to Doctor Hoskins' office, arriving at ten twenty-five. Carol announced the group to the receptionist. "Hi. We're with the Seattle Police Department. We have a ten-thirty appointment with Doctor Hoskins."

Following instructions from the young lady, the group made their way down a corridor and around the corner until they found the right door. Carol knocked and opened the door to a large, spacious office with a view of the beautiful landscaped lawns and trees to the southeast.

Doctor Hoskins rose from her chair. "Come in, please. Good to see you again Detective Tullis." She wore forest green slacks with a tan blazer over a buttercream-yellow blouse. A silk scarf in pastels of green, yellow, and brown complemented the ensemble.

Doctor Irwin stepped in front of Ramirez. "Doctor Hoskins, I'm Doctor Irwin, FBI profiler. Kind of you to take the time to meet with me."

Hoskins sat down after shaking hands with Irwin and then with Tom, almost as an afterthought. "Not at all. A pleasure. When did you get in?"

Irwin sat in one of the two a wingback chairs with a Jacobean print situated beside a small conference table. "I came in late yesterday afternoon. I'm afraid my body hasn't made the time switch yet." He paused and settled back in the chair before continuing, "I did have a chance to read over your profile work on this case to date. Very impressive."

"Thank you. I haven't worked with the FBI before, so I have to say I'm humbled at your assessment of my work."

"I suspect we're just going to stick with what you've done rather than trying to second-guess it."

"With the FBI now helping the police with the case, I would hope that we'd get some new ideas. Perhaps you could help tweak things as we learn more."

After a moment of silence, Irwin said, "I have to tell you, Doctor, I was really anxious to get up here and meet you. Back in grad school, I read an article you published in the APA Journal on grief and resilience in adolescents. I remember being impressed with the attention to detail in your methodology."

Hoskins furrowed her brow for a moment before widening her eyes and laughing. "Oh my gosh. So long ago. For a moment there you had me at a loss. I have to tell you though; I left the adolescent work behind. There are some great things going on there but, my God, the politics of kids is crazy." She shook her head.

Irwin nodded but his eyes conveyed a troubled or concerned look. The two continued to talk, although to Carol it seemed they were each being careful of their words. *Typical eggheads.* Although, she liked Hoskins, who seemed more human than most of them.

After about thirty minutes of what Carol thought was meaningless banter, Irwin stood. "We should get going, maybe grab some lunch before we head back. Again, thank you for meeting with me today." His face had reverted to deadpan.

"Of course. It was my pleasure and an honor to meet you, Doctor." She stood and shook his hand. "Oh, I meant to ask you. Are the Seattle Police treating you well down there? Where did they put you up?"

"It's not too bad. But I guess there's some kind of convention going on in Seattle this week. They ended up sticking me out at the Marriott in Bellevue. Great place, though." He grinned. "Could never afford those prices if I was here in my own."

Ramirez spoke for the first time since arriving. "You know, Doc, I live out near that area. If you need a ride into town in the mornings, it's right on my way."

Irwin turned to him looking as though he was just noticing the detective for the first time. "Very kind of you. Certainly. Save the cab fare."

"No problem. I can pick you up about seven or maybe ten till. There's a great bistro near there. We can grab some coffee and a pastry."

Carol glared at Tom. *You better not let Dani find out you're eating pastries for breakfast.*

Ramirez stood. "If you want to get some lunch, I noticed a diner on the drive in, about five minutes from here."

A thought crossed Carol's mind. "Guys, would you mind going without me, maybe swinging by here when you're done." She turned to Doctor Hoskins. "I wonder if you have about ten minutes. Something I wanted to run by you."

"Of course. I've got a twelve-thirty meeting with the provost so we're good."

Chapter 46

Carol took a seat across the small table from the profiler. "Thanks, Doctor. I really appreciate this."

"A pleasure. And please, call me Marge. I've got so many people calling me 'doctor' around here that I sometimes feel as though I've lost my first name." She glanced over at the window and then at Carol. "Oh, I was going to ask you, what do you think of our good Doctor Irwin?"

Carol thought about it for a moment, not quite sure what the question was getting at. "Well, not being a psychologist, I don't know. But in general, and I don't mean to speak ill of him, he seems a bit cold." She thought about the comment and then added, "On the other hand, he seemed okay here. Maybe it was just that he didn't find Ramirez and me particularly interesting." She thought to mention the Captain Fredericks connection but decided against it for the moment.

Hoskins laughed. "Touché. I think sometimes Ph.D.s can be that way. They, well, we get caught up in ourselves." Her face relaxed. "I'm glad he's here. This case has been wearing on for two years now and I have to admit that I'm feeling the pressure of having everyone rely on my profiling. At least now we have someone else that can second-guess me. Hopefully he'll see something I've missed."

She re-focused on Carol. "I'm sorry. I got off on a tangent. You wanted to talk to me about something?"

"I wonder if perhaps we might be able to keep this between the two of us. I'm not enjoying the confidence of some key people around the department. Something like this probably wouldn't sit well with them."

Hoskins furrowed her brow and tilted her head. She leaned back in her chair, folding her hands in her lap. "I'm not sure I totally understand but, of course we can keep this private. What's on your mind?"

Carol gave it one more thought. *The point of no return.* "I've just been wondering if there might be a connection between this case and the child serial killer case a decade ago. Before you say anything, yes, that was my daughter's case. And, yes, I do accept that a part of me is probably invested in solving that. But there's something else."

"I'm guessing that any time you mention your daughter's case in any context you get accused of inserting your own baggage, right?"

"Well, in a word, yes. That's why I'd just as soon this not get back to the department. I mean, I may be completely off the wall here. At least if you can set me straight, then I can course correct without catching any flak, if that makes sense."

Hoskins reached over and grabbed a pad of paper and pen from her desk. "Of course, it does. Tell me, why do you suspect the connection?" She poised, ready to write.

Carol stood and walked over to the window. She looked out across the lawn and could see the sunlight filtering through the now bare trees creating intricate designs on the brown grass. "First, the physical evidence. The blue tarp used in our current case is the same type used in the child killings." She was careful not to refer to her daughter specifically. "And the bodies in both sets were laid out almost like a display."

Hoskins scribbled on the pad. At Carol's pause, she glanced up. "Go on."

Carol shifted her weight, suddenly aware of the lingering pain in her knee. "And, I don't know, I just keep trying to imagine a sequence. We have the killer ten years ago just stopping. Nothing since then. And now the killing starts back up but this time with adults."

The doctor looked up, eyebrows raised. "I'm afraid I'm not seeing the point. We had a set of killings ten years ago. We have some killings now. I just don't see how that connects other than the evidence similarities."

"I just, I mean, I try to envision what might have happened. Maybe this guy ten years ago went to prison for something totally unrelated. And now he's out and his tastes have changed." As the words came out, Carol realized how stupid they sounded. None of it made sense.

"Okay, let's work with this. Assume for a moment that our killer ten years ago decided to stop killing. We don't know why. Maybe he went to prison, which would have forced the cessation. Or he might have had some kind of injury or illness that debilitated him for a time and took him out of it. Maybe he just took his time getting back in. And, just to be clear, I'm not a police detective or forensics expert so I can only speak to the psychology."

She stood and began pacing the room, looking down at the floor as she walked back and forth. "If we use our current profile, and let's also call that an assumption, we conclude that our person is doing this as a means of showing what he considers to be love. It's worth noting that none of our victims to date have had sexually *questionable* lifestyles such as prostitution or exotic dancing. These are all women who, as best we can tell, are average. Given that some of them have been married and others had boyfriends, I think it's safe to assume that few, if any of them, were virgins. So, while he may view them as women of good character and worthy of his gifts, he would not view them as pure or pristine." She turned and looked at Carol. "Again, this is an assumption, but I think it an important point."

She resumed the pacing. "If we consider the psychology of a change in target, I posit that it would go the other way. In other words, a man like this would, at some point, long to give his gift to victims who are more deserving, more pristine. And what could be more pure and pristine than a child? So logically, a change might occur should he decide to move from adult women to female children. Not the other way around."

"I see your point." Carol slumped in her chair. That made far more sense than her scattered conjecture.

Hoskins took her seat once again. Smiling, she leaned forward into the table. "On the other hand, you will notice that I used the word 'assumption' a number of times. I could be wrong. And, to be fair, I haven't looked at my profiling notes for the children's cases in years." She looked down at the table as if collecting her thoughts. "Also, as I told you before. That case was my first and I regret that I made the mistake of allowing myself to get emotionally involved. I fear that colored my work." She looked up and took a deep breath. "Tell you what. This weekend, I'll pull those notes out and go through them again with an eye to what we've talked about. Who knows, something that we're seeing in the current case may well spur some additional insight in the older one. And I promise, I will keep this between us. If I come to an epiphany, I'll just say that I came up with it myself if that's okay with you."

Carol felt comforted. She knew that her attempts to connect the two were largely based on her desire to get justice for Jenny. She was pretty sure that Doctor Hoskins knew that and was humoring her. Still, she felt good giving voice to her concerns and having someone actually listen. "Thank you. And thanks again for taking time to talk to me."

Hoskins stood and offered a hand. "A pleasure, Carol. Oh, by the way, how is Doctor Sturgis doing?"

"He's fine. A little quirky but fine."

The doctor laughed. "Ah yes. Well, I suspect you are being kind. Quirky indeed. Well, if you happen to remember, please give him my regards."

Chapter 47

Despite her best intentions, Carol left the house later than she intended the next morning. She got caught in work traffic further complicated by I-5 construction and hoofed it from the parking lot, pushing through the double doors into the bullpen at eight-thirty. The first thing she noticed was Ramirez's empty chair. Then she remembered that he was picking up Doctor Irwin and probably stopping for a pastry. She put her purse in the drawer and hung her raincoat up on the wall hook.

A loud voice summoned her. "Tullis. Come."

She wiped a bead of sweat from her forehead as she strode to the captain's office. She stopped just inside the room. "Yes sir." The look on Peterman's face told her something was up and that something was not good.

He motioned her to a chair beside the desk. "Have a seat."

Her uncertainty building by the second, she eased into the chair, never taking her eyes from the captain's face. He looked frightened.

"Shooting over in Bellevue this morning." He paused. "Doctor Irwin died at the scene. Ramirez has been taken to Overlake. Not sure of his condition yet."

Carol felt her stomach tighten and her head lighten. That couldn't be right. Tom would never get involved in a shooting in another jurisdiction. There had to be some mistake. He would walk through that door any minute. She stared at the captain waiting for him to tell her that it was just a joke or a mistake or something.

His voice grew soft and gentle, a side of him she'd never seen. "Get over to the hospital." He gestured toward the door.

Carol stood but could feel her legs threaten to give way on her. She swallowed hard. "Yes sir. Uh, nothing at all on his condition?"

He looked down at this desk and shook his head. "No word yet."

"On my way." She turned for the door and heard the captain's voice over her shoulder.

"Tullis, keep me posted."

***

Carol parked the car and bolted, running at full tilt toward the emergency room entrance. Scores of different scenarios coursed through her mind, none of them good. Hovering at the edge of her mind was the knowledge that she was about to face Dani and try to explain why she had failed to keep Tom safe.

As she crossed the threshold, she saw Dani standing outside one of the exam/treatment areas. She slowed her pace and walked over, trying to read the expression on the woman's face. "Dani, how is he?"

A smile lit the wife's face contrasting with her red, swollen eyes. She threw her arms around Carol's neck and squeezed tightly. After a moment, she pulled back. "I knew you would save his life. I knew that I could count on you."

Confusion set in. "I wasn't even there. I mean, I assume he's okay then. But I didn't have anything to do with it." She tried to look around Dani and get a glimpse of what was going on in the room.

"Last night when Tommy got home, he was wearing his vest. He said you nagged him into wearing it and he just forgot to take it off before leaving the precinct. This morning, for some reason, he put it on rather than just taking it with him. The man shot him in the back and the vest saved him." She hugged Carol again.

Hmmm. I'll be damned. "Can I see him?"

"I guess so. I think they're going to release him later this morning. But you should be able to talk to him."

Carol walked toward the cubicle but a nurse intercepted her. A flash of the badge resolved that and she quickly found Ramirez sitting up on an exam bed, his shirt off but still wearing his trousers. From the front, he looked as if nothing had happened. She imagined that, depending on the caliber gun used, he could have a very nasty bruise on his back. She tried to make light of things. "See there. You need to listen to Mother more often."

But Ramirez wasn't smiling. "Tullis, I saw him. I looked right into his eyes."

As Carol left the emergency room, she heard a ping on her phone. Looking at the display, she saw that a meeting of the serial case had been calendared for eleven in the Sex Crimes conference room. She had little doubt about the topic.

But more to the point, that gave her about an hour and a half. She considered calling Captain Peterman to update him but decided to swing by his office instead. She knocked on the doorframe and stepped across the threshold. "Captain, I wanted to update you on Ramirez."

He looked up, his eyes engaged and his face tense. "Yes?"

"Well, as it turns out, he had his vest on and the shooter caught him straight in the back. He's gonna have one hell of a bruise but I think they're going to let him go home this afternoon."

She watched tension melt from his face. His shoulders slumped as he leaned back in his chair. "The doc?"

"I didn't hear anything at the hospital beyond what you told me. I'll let you know if I find out anything else."

He returned to his work without speaking.

Chapter 48

Badge clearly displayed on a strap around her neck, Carol wandered cautiously into the forensics lab. Looking around, she spied a familiar face. "Hey Sam. Can you spare a few minutes?"

The young man with shaggy hair and a clean-shaven face turned to face her as she spoke. His eyes lit up and he offered a grin. "*Deeeeetective* Tullis. And how does this day find you, Ma'am?" The strong southern drawl evoked a sense of easiness in Carol.

"I'm okay but I expect Ramirez has had better days."

"Yeah, but you have to admit, Jose was one lucky wetback."

Carol flinched at the language but remembered that the two of them went back and forth with almost a kindred tie. "Indeed. I'll bet he doesn't argue with me about the vest again."

Sam burst out laughing. "Well, that'll do it every time." He paused before continuing. "So, what can I do for you this fine morning?"

She leaned back on one of the tables. "I was wondering if you've been out to the shooting site?"

He shook his head. "Nope. That's Bellevue territory. Don't think they'd appreciate me snooping around their chicken coop. Anyway, that psych was a fed. The FBI's gonna be all over that like butter on grits."

Carol nodded in agreement.

"But I did talk to my buddy over there in the Bellevue lab. The doc took a clean shot to the back of the head, dead before he hit the ground. They're thinking a thirty-two but not sure yet. My guess is that the feds are gonna scarf everything up before the lab runs an analysis."

She considered the information. *Nothing really.*

"Oh, and one other thing." Sam reached up and scratched his scalp. "Odd. The killer took both of their cellphones. Don't make any sense, really. Unless he's some tech whiz, he won't be able to access them. Also, ours have GPS tracking enabled and I'm sure the feds have it too. That means that taking them would create a problem for the guy, unless he's just too stupid to realize it." He shook his head. "Not betting on that, though."

Carol thought about it. *That does seem strange.* "I'm assuming that the tech guys have already terminated the service for the phone and blocked access to our network?"

"Dunno, but I assume so. You might check with IT. They might even be able to tell you where the phone is if the GPS is still enabled."

She looked at her watch. "I need to get back to work."

"Any time, *Deeeeetective.* And tell Jose to stop by so I can laugh at him."

"Will do, and thanks again, Sam." As she strode out of the lab and into the corridor, she thought about her unavoidable interaction with Sullivan later in the morning. A sudden sense of purpose infused her with energy.

This crap with Sullivan ends today.

Chapter 49

When Carol took her seat at the conference room table, she noticed a host of new faces. She assumed them to be FBI since they all grouped with the agents that she'd already met. Detective Sullivan sat alone at one corner, apart from the feds. She looked beaten.

What struck her even more, though, was Captain Fredericks' absence. The wheels in her head kicked into high gear. This could not be a coincidence. But if Sullivan suspected anything, she didn't show it.

Doctor Hoskins sat several chairs down from Sullivan. She seemed to be staring blankly at the tabletop as though in shock. Wrinkles emanated from the corners of her eyes and mouth. Puffy bags sat beneath her eyes, which were rimmed in red.

At eleven, Special Agent Slattery stood. "I think we're all here. I'm guessing that everyone knows about the morning's events so I'm not going to go through them in detail. It should go without saying that the game has changed. We now have two cases. One is the ongoing serial rape and killing case. The other is the straight-up murder of a federal officer. We believe they are connected and will move forward on that assumption. Fortunately, we have a reliable eyewitness to this morning's shootings. We're passing around the artist sketch. This is our man." He paused and shot a quick glance at Sullivan, a look that seemed to convey a degree of sympathy.

When the sketches came to her, Carol took a copy and passed the stack along. *I've seen him.* She studied the rendering—white male, forties maybe, brown hair on the sides, bald on top with a moustache. Beard on the chin. *Where have I seen this guy?* The recollection was vague and distant. She ground her teeth as she tried to pull up the connection— nothing. The image looked like no one that she could recall. She put her hand over the moustache and beard to see if the eyes and hair registered. Again, she came up empty.

Slattery droned on. "This creates unavoidable jurisdictional issues. The serial case remains with Seattle PD for the time being. Doctor Irwin's murder is federal. Needless to say, we will have to coordinate closely. The Seattle field office of the bureau has the murder case. We have to keep sight of the fact that if they solve their case, then it likely solves the serial case as well. To that end, I suggest that we focus all of our combined effort and resources under the leadership of Special Agent-in-Charge Lucas." He nodded at a fortyish woman with close-cropped brown and gray hair sitting several chairs down from him. "She's indicated that once she gets her team organized, she'll call a meeting of the group to outline status and strategy."

Slattery paused for a few seconds, surveying the room. "Right now, I'd like to hear from Doctor Hoskins. I think we're interested in hearing how the morning's events play into the existing profile."

Hoskins met his eyes but remained slouched in her chair for a moment. She used her hands on the arms of the chair to help herself up. Her face looked blank, but her eyes conveyed deep worry. She looked around the room and then briefly down at the table. She cleared her throat. "The profile? What happened today is completely outside the boundaries of the profile. Everything we thought we knew seems inconsistent with his actions today. Up until now, our subject has shown no interest at all in the police. All of a sudden, he assassinates a federal officer, assaults a detective in plain view, and allows himself to be seen. Our notion to this point has been that he makes few, if any mistakes and has always remained unseen. Now, well…." She shook her head.

Slattery considered her for a moment before responding. "We have a couple more psychologists back in DC. I can have one of them out here within a few days if you see the need."

"I'd love to say that I have complete confidence in my work. But, honestly, I'm feeling out on a limb right now. First, what happened today, it is so out of character with what we thought that it makes me question everything. Second, and well, I have to say that I'm more than a little frightened. I've always thought of myself as being on the sidelines giving advice. But all of a sudden with no warning or indication…."

"I'll make the arrangements. In the meantime, we'll set up our command center at the Seattle Bureau office. Our local IT team will coordinate a communications network that will allow us to move information back and forth quickly. For both effectiveness and efficiency, I recommend we consolidate all forensic analysis in the Bureau team. We'll contact everyone over the next twenty-four hours." Slattery paused and looked around the room again.

"So, if there's nothing else, let's get to it. We have a killer to catch."

Carol looked down at the image that seemed to be taunting her. Giving up on that, she turned her attention to a completely defeated Sullivan.

Chapter 50

Carol gave Sullivan about ten minutes after the close of the meeting and then headed back to the detective's cubicle. As she entered the space, she saw that most of the desks were empty. Finding her way back, she plopped down in a chair next to the woman and waited for the pushback.

It didn't take long. Sullivan spun around in her chair and glared. "Excuse me. I don't recall asking you to come back here."

"No, I don't believe you did." She pulled her chair up closer to the detective, sitting with their faces only inches apart. "But whatever's got your panties in a bunch is going to end right now."

The woman laughed, although it came out as half-hearted. "If you think you can intimidate me, you're delusional." The daggers from her eyes came fast and furious.

"Oh, I have no intention of intimidating you. We're going to have a little chat and when we're done, you and I are going to work together just fine."

Sullivan glared for a moment and then the hatred morphed into something akin to curiosity. "Okay. Say your piece and get out."

Tullis began softly. "I'm going to go out on a limb here and say that you don't like me very much. Now, given that I don't even know you, I found myself questioning why the hostility. Sure, I have a soiled reputation. I know that. But it's more than that, isn't it?"

"Why should you care? All you need to know is that I'll tolerate you if I have to." Sullivan's words came out very matter-of-factly.

A moment of silence encompassed them. Carol nodded in the direction of the conference room. "You know they just hijacked your case, don't you?"

The daggers returned. "We're working together. It's dual jurisdiction."

Carol laughed. "Really? You buy that? Those guys in there just told you to chill and they'll call you if they need you. They're taking control of forensics. All of your evidence will be in their lab by close of business today. Your case files will be moved to their spaces. They'll call the meetings. They'll do the assignments. You're nothing but a piece of furniture to them. If there's a bright side for you, I mean even less to them. But, if you want more, my partner got shot this morning chauffeuring your doctor around. I'm not taking your shit anymore." Carol's face turned serious. "Right now, I'm about the only person in your corner. Even your captain has deserted you. So, here's the deal. You and I are going to air the dirty laundry and get on with it."

Silence.

Carol exhaled. *Here goes.* "Joe Royston."

She watched the woman's face darken, eyes shooting bolts of hatred. "Screw you."

Carol softened. "I know. You've heard the story. I heard it myself when I returned to work a few weeks ago." She cleared her throat. "Brenda, I'm going to tell you straight up that rarely a day goes by when I don't regret… that. What I did was beyond despicable. There is no possible justification that I could ever give, and believe me, I've tried to think of one. But the thing is, you need to know the real story, which unfortunately is not the most popular one." She got up from the chair and walked over to the window looking out on downtown Seattle. The rain fell steadily from low-hanging gray clouds on the black and gray streets. She took a deep breath and turned to face the sitting detective.

"I lost my daughter to a serial killer, who was never caught. I started drinking and then drinking more. I destroyed my marriage, deserting my husband and son. I was well on my way to losing my job and ending any chance of a career. But the bottle was still my best friend. And then I crossed paths with Joe Royston. Joe was like a kindred spirit in that he had a taste for the sauce as well. Here's where the two versions of the story differ. Joe and I hooked up once a week for about three months. We'd check into a hotel with our respective bottles. We'd have sex and drink until the booze ran out. Then we'd get up and go our separate ways. How his wife found out I don't know."

The fire had left her eyes. Sullivan stared, her lower lip trembling.

"Brenda, that was over eight years ago. I lost my job over the drinking and got sober a few months after that. The story you heard is a lie. Not that what I did was any better. I knowingly slept with a married man. I'm not proud of that. To make matters worse, this whole mess, or at least the version you know, is common knowledge around my bullpen. I have to deal with it every day. And that's fine. It's my own fault and I accept it. So, if you want to hate me, fine. Just do it for the right reason."

When the words came, Sullivan uttered them in a tone so soft and fragile that Carol was unsure of what she was hearing. "Joe got sober two years ago. He's a good man." She lowered her eyes. Tears dropped on to her tan slacks. "He's the best thing that's ever happened to me."

Carol came over and sat down again, putting her hand on Sullivan's shoulder. "I haven't seen him, well, since back then. I have no idea what he's like now. But I can tell you that when I quit the bottle, I changed in a lot of ways. I'm not trying to lay this on Joe, not at all. And I'm in no way suggesting that he's not a good man. That lie apparently took form many years ago and I suspect he was bitter at his divorce and still drinking. If he's the right guy for you, I sincerely hope that this doesn't change how you feel about him. I'm just asking that you give me a chance professionally. I'm not asking you to like me."

Sullivan nodded without speaking.

Carol pulled her chair up so that the two were almost in each other's faces. "Look, Sullivan, those suits in there want to take this over. But you know this case better than anyone. I believe, I really do, that if we solve it, you're going to be the key. I'm here to work for you. I'll do what you need me to do. But please give me a chance."

Chapter 51

Carol closed the door behind her and sat down in the chair beside the captain's desk. "I guess you probably know by now that the feds are pretty much taking the case over?"

Peterman took his glasses off and wiped them with a piece of cloth. "Bound to happen. Anything new, other than the sketch?"

She shook her head. "No, well unless you consider Sullivan and I making nice with each other to be new. Otherwise, they've shoved her aside."

He smirked. "I take it you don't approve."

Carol considered him for a moment. "I don't know. I guess it's nice to have their resources at hand. Still, you have to admit, they're an arrogant bunch of guys. I suppose we'll see how it goes." She paused and looked down for a moment. "Captain, I need to know what's up with Captain Fredericks." She prepared for a verbal head slap.

Peterman narrowed his eyes, drumming his fingers on his desk. "Why?"

Carol, exasperated, exhaled. "You know why. Irwin's dead, Ramirez barely escaped with his life, and Captain Fredericks nearly had a meltdown the other day when he heard the doc's name. So, he doesn't show up for work today and his people don't know where he is. I figure that's enough to justify my interest."

The captain slid the sketch of the suspect across the table. "That look like Fredericks to you?"

"No, but he could have been wearing a disguise. And maybe he wasn't the shooter, but something's up." Carol pushed the sketch back at the captain.

215

"He wasn't involved in this. That's all you need to know. He has history with Irwin but that's as far as it goes. As for today, he's up north in a small cabin trying to make sense of things. He went up there last night."

She steepled her fingers beneath her chin. "If I might ask, how do you know so much about this?"

Peterman motioned toward the door. "We're done here. Keep me posted."

***

Carol sat at her desk trying to focus. The conversation with the captain still irritated her but she knew better than to press her luck at this point. What little he had told her was more than she had expected.

She tapped her finger on the piece of paper in front of her and tried to approach it systematically. She didn't know anyone that looked like that. She hadn't seen an image like that since she'd returned. Unlikely she'd have seen it during her hiatus. It must have been before she was fired. But that was over eight years ago.

They were running the sketch through the cases over in Sex Crimes. The FBI was running it through every database they had. Maybe they'd come up with something. Still, the image tugged at her mind.

Maybe....

She flipped through the department directory until she found the number she was looking for. She picked up the phone and dialed, shuddering as she considered what she was about to do.

"Detective Slovak." The voice came out as bored and mechanical.

Carol closed her eyes and prayed she wasn't sinking into a black hole. "Hey there, Les. This is Carol Tullis from down in Homicide. Remember you offered to help me with that serial killing file? Well, if you like, I can come up this afternoon. We could work on it together." She poured her sweetest voice forth and then grew more and more disgusted with herself every second.

A markedly more enthusiastic voice followed the short pause. "Certainly. Would, say, five or five-fifteen be okay? I could order us some dinner if you think it'll take a while."

She almost threw up. "You know, why don't we just wait until I get up there and see how it goes. See you at five. Bye." She hung up and closed her eyes. This could go wrong in so many different ways.

Carol breathed deep and tried to shake off her disgust. She felt dirty just talking to the guy on the phone. Switching gears, she dialed Tom's home phone, remembering that his cell phone had been taken. Hopefully he'd be home by now.

Dani answered. "Hello."

"Hi Dani. How's Tom doing? Is he home from the hospital yet?"

She heard a deep sigh from the other end. "Yes. He's home and he's milking this for all it's worth. He's asking for burgers, fries, and chocolate cake for dinner."

"Don't give in, Dani. You'd just be rewarding bad behavior."

"Don't you worry. I've handled worse than this guy. He's a lightweight compared to my brothers."

"Look, the reason I called, I was wondering if it'd be okay if I stopped over tonight?"

Dani laughed. "Of course, it is, and you don't have to call to get permission. You know you're welcome here any time."

"Thanks Dani. I have to work a little late so it'll probably be around seven, if that's okay."

Chapter 52

Carol stepped off the elevator on the third floor. Halfway down the corridor she stopped and closed her eyes. *Do I really want to do this?* She felt as though this particular venture would take her backward rather than forward in trying to rebuild relationships in the department. She took a deep breath and shook her head. She needed to know.

She entered the large open area occupied by the Aged Cases division to find all but one of the desks empty. Detective Les Slovak turned to watch her walk in.

A wave of revulsion swept over her. *I can do this.* She shot him her best smile and sauntered over. "I see you have the file box." She gestured toward a portable container. "Why don't we take it over to the table where we can look through it *together*." She almost puked.

Slovak looked like Pavlov's dog salivating at the bell. He picked up the box. "Sure thing." He set the box on the table and pulled up two chairs, sitting them side-by-side.

Carol sat. "Thanks, Les. You have no idea how much I appreciate this." She took the lid off the box and glanced inside—it was stuffed to capacity with file folders, random pieces of paper, and a section of photographs. She figured the physical evidence was likely in a different box.

Slovak sat beside her and scooted his chair over closer to hers so that their legs were almost touching. "Gosh. It looks like this is going to take a while." He looked around the space as though checking for witnesses. "Hang on. I have something special." He stood and ambled over to his desk, returning with a bottle of Bourbon. On his way, he diverted to the coffee area and picked up a couple of disposable cups. "Here, this'll grease the skids a little."

That makes no sense at all. Or maybe it did, knowing him. "Uh, I'm sorry, Les. I guess I should have told you before. I'm afraid that stuff is off-limits to me." She figured the excuse would work, since her bout with the bottle was common knowledge at the precinct.

"Since there's so much, let's try to sort out the stuff that's likely not going to be helpful. How about the artist sketches, you know, from people who thought they saw something?"

He stared at her thighs. She shuddered and reached into a section of the box and pulled out what looked to be about fifteen documents. *Hopefully it's right here.*

Slovak leaned over toward her, as if wanting to get a better look at the sheets. But she knew he was looking down at her chest. He put his hand on her arm. *Ugh.*

Carol flipped through the set of sketches. *Nothing, nothing, no, nothing. It's not here.* The only thing left was to extricate herself.

She reached into her trouser pocket and retrieved her phone and looked at the display. "Oh crap. I forgot. I have to pick up my son." She looked at the box of documents. "And we haven't even gotten started good yet." *Just a few more seconds.* She put her hand on his shoulder as she stood. "I'm so sorry. Can we continue this another night, when I have *plenty of time*?" She strode toward the door without waiting for his answer, which was irrelevant anyway. Just as she reached the threshold, she almost collided with Captain Tarrant, who was coming into the area.

"Ah, Detective Tullis. Lost again? He smirked.

"No. I needed to bring something up to Detective Slovak. She sidestepped him and scurried down the corridor to the elevator.

Chapter 53

By the time she arrived at the Ramirez house, Carol had regained some of her sense of self. The brief foray into Aged Cases had left her rattled, not only because of the repulsive Slovak and his unashamed hits but also the chance encounter with Captain Tarrant. No doubt she would hear about it the next morning. *But that's tomorrow.* She was anxious to see how Tom was faring after his brush with death.

Dani greeted her at the door. "Come in. Can I take your coat?"

Carol shed her raincoat and handed it over. "How's he doing?"

"Ha. You'd think he was at death's doorstep—the poor boy. He has a nice bruise on his back, that's for sure. But he's going to be fine. He's in the den parked on the sofa watching TV." Dani stepped toward the kitchen. "If you want to go on in, I can get you a cup of tea or coffee." She looked back over her shoulder.

"Thanks. Tea would be great." Carol wandered down the hall toward the direction of the television. She could see the dancing light coming from an open door on the left. As she entered, she found Tom sitting up with Bella in his lap. Roberto and Alex flanked him on either side. The four sat engrossed in some action TV show.

"Hey, kids. It's Miz Tullis."

Bella jumped from her father's lap and ran to her, hugging her around the waist. "Hi again."

Carol rubbed the girl's hair. "Hi there, Bella. It's so good to see you." She looked up at Tom. "And, how are you?"

He shrugged. "Lucky. Very lucky." He glanced to both sides where the boys sat parked. "Jump up now, kids, I need to talk to Detective Tullis. Go ask Mom to send us in some of those oatmeal cookies, okay?"

The two boys shot out of the room. Bella left reluctantly, waving from the door as she turned to go down the hall. Carol parked in a chair kitty-corner from the couch.

Tom grew deadly serious. "I swear, Tullis, I saw him. After he shot me, the son of a bitch turned me over and took the cellphone from my pocket while he looked me in the face. Christ! There was nothing in his eyes. He's got no soul." He shook his head.

Carol considered his account. Not that she doubted him, but why would this guy look a cop in the face after assassinating a federal officer? Why not kill him too? "Yeah, they got the sketch circulated. Hopefully they'll get a hit on it." None of this made sense.

"Oh, yeah, the doc says I can return to duty next Monday. So, you're going to have to keep me filled in until then. Peterman won't even let me hang out in the bullpen without a fit-for-duty slip." He shifted on the couch, a painful move by the look on his face.

"Tom, I've seen that face before. I know it. Just can't place it."

Ramirez's eyes grew wide. "You think you know the guy?"

"No. It's not anyone I know. I've seen the sketch somewhere. It's so fuzzy that I'm sure it's from before I returned." She paused, questioning the wisdom of telling him about her adventure earlier in the evening. *Honesty, that was part of the deal.* "I thought it might have been one of the

223

sketches from the child serial case. I looked at those way back when. I went up there this afternoon and pored through the ones in the box. Nada. You know, part of the problem is that the last year or so I was on the force I stayed drunk. Not much wonder that I can't remember."

He snickered. "So, you went up to see Slovak. Aside from not finding what you wanted, was it otherwise rewarding?"

She broke out laughing. "I have to tell you, if he wasn't so repulsive and blatant about his intent, I might feel sorry for him."

Tom shifted and lay down, his head facing Carol. "So, anything else happening?"

"Well, let's see, Sullivan and I are talking now, and the FBI has pretty much taken over everything."

"No surprise there. On the bright side, you and I can get back to solving our own cases. It's not that I haven't enjoyed it. I mean, heck, I love getting shot and talked down to by obnoxious detectives. But it'll be good to just be yelled at by our own captain for a change."

"I hate to say this, but honestly, I don't think the feds are going to solve this one. I know they're good and they have lots of resources. But I get the sense that they're going to hit the same predictable dead ends that Sullivan found." She paused for a moment. "Oh yeah, I have to tell you. Doctor Hoskins was rattled. I don't know that I've ever seen anyone react that way. She even admitted that she was frightened. Can't say as I blame her. But you should have seen her. She looked like she was ready to crumble."

Tom acted as though he hadn't heard anything she'd said. "You know, Tullis, that guy came out of nowhere. We were just walking to the car with our coffee and, pop, I heard the one shot and then felt myself hurtling forward when the next one came. We never heard or saw anything ahead of time. That was just plain crazy."

***

Carol pulled her car into the garage just after ten that evening. As she entered the kitchen lit only by a small nightlight, she saw the message light blinking on her landline phone. Switching on the lights, she took off her coat and tossed her keys into the basket in the hallway.

Returning to the kitchen, she hit the play button. "Hi Carol. This is Tony. Wanted to let you know that Ben Sturgis dropped by the office today and gave his notice. He's paid to the end of the month but said he will be out by early next week. I reminded him that he's on a one-year lease and would face a financial penalty. He seemed okay with that. Anyway, so if I don't hear from you otherwise, I'll go ahead and advertise. There's no maintenance needed so we should be able to fill it right away. Talk to you later. Bye."

She turned and looked out the back window at the apartment. The place was a good deal for renters. Good location and reasonable rent plus parking. Why would he give it up? Maybe because of her intrusion. Still, vacating seemed a bit extreme just for one misunderstanding.

Chapter 54

Carol tossed and turned all night. Nothing fit. Everything seemed disconnected—important but disconnected. What was up with Ben? Was there a connection, or better yet, what was the connection between Fredericks and Irwin? Despite Peterman's assurances, she wasn't convinced that the Fredericks/Irwin relationship wasn't somehow linked to the murder. And why did the murderer let Ramirez see his face? Where had she seen that face before? And the worse part of it was that, unless things took some kind of dramatic turn, her role in all of this was over. The FBI would work the case, either moving it forward to solution or forever losing it in the mire.

Six o'clock came before the daylight. When she got up to make coffee, she glanced at the apartment through the kitchen window. The stoop light still shone but the interior was dark. *Is Ben somehow connected to all of this?* She banished the thought temporarily. She knew of nothing that in any way remotely linked him to the killings. Nothing except a gnawing in her gut that told her there was more to him than met the eye.

She made it from her house to the precinct on coffee and autopilot. She felt tired but not sleepy. Most frustrating, though, was that they couldn't follow one thread for any length of time without losing it among the other threads, all of which seemed moving in different directions.

Carol walked in with a plan fixed in her mind. Not even stopping at her desk, she went straight to Peterman's office. So focused was she on what she needed to ask him,

226

she forgot that he was likely to have something to say to her. "Captain, sorry to interrupt. I was wondering if I...."

He pointed to the chair beside his desk. "Sit."

The previous evening's foray into Aged Cases came back to her immediately. *Here it comes.* She sat down and kept silent. Her question would have to wait.

He stared at her for a moment, a look that signaled curiosity more than anger or frustration. "I assume you have an explanation."

She knew that question, or one resembling it, would be thrown at her. Still, she didn't have a great answer. "I just wanted to check something."

He narrowed his eyes and kept his hands folded on the desk in front of him perfectly still. "And what would that be?"

"Something that wasn't there, as it turned out."

"It apparently didn't occur to you that I would find out?" The upward inflection in the last few words signaled an expectation of an answer.

Despite her best effort, a brief laugh escaped her mouth. "I guess I was hoping." She regretted the words the instant they left her mouth.

He glared at her, but she could see him fighting to keep the corners of his mouth from turning up in a smile.

Maybe I dodged a bullet here.

Peterman opened his mouth and then closed it slowly. Whatever was about to come out never made an appearance. "So, what was it you wanted?'

"I wanted to take PTO today. I've got some personal things to attend to." Mostly a lie.

He smirked. "You've been here, what, three weeks? I guess you have a day on the books. If I'm not mistaken, though, you're not allowed to take personal time off until your first three months are up."

"What if I made up the time by working a couple hours extra every day for four days. We could call it even."

The captain rolled his eyes. "What is this—*Let's make a deal*? What's so important that you need off today?"

Carol fell back on the tried and true favorite. "It's just personal business. I have to take care of it during business hours, you know."

He gestured her out of the office with a flick of his hand. "Go. I'm confident you'll make it up to me."

Once outside his office, Carol made a beeline for the hallway to the elevator that would take her down to the parking garage. Before getting in, though, she retrieved her cellphone. Pulling up her directory, she clicked on a name.

After two rings, a familiar voice came over. "Good morning. This is Doctor Hoskins."

Chapter 55

Carol settled into one of the wing-back chairs in the well-appointed office. "Thanks, Doctor. I guess this is getting to be a habit. Maybe you should start charging me." It occurred to her that she'd almost begun to think of the doc as her personal consultant.

Hoskins laughed. "Well, if I wasn't afraid it would put me in a higher tax bracket, I might consider it." She waved her hand as if to wash away the concern. "So, what brings you here *today*?"

The detective took a few seconds to organize her thoughts. "Well, first I need to tell you that I'm here on personal time off, so this isn't what you'd call official business."

The doctor arched her eyebrows and sat back in her chair.

The moment of silence was punctuated with clicks from a pendulum clock on top of a bookcase. "But it's about the case. It's just that I.... Look, I'm sure that you can see the FBI taking control of things. And I'm not sure that's a bad thing. I mean, they can ease me out the door and I won't be that sorry to go. But there are a few things that are eating at me." Carol paused, trying to put the next few thoughts together.

"Thing is, though, they're kind of crazy, *out there*, things. And, truthfully, you're the only one I can count on to tell me that I'm completely screwed up without making me feel stupid, if that makes any sense." Surprisingly, it did make sense to Carol when she said it.

Hoskins laughed aloud. "Yes, I do understand what you're saying. Also, I would guess that the fact that you and I are able to speak in confidence reassures you that nothing will be held against you. But I can tell you that these kinds of discussions often produce remarkable results precisely because they occur without fear of reprisal. The free exchange of ideas, no matter how seemingly ridiculous at the time, sometimes lead to new insights and ways of looking at things." She paused before adding, "And heaven knows we need a new way of looking at this case."

Carol relaxed and relief flooded over her. This is exactly what she had hoped for. "Thanks, Doctor. So, in a nutshell, it's about Doctor Sturgis."

The doctor's eyes widened, and her chin dropped, resulting in an open mouth. After a moment of what looked like shock, she recovered. "Are you suggesting that Ben might somehow be involved?" She narrowed her eyes and shook her head slowly.

"No. Not really. Well, maybe. I don't know." She relayed the string of events to the doctor, beginning at the start with his desire to interview her about serial killings and police procedures.

Hoskins stared down at the desk as she listened, tapping her fingers quietly. To Carol's relief, the doctor did not take notes. When the account of events finished, another brief silence fell over the room with the exception of the clock, which was now joined by the patter of rain on the window.

"Let me ask for a clarification if I might. Are the two of you intimate?" Hoskins facial expression seemed neutral.

Carol shook her head vigorously. "No. Like I said, he did flirt a bit and made a pretty intense pass, I guess you'd call it. And I have to say, he is attractive and likeable but, no, we were not."

"Good. I don't mean that to sound judgmental or in any way disapproving if you were. I just need to know so that I can assess what you've told me." She tilted her head back and looked at the ceiling for a moment. She swiveled ever so slightly back and forth in her chair as she thought.

"Let me give you a bottom line first. I don't think he's involved. I'll go over some points on both sides of the argument. Honestly, the man is quirky but I believe he falls well outside any profile that I could think of for this case."

Carol felt relieved to hear those words. "That's actually good to know. The thought of a serial killer sleeping in my apartment is a little unnerving to say the least."

Hoskins linked her fingers behind her head. "First, I can tell you that Ben is a flirt and is drawn to attractive women. It's no surprise that he would approach you. I never received any formal complaints about him. It was common knowledge, though, that he pursued different staff members, both single and married. I have no idea of his success rate, but odds are he managed something while he was here."

For some reason at that time, Carol began to look at the doctor more as a woman than a psychologist. She wondered in passing if Hoskins might have been attracted to Sturgis. She noticed that the doctor didn't wear a wedding band. *So, neither do I.* There were no pictures of family or friends hanging on the walls. The only framed items were diplomas, certificates, and testimonials. This woman lived her work.

The doctor continued speaking, this time more slowly. "So, that's the easy part. There is one particular thing of notice about Ben, although I'm not sure how it would move him any closer to this case. He's very conflict averse." She paused and eyed Carol for a moment.

"What I'm going to discuss with you now is privileged information, so I ask that you do not repeat it. If we find any evidence that connects Ben, then of course I'll bring this forward. Doctor Sturgis was an excellent teacher but a less than adequate researcher. That was at the heart of his problem here. Faculty are tasked with research as a part of their workload and are expected to publish aggressively. Ben, I'm afraid, was not up to the task. His qualitative skills were fair, but his quant skills were completely in the trash."

"He did have value to the school and had he been willing to put more effort forth, we might have reached some accommodation. But he was up for tenure review next year and, rather than engage in problem solving, he chose to chuck it all and quit. Staying on would have meant conflict with the provost and the review committee. I just don't think he was up to that."

Carol tried to put this insight into the picture but could only see a vague connection. "Why might this be important?"

"I'm not saying it is. But it explains a few things. He failed in his romantic pursuit of you. From what you said, though, you didn't so much slam the door in his face as just put him off for the moment. Most men might have continued to try, maybe use different approaches. His reaction to your intrusion was vastly out of proportion to the crime, so to speak. I think what you were seeing was his aversion to conflict. Rather than continue to try and woo you, he chose to alienate you and now he's vacating, at a significant financial cost, I might add. It does fit."

"Yeah. I have to admit that makes sense. Maybe that's the extent of it and there's no connection to the case, like you said."

Hoskins adjusted herself in the chair. "But since we're alone, speaking in confidence, and I have a little bit of time, let's run this forward and just play with it. It will probably come to nothing but maybe it'll stimulate our thinking in other ways."

"Sure. Fine with me." Carol had no place else to be.

The doctor stood and cleared her throat as if she were going to deliver a classroom lecture. She paced over to the window and turned back to Carol. "Let's take a look at the conflict aversion for a moment within the context of romance. Our unsub, as they like to call him, seems to be driven primarily by a romantic or perceived romantic connection to his victims. Two things strike me. First, if he was generally unsuccessful in his pursuit of women in the more traditional way, the current method would avoid the pain and humiliation of rejection, which often lies at the heart of conflict aversion. Second, his MO is to disable the victim with a toxin that renders them unable to move and, more importantly, unable to speak. In this situation, he can enjoy sexual activity without fear of criticism or objection." She reached up and scratched idly at her temple.

"I'm going to engage in some intellectual machinations here that are purely speculative and, quite frankly, highly unlikely. Men and women behave differently at the conclusion of sexual intercourse. Women enjoy the closeness, cuddling, whispering, light kissing, and just being held. Men, on the other hand, want to fall asleep, get something to eat, or just get up and leave. Let's assume that when our man finishes, he is no different. But rather than learning to deal with his partner and find common ground, he simply eliminates them and starts over with a new victim."

She paused, as though composing words, before continuing. "Let me repeat, though. This is pure conjecture combined with some psychological contortions. There's no way I would ever advance this notion in a serious forum. As I said, I don't think Ben's involved. He has his eccentricities, but I have never seen anything to indicate that he would consider violence. Just not in his nature." She walked over and sat down, leaning back in her chair.

As Carol considered the information, the whole notion of Ben being involved seemed sillier and sillier. "That makes sense, I guess. Actually, I feel better. Thanks for taking the time on this. At least now I can let go of it. And since I don't have any other great ideas, I guess it won't feel so bad when the feds cut me loose."

Hoskins laughed. "I hear you. And, between you and me, it wouldn't hurt my feelings much if they dump me as well." Her eyes became intense. "But, really, I'd like to see it through. This has destroyed so many people. It has to end."

Chapter 56

When Carol arrived at work the next morning, something different about the place struck her. It felt like home. Several of the guys nodded greetings to her, Mulroney chief among them. She smiled in return. At least as far as relationships went, things had steadily improved over the past three weeks.

After hanging up her coat, she strode toward the coffee room and poured a cup of what smelled like reasonably fresh brew. As she made her way across the bullpen, she noted that it seemed a subdued but relaxed environment. Detectives worked at their monitors, had phones to their ears, or scribbled notes on paper. Even Captain Peterman, visible in his office, seemed immersed in his work and oblivious to distractions.

About a half-hour into the day, the phone on her desk rang. She checked the caller ID readout before answering. *Hmmm. Things must indeed be better.* "Morning, Sullivan."

The voice emerging from the handset sounded tired with a feeble attempt at excitement. "You may want to drop over. The feds just delivered a pile of documents for me. Unfortunately, they didn't make copies for all of us."

Carol stood as she finished the conversation. "Be right there."

***

"I hate to break it to you but that's not a *pile*. That's more like a mountain of paper." Carol took stock of the mass of photocopied documents. "Anything good?"

Brenda smirked. "What do you think? They had a flunky run them over. That's the only thing I've heard from them in two days. At a glance, it looks mostly like background information on Irwin."

Carol scratched her head. "Well, I guess it's good that we have at least something. Although I'm not sure what we hope to find." She sighed. "But you never know. Do you mind if I take a look?" Deference might help keep this relationship alive.

Sullivan laughed. "Knock yourself out."

Carol pulled a chair up to the desk and sat beside the detective. Taking a couple of inches off the pile, she sat them on the desk and started to browse through them. "Oh good. We see all the places he worked. And look at this. We know where he went to school." She shook her head and exhaled. "At this rate, we should solve the case within the next ten minutes." The attempt at sarcasm didn't sound as good to her ears as it had inside her head.

The two women fell silent as they continued to go through the stack, one page at a time. Carol found it hard to focus given the seeming irrelevance of the material. She noted very quickly that there was nothing in the stack about any of the evidence, the results of the database searches on the sketch, or even about the serial case. "And here. Just what I was looking for. He taught some classes fifteen years ago. And, graduate classes at that." *Maybe I should cool the sarcasm.*

Actually, it looked like he taught the same course over the span of several years. The title caught her eye—"Mental Health Issues Manifesting in Serial Killers." Something about the title seemed familiar. But like the sketch, Carol couldn't put her finger on it. Setting that aside, she continued going through the pages. Each page was a particular offering of the class. It showed the date and the list of students. Page after page of meaningless names began to numb her mind until she saw it. Her eyes opened wide and she did a double take.

Jackpot!

Chapter 57

Carol watched as Sullivan stared at the class roster. "I know, it's all completely circumstantial and relies on a lot of assumptions. It's seems to be the only thing we have so far, though." She had recounted her concerns about Ben Sturgis, leaving out, of course, all information given her by Doctor Hoskins.

Sullivan sighed and shook her head. "I'd say that calling it circumstantial is being generous. It looks to me like a quirky psychologist who likes to chase women happened to take a course fifteen years ago from our dead doctor. I'm not even sure where we'd go from here, even if we wanted to."

"Yeah. I know. Well, there is the fact that Sturgis is writing a book with almost exactly the same title as the course and it does relate to serial killers."

"So, what? Irwin was killed over plagiarism?"

Carol ignored the humor, narrowing her eyes and turning her head to the side. "I may have one source I can talk to. It's really a long shot but I'll try. Other than that, I guess we could just dump it all on the feds and let them sort it out."

***

With the phone to her ear, Carol grimaced as she waited for the connection. She dreaded asking.

"Good afternoon, this is Doctor Hoskins."

She closed her eyes. *Here goes.* "Good afternoon, Doctor. This is Carol Tullis. I'm looking for a really big favor. It's kind of a big one and if you can't do it, I certainly understand."

After an initial pause a tentative voice came over. "And what is it you're looking for?"

Carol went over everything she'd found. With the foresight of making an outline, it came out more or less coherent. "So that's what we have right now."

"And what do you need of me?"

"Since Doctor Sturgis worked for you, I wonder if you might have access to his transcripts from college?" Carol knew she was wandering on to some very thin ice. And if Hoskins agreed to this, they would both be out there together.

"Of course, I do. I have a copy in my file cabinet but without a court order or Doctor Sturgis' approval, I could not release them to you." The tone left little room for debate.

Carol slouched in her chair. "I understand. Just thought it might be worth a try. So far, this is the only thing we have going for us. Although they haven't said anything, I suspect that the FBI is not doing any better."

"So, this class, it was at George Mason University, you say?"

"Yes. That's the only connection we find between the two men." Carol eased herself back up in the chair, her eyes narrowing. The tone of the question gave her hope.

"And what is it you hope to learn? I mean, you know he took the class. You've spotted the similarities in the titles. I'm not sure what a transcript would do for you."

Carol thought about it. "I guess at this point, the only thing we might get of interest would be his grade in the class." She had no idea how that might help.

After a moment of silence, Hoskins responded. "Interesting. Look, Carol, you know that we're both out there on a limb with this. I'm going to tell you something. It is for you alone. You can use it to make decisions about how you want to proceed but I must ask you, please, do not share this information with anyone. Is that acceptable?"

A wave of optimism swept over Carol. "Of course, I will certainly respect that."

"Our Doctor Sturgis didn't do that well in the class. He came out with a C and this was in graduate school before he went for his Ph.D. Most grad schools count a C as passing provided that the overall GPA of the student ends up at three-point-oh or better. Sturgis was generally an exemplary student with the exception of this one class. And before you ask, the transcript gives me no clue as to why he got a C."

Carol thought about it. "That would be interesting to know. Irwin obviously can't tell us. I'm not sure whether tipping our hand to Sturgis right now is a good idea. I'm pretty sure that there's no way that I could get any kind of authority to get his records from George Mason but maybe the feds can pull strings. Hopefully, I can give them enough circumstantial evidence that they'll have some success."

Another moment of silence followed. "Carol, I'm not sure about this. I understand everything you've told me. But I just don't see Ben as a killer. The worry I have is that, if you move forward with this and you're wrong, you may well wreck his reputation and career, not to mention his life."

Carol felt a knot form in her stomach. "I understand, Doctor. I think I might sit on this for a day or so. And thank you. I'll keep this information private."

Chapter 58

Carol found herself back in Sex Crimes sitting beside Sullivan after another fitful night. "Seems we're running out of options." She reminded herself to keep Hoskins' confidence as she pored over the case with the detective. "I ran it by my captain today. I hoped he might have a magic wand. He had nothing."

Sullivan's demeanor appeared more and more despondent. Carol could see the toll it took on her. Bags beneath her bloodshot eyes spoke to a lack of sleep. The look of defeat on her face—the blank stare, the tight line of her lips, the slight tilt of her head as if were about to topple over—added to the concern.

Carol took a deep breath. "So, it comes down to a choice. We can take what we have to the feds or just drop it. As much as it galls me, taking it to the feds seems the right thing to do. Dropping it seems tantamount to covering up."

"You're right. We can't not tell them. I'll give Slattery a call and set up a meeting."

***

After detailing what they'd found, minus the information from Hoskins, Carol watched Slattery tap his pen on the tabletop without speaking for a moment.

"So, what do you expect from me?" He leaned back in his chair, idly twirling his pen in front of him.

"Nothing. I work for Detective Sullivan. I understand that my job is to report anything I find. When I spoke with her about it, she indicated that we have a responsibility to make sure that you're aware of it." She glanced over at her partner in crime.

Sitting across from Slattery, she pulled her chair up closer and leaned into the table. "Agent Slattery, I'm not stupid. I know that I'm pretty far down on the food chain here. I know that you see a much bigger picture than I do. That's why I'm bringing this to you. I could certainly come up with all kinds of ideas but, frankly, you're in a much better position to make these calls. I'll do anything I can to help but my goal here today is to be a good team player. You're calling the shots." She offered the sincerest look she could muster. She knew, from the look on his face, that she'd hooked him.

***

Carol smirked to herself as she and Sullivan walked down the corridor to the Sex Crimes office. Her ploy had worked better than she had anticipated.

Sullivan, who had remained quiet to this point, interjected. "Did we really accomplish anything back there?"

"Absolutely. Look at it this way, Brenda, he's got a dead federal agent and twenty-four dead women and they're all sitting on his shoulder. We just put another monkey on his back. And unless he's got a really good poker face, I'd say that our monkey is the only one in the dance right now." She paused, mentally patting herself on the back. "Yeah, he's not going to let that one go. And the beauty is, no matter how it turns out, all we've done is to bring information to his attention that he'd provided us to begin with."

***

Carol oozed optimism but the speed with which results poured forth surprised her. The first inkling that things had moved along was a phone call just after eight the next morning.

"Detective Tullis, how can I help you?" She leaned back in her chair waiting for Doctor Hoskins, whose name had shown up on her caller ID, to speak.

The voice came out soft and serious. "Carol, I wanted to give you a heads up. I just talked to Slattery, who swore me to secrecy by the way. They got into the George Mason archives with a federal warrant issued by a judge in northern Virginia. The C grade stemmed from a paper that Doctor Sturgis wrote. The subject of that paper was centered around the notion that some rapist serial killers were motivated by romantic factors rather than power and violence. No surprise, that paper meshed almost perfectly with our profile. He's going to call a meeting for early afternoon. I assume you'll be invited but I wanted to give you some advance notice, given the feds' occasional tendency to exclusion."

Carol had come alive. She sat straight up in her chair, her eyes wide and her pulse quickened. "Thank you. And I'll remember to act surprised."

Chapter 59

Carol and Sullivan arrived early and found seats around the crowded table. Tullis whispered to her companion, "These guys know how to throw a party." The FBI Seattle field office was well-appointed, to put it lightly. The conference room looked like it would easily accommodate thirty people. At the far end of the room, small, flat metal panels in the ceiling suggested drop-down screens. Several large monitors sat atop expensive looking stands with a video camera mounted between them. A cart sat back against the wall with two carafes and a stack of ceramic mugs bearing the FBI logo. *Tax dollars hard at work.*

Although the Irwin case technically belonged to the Seattle office, Agent Slattery ran the meeting while Agent Lucas, in charge of the local office, sat expressionless. There was little doubt who was calling the shots. After introductions and reminding everyone of the need for secrecy, he reviewed the evidence, including his findings from George Mason. He'd also managed to get a court order for Sturgis' records at Western Washington.

Doctor Hoskins sat on the periphery of the federal team, her face ashen. She avoided looking at the federal officer as he spoke.

Carol understood. After all, she herself had nearly been seduced by the man. But something struck her as odd. If he was regularly abducting women to play out his sex or romance fantasy, as Hoskins suggested, why make passes at other women? And his attempts seemed, well, almost desperate. Another thing—back at WWU, he routinely flirted and pursued women, according to the doctor. Why do that if

244

he was able to act out his desires with captive women? That part didn't make sense. On the other hand, nothing about this case made a lot of sense anyway.

Captain Fredericks sat at the far end of the long oval table opposite the FBI contingent. The skin on his face seemed to sag and his vacant eyes sank back into their sockets with puffy bags providing support below them. Carol found it odd, even alarming, that he hadn't acknowledged Sullivan when she entered the room.

Agent Slattery's words brought her back to the present. "We're moving this afternoon to get a search warrant for Sturgis' apartment. Given the hour of the day, I don't expect it until tomorrow morning. Once we have it in hand, we'll move in." He paused and looked at Carol.

"Detective Tullis, as I understand Doctor Sturgis rents an apartment from you."

"That's right. It's detached, sits behind my house."

"Okay. I want to be very clear on this. You are not to have any contact with him. Is that understood?"

Despite the annoyance she felt toward the condescending jerk, Carol stifled her desire to retort sarcastically. "Got it."

***

That evening, Carol stood for about fifteen minutes at her kitchen window staring at the apartment. The stoop was lit but the inside was dark. Ben's car sat parked in its usual spot in the driveway.

She opened the pantry door and pulled out her box of cereal. With a splash of milk to dampen it, she sat down to dinner. But her thoughts remained on Sturgis and the case. She still saw so many inconsistencies. And Hoskins' warning haunted her. This could ruin Sturgis. Nothing that she'd seen even closely approximated a smoking gun. Everything was predicated on assumptions, speculation, and what could well turn out to be nothing but coincidence. Despite her success at punting the responsibility to the feds, she felt a pang of guilt. Then again, guilt was something she was good at.

Tomorrow will tell.

Chapter 60

By the time the alarm went off at six, Carol was already up, showered, and halfway through her first cup of coffee. The bedcovers were a wreck from her tossing and turning. The night had not been kind to her.

Peterman had suggested that she stay home and keep an eye on the apartment until the FBI arrived with the search warrant. Agent Slattery had made it crystal clear that only FBI personnel would be involved in the search of the premises.

Back in the kitchen, Carol poured a second cup. Sullivan would be arriving around eight-thirty. They had agreed, the day before, that Carol's house would serve as their makeshift headquarters for the day. Most likely, they would need another pot of coffee.

Neither of them had broached the subject of Captain Fredericks. If Sullivan had thoughts or concerns about him, she kept them to herself. For her part, Carol put her faith in Peterman's assertion that Fredericks was not involved. Sitting there in the quiet of the kitchen on this dark, wet morning, she wondered if perhaps she accepted it too easily. *What else can I do?*

Brenda showed up about ten minutes early. Outfitted in her vest that showed beneath her open raincoat, she looked ready for action that, in all probability, neither of them would see. "Come in. Let me take your coat. There's coffee in the kitchen. Mugs are on the counter." Carol took the mostly dry coat and draped it on a hanger. "There's milk in the fridge if you need it and sugar's right there with the mugs."

By the time Carol returned to the kitchen, Sullivan had a mug cupped in both hands in front of her face. She blew

247

lightly across the steaming surface. "It's turning colder. The damp just eats through the clothes and chills to the bone. November's definitely on the way." She shivered and took a drink.

As the two sat, a brief silence dropped over the room. The darkness of six in the morning had given way grudgingly to a subdued gray lighting. The apartment remained dark. Carol had still seen no signs of movement.

Sullivan broke the silence. "You seem preoccupied. Everything okay?"

Carol set her cup down on the table and let her head tilt back. "I just can't shake the feeling that this might be a mistake. I know it wasn't my call. And I know that there are some things pointing in this direction, but here in the morning light, it all seems so, I don't know, thin and circumstantial. This could wreck the guy's life all because I had a hunch."

"Like you said, though, you didn't make the call. In fact, it wasn't even the FBI. A judge signed off on the original order. And if the evidence is that thin, then it's not likely that they'll find a judge here to issue the search warrant for the apartment. You just have to trust."

Tullis closed her eyes. "Yeah. I guess."

More silence. The combatants-turned-companions sat and alternately sipped their coffee and stared out the window. Carol's thoughts swung wildly from concerns about Sturgis to memories of the days following Jenny's death. She thought about her struggle to rehabilitate herself and her return to work.

Sullivan interrupted her roller coaster ride. "Carol, I haven't ever apologized to you." The words came out soft and sad. "What I did…the way I treated you…"

Carol reached across the table and touched the woman's hand. "No need." She allowed silence to intrude for a moment. "What I did was, well, I deserved it. It's taken me a lot of years to try and gain some degree of peace. But it's just not something that can be easily left behind."

"I didn't talk to Joe about it. I'm sorry. I was going to confront him about the lie. But he seems to be trying so hard to make this work. And I need it to work. I haven't had the best luck in men. When I looked at him, I just couldn't bring myself to do it. I guess maybe part of it is that, when I think about it, he's never repeated the lie since he got sober." Sullivan refilled her cup. Rather than returning to her seat, she leaned back against the counter, cup in hand. "I thought about it. When I told him that you were on the case with me, he just nodded. He never really said anything at all. I honestly think, in his heart, he's sorry."

Carol thought about it for a moment. "It's okay, really. I can tell you from experience, when you have something that's dear to you, something you love, you have to hold on to it. You do what you have to. I'm glad Joe's working out." She wanted to say more but the words didn't come. She glanced over at the clock—nine-thirty.

Any time now.

Chapter 61

Carol wasn't sure what she expected. Maybe they would sneak around so as not to be seen and then knock on the door. Or perhaps they would rush the small apartment like an army assaulting a strategic position. The uncertainty ended with a ring of the doorbell.

"Special Agent Slattery, good morning." She noted the small contingent waiting out at curbside. Four large black SUVs and about fifteen men and women wearing vests with FBI emblazoned on the front and back. About half of them carried shoulder weapons. The remainder, presumably, would wield their side arms. She stepped aside to let the agent in.

"Thank you." He entered and, after greeting Sullivan, he turned to Carol, his demeanor calm—all business. "Do you have a key to the apartment, just in case."

"Do you want me to come along and open the door, *just in case?*' She knew the sarcasm didn't help. But it sure felt good.

"No. Just the key please. You and Sullivan remain here until we secure the scene." If Slattery had recognized the jibe, he didn't show it.

His words bothered Carol. "I thought this was just a search. You make it sound like an all-out assault."

The agent turned toward the front door. "I'll send someone for you." And with that, he was out the door.

Sullivan shook her head. "Sometimes I wish I had your quick wit."

"Be careful what you wish for. It gets me into a lot of trouble."

The two women returned to the kitchen where they could observe the FBI's approach to the apartment. The *assault* turned out to be anticlimactic. Slattery pounded on the door a few times, shouted out, identifying himself and demanding that Sturgis open up. Finally, he unlocked and opened the door himself. One by one, the agents slid inside, weapons drawn and ready.

Within a couple of minutes, one of the underlings emerged and approached the back door of the house. Carol greeted him and stood in the threshold with Sullivan standing behind her.

The man gestured toward the apartment. "Come on."

Chapter 62

Carol stood in the center of the room transfixed by the scene before her. Ben Sturgis, or rather his body, sat hunched over in a chair, his head resting on the dining room table. His right arm hung loose at his side and what appeared to be a thirty-two-caliber pistol rested on the floor below his right hand. Dressed in jeans and a tee-shirt similar to what he'd worn when they met, he had a small wound on the right side of his head. From her vantage point, she couldn't see the left side, but blood splatter decorated the table to the left of him and a part of the adjacent wall.

Sullivan interrupted her mental and emotional processing of the scene. "Oh shit." She touched Carol's arm. "Hey, you okay?"

Carol started, looked around, and shook her head. "Yeah. I just wasn't expecting this."

Agent Slattery finished up issuing instructions with a member of his team and slid over to the two SPD detectives. "You can look around but don't touch anything. I've got the lab guys from our office on the way. The Seattle ME should be here shortly." He paused and addressed Carol, "You hear anything last night or early this morning?"

"No. Nothing." As she eased around the room trying to avoid the sea of federal agents, she felt almost overwhelmed at the amount of evidence they were securing. The door to the pot-bellied wood stove stood open and an agent raked through the contents. A bottle of Glenlivet Scotch and an empty glass sat on the table to the right of Sturgis' head.

252

She stared at the pattern of blood spatter, first looking closely and then standing back and allowing her eyes to lose focus. She retrieved her cellphone from her pocket and began taking photographs.

A voice filtered from the bedroom. "Agent Slattery, you need to see this."

Carol followed him to the bedroom door. A female agent met them and stood aside, gesturing at the bed. Sitting among a set of four items, sat a small pink sweatshirt with a yellow, blue, and green flower print on the front.

A wave of nausea flooded over the detective. "That's…." She felt her legs tremble and threaten to give way. Her vision darkened at the periphery and the garment occupied her attention. *Jenny.* Sounds faded to a dull hum and blackness washed over her.

***

Sounds returned first. Then grayness nibbled at the edge of the darkness. Carol opened her eyes but couldn't focus. And then the memory returned. She squeezed her eyes shut and shook her head.

"Hey, Tullis, you still with us?" Sullivan's soft voice cut through the hum of the background noise.

Carol opened her eyes again. "Yes. I'm fine. Sorry." She rolled on to her side and then sat up. They had apparently stretched her out on the floor and put a jacket under her head. She tried to clear her head with a quick shake. "The sweatshirt, I think that belonged to my daughter. She was wearing it the day she…." She felt a hand on her arm.

Brenda dropped down to the floor beside her. Carol felt gentle hands press on the back of her head, pulling her closer. She broke into sobs as she lay in Sullivan's embrace.

Chapter 63

Carol regrouped and sat on the couch holding her hands between her knees and staring at the floor. She felt rage building in her. *How dare he rent an apartment from me after.... How dare he kiss me.* She felt physically ill. If there had been anything in her stomach, it surely would have come back up. Jenny's killer had lived right behind her and then, as if to mock her pain, tried to seduce her. His death was not enough. Suicide robbed her. She forced the rage back down and turned her attention back to the activity in the room.

By this time, the lab guys were poring over the place, photographing, retrieving, bagging, and dusting for prints. She stood beside the wood stove where one of the techs was using a pair of tweezers to extract partially burnt pages of paper. As he pulled them out and put them in the large plastic baggie, she could see that they were copies of news stories about the abductions and killings.

She pulled her phone out and resumed photographing the scene. She sensed something important here.

Carol noticed Sullivan sitting in one of the living room chairs writing in her notepad. She approached and touched her fellow detective on the shoulder, motioning her outside. As they stood in the afternoon mist, she lowered her head and mumbled, "Thanks for... you know." She wasn't sure what else to say.

She steeled herself and re-focused her attention on the case. "I'm trying to get photos of everything. We need to make sure we have our own notes. I don't expect to get much out of these guys." She paused. "Something seems, I don't know, off. Nothing specific but it doesn't feel right."

Sullivan arched her eyebrows. "Like what?"

Carol turned briefly toward the door to check for listening ears. "Nothing big. Just little things." She wondered, though, whether her emotions were playing tricks on her. "I don't know. Maybe it's nothing. I'm going to finish up with the photos." She turned and re-entered the apartment.

***

By the time darkness had fallen, the horde of federal agents had abandoned the small apartment leaving in their wake strips of yellow crime scene tape. The stoop light had been left on and the interior lights were out. Carol stared out the window from her darkened kitchen at the surreal scene. An unpleasant memory invaded her mind. She recalled standing at that very window looking out and agonizing over whether or not to make the walk across the lawn and climb into bed with her daughter's killer. The wave of sickness forced her to sit.

As she gathered her composure, she considered calling Chris. After all, he had a right to know that his daughter's killer had been.... Had been what? Identified? Killed? Caught? As if on cue, her home phone rang. She stood, walked over to the counter, and glanced at the caller ID.

She tried to summon some enthusiasm. "Hi Chris."

"Is it true?" His voice sounded incredulous.

She shook her head. Was it true? "Well, yes. It appears so." The answer didn't sound very convincing. She wasn't very convinced.

"You sound, I don't know, pretty ambivalent."

256

"It's been a long day. I'm still trying to work through it all. They found Jenny's shirt."

Silence.

"I'm sorry, Chris. I guess I'm not handling this as well as I should." She stood on the verge of tears, yet again.

"Carol, are you okay? You need me to come over?" That voice, so genuine, so caring.

She forced a laugh. "No. Thanks, but I'm fine. I just need to work through it." All the while, she was shaking her head, knowing that working through it would not be that easy.

A moment of silence. "If you need me, please call, okay? You don't have to do this alone."

"Thanks. I'm headed off to bed pretty quick. How about I call you tomorrow or the next day and fill you in. I just need to get it all straight in my own head."

As she disconnected, Carol's thoughts returned to the bottle of scotch that had been sitting on the table. *If ever there was a moment for a drink.*

She checked the clock—just after seven, still early. Would it have been *so* wrong for her to take Chris up on his offer to come over? The darkness in her house seeped into her soul. With every passing second, she felt herself slipping a little bit more into that black abyss.

In her heart she knew why she couldn't ask him over to help. He had found happiness. Shelley now filled the empty spot in his life. Carol had abandoned her family. Calling on him now would be like dragging him back into her nightmare. No. She couldn't do it.

Shaking her head, she flipped on the kitchen light and retrieved her cellphone.

Chapter 64

Carol made her way from the car to the porch just as the front door opened. "Hi. Thanks for letting me intrude." She forced a quiet laugh.

"You're not an intrusion and you know it." Dani embraced her. "Come in, please. Tommy's in the living room and I just put on a pot of coffee." She stepped aside and gestured Carol in.

Tom sat on the couch in a pair of flannel pajama bottoms featuring the Road Runner and Wiley Coyote along with a UW sweatshirt. "Tullis. Congratulations. See, all I had to do was take off work and leave you alone. I knew you'd solve it." He stood with apparent difficulty using the arm of the sofa to push up.

Carol stepped over to him and gave him a very gentle hug. "Thanks." She almost added a humorous retort but decided against it. She felt little enthusiasm for the "victory." It didn't feel very *victorious*. As she was taking a seat, she heard a small voice from down the hall.

"I heard Miz Tully."

Carol turned to see a little girl trudging from the bedroom in her pink long-sleeved pajamas with blue, yellow, and green unicorns and stars.

"Hey, Bella. What beautiful pajamas. Do you like unicorns?" She got up and met the girl at the threshold of the living room.

Bella threw her arms around her neck and squeezed hard. Thoughts of Jenny intruded as Carol returned the hug.

The two wandered back over to the chair. As Carol sat, Bella climbed up in her lap. "Miz Tully, Mommy made

258

hamburgerers tonight and she put love in them. I tasted it. But Roberto and Alex don't believe me." The young girl looked at Carol with wide eyes filled with a combination of wonder and questioning.

"Do you think that your mommy would ever make anything for you and not put love in it?"

The young girl, eyes widening even more, looked over at Dani and then at Carol, shaking her head.

"So, that must mean that you know more than your brothers about this, doesn't it?"

Bella blinked her soft brown eyes and nodded with her mouth slightly open.

Carol laughed. "And tell you what, 'Tullis' is kind of hard to say, isn't it? So, if it's okay with your mommy and daddy, you can call me 'Carol.' Would that be easier?"

The young girl looked over at Dani, who returned a barely perceptible nod. "Okay, young lady, it's time for you to be back in bed." The veneer of severity on the mother's face barely obscured her pride and love.

Bella slid down from Carol's lap. "Do you like stories, Miz Carol?"

"I love stories."

"Me too." The young girl took her hand. "Would you read me a story? I like the Free Pigs and the Woof best."

Carol stood and allowed herself to be guided down the hall. "I like that story too." The emotion coursing through her heart felt an unlikely combination of love and grief. She had read that story to Jenny. *I also read that story to Jason.* She realized at that moment that the sadness was just as much about her son as about her daughter.

***

Carol rested the cup on her knees, cupping it with both hands. She desperately wanted to tell these two parents to hold on to these children and love them fiercely. She knew better. Tom and Dani made no secret of their devotion to their kids. Instead, she kept it light. "At least it's good to know I haven't forgotten how to read stories."

After a moment of silence, Tom moved the conversation on. "So, Tullis, let's hear it."

Carol took a sip of coffee. "I don't know. What's to say? I mean, he shot himself. He left a bunch of evidence around the place." She found it hard to be convincing.

Tom shifted on the couch, the grimace on his face betraying his discomfort from the bruising on his back. "Yeah, but kind of creepy, what with him renting the apartment from you and all."

"Yeah, more than just *kind of creepy*. More like *really, really creepy*."

He tilted his head, his eyes narrowed. "I guess I thought you'd be happier about it, I mean, since you finally got...." He seemed to catch himself on the verge of mentioning Jenny.

"I am, I suppose. Maybe I just need some time to let it sink in. I don't know." She ran her finger around the rim of the cup.

They sat in silence for a moment. When Tom spoke again, his words came out soft and slow. "No. It's more than that. Something else is bothering you."

Carol detected a look of concern in his eyes. Before she could stop herself, she gave voice to her doubts, which came out sounding disconnected and trivial.

"Maybe." He stroked his chin and leaned forward as he spoke, "What's the FBI and Sex Crimes saying about it? Do they think they got their guy?"

"I suppose tomorrow will tell. But from what I saw today they were connecting the dots with some rather smug faces. I'm not sure they're asking a lot of hard questions at this point."

Tom eyed her with a look of concern. "You've carried the weight of your daughter's death along with the fact that it went unsolved. Is it possible that you're having trouble letting go?" He cleared his throat.

"Possible? Yes." She leaned back in the chair. "You're right. That's probably it. I mean, this just happened today so, yeah, it might take me a while to deal with it." She raised the cup to her lips to hide the doubt that she knew was written on her face.

After another hour in which the trio alternated between small talk and silence Carol stood. "I need to get home. *Some of us* have to work tomorrow."

Dani laughed and Tom presented an injured, insulted look. "Have you no shame, Madame? I am at death's door and you slander me."

His wife just shook her head. "Saints preserve us." She retrieved Carol's raincoat from the closet and walked her to the door. "Thanks for coming over tonight. I enjoyed it. We all enjoyed it."

The women embraced.

Chapter 65

After another fitful night, Carol dragged herself into the bullpen just after eight the next morning. In addition to the doubts that had nagged her all night, a new worry invaded. If her present suspicions turned out to be right, then Sturgis' death was on her. She had instigated everything. Not only that, but Doctor Hoskins had pointedly warned her about that possibility. The nightmare loomed over her like a dreadful shadow threatening to block out all light.

Hanging her raincoat up, she plopped into her seat and slouched down. A part of her didn't want to believe Sturgis was guilty. Aside from the inconsistencies that plagued the scene, she remembered him as an affable kid-like guy with an easy smile. On the other hand, Ted Bundy was reputed to be quite likeable.

After sitting for less than a minute, she stood and strode through the double doors toward Sex Crimes. She found Sullivan in her cubicle putting the case files together. "Hey. How's it going?"

The Sex Crimes detective swiveled around and grinned. What struck Carol was that this was the most relaxed that she'd seen the woman.

"Pretty good, I guess. Just trying to put all the pieces together and fill in the blanks."

Carol stood beside her, looking down at the case file. "So, what do you think? You guys going to close this?"

"Don't know yet. That's the captain's call. I suspect that he's going to wait and see what drops out from the FBI. If they call it closed for the Irwin murder, then I suspect the boss will close this one too."

262

Carol considered the woman's relaxed disposition. She decided not to voice any doubts yet. *Wait and see what the feds say.*

***

She knocked on the open door to Peterman's office. "Captain, you have a minute?"

He stopped reading the document on his monitor and turned to her. "Oh. Tullis. Nice work. Congratulations." His demeanor seemed pleasant enough, but something in his eyes seemed off—caution, suspicion, or maybe even hostility.

The look took Carol aback. She'd come in to voice her concerns over the case and possibly get some feedback. All of a sudden, she felt nervous, reluctant to speak. "Thanks." Nothing else came to mind. She wondered why she felt so threatened.

The captain's voice interrupted her thoughts. "You wanted something?"

It's just his way. The demons chewed at her—the inconsistencies at the scene and the possibility that she had facilitated the murder of an innocent man. *I can talk to him.* "Yes, actually, I wanted to bounce some things off you."

She threw out a few of her concerns before Peterman waved her off. "Let it go, Tullis. The FBI just held a press conference. They're deferring closure of the case pending the analysis of the physical evidence but the look on their faces and their language suggested that this is a done deal. If they're closing, then you can bet that Sex Crimes is going to close too. So, you're finished. Ramirez will be back next week, and I'll have more work for you then. Finish up your case notes

263

and make sure you give Sullivan everything she needs." He leaned back in his chair, arms up and his fingers laced behind his head.

"Yes sir. I'll get to work on that. But Captain, I'm not sure that those guys are considering any of these inconsistencies. Some of this stuff just doesn't add up."

His eyes turned icy and his face serious. "Do you need a refresher here? I'm the captain and you're the detective. Remember? You need me to go on?"

She slumped in the chair. "No sir."

"Good, drop this and get back to work, now." He gestured toward the door with a flick of his hand and turned back toward the monitor.

As Carol left, though, she felt his cold stare on her back. Her stomach churned. It felt like something had just changed.

Chapter 66

Carol knew better. Or at least she should have. The captain had told her to leave it alone—to move on to other things. He had finally gotten around to, at the very least, tolerating her. There was no doubt in her mind that disregarding his orders would land her right back in hot water again. Sooner or later, her luck was bound to run out. She knew better.

But she couldn't shake it. Maybe Sturgis was the right guy… maybe not. But the fact that she had instigated the interest in him gnawed at her. Where had the suspicion started? When did he move from an attractive, albeit odd, man to being a suspect in a string of grisly murders? The answer popped into her head—the journal and his reaction to her reading it. She'd only seen snippets, and yet….

Unfortunately, the Feds had the journal, along with all of the other evidence collected at the apartment. She considered asking Sam Johnson for help. After all, the forensic tech had used his connections with the Bellevue Police to get some information. No. She needed to leave him out of it.

With the phone to her ear, she kept an eye out for Peterman. If he came out of his office and caught her at this, it would be all over. A voice on the other end of the connection pulled her out of her thoughts.

"Special Agent Slattery."

"Hi, this is Detective Tullis over at Seattle PD." Carol invoked her best meek and grief-ridden persona. "I was wondering if you might do me a big favor."

The response carried a note of suspicion, but short of outright hostility. "What might that be?"

"I'm sorry, I'm just trying to sort out some personal stuff… you know… after the thing at the apartment."

"What can I do for you?"

"I'm trying to put some things together, you know, like why I became suspicious of Sturgis. I know that you jumped through a lot of hoops to get the search warrant. And I appreciate how you handled it, taking the responsibility and all. I just wanted to go over, for my own benefit, how I fit into all of it, if that makes sense."

The subdued question followed a brief pause. "What do you need?"

"I was wondering if I could take a look at Sturgis' journal. That was the thing that first alerted me. At the time, I didn't get a good look. I think it would help me resolve all of this if I could read through it in its entirety." The flimsy attempt at manipulation felt dirty, but she was pretty sure it was the only way she'd ever see what she needed to.

"I'm sorry. I can't release that to you. Technically, it's not even my call. The case belongs to the Seattle field office. They have custody of all evidence."

"I'd be happy to come by there and read it at their offices. They can even sit with me while I go through it."

"I'll check and get back to you."

***

It had taken less than an hour. And by one o'clock, Carol sat alone in one of their small offices with the leather-bound journal in front of her. She stared at the cover, running her hand over the worn surface. She thumbed through looking for a good starting point. Less than a minute later, she found herself looking at the familiar page.

> *Damned editors. They think they know everything. She's full of shit. I think she suspects that the stuff about emotional motivation of serial killers is plagiarized. How fucking crazy is that? If she'd check the citations, she'd see. But unfortunately, I need her on my side. I've got to get this book out the door. Will just have to change things. Not big things, of course. But I guess I at least need to listen to her concerns. I'll talk to her and iron things out. I don't have a lot of options.*

So, there it was. His editor had suspected him of copying someone's else's work. And he needed to change the way he was dealing with her. *Shit!* But why had he been so angry? Carol kind of understood. Sturgis was an academic. Plagiarism was a big deal to these guys. And for that, she'd started the ball rolling, and he died because of it.

Still, regardless of what had started the process, the evidence was overwhelming—Jenny's shirt. Did it really matter what made her suspicious? The bastard had killed her daughter, along with dozens of other girls and women. Yes, there was the evidence….

Chapter 67

For what little remained of the day, Carol worked on putting things into perspective. She had no control over the case. Sex Crimes called the shots for the Seattle PD. It appeared as though they would follow the FBI's lead. She had questions about their captain. She had questions about the evidence they had gathered at the apartment. Mostly she had questions about whether she had done the right thing. Sturgis was dead. Perhaps he was guilty or maybe not. Either way, she had put the spotlight on him.

As she prepared to leave work, she paused. Some of the desks in the bullpen sat vacant, their usual occupants gone for the night. Other detectives plodded on staring at computer screens, making notes in files, and looking out into space with telephone handsets glued to their ears. She liked this place. She resolved to finish up her notes the next day. This case was over as far as she was concerned.

This would be the night. She would venture into an area that she had avoided for nearly a decade.

***

Carol moved pensively down the hall from the living room, stopping beneath the pull-down door to the attic. She stared up at the chain for a moment before reaching up and grabbing it. The door swung down revealing a set of folded steps. She unfolded them creating a ladder. She peered up into the darkness dreading what she would find there.

Turning on the light as she ascended into the space, she made her way across the rafters to her destination. There it was, exactly where she had left it the night she moved it to get to her shoulder holster. She found it hard to believe that had been only a month ago.

Kneeling down beside the box, Carol gently brushed dust from the top. She picked it up and held it in her left hand, allowing her right to rest on the lid. Closing her eyes, she tried to conjure a vision of what she would find inside. The photos in the box documented her life, their life before…. *I have to do this.*

Back at the dining room table, she sat staring at the box. She wondered why she had not looked through it before. It was as though she had shunned the visual images in the same way that she had pushed her husband and son away. The difference was that the photos had waited patiently for her to return. She had lost her family forever.

Carol gently removed the lid with both hands and set it on the table. Closing her eyes and taking a deep breath, she reached in and took out a photo. She opened her eyes to a shot of Jenny and Jason sitting around a Christmas tree, their Christmas tree. They looked to be about ten and five. Jason's eyes were wide with excitement. Jenny, who still believed in Santa Claus, sort of, smiled that shy, heart-melting smile of hers.

No. I can't stop.

She stared at the picture and something strange happened to her. She found herself staring not at Jenny but at Jason. Five years old and dependent on his parents for everything—food, clothing, and love. Two years after this, she would lose Jenny. But Jason she would push away, wallowing in her own sorrow and completely ignoring him.

On to the next one. Chris held on to Jason, who sat on his bicycle for the first time, training wheels and all. She turned the photo over—"June 2006. Jason's First Ride." The camera had captured the boy staring back with a look that included both fear and excitement. Carol remembered that she'd taken the shot. Her son was looking at her. She reached for a tissue, wiped her eyes and cheeks, and retrieved the next photo.

Her thoughts became spoken words. "I remember this. Vacation down in Oregon." She gazed at the photo of the four of them, taken by another tourist. The two kids in the middle with her and Chris on the ends. The Columbia River served as a majestic backdrop. Her eyes were drawn to her son. Her finger found its way to his image and gently rubbed it.

For all these years, she'd thought only of Jenny. But this night Jason's likeness spoke to her. "Why didn't you love me, Mommy?" Another bunch of tissues.

Her attention moved to the image of her husband. God, she had loved him so much. And then she….

I can't do this. She put the photos back and replaced the lid. Leaning back in her chair, she closed her eyes and allowed the tears to flow. Finally, she stood and picked up the box. It needed to go back into the attic for the time being. *Maybe some other time.*

The doorbell chimed. She glanced at the living room clock—nine-thirty. The hackles went up on the back of her neck. Who would ring her bell at this hour? She slid into the bedroom and retrieved her weapon from its case. Sliding a full clip in, she chambered a round and set the safety. Easing down the hall to the living room, she held the weapon behind her back as she approached the door.

She moved the curtain slightly to the side and peeked out a small vertical window situated adjacent to the door. *What the hell?*

Chapter 68

Carol felt a cold sweat on her brow. She struggled to control her trembling. Her legs felt as though they would give way any moment. She placed her thumb on the safety of the Glock, ready to click it off. Keeping the weapon behind her, she opened the door with her left hand, cracking it about the width of her face. She looked out at the man standing in front of her. "Captain Peterman?"

His eyes betrayed no emotion, his affect totally flat. His arms hung loosely at his side. "We need to talk, Tullis."

A burning question nagged at her mind. At *what point would I be justified in pointing my weapon at him?* She hesitated for a moment and then tried to stall. "Uh, Captain, I was just getting ready for bed. Can we do this in the morning?" *Please.*

His face remained stony not reacting at all to her response. Surely he could see that she was nervous, even panicked. But, no, he seemed to notice nothing. "No. We need to talk tonight." He edged closer to the door.

Here it comes. She expected him to push his way in any second. She eased away from the door slightly to make sure his push wouldn't throw her backwards.

In an instant, everything changed. Peterman rolled his eyes and let out an exasperated sounding sigh. "Oh for God's sake, Tullis, I'm not here to seduce you or kill you. Let me in the Goddamn house."

She stepped back, opening the door to allow him in. She shook her head in bewilderment. Why had that simple statement washed away all of her concerns? It made no sense. And yet, she somehow felt okay with it.

He entered the house and shuffled toward the dining room. He spoke over his shoulder as he walked. "And put that damn gun away before you shoot yourself."

She stood there staring, her right arm hanging loosely at her side with the Glock in her hand. "How did you find out where I live?"

Peterman turned and laughed. "Really? You have to ask? I'm the chief of Homicide. I was detecting before you were even a cop. I think I know how to find out where my employees live. They're called personnel records, to which I have access." He shook his head and turned toward the dining room table. "We're going to need something to drink."

Carol looked at him with puzzlement. He knew she was an alcoholic. There's no way he was that dumb.

"You got any French roast?"

She rolled her eyes and breathed a sigh of relief. *I should have known.* "Breakfast blend."

"Cheap swill, but it'll have to do. Better make a whole pot."

***

Each with steaming cups of coffee in front of them, Carol engaged in some basic damage control. "Sorry about the awkward greeting. I'm a bit off tonight."

He waved her apology aside with a flick of his hand. "You know why I'm here instead of talking to you in the office?"

"No, but I admit I wondered about that."

Peterman's words came out sounding tired. "I know that I'm not the killer. And I'm pretty sure that you're not

273

either. Beyond that, I'm beginning to wonder who I can trust. Something about this hasn't felt right ever since we received our invitation to join the club."

"And so, what is it you want to talk about?" This was the most forthcoming she'd ever seen the captain.

"Well, you're the one who had concerns about the case and Sturgis. I guess that's as good a place as any to start." His expression grew serious. "Before we start, though, was there anything between the two of you?"

Her back grew rigid and she clenched her jaw. "You mean was I sleeping with him? That's kind of personal, wouldn't you say?"

"Look, Tullis, I'm not interested in the lurid details. I just need to know about the relationship because that will color whatever you tell me. It doesn't matter one whit how objective you try to be." He folded his hands on the table and waited.

She had to admit he had a point. How people feel about others definitely affects descriptions. "There was no relationship other than tenant and landlord."

"Okay. Talk to me."

Chapter 69

She pulled a couple of lined yellow notepads from the end table next to the sofa. Sliding one across the dining room table to Peterman, she retrieved a pen from a kitchen drawer. "I guess to start, I'd have to say that something just didn't feel right. I was standing there looking at the scene and everything seemed all wrong."

The captain cocked his head and rolled his eyes. "I tried that line of reasoning in court once. Didn't get me very far. You're going to have to do better than that." He leaned back, arms folded on his chest.

Carol leaned into the table, her hands flat on the top. "Yeah. I know. So, for starters, the clippings he tried to burn in the wood stove. What was that all about? If you're committing suicide, why go to the trouble of trying to destroy evidence?"

"I don't know. Maybe he has family and didn't want them to know about him. So, he wanted to end it but go out with a clean reputation. I've seen stranger things."

She smirked. "Oh, come on, Captain. That's crap and you know it. But, okay, let's assume it's strange but true. Why screw it up? He threw the papers into the woodstove in a stack and lit some of the pages. It doesn't take a physicist to know that it wouldn't work. And, why not a shredder? It's not as if that's new technology. But the way he did it was the worst possible way."

"The guy was a shrink. What do you expect? They're not known for their practicality."

She shook her head. "No. That doesn't fly. This guy's been flawless for two years—never a misstep or mistake.

275

Then all of a sudden… bam. It doesn't make any sense." She jotted down a bullet note on her pad—"Burning evidence." Narrowing her eyes, she tapped her pen on the pad. "And they were photocopies. Where are the original clippings?"

The captain chewed on his bottom lip. "Maybe he destroyed those earlier and saved the photocopies."

Carol scrunched her face and shook her head. "That's stupid. If anything, he would have destroyed the photocopies first and then the originals. And, come to think of it, why even have photocopies if he had the originals, which he had to have had."

Peterman picked up his cup and took a deep draught. "Okay. Put that in the 'very interesting' column. Next?"

She closed her eyes, barely trusting herself with the next topic. "The, uh, things…."

The captain's eyes softened as he leaned forward. "Your daughter's sweatshirt and the other items. Yes."

"Yes. Why those? The sweatshirt seems to suggest that this is the same killer as the child case." She avoided referring to *Jenny's sweatshirt*. "The combined number of murders, adults and children is, what, thirty-seven? Why just these four? Where are the keepsakes from the others?" She almost called them "trophies," but something inside would have no part of that.

Peterman stood. "Ready for a refill?" He picked up his empty cup.

She looked down at her still full mug. "I'm fine."

As he ambled toward the kitchen, he spoke over his shoulder. "Maybe the others are in a storage unit somewhere. Or maybe these are the only ones he kept. Maybe he destroyed the others already. Lot of 'maybes' there."

Carol knew she was on the right track. His speculation wasn't even logical. "Then why keep these four?" She raised her voice to carry into the kitchen. "And why the sweatshirt?"

The captain wandered back in, sipping his drink as he walked. "Random chance. Assuming he had thirty-seven items. He held on to four, one of which was the sweatshirt. Or maybe he wanted to give you closure. If it was random, then it had the same probability as any other item. As to why he kept them and not the others...." He shrugged as he sat.

Score another one for me. She knew she was on a roll. "You have to admit, that's a pretty lame response. I'll just put that over in the 'very interesting column' as well."

Carol stood. "I'll be just a sec. I have something to show you." She retrieved a set of photographs from the bedroom. "I took these with my phone and had them printed." She set them in front of the captain. "With the light finish on the table, you can see the blood splatter. Since it was a thirty-two, it's not as dramatic as, say, a forty-four. But you can still make it out. Now, if you look at it and let your eyes lose focus, what do you see?" She leaned back in her chair and waited.

Peterman stared at the photograph on top for a few seconds, turning his head first one way and then the other. "Seems to be a gap, maybe two, in the pattern." He tapped his finger on two different spots. "Here and, maybe here, too."

"Yes. The one there on the adjacent edge of the table, where a guest might have sat, it looks like there could have been another glass there. Also, here, it's not as well defined since it was not in the main pattern, but it looks like it could be where a bottle was sitting between Sturgis and where a guest might have been seated." She paused for a moment before adding, "And you can see here, where the bottle was found, there's no gap in the pattern at all. It is as though it was placed there after the fact."

He stroked his chin as he stared at the photos. "Okay. I don't have a good answer for that one. Anything else?"

"The weapon ended up on the floor below his right hand, which hung down at his side. The entry wound was at the right temple, hence the splatter pattern to the left. The only problem is that Sturgis was left-handed." The image of the young man contorting himself to fix the light, all the while complaining about the difficulties shot across her mind.

"How would you know that?"

"I watched him, or rather helped him repair a light fixture in the bedroom one evening. He mentioned it then and I did notice that he used his left hand."

Peterman narrowed his eyes. "I thought you said there was nothing between the two of you. How did you come to be in the bedroom with him?"

Carol rolled her eyes and stood. "Oh, for God's sake. He was repairing the damn light fixture and needed me to hold the flashlight. Hardly the stuff of adult movies."

The captain sat still. Silence washed over them. The captain picked up the photos and examined each. When he finished, he slid them across the table. "Okay then. Let us assume, for argument's sake, that young Doctor Sturgis is not our killer and that he was murdered. This brings us to a rather challenging inconsistency." He leaned back in his chair and tilted his head back, looking at the ceiling. "Why?" Peterman stood and began pacing around the room. "We're talking a serial killer here. He kills once a month. Why frame a guy? He's due to kill in another couple of weeks. The entire set-up goes away when he strikes again. Why bother?"

Carol had anticipated this. The question had troubled her the night before. It was only with a dawn that followed the tossing and turning had the answer flashed before her. She leaned into the table. "I'll tell you why." Before she could continue, though, her landline telephone rang. *Who would be calling at midnight?* "Let me get that." She felt a knot in her chest and a rising sense of dread as she made her way into the kitchen.

The caller ID unit confirmed her worst fears—Her ex-husband's cellphone. "Chris? What's wrong? Is Jason okay?" That familiar sense of panic that had invaded her life before when....

"Carol. I'm here at the Overlake Emergency Room."

Chapter 70

God, please do not let this be happening. Not again. The traffic on I-5 north was predictably light. Her car maneuvered itself around the slower traffic while she stepped through every conceivable possibility.

Carol tried to summon up her store of knowledge about appendicitis. *Something about pain in the abdomen, maybe surgery. Not fatal, usually.* The car increased its speed. She watched for the signs she knew would mark the right exit—the blue "Hospital" signs that she'd ignored so many times before.

Her Honda had barely parked itself when she unbuckled her harness and shot out the door, sprinting toward the emergency room entrance. As she bolted through the self-operating double doors, Chris rushed forward to meet her, wrapping his arms around her.

She held him tight for just a second before letting go and stepping back. "How is he? What are they saying? Can I see him?'

He held her shoulders with his hands. "He's still in surgery. They said that we got here in plenty of time. He should be fine." His face looked haggard and tired but his eyes shone with what she could only assume was relief.

Carol's legs began to tremble, her knees feeling wobbly. Her body started to shake. She started to ask something else, but it escaped her mind. Truthfully, she didn't want to hear anything else. *He should be fine.*

The two slipped over to a row of chairs set back against the wall. As they sat, Chris held her hand. "He just had this intense pain in his side and, well, I panicked so here we are."

Relief, gratitude, and guilt all competed for sway over her mind. Once again, Chris was there while she was off doing something else. He was taking care of their son, saving his life, while she was drinking coffee and engaging in shoptalk with her boss. "Thank you." She wanted to say more but knew that translating her feelings into words would only unleash the tears. She squeezed his hand.

They sat in relative silence for the next hour. He made a few light comments—the weather, Jason's grades, and her job. Nothing mattered to Carol except hearing that her son was going to be fine. Every once in a while, the double doors to the waiting area would open as people made their way in, likely with the same concerns and worries that she had. The small gusts of damp, cold air signaled their entrance.

A tall, thin fortyish doctor emerged around three a.m. to announce that Jason was out of surgery and would be fine. They had moved him into recovery, and they could see him in a few hours. Daylight made an appearance around seven. Chris had dozed off a couple of times. Carol, on the other hand, still felt the residual effect of the caffeine. She powered through the night, alternately sitting, pacing, and going to the restroom.

Finally, a nurse came over and announced that Jason was awake and that they could go in. Carol stepped out in front of Chris as they strode toward the recovery area.

Her heart revolted and rejoiced at the same time seeing her son in a hospital gown, the covers pulled up to his chest, his face an ashen shade of gray—and yet alive and well. She shot over to his bed and hugged him the best she could, given the myriad of electronic leads and tubes connected to him. "Hey you. You scared me to death, you know." She moved back from him, wiping the tears.

"Hi Mom."

God, those words sound great! A sense of peace and happiness that she'd not felt for years settled over her. Her son was going to be all right.

After about thirty minutes, he started to doze off, his eyelids looking heavy. Chris, who had parked in a straight-back chair against the wall, stood. "Let's let the kid get some sleep. How about I buy you breakfast. And, you're going to be late for work."

Carol, sitting beside the bed, tightened her hold on Jason's hand. "I'm not going to work. I need to be here." She glanced over at Chris.

He arched his eyebrows. "Okay. So, we can have a more leisurely breakfast then." He eased over to her side and put his hand on her shoulder.

"Some coffee would be good, I guess, but I'm not really hungry. I'm going to hit the restroom and I'll meet you in the lobby." She reluctantly stood and released her son's hand.

Standing at the sink in the restroom, she splashed cold water on her face. As she looked into the mirror, what she saw looking back sent chills down her spine. Her gaunt face was lined at the corners of her eyes and mouth. Her eyes sank deep into the sockets with puffy bags beneath them. She stepped back and took in the image of her body—thin and frail looking. Her shoulders sagged and her bony wrists and hands protruded from her coat. She closed her eyes.

She found Chris waiting outside the restroom, pacing. "All set?"

Carol took a deep breath. "Yes. And you know, breakfast does sound good."

Chapter 71

The hot oatmeal, fresh blueberries, and whole-wheat toast tasted good. Carol had to admit, though, it left her feeling bloated. She wasn't used to eating so much. Still, on the way out of the hospital cafeteria, she detoured over to the food line and picked up an apple for later. *I can't continue to exist on cold cereal and coffee.* The memory of the image in the mirror haunted her.

Back in the hallway, she pulled out her phone. "I need to check in with the captain. I'll meet you back at Jason's room."

Chris's eyes were red and puffy. His hair disheveled. It had been a long night for her ex-husband, too, but he had pulled through it with grace, as he always did. He headed off down the hall.

The phone call to her boss cleared her for the rest of the day and the next day. Peterman, without saying much, signaled that her immediate duty was with her son. "Keep your cellphone turned on. I'll call you if anything comes up. If you're up to it, we can continue our conversation tomorrow evening. Maybe you can even get some French roast by then."

When Carol reached the recovery area, Chris was waiting to tell her that they'd moved him up to a regular bed. "They said they'd keep him overnight and depending on what the doctors say at rounds in the morning, he could conceivably be home by lunch time tomorrow."

She uttered a sigh of relief. *Going home.* That sounded so… perfect.

By early afternoon, the activity around Jason's room had taken on the tempo of routine. Nurses came and went, first at half-hourly intervals then decreasing to hourly. Chris went home to clean up and get a few hours' sleep while Carol sat with her son, who drifted in and out.

When Chris returned just after five, they jointly agreed that she should go home and try to rest up. "I'll be back before midnight."

Chris narrowed his eyes and glanced over at Jason, who was asleep. "You know, I'm not sure that we need to be here all night. Let me check with the nurse."

As he left the room, Carol sat in the bedside chair and fought back the urge to take her son's hand and squeeze. He needed the sleep. *But I need to hold him.* She had fought that battle all afternoon. She sighed and leaned back in the chair just as Chris entered.

"Just as I thought. He'll be asleep during the night. They'll be in and out watching him. The techs will draw blood for labs around four tomorrow morning. There's no point in us being here past about ten. So why don't you go home, get some dinner, and try to sleep. I'll be here early in the morning, so we'll be ready to go when they release him."

She frowned. Should she leave her son there all night without her? Chris was always there for Jason. She, on the other hand, had never been there for him. "Why don't I just stay for a while?" She revolted against the idea of deserting her son yet again.

Chris took her hand. "Carol, you've been here since last night. You're not doing Jason or yourself any favors by running yourself into the ground. I'll call you once we're home and you can come over."

She felt a surge of weariness. "Please call me from the hospital before you leave. I'll meet you at your place."

285

"Go home. Get some rest."

***

Carol considered the food on her plate—a departure from her regular fare of cold cereal. She'd stopped at the market on the way home and picked up a few items. Sitting in front of her on the kitchen table, curried lentils over a bed of brown rice gave off wisps of aromatic steam. A small avocado tomato salad complemented the unusual meal.

Taking her first bite, she felt as though she was embarking on a long journey. Despite the odd unfamiliar meal, a sense of rightness, of renewal set in like a piece of a puzzle that she had been looking for.

Chapter 72

Carol pulled the covers up to her son's chest and took his hand. "I'll just be in the next room with Dad if you need anything."

"I'm okay, Mom. Really." He closed his eyes and turned his head to the side.

She couldn't resist. She bent down and kissed his cheek, rubbing her hand through his shaggy brown hair. "See you in a bit. I love you."

Chris closed Jason's bedroom door behind them as they left. "Let's get a cup of coffee."

The neatness of the house struck her. Not so much that it was immaculate, but everything seemed in its place. She saw no dust on tables or shelves. The carpet looked clean and the house had a generally pleasant odor that she could only identify as "fresh." Leave it to Chris to make a good living, be a good father, and keep a reasonably straight house.

She wondered in passing if Shelley ever came over and helped. Carol just assumed that the woman spent a great deal of time there since she and Chris were close, well, engaged if Jason was to be believed. But there was no evidence of the woman to be seen. The family photos that adorned the walls included old ones of the entire family before… as well as more recent ones.

Chris interrupted her musings. "I'll put a fresh pot on. And I picked up some almond scones on the way to the hospital this morning." He shuffled into the kitchen while she waited in the dining room. Looking at the table only deepened her sorrow. She imagined sitting down with her family for dinner or a hurried breakfast before everyone went their own way. How many evenings had Chris and Jason sat there eating and discussing their day while her chair, or what would have been her chair, sat empty? Had Shelley filled in for her? Had they laughed together? Had Chris' new love been good to Jason? Would he start calling Shelley "Mom" once they were…?

Chris came back into the room with a plate of scones and set them on the coffee table in front of the couch. "Have a seat. The coffee will be just a minute." He went back into the kitchen. She could hear dishware clinking.

She felt better knowing that at least he hadn't been up all night baking in addition to everything else he did. She called into the kitchen, "The place looks really great. I don't know how you keep up with everything."

A laugh floated into the living room. "Not just me. Jason does his share. It's either that or no car. His driver's license has given me a lot of leverage in the chore department."

How does he do it? How can he handle all of this, work full-time in a busy law office, and manage a kind word and a smile for me?

***

Carol set the cup of steaming liquid in front of Peterman before sitting with her own cup. "There you go."

The captain closed his eyes and took a deep breath through his nose. "Ah, French roast. You can take a hint when you try." He blew across the surface and then took a drink. "How's your son?"

"He's good. He went home this morning. He'll be laid up for a while but he's going to be fine. Thanks."

He eyed her quietly. "Good." Setting his cup to the side, he leaned into the table. "So, tell me why it made sense for the killer to set up Sturgis."

She mentally shifted gears, clearing her throat. "Okay, first, let's talk about the child serial killer case. And please bear with me. This isn't because of my daughter. Remember, we found her sweatshirt among the items in the apartment, which, on the face of it, connects the two cases. So, I know that you weren't at the department then but I'm sure that you've heard about it. He stopped killing for no apparent reason. He could have gotten sick, gone to jail, or... who knows. But he stopped. How long would you say the full investigation went on after he quit?" She placed her hands flat on the table and stared him in the eye.

"I don't know. If I had to guess, I'd probably say it went full speed ahead for maybe four to six months. After that, resources likely got re-programmed leaving a small contingent still working on it. But it had already made its way up to Aged Cases before I got here."

"Exactly. We had a killer that we didn't catch. We had no reason to believe that anything happened to him. And within months, the pressure was off. Within a few years, the case was put on the back burner awaiting *further developments*."

"So?" Peterman narrowed his eyes and shifted his head slightly to the side. Carol could see the beginning of understanding, despite his challenge.

She grinned. "So, right now we have a dead body that some would argue was the killer. Granted, we've sat here and picked that apart. But suppose that in two weeks, there is no killing. And then the next month—no killing. And the month after that. What do you think will happen?"

"We have a body. We have no more killings. Yeah, I could see a strong motivation to close the case, practically as well as politically. We need resources on active cases. The politicians need to reassure the public. The chief and top management need the confidence of the machinery. So I see your point. I guess we can assume that the real killer intends to take some time off, maybe change things."

Carol had seen this coming for some time. She could put it off no longer. "Captain, I have to ask you. Why are we ruling Captain Fredericks out?"

He looked directly at her although his eyes seemed to lack focus. When he spoke, the words came slowly. "Let me say up front that I realize that, here in your home, this is not a 'me captain, you detective' moment. So, I'm going to ask you to trust me on this. I am not at liberty to explain it, but I can personally assure that he's not a part of it."

This was essentially the same thing he'd told her before. "So what? Is it classified or something—above my pay grade?"

He shook his head. "No. It's a personal issue."

She stood her ground, determined not to buckle under. "Captain, with all due respect, this is not personal. We have a lot of bodies stacked up. It may well be that he's not involved, but given that we're putting everything on the table, so to speak, I don't think it's unreasonable for you to tell me how you've managed to rule him out. Because what I've seen so far doesn't seem to justify it."

The initial silence discomforted her. When he began, the words came softly. "Fredericks and Irwin had history. It goes all the way back to when the two of them worked together back east. He was fresh out of the academy and Irwin was a newly minted Ph.D. They got crossways over a woman and Fredericks won. But Irwin was a vindictive bastard. He used his position as the department's psychologist and spared no effort to try and discredit the young cop. At one point, the doc even tried to implicate Fredericks in an unsolved rape/murder case."

Peterman shook his head and took a deep breath. "It went nowhere, of course, but the innuendo was like a thorn that would never go away. It just dug deeper. Finally, Fredericks quit and moved out west. That's where I met him. The two of us became good friends over drinks—many drinks. We drank ourselves to the edge of personal and professional destruction. He pulled back in time to save his marriage and career."

"So that's it? They had a falling out over a woman? Didn't his reaction seem a little extreme to you, if that's the only reason?"

"Not at all. Remember, Fredericks was sitting on a two-year old case that was going nowhere. And then his old nemesis who had once tried to falsely implicate him was joining the investigation. He could see his career, even his life, going up in smoke. His wife called me the other night and told me that he was crumbling. I knew what she meant. The bottle was calling. You, of all people, should understand that. He retreated to his cabin up north to try and keep the demons at bay. That's it."

"And so, I'm supposed to just give him a pass?"

"You don't have to give him anything. I provided an explanation. You can either accept it or not. For me, I'm satisfied and ready to move on to another line of inquiry."

Carol turned his words over in her mind. While she wasn't totally mollified, it seemed there was no place to take the discussion that didn't devolve into a spitting contest. "So, what next, then?"

Peterman leaned back in his chair, coffee cup in hand. "It's time that we actually get to work. You've done a masterful job of convincing me that Sturgis is not our man. And, at least in my mind, we've eliminated Fredericks. But that simply tells us more about who didn't do it. It doesn't move us one step closer to knowing who the murderer is."

Chapter 73

Carol's ecstasy at proving her point gave way to the realization that she was no further along in the case than she had been before she suspected Sturgis. Still, a part of her rejoiced that the man living in the apartment behind her house, the man who had made nearly successful advances, was not the killer. A wave of guilt swept over her. Ben had been killed, very likely as a result of her bringing him into the case.

Peterman's voice interrupted her emotional processing. "Are you ready to get started?

The voice, more than the words, startled her. She blinked to bring her eyes back into focus. "Excuse me?"

He shook his head. "I don't have all night. I'm an old man and need my sleep. We've spent an evening and a half ruling out Sturgis. Time to move on."

Carol sighed. "I guess we need to step back and look at the big picture." The line sounded good, but she had no idea what it really meant. The truth was that she didn't know where to look next.

"No." The captain spit the word out and then raised his mug to his lips. After a deep draught, he continued, "That, Tullis, is your problem. You and the others have spent entirely too much time trying to solve this by looking at the *big picture,* as you call it. It's time to get into the weeds."

She rolled her eyes. Standing, she began to pace the length of the combined living room/dining room. "We've been through these details again and again. They always take us to the same place." She balled her fists tight as she strode back and forth.

Her declaration produced only a few seconds of silence before the captain waded back in. "Then let's start with something that you likely haven't beaten to death."

She whirled around to face him. "And what, pray tell, would that be?" His vague recriminations were starting to annoy her.

He turned his chair to face her. Cradling the cup in both hands, he arched his eyebrows. "How about we look at the Irwin/Ramirez shooting?"

"What about it?" She had to admit, though, that the group had spent almost no time on that. The event had heralded a full takeover of the case by the FBI.

"Sit down before you trip on something. Besides, your pacing is making me nervous." He shifted back around to face the table as she sat. "Let's work the facts and assumptions. First question—was this shooting related to the serial killings?"

What a stupid question. "Of course, it was." As the words came out, though, a twinge of doubt crept in. "What other explanation could there be?"

Peterman burst out laughing. "That's your problem right there. The moment you assume things, you start to rule out everything else. I'm not saying it's not connected. I'm asking you to tell me whether you think it is or not and why?"

Carol searched her memory of the event looking for something that might suggest that it was not connected. She came up blank. "I guess it could be random or some kind of coincidence but that seems a little far-fetched to me."

Tapping his fingers on the table, he peered at her through narrowed eyes. "Let's start with the *random* explanation. Why is that far-fetched? I mean, it happened in a parking lot early in the morning before a lot of foot traffic was around. It's not like this was a scheduled appearance or something. Maybe just a killer looking for a victim."

Carol scrunched her face. "No. Doesn't wash. Beyond sounding absurd, why kill Irwin but not Ramirez? Why leave a witness alive? After all, he just killed a federal officer. Why not finish the job?" She shook her head and gestured with her hand, waving away the idea.

"Okay. Kind of makes sense. Second possibility, that Irwin was the target, but it was something personal—not related to the case."

That thought had not occurred to her before. "Could be, but why do it here? Irwin lived in DC. Why come all the way out to the west coast. It would be much easier to predict his movement and catch him alone back there. And why kill him in the presence of another person and then leave that person alive?"

"Okay, then, moving on. Maybe it was related to another case. The FBI is working on a number of things. Perhaps the doc was getting close to something and they chose to remove him"

"Again, possible but the east coast-west coast argument is the same. Why follow him out here? It would be much easier to get him on his home turf."

"Which brings us back to where we started. The killing is related to our serial killer case."

Carol let her open hands fall on to the tabletop as she exhaled loudly. "And so, what was the point of all that?" Wasting time going in circles frustrated her.

"It forces us to think, Detective, you know, comb over the details. Allow me to offer a constructive criticism to what your group has been doing. You've been working with assumptions without questioning them. And, I might add, you've continued to come up empty. It's time to start challenging what you think you know."

She had to admit that he was right. The group had yet to challenge any assumptions at all. They had just kept on with their approach despite going nowhere. "Point taken. What next?'

He stood. "Hold that thought. I need to hit the restroom." He gestured toward the hallway. "Down there?"

She watched him as he shuffled toward the guest bathroom. As he shut the door, she tilted her head back and gazed at the ceiling. The details of the shooting began to arrange themselves in her mind. The opening of the bathroom door brought her back to the present.

Peterman returned and sat. "You solve it yet?"

Carol couldn't tell whether it was a genuine question or a snarky jibe. Either way, she didn't have a good answer. "No, but here's what we know. The killer hit Irwin from behind with a thirty-two—clean headshot, instant kill. Before Ramirez could react, he took a round to the back, which was stopped by his vest."

The retort came quickly. "Did the killer know he was wearing a vest?"

She narrowed her eyes. "Yes. Tom's wife said that he was wearing it over his shirt and had no jacket. So, the killer would have easily seen it. And, if he was the least bit knowledgeable about his weapon, he would have known that it wouldn't penetrate."

Peterman's response came out as a challenge. "And so rather than putting a bullet in his head, the killer chose to put a single round of an underpowered weapon into a vest."

The light clicked on. "He had no intention of killing Ramirez. But why leave a witness, especially a trained and experienced cop?"

The captain pressed on. "Why indeed? Go on. What else do we know?"

The facts began to align themselves painting a more vivid mental picture than she had previously seen. "The killer took Irwin's cellphone. He then turned Tom over onto his back, reached down and took his cellphone from his shirt pocket. That's when Ramirez saw his face."

"Yes. Ramirez saw his face. And tell me, Detective, why would a perfectionist serial killer make the novice mistake of letting a cop see his face?"

The clarity shook Carol. "Because it was no mistake. The killer deliberately allowed Tom to see."

"No. He didn't allow it. He forced Ramirez to see him. He stood over him, bent down, and looked into his eyes as he took the cellphone. There was no way that Ramirez could have not seen. Why, Tullis, why?"

She should have seen the question coming but it still stunned her. *Why would a killer force a witness to see his face?* "Let me think a minute." She chewed on her thumbnail as she ran various explanations through her head. *No, he hasn't taunted the police. There's nothing to suggest he's playing a game with us. Why?* "The only thing I can think of, assuming he doesn't have some underlying need to be caught, is that he wants us to be looking for the man that Ramirez saw."

Peterman reached down to his portfolio that sat beside his chair. He retrieved a piece of paper and slid it across to Carol. "You mean this man?"

She stared down at the sketch artist rendering of the suspect. Something tickled the back of her mind but, once again, she couldn't grab hold. "Yes. This man. The killer wants us looking for him. But, since he's the killer, that makes no sense."

"Something about this is bothering you, isn't it?"

"Yes, but I don't know exactly what. I could swear that I've seen this before but...I don't know."

He reached down, got another piece of paper and placed in front of her. "Is this what you remember?"

Chapter 74

Carol stared at the two images, shifting her gaze back and forth between them. "Where did you get this one?"

Peterman gave the pictures a cursory look, then back at her. "The same place you were looking for it. I'm just quicker."

She stared in disbelief. "You got this from the child serial killer case file?" It struck her that he must have already had the drawing when he warned her off, back in the office.

He leaned back and stroked his chin. "This may come as a surprise to you, Detective, but I make it my business to stay informed. I've looked at the case a number of times over the years. You and I both know it's been going nowhere up in Aged Cases. Not their fault, I'm sure. They're overloaded and their staff is, well, shall we say, not the sharpest bunch of icicles on the roof. I've gone through those images on several occasions. When I saw this latest one, I knew exactly where to look." He grinned as he reached for his cup.

"Why didn't you say something when I told you about my suspicions? Why tell me to back off?"

"Like I told you the other evening, I'm not completely comfortable discussing this in the office right now."

Carol considered his explanation for a moment, trying to shake off the sense of betrayal. She went back to comparing the two images. "It's the same guy." She stared at the likeness of the man who killed Jenny. Now she had a focal point for her rage.

Swallowing his gulp of coffee, Peterman cleared his throat. "What makes you think it's the same guy?"

"What? Of course, it's the same guy. Look at him." Her eyes widened with incredulity.

He studied the two documents for a moment, shifting his attention back and forth between them. "Okay. I'm looking. Again, why do you say it's the same guy?"

Carol threw her hands up and exhaled. "Look. The beard, mustache, and the bald head—they're identical." She teetered on the verge of a snarky remark about his ability to observe. A gnawing doubt cautioned her. The captain had thus far proven intuitive. She had a sneaky suspicion that he was building to a point. "Maybe we should ask, why wouldn't we consider this the same person?"

Peterman pursed his lips. "And maybe a better question is, do we really know what these tell us? Remember, the killer willingly and purposely gave us this. I surmise that he did the same thing ten years ago. So, what we have here is exactly what he wanted us to have."

She peered through the living room window into the darkness, allowing her eyes to lose focus as she turned the problem over in her mind. "It's the beard, mustache, and bald head. That's what he showed us. But even so, we have the artist rendering. And with today's software, we can remove those, and we have what may be a more accurate drawing."

The captain guffawed. "Do we really, now?" He tore off six pieces of paper from his yellow pad. He positioned one of the sheets over the latest image, covering the subject's bald head. He then placed scraps covering the subject's beard and moustache. This left only an image of eyes, nose, and ears. He repeated the process with the older image. "Now, tell me. Are these two the same person?"

Carol's heart fell. As she looked at the two sheets of paper, there was very little similarity between the two images. "I see. Hmmm. So, if we used software to remove the features, then we end up with two different faces."

"Don't sound so beaten. There's a good reason. Take Ramirez. How long did he have to look at the man?"

Carol furrowed her brow and stared at the images. "I don't know. What, maybe five to ten seconds? Come to think of it, that might even be on the high side."

"Right. And in that brief period, what do you think Ramirez saw?"

"A beard, a mustache, and a bald head." The light went on in Carol's head. "He wants us looking for those things. Without those, there's nothing in the image that helps us. Would hypnosis work? I mean, is it possible that Tom saw something in the man's face but can't recall it because the dominant features get in the way?"

"Maybe. Maybe not. In any event, let's take this information and use it. So, we know that the killer wanted us to see those features. Tell me, Detective, when our profiler gave us the rundown on this guy, what was the first set of descriptors?"

She tilted her head back as she summoned up the memory of that briefing. "Let's see, if I remember correctly, she said he was a white male in his early to mid-thirties. She went on to say that there were some assumptions involved, you know, statistical probability stuff."

The captain shot back quickly, "Assumptions about what?"

Carol mulled over the question. What was the assumption in that first descriptor? "I believe it was about race. She said that most serial killers are Caucasian. So, her conclusion was white male." She toyed with the new perspective. "But she didn't say how she got to the male part."

"Right. But I'm figuring that she used the same logic the rest of us bought into. Statistically, serial killers are far more likely to be male. And we do have the rape factor. There was penetration. Still, the killer went to great lengths to reinforce that we are looking for a man. Any thoughts?"

Whatever confidence she had built up over the course of these sessions evaporated. "Crap. I'm confused. Are we or are we not looking for a man?"

"Possibly. But let's put that assumption over in the 'don't know' category for now. I mean, we *could* be looking for a female. Maybe she hates other women and uses a sex toy for penetration. With a condom, we wouldn't see the difference."

"But Ramirez saw a man. We have a drawing from ten years ago. Would it make sense for a woman to dress up as a man to mislead us?"

"It's possible."

Another idea hit Carol. "What if we're looking for two people—a man and a woman? Maybe the man dominates the woman like with brainwashing. It wouldn't be the first time. Maybe he selects the victims and then has his accomplice go out and do the abduction."

The captain raised his index finger. "Yes. That is a distinct possibility. Think about it. With all of the publicity of this case, what's the likelihood that a man could get close enough to a woman he doesn't know to spike her drink and then convince her to leave with him without anyone noticing?" His eyes were ablaze with excitement and the tempo of his discussion picked up.

The excitement proved infectious. Carol quickly interjected, "But a woman, yes, no one would notice a woman sitting down with another woman. She could offer any number of reasons. Maybe she is a little older and tries to come across as frail. Maybe she sits under the pretense of asking directions or maybe saying she's tired. Or maybe she says she's afraid of being out alone with all of the killings going on. She would need very little time if she was practiced."

Peterman leaned back, arms folded on his chest. "Okay. That's one possible alternative. Let's not fall into the same trap again—grabbing an assumption and moving forward without looking at other possibilities. How about a cross-dresser?"

She mentally shifted gears again. "Hmmm. Maybe. And I have to admit I'm not an authority on this, but from what I've seen, most cross-dressers aren't that passable. They look okay at a glance but up close, it tends to break down. I'm sure there are some out there that are very good at it and it's a possibility. But I'd think that a marginally passable dresser would be apt to draw more attention than a man. Even so, if this were the case, we'd be looking for someone who shifts easily between a male and female persona, complete with convincing looks. This doesn't seem as likely to me."

"While I might agree with that, let's not fall into the trap of ruling things out before we have the evidence to support it." Peterman shook his head and stood. "Okay. I think we've beat this horse to death. We now have four possibilities—a male working alone, a female working alone, a man and woman working together, and a cross-dresser. And with that, I'm off. Hell of a way to spend a Friday night." He stretched his arms out and twisted his body. "Years are catching up with me."

The abrupt ending caught Carol off guard. "So, what do we do now?" She stood to accompany her boss to the door.

He laughed. "What's this 'we' crap? You got a mouse in your pocket? I'm the chief of Homicide. I don't investigate, remember? I'm the captain and you're the detective."

Carol sighed and shook her head. "Okay. So, what am *I* supposed to do? I get the sense that Sex Crimes wants this one put to bed. All we have here, other than our work on Sturgis, is more conjecture. And the FBI, those guys have all but declared victory."

The captain put his hand on her shoulder. "Strategy, Tullis, strategy. The FBI has its assassin case wrapped up, or so they think. Sex Crimes has hitched their serial killer wagon to the bureau's star. They'll go where the feds take them. But remember, if Sturgis isn't the killer, then he's the victim of a homicide. Not a sex crime. And he's not a federal employee. As it turns out, I am the chief of Homicide and I assign cases."

A newfound respect for her boss swept over her. "So, you assign the case to Ramirez and me. He's supposed to be back on Monday."

He shook his head. "Oh, come on now, Tullis, you know better than that. This murder happened to a man renting an apartment you own. You're too close to it. Try again.

Carol considered the problem. The sane, reasonable part of her understood even if the fiercely passionate part of her pushed back. "Can I put in my two-cents worth?"

"You can say anything you want. Whether I take your advice or not is another matter."

She paused before responding. "Mulroney and Collins."

He laughed. "What, you and Mulroney made nice already?"

Despite the laugh, she could see concern in his eyes. "Let's just say we're working on it. And this isn't about him and me. This is about the case and who would be best. He's got the experience and knowledge. I'd trust him with it." She knew that what she was saying is that she would trust him with her daughter's case. *How ironic.*

Carol went to the closet and retrieved his coat. She handed it to him just as the phone starting ringing. "Let me check that." She strode toward the kitchen where her landline phone resided.

"I'll show myself out. See you on Monday."

She heard the door open and close as she looked at the caller ID. Panic set in. She grabbed the handset. "Chris? What is it? Is Jason okay?"

Chapter 75

Saturday morning brought a crisp wind from the north accompanied by brilliant azure skies. Carol made her way north on I-5 in light traffic. The late-night phone call that had produced panic was Chris wanting her to sit with Jason for a few hours—he had an unexpected work commitment.

She rolled into his driveway just after eight. She'd considered stopping for a cup of coffee but knew that her ex had a taste for the good stuff. *Might as well mooch off him.*

Chris answered the door in a pair of faded jeans, a yellow shirt, and a navy fleece vest. "Come in. Thanks, Carol. I really appreciate this. I shouldn't be more than three hours."

"A pleasure. Where's the invalid?"

He chortled and pointed toward the stairs. "Still sleeping, I suspect. I haven't heard a peep from him yet." He walked into the kitchen and picked up a cup of coffee, draining the last of it. "Half a pot left. Help yourself. If you want to make more, the beans are in the freezer. The grinder's down in that cabinet." He pointed to a set of double doors next to the oven.

"Then I'm all set, I guess. Go. I'll hold down the fort." She a cornflower blue mug with a yellow and pink floral design from the mug tree on the counter. As she poured the coffee, an uncomfortable thought occurred to her. *God, I hope this isn't Shelley's cup.*

If Chris noticed he didn't let on. "Okay, then, I'm off. I'll leave my cellphone on just in case. Give me a call if anything comes up."

After checking on her sleeping son, Carol settled into one of the overstuffed living room chairs, cradling the mug in her hands. A collage of framed family photos adorned the wall adjacent to the stairway. She fought back the urge to go over and look at them more closely. She knew what they were and didn't need to be reminded. That was her old life. She needed to stay focused on her new reality.

Halfway through her second cup, she heard footfalls on the carpeted stairway. Turning, she was surprised to see Jason coming down dressed in jeans, a sweatshirt, and sneakers. "Hey you. Shouldn't you be in bed?" She stood and walked over, hugging him gingerly.

He half-heartedly returned the hug. "I'm okay."

He's gotten so big. She reminded herself that he was a senior in high school. Next year he would traipse off to college and start his own life. She'd missed the opportunity to be a part of his past ten years. No, that wasn't right. She hadn't *missed* them. She'd wallowed in her own grief and thrown those years away for a drink.

"How about I fix you some breakfast?"

He shuffled his feet as he stood, staring at the floor. "I'm okay. Thanks." The words came out as a mumble. He put his hands in his pockets.

"Is something wrong? Are you feeling okay?"

"When is Dad going to be home?"

Ah, so that's it. He doesn't want me here. She couldn't really blame him. "He won't be that long, maybe a few hours."

His face changed. He locked gazes with her, the corners of his mouth turning up ever so slightly. His eyes sparkled. "Okay. Well, hmmm, I was wondering if it would be okay if I used your car for about an hour. I need to go out."

Carol stared at him in stunned silence. Of all the things she imagined, this was nowhere on the list. "Jason, you're not supposed to even be up and around that much. Going out? No. That's not a good idea." As an afterthought, she added, "Why do you need to go out?"

His smiling eyes flared with a touch of anger. "I'm fine. You can see, I'm doing good. I just need to see somebody. I promise, I'll come right back. It'll be okay."

"No, Jason. I can't let you do that." She started to invoke Chris' mandate but realized that he hadn't actually given her one. This was on her. "Who do you need to see? They could just come over here and see you."

His voice grew louder. Hands out of his pockets, he stood with arms crossed. "Mom, you can't keep treating me like I'm seven. I've grown up since… then. I need to go out. You don't have any right to keep me here."

His attack shocked her. "I'm not doing anything but trying to keep you safe." She moved closer to him and tried to hug him. He pulled away.

"I don't need anybody to keep me safe. And if I did, it wouldn't be you." He blinked and shook his head, as if trying to clear something from his mind. "I'm sorry, Mom. I didn't mean that. I just need to go out. Please."

Still reeling from the harsh words, Carol fought to stifle her emotions. *I'm the adult here.* "The answer is still no. You can say all the hurtful things you want. And yes, they do hurt. But there is nothing you can say that will change my mind. I'd rather have you alive and mad at me than…." She couldn't finish the sentence.

He spit his response out. "That's bullshit." He turned and stomped back up the stairs. She heard his bedroom door slam. In fact, Carol was sure that the neighbors probably heard it as well.

She sat in the chair staring at the window, seeing nothing. She unconsciously picked up her coffee. The cold feel of the ceramic mug changed her mind about drinking what was left. She set it down on the small table beside her chair.

After an hour of wringing her hands and alternating between sadness and anger, toward herself and her son, she stood and climbed the stairs. She knocked on the door and then opened it to find her son sitting on the bed apparently sending a text on his phone.

She sat beside him, allowing a brief silence to envelope them. "Jason, I'm sorry about all of this, really, I am. And I know you're angry at me, probably for a lot more than just today."

He shrugged and stared at the phone in his lap.

"You know, you're right about me not being the person to protect you. After all, it was me that let Jenny get away. And there's not a day that goes by that I don't hate myself for that. There's not a night that goes by that I don't cry and think of all the different things I might have done." She fought to keep the tears at bay.

"So, yes, I may be overprotective of you. I understand why that might upset you. I get that you may never forgive me for everything. That's part of what I have to live with. But whatever else you think, I love you and I will never let go of that." She put her arm around his shoulders and pulled him close. He didn't resist.

The sound of the front door opening interrupted the moment. A voice floated in from downstairs. "I'm home."

Carol closed her eyes and took a deep breath. "That would be your father. Perhaps you'll have better luck with him." She tightened her hug on him and then stood.

Jason sat there staring at his phone.

Downstairs, she retrieved her jacket from the hall closet. "You got done faster than I expected."

"Yeah. Things went pretty quick. Say, I was going to order a pizza for lunch. Want to join us?"

Her heart jumped at the idea—the three of them sitting around the table munching on unhealthy food and laughing. Then reality set in. "You know, I'd better head home. I need to do some shopping on the way." A lie.

He furrowed his brow. "Everything okay? You look pale. Things go okay with the kid?"

"Yes. Things went fine." She started to mention the disagreement but stopped herself. *What would be the point?*

"I guess I should have told you. He has a girlfriend now and I was worried that he might try to con his way out of the house. Anyway, glad it wasn't an issue."

Chapter 76

He relaxed in his lair. Despite the inner conflict, it was done. He had committed. Recollections of the passionate affairs with his lovers danced through his head. *So many wonderful evenings. Gone forever.* Except, of course, for the memories and souvenirs.

But not really gone *forever.* The notion of new beginnings intoxicated him. The research and the planning would take years. And what a delicious process it would be. A new home—somewhere drier, perhaps Arizona or New Mexico. A new approach to love, although he couldn't think of anything more perfect than what he had been doing for the past two years.

He stared at the sofa, which pulled out into the bed that he used for his encounters. The preparation for the special nights took hours—affixing the visqueen cover, fitting it with a disposable mattress pad and sheets, and placing a disposable area rug beneath it. This all seemed like a lot of work for that one moment. But he prided himself on the ability to think ahead. When he vacated, which he would be doing within a few years, he needed to leave a pristine space behind.

A part of him felt sorry for Sturgis—regret that the unfortunate, relatively unoffending soul had died taking the fall for him. On the other hand, a degree of fame and notoriety would accrue to the man that he really didn't earn. *I guess it all evens out in the end.*

If his mental timeline held, the FBI and the police would grapple with the inconsistencies of the case for a few months. But with no activity to motivate them, enthusiasm

and effort would wane. It was truly a win-win. They would
have solved their cases. He would have a new beginning.

Chapter 77

Carol settled into her desk on Monday morning not quite sure what to expect. The captain's intention to open a case on Sturgis as a homicide had percolated in her mind all weekend, or at least that part of it not dominated by her relationship with Jason.

The opening of the double doors into the bullpen roused her. She turned to see Ramirez shuffling toward her. "Ah, the malingerer returns." She stood, walked over, and hugged her partner. "How you doing?"

"Could use another week off. After all, I did get shot in the back."

She chortled her reply. "No, your vest got shot. You got bruised."

He took off his jacket and hung it up. "Details, details, Tullis. You spend too much time on the inane." Walking over to his desk, he sorted through a few pieces of paper that had been dropped into his inbox. "So, you solve all the murders while I was gone?"

Carol shuddered. She wondered if she should have talked to him before today. "Working on it." She glanced around the bullpen. Both Mulroney and Collins sat at their desks engrossed in whatever work sat on the top of their piles. *When's the shoe going to drop?*

The answer to that question came in the form of her boss' booming voice "Mulroney. Collins. Ramirez. Tullis. Come." But rather than remaining in his office, Peterman strode across the bullpen toward the door. "And bring your coffee," he shot over his shoulder. He carried a mug emitting wafts of steam in one hand and a thin file folder in the other.

Carol shot a glance at Mulroney and Collins, both of whom stared at the captain's back as he receded through the doors and down the hall. The two, almost as if of a single mind, turned toward Carol.

Mulroney arched his brow. Carol tried to summon up her best *I have no idea* shrug. But of course, she did have an idea. Instead, she stood, picked up a pad and pen, and followed the captain.

***

Carol settled into a comfortable chair in a small, well-appointed main floor conference room. The steel blue gray carpet appeared to be years newer than the floor covering in homicide. The table was simple, classic oak. The finish and the notable absence of coffee cup ring stains left no doubt that this was not the domain of the unwashed. And the tweed fabric chairs exuded luxury. *This must be where management hangs out.*

Peterman dropped the file folder on the table. "There is a quaint, old saying—into each life a little rain must fall. And today is your day, collectively that is." He glanced around at each of the participants, three of whom had no idea what was about to come their way.

He slid the folder across the table. "Detectives Mulroney and Collins. I'd like you to meet your new case—your highest priority case."

Collins opened the folder and the two of them stared down at the document. Mulroney broke the silence. "What's this? Looks like an autopsy report for Sturgis. Says here it was suicide." He glanced at Carol and then back to Peterman.

314

The captain's words came out matter-of-factly. "Yes. That's what it says. I read it before I handed it you." He picked up his mug and took a deep draught.

Mulroney furrowed his brow and shook his head. "And isn't this the perp from the serial killer case? I thought they were closing that." His eyes signaled complete and utter confusion.

"Yeah, that's what I understand." He looked down at his cup and adjusted its position on the table with both hands. "And maybe he is the perp. Whether he is or not, it may or may not be suicide. If it wasn't suicide, though, then it must have been a homicide, assuming of course that the unfortunate Doctor Sturgis was not the victim of an accidental shooting." His grin came across as mischievous, almost malicious. "And since we are in the Homicide Division, it is for us to decide. The task falls to the two of you." He stared across at the hapless detectives whom he had just ambushed.

Chapter 78

Carol expected the short-tempered, sharp-tongued Mulroney to push back against the somewhat vague presentation by the captain.

Peterman won the staring contest. Mulroney relented. "Okay."

"Glad you agree. So, I'm going to go through a few things before leaving you to your business. We are here in this room because I am certain that there are no ears other than our own here." He leaned into the table, staring at Mulroney. "I'll be blunt. Tullis and I have already concluded that neither of us is the killer. Ramirez didn't shoot himself in the back. And I'm just going to have to trust my gut that you two are not involved. Beyond that, I don't know. Take that to heart. Be careful who you talk to."

Mulroney's mouth hung open, his eyes wide. "Uh, what, you think that maybe someone in the division might be involved?" The words came out slowly as if the detective was navigating through a minefield.

Peterman tapped his fingers on the table nervously. "Let's just say that if Sturgis isn't our guy, then the only explanation for his untimely death would be that someone close to the investigation is the killer." He paused and narrowed his eyes. "Well, there could be other explanations but assuming the perp is close to us is the safest one."

Collins, who had remained quiet to this point, chimed in, "Why are Tullis and Ramirez here?" He glanced over at the pair. "No offense."

Ramirez grinned and shot back, "None taken."

Steven Hamilton

The captain looked at Carol and Tom before addressing Collins. "Good question. You can see from the case folder, that you're a little light on evidence. The best information available is in FBI custody. And given that you're about to rain on their parade, they're not going to be very forthcoming. Sex Crimes has some good background information but not much of the newer stuff. I'll call Captain Fredericks and secure their cooperation but don't expect a lot. They're going to want this case closed too. It's haunted them for two years and now they have someone they think is good for it."

He leaned back in his chair, gesturing toward Ramirez and Carol. "These two are going to be your best sources of information. I trust that you can all play nice together, so I'll go back to work." He stood to leave. "Make no mistake. You are collectively working in a swamp. A wrong move and you'll either step in quicksand or get eaten by an alligator. Keep me informed." And with that he was out the door.

Collins broke the silence. "Well that certainly was helpful." She rolled her eyes and drew her mouth into a tight line before turning to Carol. "I take it you can fill in the gaps."

Chapter 79

Carol presented her case to the other three, trying her best to be objective. She drew upon the evidence where she could and took care to be explicit where opinions and assumptions came into play. She jotted down notes as she went, mainly to serve as a checklist for herself.

Mulroney took notes furiously while Collins idly scratched at her earlobe. The two, plus Ramirez, took turns at the occasional question but, for the most part, they remained silent as she spoke.

Mulroney responded first. "I guess the part that concerns me is the assumption that someone close is involved. It seems that our options necessarily turn on that. It constrains how we gather information." He leaned back in his chair, hands laced behind his head. "Maybe we should start by trying to rule out different people so at least we know who we can go to."

"Maybe." A thousand things rummaged around in Carol's head, but she couldn't find the right way to express them.

Detective Collins looked up from her notes. "No."

Mulroney twisted his body around to face the woman sitting next to him. "What do you mean no? No to which part?"

She shook her head. "Look, guys, this perp or unsub or whatever you want to call him, has operated for two years running apparently without a mistake. I'd say that speaks to an attention to detail. If he's close to us, he will have made sure to cover every single track. Plus, we'd just end up chasing our tails if we try to start ruling people out one at a

318

time." She slid her chair closer to the table and sat with her forearms on the surface.

The words came out laced with intensity and purpose. "The key is in these last two events—the shooting of Irwin and Ramirez and the murder of Sturgis, if it was a murder. These took him out of his routine. Given what Tullis just described, these were each done with little planning. That means that our best chance of finding a chink in the armor will be there. For my money, we put these two incidents under a microscope. We look at every detail."

Ramirez looked up at the ceiling and shook his head. "But, like the captain said, the FBI has virtually all of the evidence on those and we're not in their club."

Collins replied, "Too true, Detective Ramirez, but we have something they don't. You're an eyewitness to Irwin's murder. You and Tullis were with Irwin the day before he was killed. Hell, you've spent more time with him here than anyone else. And Tullis was acquainted with Sturgis. She's the one that got the ball rolling on him. Whatever happened to put him on the killer's radar, I'd bet a paycheck that she's aware of it and just may not see it yet."

Carol considered Collins and Mulroney with newfound respect. They'd been dragged into a mess not of their own making. Yet they immediately immersed themselves as if on personal missions. "I agree. I do have one request, though. I'd like to see Sullivan pulled in on this. While I can't say with one hundred percent certainty that she's not a part of it, I'm well beyond a reasonable doubt."

Collins put the challenge on the table. "What makes you say that?"

"I'm not certain. Little things mostly. She's been battered on this for two years. And my observation is that she's taken it personally. Lately every time we spoke, she looked like defeat personified. It just seems to me that if she was a part of this perfect operation, she'd manage to keep on a more even keel."

Mulroney waded in. "Maybe that's an act."

In the past, she would have taken it personally. On this day, it seemed a logical part of the case discussion. "Good point. Could be." Carol looked around the table at the others who were clearly waiting on something else from her. "So, yes, it would be a risk. But she has access to information that we don't have. She can also bring continuity and a sense of the overall case. Ramirez and I only came in at the end. She can tell us how things proceeded, how the process unfolded, if you will. There could well be some hidden gems in that." She paused and leaned back in her chair. "Like I said, though, it's just my opinion and it falls to the two of you."

Mulroney, who had been leaning back in his chair, head tilted with a skeptical look in his eyes, interjected with a sudden and decidedly firm declaration. "Maybe. Actually, I do think it would be worth the risk." He turned to Collins, who shrugged without speaking.

He pulled his chair closer to the table and leaned in. "Okay. You got it. Talk to her and let's put a meeting together. Make sure, though, that she understands she's not to speak to anyone else about this."

She tried to picture what she was sure would be an awkward conversation with Sullivan. "Okay. I'll call her when we finish here."

Mulroney shook his head as he lifted his hands and gestured with one of his index fingers. "The key here is not in the evidence or even in the specifics of these two events. What we're looking for is in the sequencing, the events and circumstances leading up to the events. We need to revisit everything we know about what happened immediately preceding them." He let his hands drop palm down on the table.

The noise, combined with his words, stunned Carol. *Of course. How did I not see this?*

Chapter 80

Carol asked Sullivan out to lunch at a small deli located two blocks from the precinct. She used the time walking to lay out the situation to the bewildered Sex Crimes detective. "I'm sorry for doing it this way, Brenda, but I'm reluctant to discuss this any place where there could be listening ears. It may all sound paranoid right now but at least sit down with us. It'll make a lot more sense then." She continued to glance back over her shoulder to make sure that no one was within earshot. *God, this feels so stupid, like some kind of spy movie.*

Sullivan shook her head as she stared down at the sidewalk in front of her. "Geez, Tullis, I thought I was done with this." The words came out as thin and tired.

"Yeah. I know. Me too. And I need this to be over. But I'm sure that this is exactly what our unsub is counting on. I mean, think of the reaction at headquarters or in the mayor's office. Everyone wants this to be done. And if there's no killing in two weeks, well, you can imagine what route this will take."

Sullivan sighed as she walked. "Okay. What next?"

***

Carol gathered her thoughts. She visualized that epiphany from their last meeting and chose her words carefully. "So here it is. Mulroney, you nailed it. It's not in the evidence or even in the facts regarding the two recent incidents. It's about sequencing—what happened when? And thinking back on it, I have a pretty good idea who we're looking at. I just have to check one more thing. I believe the key to unlocking this lies with Doctor Hoskins. If we all agree, I'll contact her right away."

The other four stared at her, all sporting a completely dumbfounded look.

"Well, at least I have your attention. So, here's how I see it."

Chapter 81

Carol closed her eyes and mentally prepared for the conversation she dreaded. *How many times can I go to this well?* She hit the connect icon and waited.

"This is Doctor Hoskins." If the doctor had caller ID, she didn't let on.

"Good morning, Doctor. This is Carol Tullis. I'm afraid I'm in the unfortunate position of having to beg for another favor." She grimaced.

A hearty laugh came through. "Well, I have to say I love it when the police come begging. What can I do for you, Carol?"

Several run-throughs of rehearsal hadn't done that much good. A solid starting point for the discussion still eluded her. *Oh well, might as well dive in.* "I guess the best place to start is to tell you that I'm having some second thoughts about the serial killer case." She paused for a reaction.

"Oh?" A pause followed. "If I might ask, are you suggesting that Doctor Sturgis might not have been our man?"

Carol sighed. "I've been turning it over in my mind and I can't make all the pieces fit. I don't know. Do you ever get the sense that something's just not right?"

Another laugh. "Only about once a day. Seriously, though, yes. When you work with people and their emotional problems, there are always hidden issues and misdirects. Some days I go home feeling more than a little paranoid."

Carol smiled to herself. "I guess I'm in good company, then. First, I need to ask you if it would be possible to keep this private?"

"That seems to be your style, if you don't mind my saying. Every time you have something to discuss it's something you don't want to go beyond the two of us."

She leaned back in her chair and turned toward the window. She watched two birds in flight playing with each other, diving and climbing, avoiding and charging. "Yes, well, I'm afraid that this time it's a lot more serious than just me getting into trouble." She paused and took a deep breath. There would be no going back after this. "I just have the nagging sense that the real killer is someone close to the investigation. I don't know who to trust around here. I mean, just about anyone I confide in could be the one. I think that you may have something that will help me narrow the field, but I need to do this without any department involvement."

After a brief period of silence, Hoskins responded, "That's a lot to digest, I have to admit. But I guess this really all depends on what you need from me."

The hardest part was past. "Actually, not a whole lot. I think that what I need is in your profiling notes from the child serial killer case from ten years ago."

"Hmmm. What do you expect to find?"

"I'm not sure, but I believe I'll know it when I see it."

"You should have a copy of the report in the case file." The words came out as cautious but curious.

"I know. I've read it. But I'd like to see your original notes. Looking at everything we've found recently, I'm pretty sure I can make a connection. If you don't mind, I could drive up there this afternoon. Shouldn't take me but a few minutes if they're handy."

Silence. "Carol, you know I'd love to help you, but I just need to know a bit more about what you're after before I open my personal notes to you. I hope you understand. I keep these very close. When I write them, I don't filter my thoughts or hedge my words. The end result is that there are often things that, while they are helpful for me, I wouldn't necessarily want anyone else to see."

Carol tried to reassure her. "I completely understand. I give you my word that I will keep the material in confidence. And you'd be right there with me so if there was something that you prefer I not see, you can intervene. Honestly, I'll be in and out before you know it."

The tone turned suspicious. "And you haven't discussed this with anyone else? I mean, this is just some personal hunch you have?"

"I know it seems a stretch and it may well be a long-shot. In the end, there may be nothing there and the case will close. But I just feel that I owe it to Doctor Sturgis to try."

She heard a deep sigh. "Fine. But I don't keep my old notes here. I maintain a private therapy practice. My office is in University Heights, down in Seattle. All of my archives are there. Let me check my calendar. Let's see, I have a six o'clock with a client. If you show up about seven fifteen, he should be gone. I have a dinner engagement downtown at eight, so you'd have about twenty to thirty minutes. Otherwise, we can try for another time."

Carol felt the tension lift from her shoulders. "Thank you, Doctor Hoskins. I really appreciate this."

Chapter 82

The doctor's directions proved accurate and easy to follow. Carol entered the older but upscale building at ten after seven. The tiled entry gave way to a lobby with lush sapphire carpet. Hallways extended to either side of the single elevator.

In contrast to the age of the building, the elevator appeared to be the latest technology. The smooth stainless-steel doors opened with barely a swoosh, releasing a gentle waft of cool air onto her face. This didn't appear to be the kind of place to which ordinary people would bring their problems. *She must have some well-heeled clients.* As she entered the car, she noticed that her destination was on the top floor.

Once in the ninth-floor hallway, Carol encountered a mechanical room—double doors with an "Authorized Personnel Only" sign affixed. The next door was unmarked, most likely a maintenance or supply closet, she figured. Turning the corner, she found the right office—904. The door was solid wood, in contrast to many other office doors that had translucent glass windows. The name plate confirmed the location—Margaret Hoskins, Ph.D.

She tried the door but found it locked. She pressed the "Call" button on a small white plastic box mounted on the wall beside the door.

The apparatus squawked to life. "Carol?"

She moved over closer and responded. "Yes." A buzzer sounded and she heard a click in the door handle mechanism. Carol pushed the door open and entered a plush well-appointed office space. A large Hamadan Persian area rug with a geometric pattern containing indigo blues, brick reds, and subtle browns dominated the area, covering a deep maroon carpet. The art on the walls, mostly limited-edition prints, complemented the floor covering.

Taking stock of the surroundings, her eyes focused on the door locking controls. The plastic white box was larger than the one in the hallway and included a small screen that displayed the area just outside the door. "Nice security feature. Wouldn't think you'd need it in this building, though."

Hoskins, who stood over near a bookcase, laughed in response. "Yes, well, I do admit that the clientele frequenting this building aren't usually a problem. Still, with the events of the last two years, I find myself more than a little paranoid sometimes. It can be especially unnerving when I'm here alone at night."

"You know, I've been meaning to tell you—I love your scarves. You always seem to manage the perfect color combination."

Hoskins touched the end of the scarlet and cornflower blue silk material that clung to her neck. A questioning look passed over her eyes as a cloud might momentarily obscure the sun. The look vanished as quickly as it had appeared. "Thank you. I'm afraid that, if truth be told, they're mostly utilitarian. At my age, scarves hide a multitude of sins." She chuckled and shook her head before her demeanor grew serious. "I have to tell you, I'm tired. I had hoped that this mess was over."

"Well, I think one way or the other, with what I find tonight, it ends soon. I'm with you, though, I was hoping it was done." Carol walked over to a small credenza. "This is beautiful." She picked up a small statue of a woman holding a child. The base had an engraved plate.

Doctor Margaret Hoskins
In Recognition
Outstanding Contributions to Adult Mental Health
American Psychological Association

"Impressive." She held the statue in front of her. "I'm not sure why, but somehow I thought that your specialty was children or adolescents."

"I started out with kids. But in the end, I couldn't handle it. Their problems are complex and, to make matters worse, it's sometimes hard to tell which ones are real problems and which are just the normal growing pains of teenagers. I lost entirely too much sleep over that. Adults are simpler. They have problems. They either work on them or they don't. Either way, I get paid."

Pointing toward the statue in Carol's hand, she continued, "As for that thing, don't let it fool you. They give those away like popcorn to keep us paying our dues. Damn marketers." She gestured toward a padded chair with wooden arms situated beside a small work table. "Please have a seat. My client just left, and I haven't had a chance to dig the file out yet."

Carol set the award beside a potted plant on the table next to the chair. "This is a nice plant. These pink blossoms are beautiful." From her seat, she reached over and touched one of the leaves.

"That's a Christmas Cactus. It blooms this time of year. Ironic that it blooms in the winter, but it does add a bit of cheer to an otherwise dark season.

She turned toward a cabinet with glass doors. "I'm going to fix myself a drink. Sometimes I think I need the medication more than the people with the problems." Holding a crystal bottle three-quarters full of an amber liquid, she turned her head to face Carol. "Can I offer you one. All I have is Scotch and, unfortunately, no ice. I don't have occasion to offer drinks very often up here."

Carol stared at the bottle. The golden liquid sloshed gently as the bottle moved. She could taste the Scotch in her mind, robust and biting. She could almost feel its smooth, warm comfort as it slid down her throat. She knew beyond a doubt that she would breathe in the aroma as soon as the doctor removed the cork. She barely breathed. "Uh, well, sure, I guess. Just one."

Hoskins took another crystal glass from the cabinet. With her back to Carol, she poured the drinks, talking over her shoulder. "It won't take me a minute to get that file. Hopefully we can wrap this up and I can be eating salmon by nine." She walked over and offered the drink.

"Thanks." Carol closed her eyes and breathed deep. The smooth but strong aroma filled her senses. Her hand trembled as she lifted the glass to her mouth and felt the cool liquid against her upper lip.

Chapter 83

With her forearms resting on the arms of the chair, Carol watched the hand holding the empty tumbler relax. The heavy glass descended in slow motion, bouncing off one of the chair's protruding wooden legs with a distinctive clunk. It landed soundlessly on the plush carpet and tumbled over to its final resting place about two feet in front of her.

She shifted her gaze without moving her head—the tumbler, the decanter on the hutch, and the door into which Doctor Hoskins had disappeared. Carol blocked out the fear and forced herself to assess the situation.

"Detective? Is everything alright in there?" The familiar voice floated in from the other room. After a brief silence, Doctor Hoskins appeared in the doorway, her right hand behind her back. "Carol?" She looked down at the empty glass on the floor and then up at Tullis. A smile lit up her face. "My, you were a thirsty girl."

Carol answered with her eyes—rage and fear. Confusion would have been added to the mix, but she knew exactly what had happened.

Hoskins strolled into the room, allowing her right arm to drop to her side. "I guess I won't be needing this after all." She placed a revolver, a thirty-eight by the look of it, on the hutch alongside the liquor container. Shuffling over to where Carol sat rigid in the chair, she reached down inside the detective's coat and removed the nine-millimeter Glock handgun. "And you'll excuse me if I take custody of this. I know that you wouldn't be reaching for it, but I think we'll both feel a little safer if I just put it over here with mine. Okay?"

Turning, she leaned back on the cabinet. "As you can tell, the naelosaxitoxin has kicked in. You might as well relax. We've got so much to talk about, you and I." Hoskins turned and left the room, speaking over her shoulder as she went. "If you don't mind, I'm going to slip into something a little more comfortable."

Coming from the other room, Hoskins' tone was suddenly lower-pitched. "As perfect as things have been, I admit that I've often longed to have a forthright, honest discussion of this case with an associate without all of the subterfuge." The sound of drawers opening and closing punctuated the words. "Of course, with you not being able to speak, it will unfortunately be a one-sided conversation. Still, as a skilled therapist, I'm pretty good at reading emotions, if I do say so myself."

When Hoskins re-appeared, she, or rather he, was not Hoskins. A trim man with a bald head appeared in the doorway through which the somewhat frumpy female doctor had disappeared. He wore a pair of black fleece pants and a gray tee-shirt. The prominent Adam's apple confirmed the true purpose of all those beautiful scarves.

"Yes, we have much to discuss. But where are my manners? Introductions are in order." He dragged over a chair identical the one in which Carol was seated.

He rubbed his face with a towelette. "I've never understood women's fascination with makeup. And I have to admit I'm always glad to get out of that body padding." Tossing the used wipe into the trash can, which sat about three feet away, he folded his hands in his lap.

"I am, or rather used to be, Paul Cheney. Frankly, I think I'm better as Marge Hoskins. In fact, I'm a better Marge

Hoskins than the original." He arched his eyebrows. "Oh yes, there was a former Doctor Hoskins. What a cow and certainly not the brightest of the lot. We became acquainted, she and I, when she was my Ph.D. advisor at the University of Pennsylvania." He paused and looked over at the bookcase, apparently lost in thought.

"To say that we didn't get along would be an understatement. She didn't like my dissertation subject. She didn't like my literature review. She didn't approve of my research methods or my writing in general. You know, come to think of it, I don't think she liked me at all."

He turned back toward Carol and grinned. "Between the two of us, and I hope this doesn't offend your sensibilities, I think the old lady needed a good stiff dick on a regular basis. But, one look at her and you could tell that it wasn't going to happen. I would have obliged her myself, but, you know, there are some things that even I won't do."

Carol closed her eyes and tried to will an end to this encounter. A part of her wanted to shut out his words. She knew, though, that everything depended on her paying attention.

"Where was I, oh yes, Ph.D. advising. Can you imagine that an institution as reputable as UPenn would stoop to employing someone of her limited intellectual capacity? But, being a professional, I persevered. With less than a year to go, that bitch decided to take a sabbatical. Without a thought to anyone but herself, she said that she would *pass me off* to a colleague." Hoskins or Cheney or whoever he was, stood and began to pace, hands behind his back.

"And that twerp of a colleague was worse than Hoskins, if you can believe that." He stopped and turned toward her, his arms in front of him with his fingers outstretched, "That was the final straw."

Carol checked the clock. Barely ten minutes had passed.

He resumed his pacing. "And so, she left for the great American southwest. She was going to do research on mental health issues among the indigenous population there. How stupid. How pointless." He fell silent as he marched back and forth. His head nodded occasionally, and his jaw clenched.

He turned to Carol and seemed to relax. "And so, I accompanied her, at a distance of course. And it was in a small town in west Texas that we connected again. You know, I quite forget the name of that town. Anyway, it was in that place that I became Doctor Hoskins and the former version of her took up a richly deserved resting place in a shallow grave, destined to sleep in peace undisturbed for millennia."

He returned to his chair, folded his hands, and leaned forward, eyes wide. "Surely you will appreciate the genius of this. A simple letter of resignation freed me from the burden of her previous employer."

Carol wondered how long he would continue to ramble. Would he lose track of time? She fought off the urge to withdraw. She needed to stay focused.

"After that, it was mostly mechanical. Between you and me, the hardest part was learning to dress. That kind of galled me to begin with. You know, most people think that cross-dressers are all gay. Not true. Not true at all. Some men just find sexual satisfaction in wearing women's clothing. As for me, I never enjoyed it. But I'm professional and disciplined enough to pull it off." He reached up and rubbed his cheek, which still had vestiges of blush.

Carol forced herself to look at his face. She saw it now. Although he was clean-shaven, she could picture the beard and mustache. And with that, she saw the image contained on the artists' renderings.

He leaned back in his chair, crossing his legs and allowing his folded hands to rest in his lap. "Taking over someone's identity isn't as hard as you might think. It's all one step at a time. Use the existing driver's license to get a post office box. Postal workers can't be bothered with attention to detail. They never even looked at the photo on the license."

His eyes widened and his smile deepened. "Oh, let me tell you the best part. I was able to get access to all of her financial accounts, including her retirement fund. It's funny what someone will tell you when they think it will save their life." He shook his head. "Stupid woman. She should have known better."

"I got a new driver's license, with my likeness on it. I renewed the passport with an updated photo. I love working with bureaucrats. Just fill in the form and give them money. You can get anything you want. Once I got all of that done, it was simply a matter of picking up my professional life again. I started slow, teaching at a community college down in Arizona. They were only too happy to get a Ph.D. psychologist with both teaching and research experience. From there, I just re-built my career, one position at a time. Sadly, the original Hoskins had no friends or family. No one even missed her. How pathetic."

Cheney stood and went over to a file cabinet. Opening a drawer, he pulled out several bound documents. "See these?

This is all research that I, the new and improved Doctor Hoskins, published. She'd be proud of me, don't you think?"

Taking his seat again, he leaned forward, his hands resting on the arms of his chair, and grinned. His eyes sparkled with excitement. "Now that the formalities are out of the way, we can get on with it. There's lots to tell and we have, I'm afraid, limited time."

Chapter 84

Focus. Stay with him. Carol watched Cheney's every move. She concentrated mostly on his eyes, which reflected what seemed to be a manic state of mind. His gaze flitted about the room but always returned to her.

"Excuse me for a moment," he shot over his shoulder as he eased through the door into the other room. He returned a minute later with a large sheet of visqueen. "I hope you don't mind if I work while we talk. The rug," he gestured toward the area carpet, "generally works well to keep things clean, but I'm going to just throw some of this plastic around the edges to, you know, make sure." He began laying the covering around the periphery of the Hamadan carpet.

"I'm sure that the delicious irony is not wasted on you. The best minds in law enforcement, even the FBI, couldn't see what was directly in front of them. And, just to be straight for the record here, I never lied to them. The profile I gave you was dead on, pardon the pun."

Carol allowed herself a quick glance at her surroundings. Her weapon sat on the hutch next to his revolver. The empty glass tumbler rested on the floor where she'd dropped it. The award statue sat on the table to the right of her along with the Christmas Cactus. She felt as if all of these inanimate objects stared at her, waiting for instructions.

"Being the diligent and curious detective that you are, I'm sure there are questions you'd like answered. Pity that you can't ask them. In the interest of professional dialogue, though, I'll try and anticipate a few of them. First, why kill Irwin? A fair question, I suppose. After all, I didn't know him personally. He seemed harmless enough, although between you and me, maybe a tad on the dull side. No, his great sin was that he suspected me. The comment on the earlier research paper published by my predecessor clearly signaled his suspicion. I simply could not let that go unaddressed."

He paced across the room, hands clasped behind his back. On reaching the far wall, he turned. "Oh, and the Sturgis thing. I hope that you noticed the skill with which I pulled that one off. Anticipating the investigative skill of the FBI, I took care not to use a chemical restraint."

"I managed to *bump into him* at a bookstore I knew he frequented. I fed his ego by asking about his book. And, well, one thing led to another and we ended up chatting at his place."

He paused, looking as though considering what he had just said. "Strictly professional, of course—nothing sexual. We chatted, Ben and I, for a bit. After finishing my drink, I excused myself to use the bathroom. As I returned, his focus remained on the glass in front of him. It took only a second for me to put the gun to his head from behind and pull the trigger. He never saw it coming. Oh, I know what you're thinking. There was no powder residue on his hand. And that would indeed seem to be a problem. But I have complete faith in the laziness of the police. All the little inconsistencies will fade to nothing as they find themselves with no more victims. Their attention span is somewhat akin to that a of toddler, wouldn't you say?"

Cheney cleared his throat with a subtle cough. "So, I'm confident that within a few months, Doctor Sturgis and this whole affair will be in the past. But let me say, just to clear this up, that the problem with your work—and when I say 'your work,' I'm referring to the collective *you*. You allowed yourselves to be seduced by the technical details. Yes, yes, the rohypnol and the naelosaxitoxin. You cataloged the plastic cover and the silk cloth. You analyzed it, discussed it, and ran the scenario over and over. But you always came to the same empty, dead-end conclusions." He smiled with what looked like a fatherly smile from an elderly minister or priest. "You were simply asking the wrong questions, my dear. You should have been asking, 'how does a strange man get close enough to a woman to spike her drink?' You might have wondered how, even with a compliant woman, how does he get her out of the establishment with no one, not a single soul, ever noticing." He shook his head and sighed.

He's right about that. Carol thought back to early conversations with her captain. *We need to look at the problem from different perspectives.* She knew going in that they were caught up in tunnel vision. Yet she'd fallen right into the swamp with the rest of them.

"But now you have clarity, right? Two women talking and leaving together draws no interest at all, especially from bored, self-absorbed baristas." He lifted his right arm and gestured with his index finger. "As for the women themselves, this had to be handled carefully. For all of their similarities, they were all different in so many ways. This put my skills and insight to the test. I had to gain their confidence within a minute or so."

Carol understood. After all, she had also been taken in by this sensitive, intelligent, caring psychopath. She had been in good company, though. The entire task force and even the FBI had bought into her, or him as it turned out.

"I do wish that we had the time for me to go through each and every one of them. Unfortunately, I'm going to have to generalize. Otherwise, we just won't finish this. I guess I'd have to say that the best approach was always *the woman in fear* routine. What with all of the danger these days, I feared being out in public alone. I convinced them that we'd both be safer if we left together. You know, strength in numbers."

Why didn't I see it earlier? She glanced at the clock— nearly twenty-five minutes had passed. *How much longer?*

"How did I get them out of there without being seen? Oh, that's easy. It just took some planning. I picked spots with no surveillance. Actually, that was always my first decision point. Find the location and then work backwards from that. Once outside, my compliant partners followed my direction without argument. I drove them to, well, to this very office where I told them that they'd had a dizzy spell and nearly fainted. A glass of water, a cup of tea, or a stiff drink to help them regain their composure—that sealed the deal. Once the toxin kicked in, I carried them back into my special area. What went on there was personal and private, so I hope you'll understand if I'm not explicit. After all, the best intimate stories leave much to the imagination."

Carol fought off the inclination to envision what went on *in the back room*. After all, that was not going to help her here. *Thirty minutes down.*

He shifted in the chair, rubbing his chin. "And this leads to the question of how I selected my lovers. And it's a complicated question. As you know, they were not beauties, at least not in the traditional physical sense. But they all had beautiful spirits. And, I guess the thing that linked them all is that they all wanted love in their lives. Even the married women longed for something more, something that had slipped from their relationships or was perhaps never there.

They all found their way to coffee shops or bistros where they sat alone, consuming whatever was their pleasure, fantasizing about what they were missing."

Cheney shrugged. "I gave them what they wanted. Although our time together was brief, the love that we experienced was more intense, more beautiful than anything they'd ever known. I know it seems harsh to end their lives but it was only right. Nothing that came after would ever measure up. They departed this life on a positive, upbeat note."

The room fell silent. She could hear the ticking of the clock that hung on the wall between two pieces of art. She watched the second-hand jump from one mark to the next. Her mind wandered back to the older analog clocks that she'd seen—the ones where the second hand swept in a continuous motion. *Everything is twitchy now.*

He stood and walked over to the hutch where both weapons sat. Reaching up into the cabinet, he retrieved the decanter of Scotch and poured himself another drink. "I'd offer you one but, well, you understand." He raised his glass toward her as if in a toast.

"I think that should answer the most pressing questions." He paused, eyes widening. "Oh yes, one other thing. The move from children to adults." He stopped, his eyes narrowing as he considered her. "No, that's for later."

He stopped talking and stood still, looking intently at her. "But, enough about those other women. I think it's time you and I spoke about your beautiful daughter."

Chapter 85

*J*enny stood in the center of the room pouting. *"Why does Jason have to go?"*

"I told you, honey, Daddy is busy today so we can't leave your little brother here alone. Besides, think about how much fun he'll have with us."

Her intense sky-blue eyes sparkled, although the emotion conveyed seemed a mix of anger and disappointment. "But you said it was just you and me. It's our day out." The words came out as a plea.

"Next time. I promise. Just you and me."

Jenny lowered her head and drew her mouth into a tight line. "Okay."

***

"Carol?" His eyes widened and he shook his head. "I believe you were ignoring me." He continued after a brief pause. "Or, maybe you were reminiscing. Were you thinking about our Jenny?"

Rage built upon rage. She clenched her jaw and launched her most hateful arrows from her eyes. He had no right to even speak the name.

His shoulders sagged as he tilted his head. "Yes. Of course, you were. I've long wanted to talk to you about her. You might be surprised to know that Jenny was the reason I took a break and made the change to adults." He shifted in his seat and rubbed his chin. "After I ...."

Carol's thoughts blocked the rest of his words.

***

"Ewww, gross." Jenny pointed at her brother. "Mom, I told you."

He had chocolate smeared all over his face and on his light green tee shirt. He licked his fingers, apparently oblivious to his sister's revulsion.

"Jason. I told you to finish that candy at the table. Look at you." He stood still while she took a napkin from her purse, licked it, and started wiping his face.

"Mom. Don't do that. Yuck." Jenny's voice distracted Carol as she tried to focus on cleaning her son's face. The shirt was a lost cause. Maybe it would come clean in the wash.

"Just hold on a minute, Honey. I'll get done with your brother and then we'll go look at those shoes." She made a quick pass with the napkin over the hair on the side of his head.

"I'm going to look at the shoes. They're just right over there." The volume abruptly decreased signaling that she had turned away.

"No, Jenny. You wait there. I'll be done in a minute." She continued to wipe.

"I'll be right back." The words faded.

***

"Detective Tullis, that's rude and disrespectful. Here I am trying to pay homage to our beautiful young girl, and you keep phasing out on me. What would she think? Tsk." He shook his head and pursed his lips.

Carol looked down at her hands, resting limply on the arms of the chair. How she longed to wrap those hands around his neck and squeeze, watching the life drain from his eyes. She wondered whether he would beg for life.

"Like I said, after my night with Jenny, I tried with one other young girl, but it wasn't the same. I realized that it would never be the same. Our beloved young lady spoiled me for any others." He sighed as he appeared to collect his thoughts. "The other thing is that, you know, children are so precious, but they lack the ability to understand these kinds of things. I could see her fear. I could smell the terror on her as her eyes darted wildly about. Back then, I didn't use any form of chemical restraint. She called for you to come save her. She never understood that I was there to give her love."

Carol went white-hot with rage. Still her arms rested on the chair.

"It may be hard for you to hear this, but it all happened for the best, you know. If not for me, she would have lost her innocence within a few years. Some clumsy high school kid would have had her in the back seat of a car leaving her with nothing but a sticky mess to show for it. At least with me, she knew what true love was like, which is more than most women experience."

***

"Jenny? Honey, where are you?" People shuffled here and there, browsing the shelves. But no small girl with shining blonde hair.

"Jenny!" Panic seeped in. Looking frantically around. "Jenny" Louder. A shout. A scream. "Jenny get back here right now."

A middle-aged man with a blue vest and some kind of name tag approached her. "Ma'am, is everything okay?"

"Jenny!" The knot in her chest tightened. Her eyes widened. "My daughter. She was right there. I was…." She pointed to her son. Surely the man understood. "Jenny!" She bolted around the man and ran from aisle to aisle screaming for her daughter.

Something crept into her mind uninvited. No, that couldn't be. Not Jenny. Please, God, not my Jenny. The thorn dug deeper into her heart and refused to leave. "Jenny!"

***

"I can see this isn't working." Cheney exhaled and shook his head. "I thought you were stronger than this. I've so wanted to talk to you about her. But I can see that you're upset. So, out of respect, I'll leave this."

Carol focused. If only the arrows from her eyes could kill. She would relish seeing his repulsive body punctured and shredded as she fired volley after volley.

He leaned his head back, closed his eyes. "And so, that leaves us only one more subject—you and me."

Chapter 86

Carol checked the time again—forty minutes, give or take, had passed. The conversation, or rather his ramblings, seemed to be headed for a conclusion.

Cheney sat, a benevolent smile on his face along with a few traces of residual make-up. "Yes, Carol, you and me. Please don't take this as an affront, but surely you know that you are not beautiful, at least in the way society tends to define beauty. But I just can't tell you how many nights I've thought about what it would be like with you. I've longed for the intimacy that we might have shared under different circumstances. You are a curious mix of pain and passion. I assure you, it would have been a night that we would both remember." He stood and strolled over and set his empty glass on the hutch.

A wave of revulsion swept over her. The knot in her stomach tightened at the thought of his hands on her. She shifted her attention—the clock, the guns, and the statue.

Still standing, he leaned back on the hutch as he faced her. "Sadly, owing to the circumstances, I think it best that we keep our relationship professional. I hope you understand."

Then his demeanor turned serious. "I can't, of course, leave you alive. As you've no doubt figured out, I'm making another change. The weather up here is getting to be too much for me. I have complete faith that the others who are working on this will ultimately accept young Sturgis as the culprit. You, on the other hand, are just too inquisitive for your own good. I knew the first day we spoke that your grief and devotion to our Jenny would prevent you from letting go. That coupled with your intelligence, well, you're just too

346

much of a risk. And let's be honest now. You understood the scarves. Not many women have Adam's apples." He burst out in laughter. "I fear it was in your eyes, my dear. You simply do not have a good poker face. Yes, indeed, you are far too great a risk."

You have no idea how much of a risk I can be. I will rip your throat out. She began to picture the ways in which she could kill him. With each vision came the realization that whatever she could do would never be enough.

"No, I'm confident that the others will never put the pieces together. Even your disappearance won't surprise many. You are, after all, highly unstable and saddled with unbearable grief. Oh, they will ask questions. An investigation will be initiated. But, like many other cases, it will ultimately move to the back burner and then to the archives. After all, putting things in the closet to keep them from view is the easiest way to deal with them, don't you think?"

"But I promise you this, on my honor, Carol. I will not dishonor your body. I won't put you on display like the others. I have a nice secluded spot picked out for you. You will rest in peace and privacy for eternity." He began to pace again, hands behind his back. He turned and looked at her, his eyes shining. "And you know, you will be with Jenny in spirit. She's waiting for you, I'm sure. The two of you will have so much catching up to do. I so wish that I could be there with you."

Cheney shook his head and turned toward the hutch, opening a drawer. When he turned around, he held a scalpel in his hand. "I give you my word that your passing will not be painful or prolonged." He glanced up at the clock. "And

347

yes, sadly, our time together is coming to an end. The toxin, as you know, does not last forever. In just a moment, we'll need to part ways. I hope that you can hear what I'm about to say in the spirit in which I'm saying it. It will be easier for you if you relax and close your eyes. I will gently tilt your head back. A flick of the hand and in that instant, you will leave this world—no pain and no worry." He smiled warmly and tilted his head to the side. "I hate goodbyes. But change is inevitable." He walked slowly toward her. "I'm afraid it's time, my dear."

Chapter 87

Carol watched his movement. One step at a time. The knot inside tightened. Her jaw clenched. She closed her eyes for an instant and then opened them again.

Time stretched out—a fraction of a second seemed like an hour. Cheney moved in slow motion. Her eyes wandered to the weapons on the hutch, then to him, and to her hands resting on the arms of the chair.

Three steps away now. The clock ticked. The second hand jumped with rhythm marking the passing of time. The scalpel in his hand drew her eyes. He raised it in front of him. She could swear she saw a brief flash of light reflect off the blade. Another step closer.

He angled to her left. Only a single step separated them now. He continued to move, his image disappearing from her peripheral vision.

A calm almost surrealistic peace settled over her. She breathed deep. Three. Two. One. Now!

As if on its own, her right arm shot out and grabbed the statue. In a slow-motion action sequence, her body launched from the chair. She whirled. Her left arm swung around to meet the right one. She clutched the statue like a baseball bat. Her nemesis came into view.

Cheney's eyes grew wide—disbelief, panic, inevitability. His right arm moved the scalpel higher. His left arm started up in what looked like a defensive move. All in vain.

Carol focused every ounce of rage and grief into that one spot where both hands held the statue. With momentum of the whirl, she connected. The impact jolted her arms.

His head snapped to the side. Blood erupted from his left temple.

She allowed her arms to follow through with the swing before dropping the statue. Having no idea whether she'd killed him or not, Carol covered the distance to the hutch in what seemed like a single bound. The Glock in her hand, she turned to face him.

Yes, I put a round in the chamber. She clicked off the safety. Staring down the barrel, she saw Cheney waiver. His eyes still wide but alternately focusing and rolling back in his head. Blood covered the entire left side of his face. He crumbled. The scalpel fell silently to the plush carpet. He dropped to his hands and knees. His right arm buckled, and he rolled over,

Carol stepped to him and kicked the scalpel away, never taking her gun off him. "Stay down. Don't move."

Cheney ended up laying back against a bookcase facing her. A wild, almost insane grin spread across his face. "Go ahead. Do it." His eyes rolled back in his head briefly before he regained focus. His head lolled to the side. Blood dripped onto his tee-shirt.

The familiar grip of the Glock called to her. *He has a gun nearby.* The revolver sat an easy four paces away. Her palms sweated.

"You can't do it. You don't have what it takes. I took your daughter and even now you can't summon the courage."

Carol felt herself increasing the pressure on the trigger. Was he looking over at the revolver? Could he make it that far before she fired?

"I thought better of you." He reached up and wiped his mouth with his bare arm. "When I had our Jenny at the end, she called out for you. She begged for you to come save her. Her eyes pleaded with me. But did I waiver? Not for an instant. And now, look at you, nothing but an emotional train wreck." He shook his head.

Time froze. He looked down the barrel of her Glock, safety off and pressure on the trigger. Everything came down to this.

No, Mommy. Please don't.

Carol roused from her trance. She exhaled and shook her head as she became aware of her weariness. "No wonder you couldn't get your degree—lousy research. I'm a recovering alcoholic. You should have tried coffee. But hopefully your Christmas Cactus enjoyed the Scotch."

The contempt in his eyes turned to hatred and rage. "Go fuck yourself. You're like all of them. Go ahead. If you're too chicken shit to do it for yourself, then do it for Jenny." He glared defiantly through the blood.

Then, she felt her body relax. "Too much paperwork. You're not worth it." She back stepped toward the door, never taking her eyes off him. Reaching behind her, she felt for the control box and pressed the unlock button.

A buzzer sounded and the door burst open. In poured the cavalry. "You okay?" Sullivan moved quickly into the room, weapon pointed at Cheney. Behind her came the rest of the party—Collins, Mulroney, and Ramirez.

"You guys get all that?" With her left hand she felt for the microphone planted in her bra.

"Clear as a bell." Ramirez shot her a grin.

Carol lowered her weapon and re-set the safety. She felt the weight rise from her shoulders. "Can you all do the honors?" She trudged over and dropped into the seat she had occupied for the past hour.

Mulroney glanced over at her. "Good collar, Tullis."

She laughed. "Not my collar. I'm just the hired help. You guys fight over it."

Chapter 88

By the time Carol got home, it was nearly one. The weariness, both physical and emotional, had set in hours ago. She entered the dark house, flipping on the kitchen light as she made her entrance from the garage.

Her coat hung up, keys in the basket, and weapon unloaded and stored, she pondered—*bedroom or living room?* She was exhausted but strangely didn't feel sleepy. She stared at her landline phone sitting in its charging cradle on the kitchen counter. *I can tell him in the morning, or....*

She plopped down into the large, cushioned chair, phone to her ear, and waited in the darkened living room. Chris slept soundly, if memory served. The light from the street lamp made its way through the barren tree branches and the opening in the opaque curtain to cast a small sliver of light on the floor—a light in the darkness.

The voice that answered sounded groggy. "Hello?" A question rather than a greeting.

Carol closed her eyes. "Hi Chris. It's me." She kept her voice low as if to avoid waking anyone at this ungodly hour of the night.

"Carol?" The word came out crisp with a tinge of alarm. "Is everything okay?"

She sighed. "Yeah. I'm fine. Look, I'm sorry to bother you at this hour." An image flashed of her ex-husband sitting up in bed while Shelley took her arms from around him and rolled over. "I wanted you to hear this from me first." She paused. "Chris, we got the guy."

A tentative question followed a moment of silence. "You mean the guy...?"

"Yeah. Him. We got him tonight." She pondered the words that had recycled through her mind for the past few hours.

"But I thought that you already...." The voice sounded confused.

"The FBI thought they had it figured out. They were wrong. But no mistake tonight. He's the one."

"Are you okay?" The tone shifted from confusion to concern.

She considered the question. *Am I okay?* "Yeah, I think I am. I can give you the details later. I just needed to tell you tonight. That's all. I'll call you tomorrow."

Carol disconnected and continued to sit, staring out the window. Out of all that had happened that night, one thing tormented her—the voice.

She didn't count herself as a religious or even spiritual person. What little inclination in that area she had experienced earlier in life vanished with the loss of her daughter. But the voice. Was it possible? *No. It was my mind playing tricks.*

Her eyes closed, tears gathering at the corners. *No, this is stupid.* Or not. "Jenny, honey, are you here?"

Silence. Nothing.

Just as she thought. The stress and excitement of the moment. The adrenaline. All of it conspiring to deceive her.

But a wave of warmth, of love, swept over her.

***

After not falling asleep until nearly four, she wasn't surprised when she awoke an hour late. She opted for a quick shower while the coffee brewed and then grabbed a cup to go on the way out the door. With a bit of fancy driving and discrete traffic law violations, Carol managed to arrive at work only thirty minutes late.

As she parked her car and started the journey to the bullpen, she wondered what awaited her. Relations with her fellow detectives had improved but she was still no one's best friend. Would they stand and cheer for her? Would they ignore her? Did they even care?

Pushing her way through the double doors, she did a quick survey of the room. A few of the inhabitants remained focused on whatever they were doing. Most, though, glanced up. Some smiled and waved. A couple nodded. It felt right. She was no longer a freak show.

She arrived at her desk to find Ramirez intently typing. He looked up and greeted her. "Nice of you to grace us with your presence." A grin cracked the faux stern look on his face. "How does it feel?"

Opening her large desk drawer, she dropped her purse in. "Hey, you're lucky I showed up at all." She dropped into her chair and hit the power button on her computer.

A familiar booming voice echoed through the bullpen. "Tullis. Come."

"I am summoned." Carol pushed herself out of the chair and trudged to the captain's office. Knocking on the doorframe, she paused at the threshold.

As he raised his coffee cup to his lips with his right hand, he gestured her in with his left. Setting the cup down, he pointed to the door behind her. "Close the door, please."

Please? What's gotten into him? She settled into her seat and waited.

Peterman stared at her for a moment, seeming to probe her thoughts. "Why didn't you do it?"

She almost asked what he was talking about, but of course she knew. It was the same question she'd asked herself for hours after the arrest. "The thought crossed my mind. Thing is, my daughter is dead. Jenny is gone. Killing him wouldn't have brought her back. But it would have made me a murderer. Lord knows I have enough guilt without adding that to my load."

But it was more than that. She sorted through her feelings to try and make sense of it. "And I figured that shooting an unarmed suspect wouldn't go very far in building trust."

He seemed to consider the explanation for a moment before moving on. "I've got some bad news for you."

Carol was certainly no stranger to bad news. In fact, she felt as though she was constantly waiting for the other shoe to drop. "So, what's new? Can't imagine a day without bad news."

"Cheney, Hoskins or whatever you call him, has his lawyer already parked in the DA's office looking for a deal."

No surprise there. "What kind of deal?" After all, they had the evidence they needed. What could he possibly bring to the table?

Peterman set his coffee cup off to the side and leaned into his desk, his eyes meeting hers. "There are more kids, ones that weren't found. Still listed as missing. He's offering to identify them and take us to where he left them. Maybe six or seven he says. That's a bunch of parents that would…."

She held his gaze and clenched her jaw. "And in return?"

When it broke the silence, his voice came across as tired. "As you know, we have a moratorium on capital punishment here in Washington. But the feds have no such prohibition and he did kill a federal officer. Also, as I understand it, Cheney copped to a murder in west Texas. And those Texans take great pride in their ability to execute criminals. Obviously, he's going to want to avoid federal or Texas involvement. I don't know specifics but that would be my guess."

"I suppose the DA can sort that out." Her lack of engagement puzzled her. But she couldn't summon up the rage that she would have expected in another time.

"They're going to be contacting the parents of the victims we know about. I assume they'll get in touch with you."

Chapter 89

Carol found herself surprised at the speed with which the legal system churned forward on the case. Barely a week had passed since the arrest when the District Attorney organized a meeting of victims' families. The arrest had occupied center stage with Seattle media, so she figured most of those invited had an inkling of what was in store.

When she arrived at the courthouse, she was surprised to find Chris waiting outside the building in the drizzling rain for her, alone. They hugged briefly. "I thought you might have Shelley here with you."

He took her hand as they made their way into the building.

She focused her attention on the hand that held hers. *After all these years.* She became aware that he'd said something. "Excuse me?"

He stopped and turned to face her. "I said, do you have any idea what this is about?" His furrowed brow and intense look seemed to convey perplexity.

"Yeah. Cheney's looking to cut a deal. The DA wants to talk to the families of the victims before he decides."

"What kind of deal?" The look intensified.

She sighed and closed her mind, not wanting to even think about the issue. "There are some other girls, kids, that were never found. He's offering to give us the names and take us to where he left them. In return, he wants a pass on the federal death penalty for Irwin's murder." She shuddered at the thought of parents who had gone ten years or more without knowing. She shook her head to try and clear that vision from her mind.

Chris's eyes softened. They continued into the meeting room, hand-in-hand.

The two strolled into a sea of sorrow. By the looks of it, more than fifty people sat around in chairs. Few of them were talking. Most sat staring blankly at the front of the room. She could relate. There was nothing to discuss. They all shared a common bond that none of them wanted to even think about. Carol slipped into a row of chairs and took the second one in, leaving the aisle seat for Chris.

Within fifteen minutes, an entourage mounted the stage. A couple of distinguished looking gentlemen in suits entered, one of which was the District Attorney himself. Some familiar faces stood out—Detectives Sullivan, Collins, and Mulroney, who shared the arrest credit. *Good for them. They deserve it.* The notion of her colleagues being up there as a part of the system seemed right.

Introductions came and went with a somber tone. *Good. No fluff here tonight.* The DA detailed the purpose of the meeting, which drew murmurs from the crowd, most laced with anger. "I want to stress a couple of things. First, there are a lot of parties involved in this. I've spoken personally to both the governor and the mayor. This case has their full attention. The FBI has an interest as do the police and the families of victims. Second, I want to be clear that we are not here to take a vote. Our office, in concert with the other local, state, and federal entities, will make the decision that we believe is in the best interest of all citizens. That said, though, I do want to hear your thoughts. We have no time limit tonight. I'll stay and listen as long as you are willing to talk. As a matter of process, if you raise your hand, I'll call on you and you'll be given a microphone. With that, I'd like to open the floor to your comments."

Hands around the room shot up. The DA surveyed the scene and before pointing toward the back of the room. "You sir. Yes, you. And if you could, please state your name for us."

Carol turned to see a stocky man who looked to be about forty. His stooped shoulders and somber face gave the look of a defeated man. His words, though, came out laced with rage. "I'm Lawrence Turnbull. That animal took my daughter Kelley. She was only twelve. She didn't get no deal. She didn't have no lawyers going to bat for her. He don't deserve no better. I say fry the bastard." He glared at the DA for a moment before dropping into his seat. He put his hands over his eyes.

And so the evening went, one testimony after another—all similar sentiments. After about two hours, the crowd fell silent as if its rage was spent. Carol looked around. Her right hand still holding Chris's, she raised her left hand.

The DA locked gazes with her—recognition. "Yes." He motioned gently toward her.

She stood and waited until she had the microphone in her hand. "I'm Carol Tullis. My daughter Jenny was one of the girls." She cleared her throat and wondered in passing if she could do this with dry eyes. *Yes. I can. This is not about me.*

She took a deep breath and continued. "I still remember that day. The detectives walked up onto my porch and rang the doorbell. I could see them through the window. I knew why they were there. For a long time, I thought that was the worst day of my life. In fact, I felt that my life ended that day." She turned and looked out over the crowd.

"I was wrong on both counts. That day was horrible. But the two days before that were just as bad, if not worse. The not knowing. Trying desperately to hold on to some miniscule thread of hope. Fearing the worst but not having a clue as to how I would deal with it. Two days. I can't begin to imagine, in my most horrible nightmares, what it would be like to not know for ten years." She tried to imagine the lives of those parents. But it defied imagination.

"And, as it turned out, my life didn't end that day. Oh, I've had dark days and I'm sure I'll have more as time goes on. But, gradually, I've learned to focus on other things. Some of them important, like my son and my job. Sometimes it's just silly little things, like a good cup of coffee. But whatever else happens in all of this, my daughter is gone and I'm still here. Nothing, not even his execution, is going to change that."

She steeled herself and turned to face the DA. "So, two things. First, make sure that monster never walks free again. Second, give those families their closure. If you can do that, then make your deal." Carol felt Chris squeeze her hand. A tear escaped from the corner of her right eye.

Chapter 90

As little Bella took her by the hand, Carol mused that Saturday night dinner at the Ramirez household was fast becoming a tradition—three weeks in a row. As the two entered the small bedroom decorated in pastels of pink, blue, and yellow, Bella leaped into the bed.

Carol took the book from the nightstand and sat beside her. "So, as I recall, you're a fan of the three pigs. Am I right, young lady?"

The young girl narrowed her eyes and tilted her head, considering her in silence. After a brief moment, she spoke softly. "Miz Carol, Mommy says you had a little girl."

The simple statement had the effect of knocking the wind out of Carol. She struggled to get her breath. *I'm not sure I can do this.* She looked into a pair of shining brown eyes. *Yes, I will do this.* For once she needed to think of someone other than herself. She swallowed the lump in her throat and smiled. "Yes. Her name was Jennifer. We called her Jenny."

Bella looked down at the hands in her lap. After a brief consideration, she looked up at Carol. "Jenny. That's a pretty name. Was she pretty like you?" Her head tilted and the eyes widened.

The laugh almost escaped but Carol managed to hold it in. "No, Bella. She was beautiful like you." She reached over and took both of the young girl's hands in hers.

Bella bowed her head and giggled. Carol laughed.

"My daddy catches bad men." She beamed.

"I know that. But did you know that your daddy is the best bad man catcher in the world?" Carol moved in closer to the young girl.

"Nuh uh." She pulled her hands back and folded her arms on her chest. "He says you are."

A wave of emotion swept over her. After just over a month of being back to work, this family that she'd never known had stolen her heart. The partner with whom she'd had such a rocky first day brought her into his home to share the love. She searched her soul to find something she'd done to deserve this.

She moved even closer. Her words came out as a whisper. "Let me tell you a secret, Bella. He just says that to make me look good. You and I, we both know that he's the best, don't we?"

Bella looked up at her, a deadly serious look on her face. "Miz Carol, if I tell you something, will you promise not to tell Mommy and Daddy?"

Alarms went off in Carol's head. *No. You cannot make that kind of a promise.* "Bella, honey, you can always tell your mommy and daddy anything."

The young girl shook her head. "No. They would get worried."

Carol forced herself to laugh. "That's what mommies and daddies do. They worry because they love you. That's the way it works. But your job is to tell them things, okay. Keeping secrets from mommy and daddy will make them sad."

Bella looked down, fidgeting with her hands. "Well, sometimes, I get scared that a bad man will come get me."

363

She felt her heart being torn apart. *God, what do I say to that?* She took the young girl's hands again and squeezed tight. With a silent prayer to whomever or whatever might be listening, she gave it her best shot. "Remember, your daddy is the best bad man catcher in the world. And you've got the very best mommy in the world. And I'll always be here to help them. And even your brothers are going to help you, even if boys are kind of silly sometimes, huh?"

Bella giggled again and then grew quiet. Her small brow furrowed, she rubbed her hands together. Carol could almost see the wheels turning in the little girl's head. When she spoke, her voice came out soft and slow. "Did a bad man make Jenny die?"

Another rip in the heart. *Can't I just take the easy questions and leave the hard ones?* Carol took a deep breath and closed her eyes. When she opened, she found the young girl gazing at her. "Yes." She wanted to say more, or at least felt she should say more. Nothing came. She nodded her head and wiped her eyes. "Yes."

Bella nodded. "Mommy says that you're her friend. Will you be my friend too?"

Carol pulled the girl into her arms and squeezed, rocking back and forth. "Bella, I will always be your friend. Always." She eased back, holding Bella's shoulders and sniffling. "Now, about that story."

Bella rolled her eyes. "That was just a trick to get you in here so I could talk to you some more." She laughed.

"Well, let me tell you, that is the very best trick anybody's ever played on me. And you can play that any time, okay?"

364

***

Kids asleep, Carol, Tom, and Dani polished off some chocolate cake and another cup of coffee. "I'm going to have to head out. Getting hard to keep my eyes open." She stood and took her cup and plate into the kitchen. "I can't stay up until all hours of the night like I used to," she shot over her shoulder.

Tom gave her a brief hug. "Drive safe."

Dani strode over to the hall closet. "I'll get your coat." She took Carol's raincoat off the hanger but, rather than handing it to her, she walked to the front door. As Tom waved and headed off down the hall, Dani stood facing Carol. "Just so you know, she stopped wanting bedtime stories a couple of years ago." A smile teased the corners of her mouth. "She adores you, you do know that, right?"

Carol tried to shrug it off. But it wasn't something easily shrugged off—the love of a young girl and a family that had taken her in. She wanted to say something, but the words wouldn't come.

"You're good for her, Carol. I just want you to know that."

Chapter 91

Friday night. No on-call duty over the weekend. Pizza out with her son. Carol exuded joy as she navigated through the back streets to her ex-husband's house. They weren't expecting her until five but no harm in showing up a little early. She pulled into his driveway at four-thirty.

Ringing the front bell, she turned to look at the western sky where the sun had just set leaving a string of clouds painted brilliant pink and purple. A light breeze out of the north put a bite into the mid-thirties temperature, seasonable for late November.

"Come in." Chris wore a set of faded, worn jeans and a purple and gold University of Washington sweatshirt. He retreated into the living room. "I just put hot water on if you'd like some tea."

She'd been slugging down coffee all afternoon. "I'm fine. Thanks. Anything else to drink and I'm going to float away." She took off her coat and laid it over the arm of a chair. "Sorry, I know I'm early."

"Jason's not home from school yet."

Carol turned abruptly. "What? School's been out for over an hour and a half. You think maybe something's wrong?"

Her ex-husband burst out laughing. As his guffaws subsided, he shook his head. "Sorry. I guess I should have told you. He took my car today. He's giving Sunni a ride home."

She searched her memories in vain. "Sunni?"

"Girlfriend."

"Still, an hour and a half should be plenty of time to drop her off and get home." A worry gnawed at the back of her mind.

His eyes widened. "Really? You don't remember what it was like in high school? A young man does not simply pull up to the curb and wish his girlfriend a good evening. There are rituals to be observed." He broke into a chuckle. "He'll be here by five. We talked about it."

Silence found its way in. Carol wandered into the living room and eased into a corner of the couch. Chris followed, taking a seat next to her.

"Carol, I didn't have a chance the other night, but I really wanted to tell you how proud I was of you at that meeting. It took a lot of courage to say what you did."

She looked into his eyes and saw the sincerity. She had always been able to count on that. "Thank you. I can't say that it was easy. I listened to what the others said, and I felt every bit of their anguish and misery. I've lived with that rage for the last ten years. Honestly, I just don't want that kind of hate in my life any more. I'm done with it."

He opened his mouth to speak but the sound of the front door opening interrupted him. "Hi Mom. Dad."

Carol stood and floated across the room to hug her son fiercely. "Hey you. How are you? God, you've grown up." She stood back and took measure of him.

He shifted his weight back and forth from one foot to the other, the look of discomfort on his face growing with each second.

"You ready to go? We can do a movie after the pizza if you want." She relished this night with her son—no demons allowed.

Jason looked over at his dad and then sheepishly back at Carol. "Uh, Mom, something came up. I need to…." He cast his gaze down.

Chris stepped in. "Jason, we talked about this. You know—"

Carol put her hand gently on Chris's arm and turned to Jason. "What's happening tonight?"

"Well, uh, Sunni's parents want to take us to dinner." He looked up at Carol with pleading eyes. "They're like really strict. They won't let her go out with me until they get to know me. And so tonight, I don't know, maybe they'll, whatever."

"That's important stuff. Pizza can wait. You go knock 'em dead."

Jason threw his arms around her neck and squeezed tight. "Thanks, Mom. Next weekend. For sure. Thanks." And with that he bounded toward the stairs. At the second step, he stopped and turned. "Dad, can I borrow a shirt and tie?"

"Of course."

Amid the sound of closet doors opening and closing upstairs, Chris turned to Carol. "You made big points, you know."

She sighed. "I have a lot of points to make up."

Within a few minutes, Jason came down the stairs dressed in navy blue chino trousers and a light blue shirt. He carried a gray and maroon striped tie and a navy blazer over his arm. "Dad, can you help me with this?" He tossed the coat on the couch and handed the tie to his father.

Carol watched the two—father and son. Jason stood in front of the full-length mirror in the hallway with Chris behind him reaching around to tie the half-Windsor knot.

Tears came to her eyes. She reminded herself for the millionth time of how much she'd missed. Her heart pounded with a mixture of pain and pride.

Jason flew out the front door donning his coat as he went. "See you later, Mom, Dad."

Chris yelled out after him, "Midnight. And call if you have any problems." No answer. He went over and plopped down on the couch, leaning his head back and exhaling.

She marveled at this man who had managed to pull things together. He'd raised a remarkable, wonderful son on his own. And yet he always seemed to be in a positive state of mind. And here she was feeling good when she could hold it together for a month. Shelley was getting a good man, which reminded her.

"I was meaning to ask you. Have you and Shelley set a date yet?"

He looked at her for a moment and half-shrugged and offered a half-shake of his head.

She waited for more of an explanation, but none came. *None of my business, I guess.*

He sat up straight and turned to her. "You said that you didn't want that hate in your life any more. What do you want?"

The question took her by surprise. "I don't know. Maybe for starters, I hope that my son doesn't hate me. I'd love to have some kind of normal relationship with him sometime before I die. Beyond that, I guess that I'm really glad that you've found someone. It's been a long time and you deserve better. As for me, I'll be happy if my life's not as much of a train wreck as it used to be."

Her ex's laugh came out soft. "Pretty low bar, I'd say. Hoping your son doesn't hate you. Right now, he's a teenager so you can't read too much into anything. But I think he loves you more than he lets on." He sighed as he continued, "And the wreck, I'd say that you seem to have gotten the train on a track headed somewhere. At any rate, you look happier and more at peace than I've seen you since…."

She relaxed. "You're right. Now all I have to do is just keep myself from jumping the rails."

"I don't mean to seem argumentative, but that doesn't seem like much of a life. Don't you ever think of finding someone?" He sat with his arms resting on his thighs and his hands folded.

"No. I gave that up years ago. I thought about it for a while. But I came to the realization that it's just not what I want." She shuddered as she recalled exactly when that realization had struck.

He shook his head. "Whew. That must have been some realization to make you give up on love for the rest of your life."

"I'm not really comfortable talking about this. Let's just say I've learned the fine art of reasonable expectations. Modest aspirations coming true give me more joy than grandiose ones that don't." *That came out really stupid.*

He looked at her without speaking.

"It's just not something I like talking about."

He arched his eyebrows. "I'm sorry, you started the conversation—you asked about romance in my life. I thought maybe you had someone yourself."

She turned and looked out the window. "I'd rather not talk about it." The truth was that she'd not even allowed herself to go there.

"And what if I want to talk about it? After all, you comment about me going on with my life. I don't think it's unreasonable to expect you to share as well. And I'm not trying to be a jerk, really. I just don't understand what would happen that would cause you to just give up on the chance to be with someone you care about."

Tears blurred her vision. She felt her eyes filling, first at the corners and then overflowing, leaving wet lines down her cheek. *I can't do this.* Then she remembered. That was her standby line. She used it when she didn't want to deal with something painful. But she couldn't keep doing that. Sooner or later, she needed to face the demons. *Now is as good a time as any, I guess.*

She stood and walked over to the dining room table, taking a tissue from her purse. She wiped her eyes as she returned to the couch and sat at the opposite end from Chris. "Okay. I get it. You're right. After the divorce, while I was still drinking and working, I had an affair with a co-worker. At the time, I couldn't have cared less about him. After I lost my job and sobered up, I was horrified at what I'd done. I swore off men, or at least ignored them, until recently."

She collected her thoughts. "You know the guy that was renting the apartment out back?"

"You mean the young guy that got killed? The one you initially thought...."

"Yes. Him. Well, he was young, good looking, affable, and a bit on the flirty side. Anyway, one afternoon, I got some of his mail in my box and took it out to him. He answered the door fresh out of the shower, wearing only a pair of jeans." She quivered just thinking about it.

"One thing led to another and I ended up in his arms. He kissed me. I kissed him back. I had forgotten what that felt like." She took a deep breath and tried to read Chris's thoughts. He kept them well hidden but listening politely.

"I pushed back. Said no and left. I went to bed early but tossed and turned. About eleven, I said 'to hell with it.' I got up, brushed my teeth, slipped on some jeans and a tee shirt and started for his place. Chris, it had been so long. I mean, I'm an adult. He was an adult. He found me attractive. Why shouldn't I? But I stopped in the kitchen and looked out the back window at his place. The lights were still on. All I had to do was walk out across the lawn." She lowered her head and tried to put thoughts in the right order.

"As I stared, I imagined what it would be like. What it would feel like to be held, to be kissed passionately. To make love again with someone who desired me." She paused and shook her head. "Then I thought about what it would be like when it was over, laying immersed in darkness with the awkward silence. I pictured him turning on the light so I could get dressed. And more than anything else, I imagined the feeling of meaninglessness that would follow me back to the house. I knew, in that instant, that this was not what I wanted. He was not what I wanted." She shook her head, wiping the tears from her eyes again.

Chris spoke for the first time since she'd started her tale. "And what did you decide you wanted?"

She laughed. "That was the question. What did I want? You know, I tossed and turned all night trying to figure that out. Just like in the movies, enlightenment came with the dawn." She turned to him, her hands folded tightly in her lap.

"When you and I were together, we had that. We had passion. We had that love. We couldn't keep our hands off each other. And when it was over and we lay in each other's arms, it felt good. It felt right. I always felt like I was a part of something bigger and better than myself. That's what I want." She looked at him through blurry eyes, sensing that his eyes looked a bit moist as well.

"But with that came another realization. And Chris, please understand that I'm not trying to make anything out of this. You asked a question. I'm just answering. But I knew that morning that I did not want that with anyone but you. And since you were the one thing I couldn't have, then the next best thing is to live with my memories. End of story." She exhaled. *There. I've done it.*

She felt his hand on her face and realized that he had slid over to sit next to her. His lips drew close to hers. She gently moved his hands away and pulled her face back. "Please, Chris, don't. I'm carrying more than enough guilt already. I don't want to come between you and Shelley. Please." The last word came out as a whimper.

He paused for a moment before speaking softly. "Shelley and I ended what passed for a relationship a couple of months ago."

Carol's mind snapped to attention. She sat up straight, eyes wide. "What? Why? What happened. I thought everything was great. I thought the two of you were getting married. You've been going out for, what, a year or so?" She realized that she was jabbering.

He laughed. "Long story short, we wanted different things from life—too different to find a middle ground. Look, she's a nice lady and I do like her. But it was just never going to work and we both knew it. Her idea of a fun night is going out clubbing—dancing and drinking. You know me, I'm up for a disc in the blue ray player and a bowl of popcorn. She likes vacations in Vegas and on cruise ships. I like family trips to the coast." He leaned back on the couch and picked at a piece of lint on his jeans as he continued.

"Remember that weekend we were going to the Oregon coast and I asked you to take Jason? We were going to spend a nice quiet night here and then get up early and head out. Instead, we ended up talking until about eleven and then said our goodbyes, amicable ones, I might add. We both knew it was coming and, truthfully, I think she was as relieved as I was."

He paused and turned his head toward the front window. "And, truth is, I never stopped wanting what you just described. And I never wanted it with anyone but you."

Carol tried to sort it all out. "Why didn't you tell me?"

"I didn't think you cared. And, I might add, you're carrying a boatload of guilt. If I had told you, I figured it would just make you feel worse."

That's the most stupid explanation I've ever heard.

He put his hand on her face again. "So, let's try that again." His lips met hers.

Chapter 92

Carol couldn't remember ever feeling so at peace, so in love. She lay with her head resting on Chris' bare chest. She could hear the rhythmic beating of his heart and felt the gentle rise and fall of his chest. She snuggled in trying to get closer. She closed her eyes and prayed to whatever god who happened to be listening that this was not a dream. Or if it was, that she would never wake up.

A wonderful, familiar voice roused her. "Can't sleep?"

She sighed. "What's Jason going to think?"

Chris raised up and glanced over at the clock before laying back. "Well, let's see. It's eleven-fifteen. The kid's pretty good about getting home a little early so I'd say he's going to pull into the driveway about eleven-forty-five. He's going to see your car parked there and walk into a dark house with the bedroom door closed. I'm going out on a limb here and say that he's going to figure that you and I are in bed. Now, he's not a stupid kid so he's going to know what that means. But he's a teenager so the idea of his parents having sex is gross. So, to sum up, he's likely not going to think too much about it."

Carol closed her eyes and shook her head. "You're wrong. This will be a big deal for him. Deadbeat mom drops back into his life after ten years. This has trouble written all over it."

Chris lifted himself up, propping his head up with his arm. "Carol, the kid's in high school. He's got a driver's license and a girlfriend. He's thinking about graduating. He has to decide about college. And the girlfriend thing

375

complicates the college thing. Honestly, there's not a lot of room on his plate for worrying about you. You're his mother. He knows that. He knows I love you and always have. He loves you, whether you want to believe that or not. I'm telling you, this will go largely unnoticed."

"I don't know. I don't buy it."

"Bet you dinner."

***

The French roast coffee delighted Carol's sense of smell and soothed her soul going down. This Saturday morning was like no other she could remember. In fact, it felt more like a fairy tale come true than anything else. She and Chris stood at the kitchen bar holding hands, talking about the day to come, and sipping the strong brew.

The sound of soft footfalls on the stairway caught her attention. She looked up to see Jason coming down in a pair of flannel Star Wars pajama bottoms and a tee shirt. His tousled brown hair framed his sleepy face. With one hand on the stairway railing and the other scratching his backside, he glanced at the two of them. "Hi Mom. Dad." He went to the refrigerator, took out a plastic container of orange juice and a glass from the cabinet. Pouring it half full, he took a long draught. Putting the OJ back in the fridge, he finished the drink, set the glass in the sink, and trudged to the stairs. About halfway up, he turned to face the two of them. "Mom, tomorrow is Sunday. We eat pancakes and stay in our pajamas until noon on Sunday. So, if you want to sleep over again tonight, you need to find some pajamas." With that, he turned around and continued up the stairs. At the top, he called over his shoulder. "And you can't wear mine."

Carol stared for a few seconds at the spot where her son had disappeared up the stairs.

Chris's voice broke the silence. "You owe me dinner."

The End

Epilogue
Four months later

Dinner proceeded as usual. Carol and Chris chatted while they savored the meal that he had created. Jason shoveled his food in before bolting from the table, stacking his plate and silverware in the sink, and grabbing the car keys on his way out the door.

Chris called after Jason. "School night. Ten."

A faint response from the other side of the wall adjoining the kitchen and the garage. "Okay."

She marveled again that her new old husband had managed all of this by himself over the years. She heard the rumble of the garage door opener even as a sense of quiet and peace invaded their normally frenetic evening. "Doesn't that kid ever run out of energy?"

Chris returned the salad dressing to the refrigerator and the salt and pepper shakers to their resting place beside the stove. "I'm still waiting. If nothing else, old age will catch up to him. But I guess he's got a couple of good years yet."

After stacking their dishes in the sink, she turned to watch him wiping the dining room table. What struck her most is that he didn't seem to treat it as *work*. He went about these tasks—cooking, laundry, and the like—as though they were parts of life to be enjoyed, even savored.

He stalled, apparently aware that she was staring at him. "What?" She could see his eyes searching for a clue.

She shook her head and smiled. "Nothing... really." She eased over and kissed him gently on the lips. "Just thank you."

He started to say something but the ringtone on her cellphone intervened. She turned to retrieve it from the counter with a sense of trepidation. No one called on her cellphone except…. A quick look at the screen confirmed her suspicions. "Good evening, Captain."

"Sorry to bother you after hours. I need to speak with you."

She started to object. After all, she had been in the office all day with him. She would see him the next day. What was so important that he had to talk to her tonight? And the fact that he didn't state his business right away confirmed her fear that he wanted to talk in person. "Well, I live in a different place now."

"Yeah, I know. I can be there in fifteen minutes."

Carol started to ask how he knew where she lived. Then the memory clicked in. *Ah yes, he was a detective before I was out of high school. Sheesh.*

***

By the time the doorbell rang, the two of them had finished washing the dinner dishes and Chris had coffee brewed. She opened the front door and gestured. "Come in. Captain Peterman, this is my husband, Chris. Chris, Captain Peterman, my boss."

The two men shook hands and exchanged greetings. Chris moved toward the kitchen. "I've got a fresh pot of coffee here if you'd like a cup." He paused at the threshold between the kitchen and dining room.

"Thank you. Black." Peterman turned to Carol. "French roast, by the smell of it. Your husband is apparently a good influence on you."

She rolled her eyes as Chris set cups of coffee on the dining room table.

"I'll be in the study. Give me a shout if you two need anything. Good to meet you, Captain." Her husband turned and headed down the short hallway.

Peterman cradled the cup in both hands and took a sip before setting it aside. "I told you the first day we met that my main rule was that I was the captain and you were the detective. You know, I give the orders and you follow them. In general, I don't like to give my detectives choices. It complicates things. I'm here tonight because I'm going to break that rule. Actually, like they said in the movie, *they're more like guidelines than actual rules.*" He smirked at his own joke.

"I want to stress this is not an order or an assignment. I'm giving you the option. Take it or leave it." He paused and stared down at his cup for a moment before continuing.

"It seems our friend Slovak in Aged Cases hit on one too many women. He's being shown the door. That leaves a vacancy up there. What I'm going to tell you here is not for general consumption. That office is kind of a sham. Their cases are near impossible. They're old. They lack evidence or even leads. And they compete with the urgency of the present. But still, politically, the department wants to be able to say that it has a division working on them. Truth is, they never solve anything. Our mutual friend, Captain Tarrant, would like to change that. He's really not a bad guy. It's just that he's not up to the job. He was promoted and moved into that position because no one else wanted it. He has delusions of grandeur. And he figures that you are his ticket. After all, you were the one who broke the child serial killer case for him."

Carol shook her head. "You and I both know that we didn't solve that case. We solved the more current case. It just so happened that it was the same guy. Pure chance."

He smirked. "I know that, and you know that. But Tarrant is desperate. But that's not the reason I'm offering this. Carol, you were at that meeting right after the arrest, the one with all of the families. Those people deserved justice. The families and friends of all the aged cases deserve that. You have one of the finest detective minds that I've ever seen. If anyone can give these people that justice, it is you. You saw those faces. You've lived this for ten years."

She studied him for a moment. She narrowed, then closed her eyes, trying to imagine. And she could see it. When she opened her eyes, she could tell from the look on his face that he already knew. He probably knew her answer before he had even come.

Author's Notes

This is a work of fiction. All characters and events are fictional. Any similarities to real persons or events are coincidental. This work was not inspired by true events.

The paralytic agent cited in the work, naelosaxitoxin, is fictitious. It was based it on some of the properties of toxins found in contaminated shellfish.

Organizations in the novel, such as the Seattle Police Department and the FBI, are actual agencies, although I have taken great literary license in re-structuring them for the purpose of storytelling.